'I laughed, cried and cringed at the all-too-relatable moments. This is exactly the book we need.'

LUCY VINE

'A fresh, eye-opening look into the fascinating world of 'insta mums'. This smart and sassy novel is a must.'

KATY COLLINS

'A great read, especially if you've ever been a parent blogger, but also for anyone who has ever clicked into Instagram and wondered if it's all real.'

ANDREA MARA

'A really witty, sharply observed insight into influencer life.'

SUZANNE EWART

'A bitingly funny skewering of yummy mummy influencer culture, with really relatable characters and a warm heart.'

FRANCES QUINN

'A witty and thoughtful look at the world of social media while celebrating friendship and motherhood.'

LOVEREADING

'I loved this relatable tale of friendship, marriage and family life.'

LOUISE HARE

EVERYTHING'S PERFECT

NICOLE KENNEDY

HEAD *of* ZEUS

An Aria Book

First published in the UK in 2021 by Head of Zeus Ltd
This paperback edition first published in the UK in 2022 by Head of Zeus Ltd,
part of Bloomsbury Publishing Plc

9 7 5 3 1 2 4 6 8

A catalogue record for this book is available from
the British Library.

ISBN (PB): 9781800240148
ISBN (E): 9781800240155

Typeset by Divaddict Publishing Solutions Ltd

Printed and bound in Great Britain by
CPI Group (UK) Ltd, Croydon CR0 4YY

Head of Zeus Ltd
5–8 Hardwick Street
London EC1R 4RG

WWW.HEADOFZEUS.COM

For Tom, Dylan, Arthur and Felix

'So little? So little, did you say? Oh why, if there's nothing else, there's applause; I've listened backstage to people applaud. It's like... like waves of love coming over the footlights and wrapping you up. Imagine, to know every night different hundreds of people love you; they smile, their eyes shine, you please them, they want you, you belong. Just that alone is worth anything.'

Eve Harrington, *All About Eve*

So you want to be an Influencer?

Find out how with Boom! mag's guide to getting ahead…

Step 1: Speak Their Code

SoMe : Dude, if you don't know the shorthand for Social Media, where've you been?

GML: Guaranteed Minimum Likes. When you're hitting a GML of 25,000 likes per post, you're in the gang!

The CHIN: The Top 100 Chart of Influence, compiled by Mumspire HQ, the leading platform for InstaParents.

The Top Five: The gold standard of influencing, the hallowed Top Five positions of the CHIN. These have been in the vice-like grip of the key players – The Happy Hollidays, Boardroom Boss Mum, Forest Dad, Holistic Flo and Common As Mum – for the last twelve months. Could you be the one to shake it up?

Stories: Short snippets of footage posted online. Getting traction with these can take you to the next level! Get stuck in!

★ ★ ★

Step 2: Meet The Parents

Look out for our profiles of your favourite Influencers, coming soon!

Posted by Lucy Jenkins for Boom! mag © 31 August

SEPTEMBER

1

#OxygenMasks

Cassie

I've always wondered about those people, parents specifically I suppose, who, in the event of a sudden drop in cabin pressure, could make sure their own oxygen masks were securely fastened before assisting others, including children. Including *their own* children. I must have heard that audio a zillion times and the familiar robotic tone always made me eye-roll as it talked about emergencies, safety lights and kicking off your heels before jumping on the blow-up slide. I had no doubts that if oxygen masks suddenly dropped, as little mouths rasped beside me, I would be fixing *their* masks on, not mine. Especially since I've had kids. If that little mouth belonged to Birch or Scout, there's no way I wouldn't be scrambling in my last breaths to get those masks *on*. I'd hear those stupid safety videos and think, what's the point? They should give realistic advice. No one would do that. *No one* would put their own mask on before their children's. Then I met my husband. Mr Happy Holliday.

I didn't know it immediately; no one knows how a

5

beloved partner will respond to the seismic shift of first-time parenthood. It's a lottery. That sullen bloke your mate from school married, who sucks banter out of a room like an industrial vacuum cleaner, might well unfurl like a flower dipped in sunlight the second he lugs in the scent of his gunky newborn. I could never have predicted that the man I loved, the man who for a time made everything make sense, might just not be into it. That he might not have the temperament for broken sleep and projectile vomit and threenager tantrums, even though, on paper, he had all the makings of a champion father. I thought he would love it, I really did. But when I think back to the very first moment that Seb held the twins in his arms, after they were unhooked from the incubators in the Special Care Baby Unit, I don't see the soft oozing look of love in his leaf-green eyes that you see in newborn shots so widely shared online. I see fear: cold, abject fear. I see Seb backing away as I, and the twins, try to claw him closer to us. He tried, in his own way: excitedly emailing Radford so they were straight on the roll, proudly displaying the matching mini rugby kits he'd bought them before a midwife advised sticking to sleepsuits to keep them warm. I'd been home a week – nipples cracked and leaking, unwashed, undone, the sanitary-wear equivalent of the Hoover Dam still wedged up between my legs – when the warning alarm really started to clang and I found myself googling 'postnatal depression in men'. Yep. It's a thing. They couldn't even give us PND.

I'm *kidding*. Of course men are equally entitled to suffer from the cocktail of hormones and gobsmacking life changes that whack you when you meet your tiny human. Times are changing. We even have Dad Influencers now, God help us.

I just don't think that's what it was with Seb. I see him when he's with other people: happy. His lust for life undimmed. So men can have PND and can post online about how hard parenthood is (eye-roll). I should mention from the outset that I'm kind of a big deal on SoMe, so I know about this stuff, and the InstaDads? Not to be trusted. Same goes for parents who call their offspring 'mate', enjoy bath time or use the #blessed hashtag (okay, I do sometimes, but only if I'm being paid top dollar).

If we're going there, never trust a photograph. The white lacquered sideboard at Elen's – that's my own dear mum – is littered with photographs of me smiling: dressed like a fluffy pastel meringue at a wedding, in my dusky pink ballet costume, bedecked in fuchsia before my first beauty pageant. You wouldn't know about the muddy cheeks crossly swiped at with my mother's spittle seconds before the camera flashed, or the little face that deflated, like the bouncy castles I was never allowed to jump on, after the click. We were always presentation ready, Elen bristling in anticipation, in case my dad turned up. You could say that's sort of similar to how things are with Birch and Scout: it's getting harder and harder to convince them to wear the outlandish outfits and pose in the specific ways brands request after all, but I'm doing it *for* them. Not for myself, as Elen always did with me. Desperate for her fairy-tale fantasies to be realized, to be *rescued*, when I was always more interested in the dragons in those stories: fierce and fire-breathing and flying.

I want the twins to fulfil their own unique potential, not to feel like they have to conform to society's gender norms. So it's different, right? And it's more than that. I style us into a perfect family and capture us for the world to see so when they're older they won't remember the number of times their dad seethed, 'Will you just *shut up*?' Instead, they'll see us laughing together in the woods at the Big House, dressed in earthy autumnal tones, with light streaking over the den they just built (with a little help – a freebie in exchange for a post – from Forest Dad and his range of flat-pack woodland shelters), and the thousands of likes will agree. The thousands of likes will show them – in case they have any doubts – what a kick-ass, fabulous family we are. And maybe, if I keep trying, if I dress us in enough cute matching/not-matching outfits (the classic Instagram look), maybe the family in the pictures is the family we'll become? Maybe it will rub off on us? Maybe Seb will start to see us, *really see us*, the way other people do? Maybe he will see the *joy* in the twins, rather than being irritated by them all the time?

How hard is it for him, really? He's at work all week. All he has to do is play nicely at the weekend, but he'd rather be on the golf course, or having a leisurely read of the Sunday papers. I know what you're thinking: she married some old bloke; he's a geriatric dad. Not so, my friends. Thirty-eight. A couple of years *younger* than me, in fact, and believe me, when we met he had *energy* and *spark*. He was a man who *lived* his life, and when it was clear to me that I was starting to fall for him my logical brain kicked in, as it always does, and I considered his prospects much in the way I imagine Boardroom Boss Mum undertakes due diligence: likelihood of premium-grade sperm? Check. Cash in the bank? Appreciating assets? Check. Check. Cultural fit? This is where we weren't quite aligned. I knew he'd want to send them to that bonkers school he went to where they wear boaters and speak in code, but I didn't think much of it. I couldn't imagine having almost-school-age children and what it might mean; the guilt I'd feel at sending them off for their individual spirit and character to be stifled by Radford tradition. The twins adore him, of course. The more uninterested he is, the more they crave his attention. It's so drearily predictable. I graft every day and no one notices, but he gets home in time to read them a bedtime story once a week and he's a hero?

Which brings me back to the InstaDads. Any old average dad can be a success. Followers flocking in their thousands. To make it as a mum you've got to be at the top of your game, constantly working the angles, steadfastly ignoring the trolls. It's a microcosm for real-life parenting. Why should the dads get rewarded with the best brands and the best fees and the best opportunities because they deign to turn up once in a while? I turn up *every day*.

Don't get me wrong, Seb isn't all bad. He's funny and sharp and has a self-assuredness to him. He knows who he is in this world and he's good with that. I noticed it the first time we met. The twins feel it too. They often run to him if they're scared of something, like wasps or thunder, and he will begrudgingly put down his paper and lift them to his knee, tutting and sighing over their heads. I cling barnacle-like to the hope that when the twins are older and they can play golf, he might start to enjoy parenthood, but I'm still certain that in an emergency situation he would take care of himself first. Regardless of the kids, regardless of me. 'You can sort yourself out,' he would say, before reclining his seat, oxygen mask on, checking which movies were available.

★★★

My alarm sounds, breaking my thoughts. There it is, right on time.

From: Hetty@MumspireHQ.com
To: Cassie@TheHappyHollidays.com
1 September at 05:00
Influencer Update

Hola, chicas!

We're back from our jollybobs – thanks for following us and all your favourite Influencers as we tore it up at the Villa! Don't forget to use our promo code #FML to get 5% off your next break with Hobo Hotels.

The kaftan's packed away, the flamingo's been deflated… is that the first leaf of autumn falling? Don't miss our How-To-Hygge guide coming next month from Holistic Flo and Wax Attack!

Here's your Top Ten CHIN as at 31 August:

1. The Happy Hollidays
2. Holistic Flo
3. Forest Dad
4. Common As Mum
5. Mummy Likes Clean Plates
6. Middle Class Mummy
7. Skinny Bitch Mum

8. Mama Needs A Drink
9. Clean Uddies
10. Boardroom Boss Mum

Click **here** for the full list…

Hetty Says Hello!
A big Mumspire welcome to some of our new Influencers this month: The Bird With The Words, Unicorns & Fairy Dust and Mardy Mum – do go say hello! All their SoMe links are set out in the directory.

Don't forget!
London Mummies, there's still time to get tickets for today's event at the Park Keeper in Victoria Park, Hackney, sponsored by the Family Co. We have a super special panel lined up for you and one of our mamas is going to be making a big announcement – you don't want to miss it!

Hetty x

Mumspire HQ

I scan through the CHIN, wincing at Boardroom Boss Mum's fall to number ten. She's not in the Top Five any more. It's to be expected after the summer, but still, *ouch*. I skim down to 'Hetty Says Hello!', her little shout-out to new Influencers. The newbies don't worry me; most of them will drop out within six months. They can't handle the graft. They often roll into one – Mum this and Mum that. 'Mardy Mum'. Original.

Quick check online: 32,439 likes for the shot of Seb and me that I posted last night, one of the last ones left from our summer-themed family photo shoot, his tanned arms wrapped around me as I lean into his rugby-honed chest (helpfully covering his paunch), his stubble grazing my temple (#twinflames). I had to skip reading with the twins so I could hit the Chardonnay slot: knackered mums sinking on to their sofas with a glass of wine in one hand and their phones in the other. The comments have clocked up overnight:

Such a cute couple!

What a perfect family!

This is everything!

Mostly I ignore them, but sometimes I feel tiny pinpricks of guilt, like being attacked by a set of Holistic Flo's acupuncture needles. Then I remind myself that I do all this for my family and the spikes of doubt recede.

I click off Instagram and stare up at the ceiling, holding my phone against my chest. All is as it should be, and why wouldn't it be? I slide my phone back under my pillow. I should get another hour before the twins wake.

2

#MardyMum

Beth's Pinterest Feed

Save your ideas about Country Kitchens and Wood Burning Stoves!

Your pin Dream Larder Cupboard was saved 14 times

Your pin Cosy Nook was saved 131 times

Shhhhhh! Based on your Secret Board: Woodland Weddings we thought you might like: Pretty Pink Weddings and Bridal Mood Board: An Autumn Palette.

Beth

The monitor crackles to life and I hold my breath, watching the small, dark form shift on the video screen. *Please don't wake up. Please don't wake up.*

We don't need the monitor. I can hear Poppy through

the thin walls, like surround sound, but my hypno-birthing friends were so aghast when I said we didn't have one – even Jade – that I ordered one immediately. Bronagh was horrified she's in her own room already, but I was tired and desperate and willing to try anything. And it's working. This is the longest she's ever slept in her cot: one hour and thirty-eight minutes (I have the perfect baby and the perfect cot, but they will not work perfectly together).

Through the gap between the blind and the glass it's starting to lighten, summer creeping to autumn, an eerie blueing of the sky from black after dawn. The crackling stops and I release my breath into the silence of the flat – interspersed with the odd siren in the distance. I say 'flat', but it's actually the penthouse and every aspect is floor-to-ceiling glass. Joe bought it off-plan, with help from Gossy Gloria and Handsy Ron, before the property prices in East London jumped up. It must be worth a fortune now. Imagine what you could get for this in Yorkshire?

Joe stirs beside me and reflexively slips one arm under my neck and the other over the top of my belly, drawing me into the warmth of his body. His erection lodges below my bum and while one part of me's pleased this still happens even though he witnessed the horror of me in labour (what is it Robbie Williams said? Like watching your favourite pub burn down?), another part's irritated.

'Joe, I need to sleep.' I wriggle away, relieved to remove his hand from my stomach. He says I'm being silly, that I still look beautiful, but I feel like an alien in my own body. Nothing about me feels the same, not even my underwear. I tried to front it out and wear my old bras, but it was agony as my breasts filled and strained against the fabric, the quiet torture to my nipples. I had to admit defeat and embrace the boulder holders I'm wearing now.

'Of course, sorry babe.' His tone carries a soft resignation. The mattress shudders as he flops on to his back. A fresh release of sweat and beer mingles with my lavender eye mask. 'I didn't realize you'd been up again in the night.' Joe returned home around 1 a.m., entering the flat as I was heading into Poppy's bedroom. I gave him a half wave, my eyes gluey with sleep. He probably assumes I fed her and got back into bed. Like it's that simple. 'I should be getting ready for work anyway.'

I fight the tiny bubbles of rage, the sense of injustice that my life has changed irrevocably and his has changed... not so much. I was up *five* times in the night! *Five!*

But you get to do this, I think, my dry, red, itchy eyes staring up at the dark screen of the monitor. *You get to be at home with Poppy.*

Before I had a baby, I hadn't appreciated that in among all the love and the hormones and the wonder there could be something else: loneliness. How could you be lonely, I would've thought, when you have your baby with you all the time?

No one tells you about the long stretches of blackness in the night, the haunting 3 a.m. thoughts, or the days spent pinned to the sofa because your precious little bundle only likes to feed and sleep on you and you're so exhausted that you sit there for three hours, even though you need a wee and you forgot to turn the telly on. Eventually your fingers tire of creeping, spider-like, breath held as you stretch, fingertips *almost* grasping the remote, which is always, *always*, mere millimetres from your reach. Instead you watch life go by from the window, the feeling of being a ghost in your own life meeting with quiet calm as you watch your baby's eyelashes grow and marvel *again* that you made her, eyelashes and all.

I watch Joe at the foot of the bed, rubbing his eyes and stretching his arms. His boxers the same size, his skin the same texture, his life unchanged, largely, by parenthood. Have I mentioned he is *fit*? Boyish but rugged; charming but sweet. It started in the gym – our eyes kept meeting in the wall-to-wall mirrors – but he's different to the other regulars. There's a goofiness to him. He exercises to feel good, like I do, not to be the most ripped lad online.

'Tea?' Joe's whole face lifts as he smiles. He's one of those people that seem lit from within, light bouncing from his pores. Usually it's enough to make my face lift into a smile too, but today I shake my head, swallowing a yawn.

'I should try to sleep.'

Joe does something to do with 'asset-backing' in the City. Don't ask me what that means. He gets there early, does lots of shouting and head-in-hands stuff with his colleagues, but by the end of the day always seems to have come good. The upside of him starting early is he finishes around five, but he's often obligated to go to client entertainment events, which is when I get a message along the lines of *Hi babe, smashed it! Got this work thing. See you later X*. I know then not to expect him home until the early hours, like last night.

He walks round to my side of the bed and tucks my hair behind my ear. 'You're doing such a good job, Beth. Me and Pops are so lucky to have you.' He kisses me tenderly. When he pulls back, our eyes meet.

'Where'd you go last night?' I ask.

The most important thing that no one tells you about having a baby is that those things in your past, the things you thought you had dealt with, would return.

'Don't worry about that, babe. Try to get some kip.'

He bundles the duvet around me and leaves the room.

3

#SuperstarMama

Cassie

'Are you doing their breakfast?' I ask pleasantly. It's only 6.45 a.m., after all.

'Yes,' Seb exhales sharply. 'Jesus.'

I raise my eyes from my phone; I'm scrolling through the photos I've just taken of the twins, favouriting any that I might be able to use online. He ruffles a hand through his hair; I've always liked him better like this – pyjamas, messy-haired – than the sharply tailored look he sports for work, watch heavy on his wrist.

'What? I just asked if you were doing their breakfast because it looks like you're doing your own...' I wipe my right foot against my left pyjama leg; the washing machine is still leaking but I don't have time for the inevitable argument if I mention it. 'I can't be late again.'

'Am I allowed to eat too?'

'Yes, but not *first*. I wouldn't be in such a rush if Marina hadn't let me down.'

'I've told you not to trust her.'

I ignore him; I don't have time for this either. He wants *me* to hate her too. Typical of him to be so short-sighted.

'Feed the kids so they settle down and you can make—' THWACK. A hard plastic asparagus bundle hits me in my left eye. I turn to see Scout using the frying pan from the toy kitchen as a bat, whacking an assortment of pretend foodstuffs across the kitchen. Seb smirks as my vision blurs. He turns away, shoulders bobbing up and down as he resumes fussing and stirring his porridge. Adding blueberries and flaxseed and agave nectar. Things he's always berating me for buying.

'If they were eating, they wouldn't be assaulting me with toy vegetables and I could get ready!'

I pick up the offending asparagus and push it to the back of the kitchen counter to shouts of protest.

'They would be eating, if you could leave me in peace for two seconds.'

Seb moves to the kettle and I quickly unfurl the roll of paper I keep behind the microwave. I have a few of these backdrop props stashed around the house. It covers the peeling worktop with a stunning white marbled effect. Just like Marina's. I slip his porridge bowl on top, scatter some seeds, angle his spoon just so and hover my phone over the scene, my delicate love-spoon bracelet in the corner of the frame: my signature flat lay. I do it in one; breakfasts are so much easier to curate than children.

On the train I sedate the twins with iPads and quiet my stomach with a banana. 18,298 likes for my porridge shot already. Boardroom Boss Mum's having Eggs Royale at The Ned with a suit I vaguely recognize… an MP? Common As Mum's squeezing in a sausage sandwich before she sets off:

'Always time for a quick bit of sausage!' Winking face. God, I can't be bothered with today. No Forest Dad at least, and no breakfast shot. He's probably still out foraging for his.

An email notification obscures my view.

To: Cassie@TheHappyHollidays.com
From: Lucy@BoomMag.com
1 September at 08:30
Profile Feature

Cassie,

You may have seen my profile pieces on some of your fellow InstaMums (and everyone's favourite InstaDad!). They're getting great traction online. Just following up on my previous emails to see if you could spare some time for an interview? Happy to come to you. Would love to meet the twins!

Best,

Lucy

I notice a Word attachment icon at the bottom: Cassie_Holliday_Profile_Draft_Notes.doc/LucyJenkins. I click on curiously. She's obviously attached this by mistake. My mind whirrs. Unless it was on purpose; she's trying to find a way in?

• SoMe: Instagram: 1.3 million followers / Facebook likes: 800,000 / Twitter: 7,000 followers (?)

• Family: Married to Sebastian Holliday (solicitor). Two children: Birch and Scout. Gender unknown (despite multiple enquiries and media interest. Children do not attend any nursery or pre-school settings and are rarely seen outside of SoMe posts – EXPLORE).

• Brand relationships: multiple. Recently secured an arrangement with the Family Co for a three-month contract which is rumoured to be the largest fee to date paid to an Influencer in the Mumspire network.

• Media appearances: multiple. Regular contributor on television and radio discussing gender and restricting children's use of technology (no television, iPads etc.) as key to maintaining a happy home – EXPLORE.

• Own brand products: Breastfeeding Babe Bombs (energy balls for breastfeeding mothers to encourage regular supply and increased energy levels). Self-produced a range of gender-neutral slogan T-shirts last year (THEYBIES FIERCE, THEYBIES SUPERHEROES, THEYBIES THE FUTURE) but after an intensive SoMe campaign unable to sell stock owing to various ongoing trademark disputes. Rumoured that stock has since been destroyed and CH suffered a considerable financial loss.

I flush red at the last paragraph. I decide to ignore it: a reaction is confirmation, right? And if this is all she's got... she doesn't even know that my Breastfeeding Babe Bombs have been dropped by Big Mart, my last stockist. Thank God for Griff and the Family Co. Sure, the posting schedule is intense and they basically own me – and my family – for the next three months, but if I can see it through until December, to collect my fee, I can get my overdraft out of the red and start to pay Seb back after the T-shirt debacle.

I take a sip from my new Boardroom Boss Mum reusable coffee cup, but I'm too preoccupied to post a pic of it and tag her in, even though she could do with the support. Is this the reality of your late thirties? Energetic little bundles of guilt playing bumper cars in your gut: work that unsettles you, relationships you don't have the energy to maintain, the perpetual guilt that comes with having children? And all set to the thrum, thrum, thrum of your biological clock and a bombardment of targeted marketing for the perimenopause.

Am I perimenopausal? God, I hope not. I've always said that forty's the cut-off, *my cut-off*, for any more children. Forty seemed so long off when we discussed it, in St Lucia, shortly after Seb proposed: 'We'll have our kids soon, in our thirties, then our forties will be for *us*.' I cringe at my naivety. How easily I thought life could be planned and compartmentalized. Like kids would be a tick in the box that I'd move on from unchanged, unscathed. And now my fortieth is a matter of months away, in January, and Seb and I aren't in a place where we could even discuss another baby.

I sigh loudly enough to draw Scout's eyes away from her iPad. I lean my head on hers, inhaling the scent of her tangerine shampoo and ignoring the relentless beeps from my phone as we hurtle towards London, the train bumping over the tracks.

4

#InDemand

Cassie's Messages

09.15 Griff Family Co
Cassie, this is the deal of your life. Don't fuck it up. G

09.20 Seb
Sad news. Roger passed away. Died peacefully in his sleep
(nothing to do with the gout). Don't forget to set up an intro
to your boardroom chum.

09.31 Alicia Family Co
I'm not your nanny you know *laughing emoji*. Sure, I can
keep an eye on them. XOXO

09.40 Keane Bank
A/C****4038 1 SEP
You have entered an unarranged overdraft.
To avoid the Fee please repay the unarranged overdraft by
23.59 today.
For more information visit www.keanebank.com

5

#Survival

Beth

'Mitts, how many times have I told you I'm not interested?' A flush rises up my face. She says it so matter-of-factly, as if it's a totally normal thing to do, to put yourself online to be scrutinized and judged by other people. 'I don't want to be on Instagram or Twitter or anything else.'

'I don't know why you're being so weird about it.' She gives me that look that Joe gives me sometimes, which basically implies: hormones. She traces a finger over Poppy's tiny hands, fast asleep in her bouncer.

'Don't wake her!' I whisper, but it comes out in a growl. It's probably not allowed, babies sleeping in bouncers, but, well, I'm sure she won't sleep for too long. 'I'm not being weird, I just think *it's* weird, these contrived social groups and hierarchies you keep mithering me about.' My heart rate quickens at the thought. That's the warning signal: you don't need this. 'Do you want a brew?' I ask, filling the kettle, needing to shift the nervous energy beginning to bud. I don't often feel anxious at

24

home – the flat is like my cocoon – but this topic always unsettles me.

'You've read too many self-help books,' she mutters, opening various cupboards. I moved into Joe's over a year ago and she still doesn't know where anything is.

'I don't want to make *online* friends,' I say, 'I want to make real-life friends.'

'Well, that's the point,' she says as I make our drinks. 'There's this big Influencer network, Mumspire, and they hold events in Victoria Park. There's one on today.'

'*So?* I don't want to be an "Influencer", whatever that means.'

She snorts. 'No, not you. The events are for normal mums. The Influencers are like the carrot to draw them in. They do panel events and give motivational talks about their lives and brands and stuff.' She cringes a little. 'But really it's a way for you to meet other mums.' She slides the glass doors open and I carry our drinks outside. Autumn's yapping at the heels of summer, the air cooling, the wind beginning to stir.

'You pay them to make friends?' I wait while she arranges herself in the hanging egg chair on the terrace before passing her brew to her.

'Yeah. Like NCT.'

'That's exactly why I didn't do NCT.' Something I was already regretting. 'I'm on Pinterest,' I say, as I retrieve a still sleeping Poppy and carefully carry her over to the door, something else I'm probably not meant to do, and settle her on the floor. 'I'm not totally disconnected.'

'You know I love Pinterest, it's like flicking through all your favourite magazines, but you're not going to make friends on it.' She stares at me earnestly. It reminds me of the time she told me about periods and I burst into tears. 'It won't be like school. This InstaMum stuff, it's because people *want* to make friends. It's hard for mums to get out so they reach for community the easy way, through their phones. It's like dating. No one meets in a bar any more. They meet online. Then they go out to a bar. That's how it is being a mum now, too. You follow other mums, figure out which ones live nearby and then arrange to meet up with them. Why don't you try it? If you don't like it, just delete it.'

I stare fixedly down to the canal. Watch cyclists gunning along the path, some still in shorts and T-shirts, some without helmets. I think of the hours I've spent here feeling like the world's going by and I'm not a part of it. Like I've checked out. Maybe this is how I could rejoin? But I can't ignore the way my toes are wiggling, shaking off the unease trying to settle there. This is how it starts. This is always how it starts. But then another thought occurs to me: she'll be on there, won't she?

She changes tack: 'Do you know when you're going back to work?' You would not believe how many times I've been asked this. Poppy's a few weeks old. 'It can help you figure it out – who you are, who you want to be – Working Mum, Stay At Home Mum, Work From Home Mum. The options these days are endless! It could be a platform to a job you actually want to do. You should do something you enjoy, not wording promotional pensions literature.'

She's right. I know she's right, but I'm not ready to admit it. I'm not ready to start again. I'm too tired to think about it. 'What difference does joining social media make?

I'm hardly going to start working there, am I?' *Although*: I could see what she's up to, couldn't I? I could prepare myself.

'You're missing the point. Look at Holistic Flo.' She's referring to the Holistic Flo branded hot pink headbands and wristbands, like tennis players wear, that she gave me. Apparently it's a thing to take a selfie with them on, while you're in labour, and post it online with the hashtag #GoingWithTheFlo. Something I did *not* do.

Four weeks on and already I can't remember it as a seamless passage of time. I see certain moments: my bump with the monitoring strips laced over it; the greeny-brown colour of meconium after the midwife broke my waters; the thread of tubes poking from my hand. The bits between are a blur, blocked out already by the sweet centring joy I felt as I finally held Poppy, warm against my chest, limbs splayed like a frog. The very scent of her. I made a promise to Poppy that from that moment on I would keep it together for her, whatever it took; that we would be a family, the three of us; that Joe and I would give her all the things Mum and Dad gave me: stability, love, respect. The sweatbands moved from my hospital bag back to my drawer, much to my sister's disappointment.

'Or there's Boardroom Boss Mum? She's like a super cool mum of seven who's also a part-time CEO or finance director or something. She's pioneering flexible working for parents.'

'Who looks after all those kids then?' My breasts begin to tighten and on cue Poppy wakes and begins crying.

'I dunno. Her husband? Children do have two parents.' She says, springing up and scooping Poppy into a cuddle. 'I knew you'd wake and see your aunty before I left,' she says softly, but it only increases Poppy's cries. They both look at me in panic.

'She's hungry. Again.' I shift myself upright, my stitches still pulling in certain positions. I unclip my bra and reach out my arms.

'Jesus.' Her voice is low, awed. 'What's happened to your tits?'

'I know, this one looks bigger than her head!' I eye its fullness ruefully. Both my boobs are red and sore and streaked with big blue veins. 'They remind me of that A–Z of London I had that you used to laugh at.'

'You've always been weird about technology.' She smiles, but there's alarm in her eyes. 'No one tells you this stuff, do they? It's all pyjama co-ords and whimsical cot mobiles, not night sweats and constipation.' She shakes her head.

She had to rescue me a few weeks ago, holding Poppy and feeding me laxatives and Percy Pigs while I used my golden thread breath to do my first post-birth poo (at least all that pregnancy yoga came in useful for something).

'Tell me about it. I could write a book.' I drape a muslin over the top of my boobs. I don't want to put her off having children for good. Poppy will need some cousins.

'Well, you should! This is exactly what I mean! You *could* write a book about it, if you had a following online.'

'They're not ordinary mums, Mitts. They're marketing professionals who've had children.' And I don't know if that's true, but I like the way it sounds rolling off my tongue.

'*You're* a marketing professional!' She wriggles her arms into her coat and I feel the familiar stab of panic: *Please don't go, don't leave me here alone!* 'If you build up a decent following, you can do anything! And even if you keep it small, you can connect with some of the flexible working companies and still do digital marketing, but working around Poppy. There's life beyond pensions.'

'You know that's one of our key slogans?'

She ignores me. 'You're wrong, anyway. Not everything's a cynical marketing ploy. Forest Dad started posting snaps of their outdoor crafts and adventures and now he has his own Forest School franchise. You must've heard of *him*? The hot widower one?' She gazes off wistfully, as I raise an eyebrow and shake my head. 'What? His wife died, very sad. And there's The Happy Hollidays. She lives in a massive pad in the burbs somewhere, looking hot with her hot husband, and has raised her kids totally gender-neutral. No one knows if they're boys or girls. I don't know if they even know what they are!'

'All sounds a bit blooming weird if you ask me.'

'Hmm. Maybe...' She cocks her head as if considering something. 'What are you doing for the rest of the day?' she asks, swinging her bag over her shoulder.

'This and that,' I say idly, thinking of the M&S Extremely Chocolatey biscuits waiting in the cupboard and my next instalment of *The Crown*.

She reaches her arms around my shoulders and squeezes. 'I think you'd love it! This online thing – it's a community. They're always fist-pumping and high-fiving each other. Via emojis.' She lowers her voice again, gently touching the tips of Poppy's sprung hair while she feeds on, oblivious. 'From what they say, it's about survival.'

At the sound of the door closing Poppy latches off theatrically, lips kissing and smacking the air. I hold my breath but she stays sleeping, lips slightly parted, milk drunk, her closed eyelids flickering and twitching, like fast clouds scudding over her delicate peaches-and-cream skin. Love blooms and swells inside my chest. I sniff her head, breathing deeply. Sure it's hard, but it's worth every nipple-wincing, night-sweating second. *Survival?* Why would anyone need to survive this?

6

#GirlGang

Cassie

'Alicia, hi,' I say quickly, taking in her long tanned legs, offset by denim Daisy Dukes and stacked heels, and her tousled California hair. Behind her a large screen's emblazoned with '*Welcome to MUMSPIRE EVENTS sponsored by the FAMILY CO*', where Hetty's waving wildly, beckoning me to join her and the others on stage.

'Could you?' I gesture at the twins, dressed in knight tunics with sequined tutu skirts fanning out below and graffiti wellies.

'Sure, but we need to prep first for—'

I sense rows of beady eyes on the twins. See thoughts pedalling in the air: *A boy and a girl? Two girls?* I don't want to encourage any further diva behaviour in them from unnecessary attention; I've already had to promise them a treat for lunch just to get them here dressed like this.

'These things always follow the same format,' I say, propelling the twins in her direction, their alien antennae headbands wobbling. I couldn't believe it when Griff said

Alicia would be working with me on the campaign. I don't know what it is about her, but I can't take her seriously. Maybe it's the drippy LA drawl, or the way she takes taxis everywhere – literally to the end of the road (because she's always in inappropriate footwear) – but spends a chunk of her earnings on gym membership to work out with a live DJ while she's doing goat yoga or whatever it is. Just *walk*. She's never struck me as the brightest beam in the control tower.

'I'm "lifestyle". I'll give some tips on photographs, hashtags, 'theme'-ing your Instagram feed, linking back to the Family Co app, of course...' I pass her my bag and coat. There are some benefits to having an assistant.

'Right, but—'

Behind her Hetty picks up the mic, looking ready to begin.

'Boardroom Boss Mum will do empire-building and work-life balance,' – I lean in – 'although she's pared the latter down a bit since the Kid-Under-The-Desk Incident.' We all saw the tabloid coverage over the summer. That's why she's dropped so many places in the CHIN. It's a warning to us all: it doesn't matter how big you are, one false move and the whole thing can come down. 'Holistic Flo will do something on staying Zen and not losing your shit – *I know, ironic* – and Common As Mum will give some spiel around humour and connecting with your audience. Then we all go home and capitalize on the post-event traffic.' I nod towards the twins: 'H e a d p h o n e s,' I enunciate quietly, cupping my hands over my ears. God forbid the twins might be able to hear some of the crap I'm about to spout.

Alicia moves to speak. 'Didn't you read—'

I hold up my hand, not waiting for the recap from the Snowflake Guide to Getting Noticed or whatever it is. 'I don't have time to read everything that's trending this week, Alicia. Trust me, this works. Ask Hetty: at £25 a ticket for whacked-out mums trying to find a way not to return to work, it's easy pickings. I can convert them into app downloads, no problem.' The lights in the room dim. That's my cue.

'I was trying to say, didn't you read Hetty's email?' she calls after me.

I take my seat, sandwiched between Boardroom Boss Mum and Holistic Flo, who looks even thinner than usual, quite a feat. Hetty said she was a mess at the Villa, sobbing into her paella one minute and downing tequila and dancing on the table 90s-rave style the next, none of which made it online. She confided in Hetty: she recently separated from her husband and let's face it, no one wants to be *that* mum. As far as the public know, it was yoga at sunrise and extra *oms* for lunch.

I couldn't go to the Villa – there's no way I could leave Seb at home with the twins for three days. If I could, I'd be doing my old job. Obviously I made a few barbed comments about it to him, but I didn't really mind. These promo trips always look way more fun online than they are in real life; by the time you've fulfilled your posting obligations (including three hours trying to get the most natural pose against a terracotta/fresco-tiled/muralled wall), there's barely time to order a margarita.

Alicia is still looking at me uncertainly from the back of the room. Then she shakes her head, puts her hands on the twins' shoulders and scoots them out of view.

***

Flicks of red hair move like sparks of firelight across the stage as Hetty – our host, event organizer and, as the brains behind Mumspire HQ, our raison d'être – works the room in a deep-green velvet trouser suit.

'MAMAS!' She laughs as if she's just told the funniest joke. 'GOOD MORNING!!' She's like a super glossy children's TV presenter on speed. Which she might be, actually. 'I feel so – yes, I'm gonna throw it straight out there – I feel so BLESSED to have you all here today…!' She joins her hands into a prayer pose, then whoops them into the air. '…to bring together all you gorgeous mamas under one roof!'

There's cheering around the room. Hetty bounces in her pink suede pumps. She needs a clacker. Someone give the woman a clacker. At Hetty's signal the room falls to a hush, tanned arms and delicate tattoos resting on a riot of vintage floral tea dresses, leopard print and sequins.

'As you can see, our sponsor for this event is the Family Co. Now… the Family Co believe in *community*. It's at the heart of their mission. They want technology – like their new app – to *complement*, rather than *replace*, community. They're worried that we're all becoming too jaded by technology, screen time, even by social media, if you can imagine that!' Her laugh rings hollow in the high-ceilinged room. 'So our topic today is "Tell Me Something New".'

She slips her hand into her pocket and clicks a small device. Behind me, the welcome screen is replaced with #TellMeSomethingNew and my throat is filled with tiny prickly bubbles. *What's going on? Why didn't someone warn me about this?*

'Because we're getting *bored*, aren't we, mamas? We hear the same stuff and the same messages every day! We want to shake things up a little! We want to *connect* and *build community*! So try it, mamas, say hi to the woman next to you and tell her something about yourself. Something more than "I'm Hudson's mummy". Tell her something *new*.'

I pick out a few words from the hushed whispering: 'I swam the Channel', 'I produced a Bollywood movie'. The tone starts to change: 'I can't stand my husband', 'I can't stand my *kids*!' Then it's like a jet engine roaring to life and the room sounds akin to an aeroplane hangar: 'I hide from my kids in my wardrobe', 'I pretend I don't *have* kids… or a husband!'

'That's it, mamas, we're building community! We're connecting!' Hetty shouts, corralling the din. 'And I'm excited to say' – she draws it out – 'that Cassie here' – she grins at me – 'is going to share something *extra* special!'

I tilt my head towards Boardroom Boss Mum, notice that the slanted cut of her blonde bob perfectly mirrors the lapels of her 8os-style power suit; how does she have time for this shit?

'Usual format?' I ask optimistically from the side of my mouth.

'Didn't you get the email?' she asks quietly.

7

#HypnoBabes

10.15 Beth
Sorry I missed you the other day. Poppy won't settle in her cot. It's exhausting. I'm trying to get a doctor's appointment.

10.17 Priya
Are you still breastfeeding? Try cutting out dairy.

10.17 Bronagh
Is she sleeping on an incline?

10.19 Priya
White noise?

10.20 Bronagh
Established bath and bed-time routines?

10.30 Jade
You need wine! Come to the pub on Friday. No excuses!

8

#DaysLikeThese

Beth

I stay sitting outside on the terrace after my sister's left, Poppy's sleeping body warm against my belly. I've got it down to a fine art, supporting her head in the crook of an arm – with a cushion squashed underneath – leaving my other arm free. I raise my phone, hold it in front of my face to open it and think: *Now what?*

I google Amber Atkinson Instagram. I recognize her icon immediately, her voluminous hair filling the frame: @ThatGirlAmber. It's been like that since school. I click again, my breath held as the page launches and loads its heaving volumes of data. I force myself not to think about the virtual cliques swirling in the ether, the insecurities exacerbated, the cruelty inflicted in comments; made all the worse, more violent, because of the veil of anonymity the internet provides. I don't look at all the *InstaMums* and *InstaDads* my sister was blathering on about. I don't need to see other parents making things look easy; I already have that when I'm with the hypnobabes.

Instantly, I know I've made a mistake, but I can't tear my eyes away.

I sob quietly, afraid to wake Poppy, not wanting her to see me like this. I have a daughter now. I should be a strong woman, like all those pictures – memes? – that Gloria sends. But I'm not strong, I'm weak and my heart's being trampled on with Louboutin stilettos (I make a mental note to remove them from my secret Wedding Shoes Pinterest board). It's not just the bunting, or the favours, or the other wedding detail 'previews!' Amber's been excitedly posting to Instagram. It's thinking of my own bunting, my own favours, my own wedding, and all of it without Mum there.

I should've trusted my gut instincts. I knew it wouldn't be good for me. Not on a day like today, when I'm already at a low emotional ebb: tired and anxious and crabby. The 3 a.m. thoughts last night were gut-twisting: What will happen to Poppy if I die? *When* I die. What if she's still a baby? How old will she need to be to remember me, the way I remember Mum?

Before I had Poppy, I didn't worry about death: wherever Mum had gone, I'd be going too. I didn't want to die but I still took comfort from that thought. Since Poppy arrived, I'm terrified of dying. Terrified of being separated from her. And yet, in some ways, I'm terrified of living too. Terrified of days like today. Days where I still feel dismantled, like one of the old cars Dad likes to take apart and fix up. I need to be put back together properly. It's been a rush job. That's why I never told him about what happened at uni. He would want to fix me, and it would break him to know that he couldn't; whichever vintage parts he ordered, I would never fit back together quite the way I was before. I had been altered. And I couldn't confide in my sister. What if she had a relapse? Something else for me to feel responsible for.

Anything can happen on these days: why's that dog barking so loudly? Will he maul Poppy? What are those lads with beards and backpacks doing? Should I get off at the next stop? Danger is *everywhere*. And I'm the one who has to be alert to it, because Joe has no idea. How could he, growing up with his supportive parents in his Essex bubble? Nothing bad has ever happened to him. I stop my thoughts: I don't want to tempt fate.

I had my anxiety under control before I fell pregnant. With the right balance of exercise, sleep and minimum stress, I can manage it. That's why I've been at Don't Mention My Pension for so long. That's why I was still on the treadmill (walking, I'm not daft), right up until the day I went into labour. It was my way of 'keeping things on the level', as Joe would say. But that was a few weeks ago and ever since it's felt like the wheels are starting to come off. I'm just about keeping it all together. I can't work out, I hardly sleep. I'm a blooming mess.

What if they're coming back? What if I can't stop them this time?

My heart quickens as the thoughts build. My anxiety percolates like scalding, bitter coffee. Suddenly my safe space feels like a prison, a fortress I've allowed the past to penetrate. I need to get out of the flat. I need a distraction. But not something on my phone. I need something *real*.

9

#InstaAmbush

Cassie

'I've tried to keep this on the down-low...' Holistic Flo's voice breaks a little. Wow, she's good. 'But we're building community, aren't we?' She smiles weakly. *She* obviously got the email. 'So here goes: I'm single. My husband left me a few months ago.' There's a collective gasp around the room. She manages a brave smile as Hetty puts a fist to her chest in faux-solidarity.

I turn to better face Holistic Flo, my features arranged sympathetically. It's not that I don't feel sorry for her – I do – but I have a serious resting bitch face and it's never been more important that I'm seen to be at the top of my game. The Queen Bee. The linchpin of my girl gang (cringe). She reaches into her Calvin Klein athletic bag for a tissue and I detect a waft of incense and something else that I can't immediately place.

She rattles on: 'I have to accept that I'm in the right place. I'm living my best life.' Yeah, right. I feel a stabbing gratefulness for Seb, even though he's never done bath time.

She fingers her Holistic Flo rose-gold lotus necklace (fifty quid a pop). 'This is where I'm *meant* to be.' She discreetly wipes away a tear. I hear someone murmur, '*So authentic*'. Come on, is this for real? That's not where *anyone* wants to be: mid-relationship breakdown with a gaggle of kids? But as I look out across the room I see women nodding with understanding, smiling at her supportively.

'I hope you'll all download my new podcast, Holistic Flo Meets...' Okay. I get it now. There's a single-parent marketing opportunity. '...where I chat to other high-profile single parents about how they cope.' I smile, preparing to clap; you've got to hand it to her, she knows how to capitalize on a bad situation. 'And there's no app for that!' she quips.

At the word 'app' my head juts towards her, my eyes bugging out before I can stop myself. What's she *doing*? She knows what my brief is because she wanted the gig too. They all did. It's one of the few times we've all gone head to head for the same thing. But *I* got it. I need to be selling apps up here; she should stick to shifting yoga mats and healing crystals.

Hetty The Human Clacker bounces back on stage, hands clapping furiously, as Holistic Flo sits back, her high pony of ombré braids settling as she relaxes into her chair. I want to reach out and grab them, dragging her backwards to the floor.

'Next up we have... the queen of organic, free-range parenting, Cassie Holliday...!' I feel the weight of the room's collective gaze, remember I'm not quite sure what I'm going to say. That's fine. I can improvise. 'So, Cassie, tell us something new!'

I mentally flip through the app, alighting on the learning function. 'Morning, gals!' I beam, flicking a peace sign. 'I'm psyched to tell you about the fabulous new Family Co app, which has launched today! One great feature is you're able to set goals—'

'Sounds impressive, Cassie,' Hetty cuts me off, 'but today is about *community. Connection.* What we would love you to share – wouldn't we, ladies?' – she smiles eagerly at the audience – 'is what's new *for you? Tell us something new.*'

I visualize the hashtag, the volumes of tweets being sent out right now; most of the room has a phone in their hands and the Family Co will have a team tweeting as a tie-in to generate traffic. Mums leaning on kitchen worktops, bored shitless by the prospect of putting on another load of washing, will be encouraged to tweet their something new. Small parcels of data being downloaded, stacking on top of each other like Tetris blocks, each bundle not amounting to much in itself, but together creating a wall of sound, a solid picture: Cassie's got nothing. Cassie choked. Am I choking? I never choke.

There's a pregnant pause. The room is waiting. It feels like the world is waiting. Tell me something new... Where do I start? *I used to have a real career, a proper job, that I loved and I'd worked hard for against the odds and now I'm doing this because I need the money and I hate asking my husband for any... because of his stubbornness I live in a damp, mouldy cottage and not the beautiful home you see in my feed... my kids are off to school next year and I don't know how I'll cope without them there, by my side, every day...* I surprise myself with that last one.

'Shall we... bring out the twins?' Hetty asks. There's a

Machiavellian glint in her eye. Under the lights, her red hair and green trouser suit are amplified.

'Why would we?'

'Isn't it *time*?'

'Time for?' I'm not following this. 'Oh! You thought I was going to...? *No.*' I usher her over and, speaking away from the mic, whisper angrily, 'Don't use the gender of my children as a *publicity stunt*. They're not even meant to be here.'

Hetty speaks into the mic, rather than to me. 'This is about *community*, Cassie. This is about sharing with your followers. Isn't it time?'

I try to change tack. Bring this back: 'Sharing doesn't get better than with the SoMe function of the Family Co app, allowing the busy mum to schedule her posts up to two weeks in advance!'

'I don't know why you don't just tell us?' chips in Boardroom Boss Mum. 'It's getting so tedious.' Holistic Flo nods and yawns.

'You won't be able to keep it up once the twins are at school? In uniform?' Hetty renders it an indulgence with one snipe of her tongue. Suddenly it doesn't feel like we're doing one of our carefully orchestrated panels any more, it feels like me being pitted against Hetty and the other InstaMums. All the pent-up frustrations that naturally arise when you work with a group of people being aired in a very public way. I look from Hetty to the other women, my smile still plastered in place. 'And although they're delicious,' – Hetty's violet eyes fix on mine – '...I understand that the Breastfeeding Babe Bombs are no longer stocked by Big Mart?' Common As Mum guffaws. 'So what's next?'

My antennae switch into full alert. This is a code red

situation. What's going on? She's breached a golden rule. All things InstaMum-related must appear as if cast from gold and sprinkled with unicorn dust. Everything is positive and shiny and glowing. There should be no hint of failure unless included at the beginning of a caption and ending with a triumph over adversity or a two fingers up to the world: this is motherhood and I'm bossing it! I hear a girl in the front row say to her mate, 'I was thinking that too,' as her friend nods and looks at me in a way that I'm not used to… Is that sympathy?

I'm still smiling widely as if I'm totally in on this and trying to pull together a worthy response when behind me I hear a noise, muffled at first and then ear-splitting, as if someone is standing too close to a microphone. 'McDonald's!' a small voice is shouting brattishly. 'When are we going to McDonald's? Mummy said if we wore *these*,' – I picture two screwed-up button noses pinching at their tops and tutus – 'then we could go to—'

I gasp as the room comes to life, heads craning to see where the noise is coming from. *Where the fuck is Alicia?* On cue, her head pokes round the door to the right of the stage, just out of sight of the audience, a look of doe-eyed desperation, her face red and panicked. She's using her long slender legs to block the twins entering the room. One of them – Scout, I think – is dangling a microphone and Alicia's trying to wrestle it away. I'm eyeballing her, articulating the look known to all parents needing to keep their kids under control during weddings, funerals, any important event: GIVE THEM ANYTHING THEY WANT. But Alicia doesn't have kids and I'm not sure she catches my drift. Besides, does she buy into my Insta-crap? We've never spoken about it. She'll know what the official vibe is: wooden toys, no telly, gender-neutral 'littlies' (I hate that expression, but those mamas lap it up), me swishing around my beautiful home with my caramel-coloured highlights and my perfect family. But she can't think it's possible to operate like that for real?

She successfully gains control of the microphone because it's a much quieter voice I hear saying, 'Can we watch YouTube?' I just catch it because I know Birch's voice as well as my own and I nod emphatically at Alicia. She bends low, negotiating, before ushering them out of view. The other Influencers are tittering. I feel a bead of sweat slalom from my hairline down to my chin. *This is all Marina's fault.*

'Kids, eh?' laughs Hetty, eyes blazing. 'So, Holistic Flo's launching her podcast; Boardroom Boss Mum's about to tell us about the flexible working charter she's helping the Government draw up; and Common As Mum's book is out any day! How about you, Cassie? What *is* next for The Happy Hollidays? Tell us something new?'

Each time she repeats it, I want to punch her. She's right. I've got nothing. I look for Alicia. Is there something I'm supposed to say? I never think ahead to what's next these days. I didn't realize we needed a plan. I thought we were opportunists, riding this Influencer wave as long as we could and then seeing what happened next. I had a plan before and look how that turned out. I'm done with plans.

The sweat is trickling quicker now, tickling my skin. My fellow panel members lean in towards me. Boardroom Boss Mum and Common As Mum exchange a glance. Holistic Flo is smiling, her usual vibe of serenity sparking with something else – glee? As she shifts nearer, I get another whiff of incense and... I place the other smell, cigarette smoke! Ha! – but this is no time to think about that. My heart is pumping and my mouth is dry and suddenly I realize what's happening here. It's an ambush. That's what it is. It's an Insta-fucking-ambush.

10

Cassie's Twitter Feed

Trends for you

1 #Holistic_Flo_Meets
   72.1K Tweets

2 # Holistic_Flo_Meets_Cheryl
   61K Tweets

3 # Holistic_Flo_Meets_Cristiano
   59.8K Tweets

4 #TellMeSomethingNew
   55.2K Tweets

5 #MumspireEvents
   42.4K Tweets

11

#MeetCute

Beth

I grip the buggy's handlebars, enjoying the sensation of the wind boxing around my ears, as if it might clear out the negative thoughts. My mind roams with a freedom my postnatal body can't keep up with, although it's trying. I *need* something to focus on. Something *positive*.

I glance down. After briefly waking as I put on her snowsuit and placed her in her bassinet, Poppy has fallen back to sleep; it appears she will sleep anywhere other than her cot. I'm already dreading tonight. I made her a hat, a labour of love in my final weeks of pregnancy, and it finally fits. It's a shame to cover her hair – a halo of dusky blonde that fans out statically, like a lion's mane, attracting compliments wherever we go – but it's chilly out today.

I've walked half the circumference of Victoria Park, to the quiet section on the Hackney side, when I see them. Two beautiful identikit blondes duelling with sticks, their mum on a bench beside them. I know this bench. Joe and I sat there cupping mulled wine after the Christmas Market last winter. I cringe at the memory of Joe slipping his hand inside his pocket and my intake of breath as I thought: *This is it*. I recovered as he checked football scores. How much time and energy have I expended waiting for a proposal that I keep telling myself – and other people – I don't need?

I approach the woman awkwardly, tiny splinters of fear spiking over my skin. She looks almost too perfect, like the girls at school I could never fit in with. But I have an in, don't I? I'm a mum now. And this is what mums do, isn't it? They strike up conversation in the park. They don't just meet online, like my sister seems to think.

'How is it with two?' I ask, smiling. It's already crossed my mind that Poppy will need a sibling, someone to cling to if her parents get stabbed to death by a burglar masquerading as a Deliveroo driver in a bungled job. The children glance up but the woman ignores me, continuing to jab angrily at her phone. Blood rushes to my face and my scalp prickles: Did I really think it would be so easy? I'm back at school, my fingers gently sweeping across the nape of my neck, as if tracing over the keys of my flute, seeking the base of my thick rope of blonde hair, not yet comprehending. Ever so gently, my chest starts to shake. *Ignore it*. I hold my breath while I assess the tempo, fingers to my neck: *Why now?*

They're jealous, my sister always said. But that never made sense to me. Who would be jealous of the girl with the sick mum? A weird sound escapes me, something between a snort and a gag, and I tell myself: *Not here, not now*. You did not go through hours of therapy to have a panic attack in a park because you can't make a friend. It's not a big deal. But another voice, a screeching voice, repeats *They're coming back! They're coming back!*, while salty streams of saliva ripple down the inside of my cheeks.

I move off shakily, squeezing the handles of the buggy, needing to feel *something*, a texture beneath my sweating pores, anything to anchor me to the real world. I don't get far. I bend over double, dry retching, my face juddering over a mass of thick, twisting tree roots. I close my eyes. I hate this life.

Small voices float on the wind like dandelion tufts: 'Mummy, is that lady okay?' 'She looks a bit sick. Maybe we should give her some juice?'

I want to move but I'm rooted to the spot. My legs are shaking too now, sweat pooling and collecting, in my knickers, behind my knees. In my peripheral vision I see the woman stand, craning her neck as she looks at me. She puts her phone down and looks left to right as if she's weighing up whether to come over. She starts to move, then stops again. Sighs irritably. She's not perfect at all. Self-absorbed cow.

'Kids, stay there a sec,' I hear her say. She falters when she reaches me. 'Sorry. Over there. I thought you... wanted something...' Her eyes change, the lines around them creasing and gathering like pintucks as she takes me in. She must see that I'm dripping with sweat; that my body, so recently threaded together with stiches, feels like it's coming loose. 'Are you okay?' Her throaty voice drips like honey.

I nod. Unable to speak. My breath a wheeze. I haven't breathed like this in so long. This isn't how it was meant to be. Why did I go online? What good could ever come from unlocking the past?

'Put your hand on your stomach,' she soothes. 'Try it... that's it, hold it there a minute. *And breathe, come on, don't forget to breathe*. Do it with me! Like you're in labour.' She tries to connect with me, to make me smile, but when I think of labour I think of that horrible feeling of being totally out of control and another wave of panic grips me, rolling upwards through my chest. Nonetheless, I do as she says – I mirror her breathing, in and out, like we're in an antenatal class together.

A guttural shriek splits the air and I gasp, my eyes scouring the park. My brain responds: *Knife! Stabbing! Attack! Run!*

'Relax,' she says, and puts a hand on my arm. 'It's the parakeets.'

I jolt at the buzz of energy that passes between us. Something shifts inside me as I look up; the trapped, tightly coiled bands of anxiety loosening a fraction. Above me the tree is teeming with darts and flutters, emerald green and aquamarine. My breath escapes in a judder, my whole body exhaling relief.

'Ring-necked parakeets!' pipes up one of the children. My eyebrows lift in surprise.

'We love birds,' she shrugs in explanation and I smile, still concentrating on my breathing, still trying to find a way back. It's the loneliness of anxiety that gets me. The isolation of it. The feeling that no one else understands, no one else has experienced this moment, this confusion, this *sickness*. In the moment that your thoughts fracture and split, it's hard to believe that's not true.

Slowly the darts in my chest dissipate, the gentle pressure on my stomach diffusing them. My diaphragm opens and releases thick, toxic air. I visualize it, plumes of dark smoke, escaping with a hiss and snaking up to the sky. 'What is that? How did you...?'

'Tai chi, I think. Heard it at a talk at work once.' She looks wistful. 'I've done heaps of training. Stress management, disaster responses, that sort of thing.'

'I've read so many self-help... *self-improvement* books and I've never heard of that.' I pant as though I've run a marathon, almost over-egging it to mask my embarrassment. The woman turns away and I follow her eyes over the avenues of trees, the pavilion, the skate park. *Why here, why now? How long will I have to keep fighting this for?*

'It gets easier. You can't imagine it now, but it does.'

I have the startled, jumpy feeling I always get when my anxiety peaks; my perspective altered, the world in high definition. She looks too close up. I shift my head backwards.

'I hope so.'

Poppy wakes and stares up at a cross-stitch of tree branches and sky, blinking rapidly. I imagine her thoughts ticking over like a tally counter: *Where's the milk? Where's the milk?*

'I feel like a parakeet,' I say. 'Out of place in the city.' My voice splits as tears break along my eyelids. I sniff and blink to fight them away, not wanting this *got it all together* mum to see.

'*Ring-necked* parakeet!' a little voice repeats, and I try to smile.

The honey voice edges closer. She puts a hand on my shoulder and I feel it again: a ribbon of energy that wends through my muscles. 'Them? They're all over the place. They stay all year. They're thriving.'

Her kindness unsettles me. I look down to the floor, chewing on the inside of my cheeks. *This isn't normal, is it? Crying in public?*

'It was always supermarkets for me. I'd often have to find a quiet aisle – pets, usually – to have a little cry. It was the old ladies that got me. They'd catch my eye and nod, smiling, or stop me in fresh meats to say "Twins! You're *so* lucky", crinkly eyes twinkling. I'd smile back but I'd be thinking: *This Is Breaking Me. Motherhood Is Crushing Me.* I just wanted someone, *anyone*, to notice. To really see. To really see... *me*, I guess.' She trails off quietly and looks up to the sky. Something about the expression on her face makes me think maybe she doesn't have it all as together as I thought. 'To say, you know what? It's hard. But they never did. "Cherish every moment, dear!" they would cluck. Ha! No one really remembers, I guess. Something to be hopeful about?'

She tilts her head and props it on the tree bark. She's pretty. Her eyes are at the greyer end of blue, her skin clear but with small archipelagos of sun spots and a constellation of freckles, as if she's spent a lot of time outside. Her hair looks sun-kissed too, expertly highlighted. Her whole look's expensive in a laid-back way: skinny jeans, a loose white vest, multiple layered strands of gold necklaces and a brightly coloured cardigan, a rainbow of chevrons. 'Boho-luxe' they'd describe it in *Boom!* mag. I wonder how they'd describe me? Preppy spliced with indie undertones?

'Thanks,' I say, my throat sore and tight. 'Sorry, I... I'm not feeling myself at the moment.'

She holds up a hand. 'It's a total head-fuck. The whole damn thing.'

'I used to have panic attacks... before...' I gesture at Poppy. 'After my mum...' I drift off. 'And now I think they're...' I sigh, seemingly unable to complete a full sentence any more. 'It's hard, you know, once you've had a baby...'

She gives me space. Watches me before she asks, 'You lose the right to be sad about stuff?'

'Yeah, that's it. You don't have a mother, but you have a baby! Your boyfriend doesn't want to marry you, but you have a baby! I feel like I should be *grateful and happy* all the time. I feel guilty for Poppy...' (She smiles and nods at Poppy's name: 'Ah, sweet'.) 'When I'm not...'

'Welcome to parenthood!' She raises both her palms flat to the sky as I laugh.

We watch the twins, crouch-walking in tandem, following a ladybird.

'I just want to be a *good mum*... to feel *normal*.'

'You *are* normal. *Whatever that means.*' She pulls a face and we grin. 'My father-in-law died when I was pregnant. It's not easy. Be kind to yourself. Grief is... complicated.' She looks at me with sympathy. I hate that look. I don't deserve it. 'You got some mum friends? Some support?' she asks.

'A bit. I did a hypno-birthing course and we message each other a lot but, I don't know, I feel awkward with them sometimes. We've not known each other that long...' She nods as if she gets it. 'And they're so... *enthusiastic*. I feel like they all know what they're doing, and I don't.' I told Joe I was going to the hypnobabes meetup next Friday, even though I have no intention of going. I scuff my trainer in the dry mud. 'My sister tries, but she doesn't have kids. She doesn't understand why I'm not launching my own baby-zine and networking with the local InstaMums.' I can't avoid a scathing tone at the thought of Instagram and the sneak of delicate lace in Amber's last post.

She turns her head sharply, her eyes skittering over my

face, and I wonder whether she's the same – obsessed with how things look rather than how things really are.

'Don't do that,' she says eventually. 'You'll feel worse. It's all a load of rubbish.'

'That's what I said!' Words tumbling now, emboldened by a sense of connection. 'Like it's normal to put your whole life online, to monochrome your nursery to migraine-inducing levels…'

'Listen, don't worry about all that, worry about *you*. Sometimes it helps to know there's other people out there who get it. Take my number. In case you need to speak to someone, and I'm near here sometimes for work – we could have coffee?'

I feel the same relief as when Urzula nods briskly and tells me I can re-dress Poppy, noting her weight in her red book: I've passed. I produce my phone from my pocket, my hands trembling. As I do, my keys fall out.

'A love spoon!' She bends down, holds the delicate wooden key ring. 'It's beautiful. Where did you get this?' She turns it over in her hands before suspending it next to a silver charm glittering from her wrist: a small simple spoon. 'I wear mine every day,' she says. 'It's like my lucky charm! I had Welsh grandparents.'

· 'Me too!' I match her smile of recognition.

'They gave it to me for my twenty-first.'

'I've had this since I was little… from a family holiday in Anglesey.' More a fib than an outright lie. My hands are still shaking as she gives me my keys.

'Let me.' She takes my phone. 'Sandy,' she smiles as she inputs her number.

'Beth. Thank you. Again. For before. I'm not usually

like this.' I roll my lips to the left. 'Not in public anyway.' I manage a thin smile.

'Me neither.' She grins, shifting her weight away from the tree, rocking on to her toes, and I don't feel the needling unease that I do when my sister or Joe or Urzula leave. It sounds a bit weird, but I feel like this could be the start of something.

Don't get ahead of yourself, Beth. You're not exactly best friend material.

My teeth feel out the soft flesh of my cheeks again, biting down.

'Twins! Time to go!' Sandy calls. They amble over and try to play with Poppy, tickling her chubby legs while she stares at them, deadpan. Tough crowd, kids. Sandy wraps a scarf around her neck while I adjust Poppy's blanket, wondering if I should feed her here or if she'll manage until we get home, each of us returning to our own worlds. Which is probably why she doesn't think when she says, 'She would *always* pick you. You know that, right? Kids don't know if you're doing a good job or a bad job, they're just happy you're there.' She puffs out air in a whistle. 'My own mum... I mean, she...' She falters. 'She drives me crazy sometimes, but I'd still... well, I guess I would still...' She realizes her mistake, too late. 'Oh, I didn't mean to be insensitive,' she says as I snap simultaneously, 'My mum's dead. Sorry if I wasn't clear on that.' At the snarl of my voice the twins look up, concerned. 'And yeah, I would *definitely* pick her. And maybe, if she were around, *driving me crazy*, I wouldn't be finding all of this so blooming difficult!'

I'm too upset to pretend otherwise. I stare at the ground, still cracked in parts from a hot summer. I *hate* to be like this. I *hate* to be out in public and have other people seeing me like this.

'I'm sorry. I'm – my mum, we have a difficult…' She trips over her words.

My instincts on her were right. Not perfect. Not perfect at all. '*Please*…' I say. 'Just *go*.'

12

#TheUnhappyHollidays

Cassie

Hetty Mumspire, Mardy Mum and 38,632 others liked your post:

Thanks, Hetty and all my gals, for another excellent Mumspire event! Massive apols, gang, that I couldn't share my big news (yet!!), but as I said, watch this space!

#WatchThisSpace #TheHappyHollidays #PeaceAndLight

Comments:

@**Mardy_Mum** Amazing seeing Cassie today! Best day ever!

@**Cassie_No1Fan** Imagine if Cassie's big news is another baby! BETS ON THE NAME!!

#BabyNews #BirchAndScoutAnd?

★ ★ ★

'What happened?' Seb asks, when he finds me sitting in the dark. 'Did someone unfollow you on Twitter?'

A low blow. I ignore him, close my eyes. I need to stay calm. Regroup. Luckily, mindfulness comes quite easily to me. Whenever I'm feeling ruffled, I take a deep breath, close my eyes and think of all the likes.

'I was joking,' he says, intent on hanging around. 'What's the big news, anyway?'

My eyes snap open. 'So you do follow me?'

I set up Seb's account: This Happy Dad. I thought we could be one of those SoMe power couples. I started him off with a few pictures, researched the best hashtags – #BuffDaddy #MrHappyHolliday #InstaDad – and found some flattering photos. He was *so* ungrateful. Refused to give it a try and immediately changed his username to @SebHol431. He's never posted a thing.

He squeezes my shoulders with his giant hands. 'You know I do. What's wrong? It looked like it went well? Lots of…' He gropes for the right words and I feel guilty for snapping at him. 'Likes?' he ventures. I gaze up, face sullen. 'Pokes?' He tries to make me laugh.

'No one pokes any more.' I manage a tiny smile. 'It was a disaster,' I admit, rubbing my temples with my thumbs. And it was all my fault. I checked my emails and there in my Junk Folder, nestled between an offer to enlarge my penis and a discount code from The White Company, was an email from Hetty explaining the format change and telling us to have something lined up. Adding that Griff had suggested I take a lead on things since it was launch day for the app. And Alicia tried to help me, didn't she, and I wouldn't listen?

'But there's so many comments, everyone's so excited by your big news... what *is* the big news?'

He knows as well as I do that it can't be a baby. Finding the right moment to discuss it with Seb is only part of the problem; I can't remember the last time we had sex. But God, if only it were.

'There's no big news... but I need some.'

Seb shrugs and saunters out of the room. I can't be bothered to explain to him why the reality of what happened today is so different to what's online. Yes, I should have read the email, but why didn't the other mums have my back? I feel another flush of anger. Not just with them but with myself. When did my life get governed by all this? By likes and tags and charts and rankings?

In my hand, my phone fills with notifications. I click on but my interest quickly abates when I see it's someone I've never heard of called Mardy Mum, who's liked every one of my posts like an obsessive fan, clearly hoping I'll notice her and follow her back. For fuck's sake. I click on her profile, which doesn't give much away:

@Mardy_Mum
I'm E. I love sewing, my sister, and Yorkshire tea.

Her last post is an almost haunting image of stars from a projector, a mobile suspended over a cot, just visible in the stripes of light. She's only got a few hundred followers, but her follower-to-engagement ratio is massive: there's loads of comments, all posted in the small hours: *I thought it was just me feeling this way! Thank you for posting! So reassuring to know I'm not the only one!* Maybe she's on to something, posting in the night. I always hit up the US market if I need to boost my stats, but maybe I should focus on this: an untapped middle-of-the-night UK audience. She's funny too, dry and sarcastic, pulling no punches with the usual dreary mum brigade.

Hang on, Mardy Mum – wasn't she one of the newbies in Hetty's CHIN email? She's punching if she thinks she can go from zero to me following her back! I immediately hate myself for the arrogance of my thought. It's true – I can't follow everyone who follows me, popularity is my currency and why would I follow her? – but still. *What makes you think you're so special?* I hear Elen say. I click off wearily.

My thoughts return to the woman in the park. Her guilelessness, her disinterest in the whole SoMe scene. I feel fleetingly anxious: why did I tell her how hard I found motherhood in the early days? I need to be super careful with what messages I'm putting out there at the moment. Everything I've built up suddenly seems precarious. The thing is, they say when you know, you know, and there in the park, looking into her bewildered expression, her frightened eyes – I *knew*. There was something between us: a connection, a spark. She wasn't my sort of person on the face of it. Her daughter was called Poppy, for a start. I had to make the necessary coo-ing noises and feign pleasure at the consignment of this unique little person, this future leader of men, named after a *flower*. Beth herself was sporty-looking, her muscles toned despite a tiny baby, and very 'pink' – not head to toe (yuck), but hints of it here and there: a pale-pink hoody worn over a faded Stone Roses

T-shirt, sky-blue laces threading her blush-pink Converse trainers. Poppy was wearing a crocheted unicorn hat, for fuck's sake – it even looked hand-made! Beth was fresh-faced, her eyes tropical sea green and bright, despite the tell-tale new-mum tired lines. There was something about her, a girl-next-door easiness, a magnetism I can't quite put my finger on. I recognized something in her, saw myself in those early days, the bewilderment and disorientation. The shock. Mixed with the pure, blinding joy of holding your babies and wanting to protect them and keep them safe.

It was nice to interact with someone unencumbered by follower numbers or brand opportunities, the thought hovering between you: don't forget to take a selfie. I told her my name was Sandy automatically, because briefly that's how I felt – like being back at school, easily making friends, feeling part of something. They felt good, those unguarded moments. They felt normal. *Whatever that means…* I smile, but it tightens to a grimace. Why did I say what I did? And she'd just mentioned her mum. How could I ever explain to her the way I feel about Elen? The distance between us? The good intentions I have to fortify our relationship but the way my blood runs cold and I freeze when we speak? How could I ever explain *that*?

I pick up my phone to apologize, remember I don't have her number. Damn. I should've taken it. I can't even look her up online without her surname, and is she just Beth or Bethany? Bethan? Elizabeth? I doubt she has an online presence. She seemed almost *anti*-SoMe, which was… refreshing. She probably just has a private Facebook account. What I wouldn't give to go back to that. To go back to my old job and my old life. And I thought *that* was stressful.

I'll level with you. I didn't plan for The Happy Hollidays to be such a *thing*. Contrary to what you see in the squares, which looks like we live in a tastefully modernized stately home, in reality we live in a cottage in the grounds of said stately home: Seb's family home. The plan was always to renovate the cottage, or the Shed (as we affectionately called it at first, and now unaffectionately call it). When Seb's dad, Charles, died suddenly shortly after we moved in, I was pregnant with the twins. Seb was bereft. We both were: Charles was a lovely man. All renovation plans were put on hold. Seb knew that Marina, as his dad's second wife, had a right to stay in the Big House, and retain control over the trust, until she remarried or chose to move on, but he expected her to shuffle away immediately, back to Italy. Overnight, the Shed wasn't enough. He wanted the Big House. Four years on nothing's changed, and the only thing growing faster than Seb's sense of indignation is the damp patch in the corner. God knows when we'll eventually move in. Marina's so well preserved; tart and glossy like the jars of sour cherries she brings back from Sardinia. She could outlive us all.

I hadn't long left work and what with Charles passing away and supporting Seb and having the twins and then returning – briefly – to Horizon Air, I didn't have a network of friends to fall back on. I was popular at school, but my job made maintaining friendships difficult and I enjoyed my new life, my new work, too easily. Besides, those friendships were a reminder of the life I wanted to leave behind. It hadn't been my choice, the primping and preening, the fake tan and highlights (amazing the things that make you popular at sixteen – not top marks in maths and physics, that's for sure). Then there was Katya, but I had kids and she kept riding the clouds. We were friends on Facebook back when I had an account under my old name. No sign of nippers for her – just Barbados, Los Angeles, Miami. Envy twitches in my eyeballs. Not that I'd change things. You always have to add that as a mum, lest the universe thinks you're being ungrateful. Suddenly I found myself a mum of twins, with only my step-mother-in-law for company.

I had an Instagram account, but every time I logged on I was greeted with the same sad face. My account was blank. Devoid. I needed *something*. I'd been thinking a lot since having the twins about gender equality, about raising them *right*; being the best mum that I could be. Having the twins made me realize how strange my own childhood had been. What I'm trying to say is: I started with good intentions.

The twins were shrieking and toddling around outside, a blur of fair hair and podgy limbs, arms raised in delight as Marina chased them. I took a few photos from the window. They were dressed as they always used to be: for comfort and fun. Joggers and T-shirts. Pink, blue, yellow, green. Stars, stripes, spots. I scrolled through, looking for the right one. I was new to the game then: I didn't know about filters and cropping and light effects, but I knew the look I was after. There it was: bright, light and sun-streaked. I punched in the caption: 'Free-range, organic, gender-neutral littlies… reach for the sky, my darlings!' Okay, it was a bit saccharine, a bit twee, but it had been a traumatic few months; my hormones were all over the place. I wanted more for them, more than I had had.

The comments came in thick and fast:

LOVE this!

Wish I'd done this!

You are one cool mama, Mama!

I liked the sound of being a 'mama'. Was she in the US? I clicked on her profile. Oh. No, Bury.

I took another snap: my legs curled up on a cream sheepskin throw, Marina's *Vogue Italia* beside me, my love spoon bracelet just in frame as I cupped a mug of coffee. I added #PreciousMoments, when my actual moments that day had involved scraping cold porridge off a cracked, tiled floor – and believe me, porridge can really get into those cracks. It took off. I wasn't the only mum out there worrying about whether their kids were eating enough organic food, or getting enough fresh air and sunlight, or how best to shield them from society's toxic expectations.

I'd not long been posting when someone commented, asking what gender the children were. I ignored it – I mean, that was the whole point, wasn't it? It shouldn't matter. But the questions kept coming. Everyone was so *fascinated* by my refusal to confirm either way – and there were rumours of course: we keep to ourselves, but we don't live in total isolation – and it became a thing before I understood the power of it. 'Cassie Holliday has declined to say whether her children are boys or girls' turned into 'Cassie Holliday, mother of gender-neutral twins'. And yes, by power I mean a profound, unrealized, untapped marketing opportunity. You wouldn't believe what I've been offered – the sums of money – to reveal their gender in an exclusive. They've just turned four. What does it matter?

It wasn't long before the brands came calling. The twins were a sensation! After the photo shoots came the holidays. Seb would never have forked out for a family ski trip. Or the Disney cruise. Totally free (if you don't count the cost of your sanity or the demise of your relationship). Next came the merchandizing – an InstaMum is nothing without her merch – T-shirts, pin badges, a book deal if you can get it (everyone wants the book deal). I went for food. Massive error. Not even Nigella could make oats, garlic and fenugreek taste good. I should've done a clothing collaboration with one of the big brands. I tried by myself and totally bombed; out of my depth, running into copyright infringements and laborious supplier agreements I couldn't terminate when it was clear supply would far exceed demand.

My mind drifts back to the Mumspire event. Needing reassurance, I tap into SoMe. I'm met with a deathly e-quiet. You can practically hear the wind whistling across my account. A not embarrassing amount of likes for the event pic I posted (32,000) but not the usual tally of comments and no messages from brands asking to connect or would I be interested in…? In fact, the only real chatter around me is misplaced pregnancy gossip. Oh, the irony.

Is this how it starts? The beginning of being irrelevant? I shudder at the suggestion of it, because I have been *so* relevant, I truly have. I pull up the hashtag I created: #GenderNeutralLittlies. There they are, an array of kids all dressed randomly. A Matthew dressed as Elsa from *Frozen*. A little girl wearing a head-to-toe trucks-and-diggers tracksuit. Triplets – and I'll be damned if I can figure out what gender these three are – wearing primary colour T-shirts with the word 'CHILD' scrawled across them. A gender-neutral paradise. I created this. This is my community. These are my people.

A photo on the grid catches my attention. Hold up, is that...?

Noooooooo.

No, no, no.

My body pings with little beads of sweat. I breathe in, not wanting to click on it, not wanting to see the thing up close. It *can't* be.

What the —?

My heart plummets.

It *is*.

13

#Terrarium

Beth

Trees arch and bend along the canal outside as the wind ripples over the surface of the dark water, slicing the moon into segments. It feels like my heart is bleeding into the silence. I've fallen down a Pinterest hole. It started with slate floors and Agas but led to a whole new obsession with integrated appliances in a coordinated utility space. Is it healthy to have a board dedicated to how you place your washing machine and dryer: to stack or not to stack? Fearing it wasn't, I found myself searching for the inevitable, another distraction from the 3 a.m. thoughts crowding my brain: perfect wedding.

There it was. An uninvited sponsored post intruding in my secret Woodland Wedding board. A delicate sign on a rustic wooden chair reading: *We know you would be here today if heaven hadn't got so lucky.* I clicked on and up popped another suggestion: an empty chair wrapped in a sheer gauze, like a veil, and topped off with a pink taffeta bow round its circumference, presumably so no one sat there by mistake. Now I have a new secret board, worse than Utility Space: Mum. Populated with pins like 'thirty unforgettable ways to honour deceased loved ones at your wedding' and 'in memoriam signs for weddings'. Pinterest isn't helping.

Poppy latches off and I stand to wind her. The space contracts as I do, and I feel immediately claustrophobic. I quietly pace the flat instead, regretting that I didn't tidy up before bed: remote controls, empty chocolate wrappers and the last of the now dead plants litter the flat despondently. When Poppy was born, the flat briefly became a terrarium: bouquets from work, orchids from distant family, ceramic baby booties stuffed with poppies, cards scribbled with well-wishes and with... well, with love. We even got a three-foot bear made out of rolled-up vests and sleepsuits from Gloria's 'Old Gals With Balls' netball team (it took a whole afternoon to unpick). But that all feels like a long while ago now and I'm adrift in the debris.

I sink on to the sofa, keeping Poppy upright. I can't put her back down until she's burped; I can't risk another episode of projectile vomiting.

While I wait, the night presses against the glass, the darkness broken by flashes and twitches of light: aeroplanes traversing the sky, strip lights from other buildings switching on and off, reflections of street lights flaring in puddles. *Urban stars*, I think, my mind drawn back to the deeply studded skies of my youth in Yorkshire, platinum claw studs set into button-backed midnight velvet. I never thought I'd have a baby in a place like this. It still feels surreal, like it happened by accident, which I guess it did, motherhood in a cityscape. I hunger for real stars, real life, but even as I do another part of me is asking, *What's going on, Beth? Why can't you enjoy what you have?*

I bend my head against Poppy's. Feel her soft hair against my cheek and breathe her in. It's habit already that I always kiss her twice: once for me and once for Mum.

Don't slip back to that place. Don't let the bad things in the past override the good.

I don't think my sister's right about Instagram, but she is right about one thing: I need a friend.

14

#3a.m.

03.11 Beth

Sorry about earlier. I don't usually cry in parks and snap at strangers. Especially the nice ones. Any chance you still fancy that coffee sometime? I'll try to be more normal. Whatever that means! Beth x

And sorry it's late. Hopefully your phone's on silent!

03.15 Sandy

There you are!
I was worried about you after we met. Don't be sorry. I'm sorry. It was a stupid thing to say. Coffee would be great.

03.16 Beth

I didn't wake you did I?

03.17 Sandy

No, don't worry. Work emergency.

03.18 Beth

Ah you must be one of those people who love their jobs! That's commitment!

03.20 Sandy

Kind of. I do a lot of work with the US. Projects, events. I'm up at funny times.

Actually, no. I don't love it. In fact, sometimes I can't stand it. It's becoming all pervading but I need the money and it fits around my kids so I can be home with them – usual story! Modern motherhood.

Sorry, unplanned 3 a.m. rant.

03.26 Beth

I get that. I've been in my job for so long – too long – because it works for me. I could do it with my eyes closed. My sister's always mithering me to do something creative. I did art and textiles at uni. Now I do pensions marketing *grimacing emoji*.

03.28 Sandy

Is it to do with anxiety? Is that why you stay?

03.31 Beth

I guess. Pathetic, isn't it?

03.33 Sandy

It's not pathetic. Everyone's got it. Anxiety. It's an epidemic. It's modern life.

03.34 Beth

Do you think? I find it so embarrassing.

I can't even speak to my boyfriend about it, not properly. He knows – and I told him what happened in the park – but he seemed dead awkward and said I should talk to my therapist. I feel so daft.

03.35 Sandy

Maybe he's right?

03.37 Beth

Maybe. But I know if I could get Poppy into a routine and get some sleep I'd feel much better. It seems pointless to go back to therapy when I know what the problem is?

If I could talk to Joe, without feeling like he thinks I'm half mad, that would help.

03.40 Sandy

Sometimes the people closest to us are the hardest to speak to.

...

...

03.43 Sandy

But that doesn't mean we should give up trying.

Let's arrange that coffee tomorrow.

15

#Sloshed

Beth

'No, no, she's not so bad.' I jiggle Poppy up and down by the specials board, swapping hips so I can reach down and take a sip of my wine, warming on the table.

'Top-up?' Jade asks as I lower my glass, tipping the inviting pink liquid in before I have a chance to reply. I smile gratefully. Now I'm here it feels good to be out of the flat. I nearly didn't come. I kept changing my mind. Sandy convinced me. Since last week we've been messaging every day. Mostly at night, which suits me. She's almost always awake, working. She says she can power down as soon as she switches off and grabs a 'micro-nap' whenever she needs to. The thought makes me shudder. She's got such a relaxed hippyish vibe; I picture her practising tai chi, listening to the birds in her long floaty cardigan. I wish I could be more like that. I wish I could live more in the light and less in the dark.

The wine warms my cheeks and they buzz a little. Things are definitely getting better. With Sandy's messages to sustain me, warding off the middle-of-the-night feelings of loneliness and isolation *in a healthy way*, my anxiety is more in check. I'm still tired, bone tired, but I can rationalize it better: my heart's racing because I've not slept and I missed breakfast and I've had two brews. *Not* because I'm having a heart attack and leaving Poppy motherless, hungry and crying in the crook of my arm until Joe gets home (I've imagined it *hundreds* of times). I'm doing okay. That's the problem with anxiety, though. It's like the Spice Girls – you never know when it's planning its next comeback.

Jade takes a large slug of wine then scoops Ziggy up from the floor, shaking his bottle energetically. 'Multitasking!' she cackles. Then adds quickly, 'I'm still breastfeeding. Combination feeding, they call it.' Ziggy's arms jerk manically, his enthusiasm for milk matching my own for rosé. I take another swig.

We first met in our local yoga centre on a light-filled spring morning, bursting with optimism for our future positive birthing experiences. These were quickly dismantled in real time over WhatsApp as we each went into labour, one way or another, and we've been a sounding board for each other ever since: spiking temperatures, spiky partners, spiky *us* on the days our hormones are ricocheting. I survey us now – we're like a colour photograph left out in the sun, which has slowly faded, the colour bleaching out. Only our cheeks look alive, flushed by half a glass of wine.

Priya has Dingo on her left boob and a glass of rosé in her right hand. 'It's optimum timing to drink while you're feeding,' she assures us, 'so it peaks in your system just after you finish. No need to pump and dump!' Priya's an accountant and one of those people who wants to think she doesn't play by the rules, while rigidly sticking to the rules like they're a life raft.

'Well, I'm not taking any chances.' A double breast pump rests beside Bronagh's glass. 'Sure I'm shattered today,' she says, her gentle Irish timbre weary.

'Bad night?' I lean in towards the group. The sudden intake of wine and the heat of the pub has moved my cheeks from buzzing to flaming. I'm struggling to hear over the background chatter and Poppy's niggles. I circumvent the group of chairs, bobbing Poppy, the familiar sensation of not quite being a part of things, of being an outsider, creeping in. I wonder if this is how motherhood will always feel – me looking in from the periphery, not quite in and not quite out? I steel myself to speak, but each time I open my mouth I trigger a wave of hot self-consciousness. I try to bury it down with more wine.

'Godawful!' She waves her glass around. 'Would you believe it, little Noel slept through but the bleddy alarm kept going off!' She has one of those naturally loud voices. A 'carrying voice', Mum would've said. I see a few people at the next table look up and I grin wildly, a welcome distraction from my thoughts. *Welcome To The Friday Branch Of The Sloshed New Mothers Group!*

'Why don't you switch the heartbeat sensor mat off? You've got the video monitor,' Jade asks impatiently while she winds Ziggy face down over her knees.

'And what if the one time I do the worst happens? I'd never forgive myself! My great-auntie Una's little one was thirteen months old!' She fervently cups her wine glass. 'I don't know how ye get a wink of sleep.' She shakes her head.

'But you don't sleep!' Jade spits. 'Even when Noel

does!' She returns Ziggy to the floor, quickly gulps a large mouthful of wine, then picks up Zelda. 'You lot have no idea! You should hear some of the things we talk about in our twin group.' As she yanks Zelda's bottle out of her changing bag, a sharp pair of scissors pokes out.

'Watch out!' I shout, finding my voice as her wrist glances over its tip.

She glares. 'It's the poo bombs. Unless it's designer, I hack it right off, straight down the middle and in the bin.'

Priya looks on in horror. She's a zealous recycler and the only one among us who's managed to stick at reusable nappies.

'I had a terrible night too.' I force myself to speak, grateful I've not experienced a 'poo bomb'. Not just to defuse the tension, but to ward off the gentle vibrations: in my ears, my chest, my feet. *The pub is hot and noisy and you're tired. Nothing bad is going to happen.*

The hypnobabes are familiar with Poppy and her little idiosyncrasies, like hysterical crying for no obvious reason.

'Did you take her back to the doctor?' Priya asks.

'I keep going back,' I nod, too fast. 'It might be colic. Or silent reflux. Which would be ironic, wouldn't it? He said it's too early to tell. Told me to speak to the health visitor.' We all roll our eyes.

'Did you see Doctor Shah?' asks Jade, eyebrows raised. She whistles as we laugh.

'It can't be easy having a difficult baby.' Priya smiles at Dingo beatifically; he stares gormlessly into the middle distance, hypnotized by the pub's lights.

'She's not difficult! She's lovely, she's—' My voice starts to crack.

The conversation shifts; they begin gossiping about The Happy Hollidays and a post on *Boom!* and I can't join in, even though I have so much to say.

My friends don't like my baby.

'Have you seen Cassie's husband?' Priya licks her lips. 'Seriously hot. I asked Georgina, my lawyer friend, if she's come across him, but apparently he only represents super-high net-worth individuals,' she swoons. 'They must be worth a *fortune* between them.'

She talks about these people as if they're minor celebrities, which I guess in the mum bubble they are. How weird to be famous in one little pocket of life, on people's phones, but not in the real world. I point it out to the others, bitterness sticking to my words, knowing the heat of debate will be the distraction I need. *She's unlikeable. Like you.*

'Isn't that how the world works, though?' asserts Priya a little defensively, and I realize the hot pink graffiti on her T-shirt says 'Holistic Flo'. 'There'll be countless "famous" footballers that Joe would do a double take at if he walked past them on the street, but you wouldn't have a clue.'

'But footballers exist outside of people's phones. They have a talent – they play football at packed stadiums and their "celebrity" is just a by-product.'

'Well, I think looking after kids and keeping your home immaculate is a bloody talent. You should see the state of mine,' Jade says wearily. Her Afro hair fans out from a thick orange hairband with an abstract print. She's one of those cool, artistic-looking people, who talks about 'the agency' and always has a MacBook poking out of her bag, but you're never quite sure what she does.

'I didn't think *you'd* be into the InstaMums?' I say, realizing I see it as a compliment.

'The agency uses them,' she shrugs. 'I think fair play to them. It smacks of bored, frustrated women, wanting to be at home, probably under-estimated at work, utilizing their talents and earning a bit of cash for their families in the process. No harm in that? But you've got to take it for what it is. You can't buy into it, or compare your life to theirs. They're running a business.'

'It doesn't bother you the whole thing's fake? And they're using their kids to do it?' I shake my head. 'It's all wrong.' I feel stirred up. 'They're just another clique – the cool gang at school – trying to make the rest of us feel inadequate and making money out of it!'

An awkward silence ensues. I have to remind myself: they don't really know me. They don't know about what happened at school. I make the connection with a start – is that why I find the night-times so hard? The way the silence seems to reverberate around me, like it did on the steps alone at lunchtime?

I didn't realize until after Mum died how much what happened at school had affected me. That's the thing you learn with therapy: it's never about the thing you thought it was. I thought I was grieving for Mum, my body literally crippling with guilt at what happened. I thought the anxiety, the intrusive thoughts, the panic attacks that made me think I was dying too were because she was gone and it was my fault. But Russell, my therapist (arranged by the university counsellor) made me realize it wasn't just about that – it was about what happened at school. It was about not having a safety net when bad things happen.

Like the day Caitlin Oxenbury reached right over her desk in Textiles and, with sharp fabric scissors, chopped my plait clean off. I remember the quick, strange tugging feeling and her big grin, her teeth still with bits of crisps stuck between them from lunch, the thick rope of blonde hair on the floor.

Mum was amazing. I still ache for her when I think of it. She came straight to school and whisked me to Leeds. I sobbed all the way, not wanting to get out of the car. 'I look like a scarecrow!' I'd cried. 'Life gets a lot tougher than this,' she said, and she'd already had her diagnosis by then so I couldn't disagree. She marched me into Kit Cuts It, the coolest salon in Yorkshire, which I wouldn't have expected Mum even to have heard of. Kitty herself enveloped me in a hug: 'Beth, your mum called. What a day you've had! C'mere, love.' She smoothed and patted my hair, ushering me to a chair and assessing the damage with a frown. Next to me, a woman I recognized from the gossip mags gave me a smile from under her foils. I didn't see Caitlin again as she was expelled, but she would've heard about how the woman *and* her Leeds United football player husband came into school the next day to talk to everyone about bullying and said hello to me by name. I thought I'd got over it until Mum died the summer before uni and the world – my world – started to close in.

'I think you're reading too much into it.' Jade scrutinizes me. 'You know you're doing a great job, right?' I sniff and smile as wide as I can without triggering tears. She squeezes my leg. 'You've got this.'

I put a hand on my stomach and remind myself to breathe, like Sandy showed me. The knots around my chest stop tightening. The tiny vibrations recede. Is Jade right? Have I got this? I'm here in the pub with my friends and our babies, aren't I? I've become friends with Sandy. I live in a nice flat with my nice boyfriend and my beautiful baby. From the outside, at least, I'm doing okay. So why doesn't it feel like it?

Something at the table has shifted. We finish our drinks quietly, the noise from Bronagh's nursing pump the only sound breaking the silence at our table.

16

#Papped

To: Cassie@TheHappyHollidays.com
From: Lucy@BoomMag.com
15 September at 11:35
Harassment

Hi Cassie,

Great to hear from you! I wondered if I had the correct email address for you.

I was approached with the photograph from an unnamed source (see below). Don't worry, I'm not looking to do a profile piece on you now since I have a feeling I'll be getting a lot more material from my new friend here which will be of considerable public interest.

All best wishes

Lucy

★ ★ ★

—— Forwarded email ——

To: Lucy@BoomMag.com
From: theunhappyhollidays@mail.com
1 September at 16:40
The Unhappy Hollidays

Hey there, Lucy,

I've seen your coverage on the InstaMums and wanted to reach out. I always thought there was something odd about Cassie Holliday and now I know – she's a total fraud.

There's more where this came from but I have one condition: I want you to use the hashtag #TheUnhappyHollidays – let's get this trending!

TUH xoxo

17

#MudKitchen

Cassie

Boardroom Boss Mum and 1,465 others liked **Common As Mum**'s post:

I love this woman! Check out @Mardy_Mum for hilarity and honesty from a first-time mum!

#MardyMum #TheSloshedNewMothersGroup

Boardroom Boss Mum, Holistic Flo, Forest Dad and 2,809 others started following **Mardy Mum**

I take my frustrations out on the broom, but it only aggravates the mud, flurrying it further into the air. Tiny brown particles contrast with the gleaming surfaces.

'Thanks, Ruby,' I mutter. Ruby lives in the village. Her mum runs the post office, which is handy because Ruby runs a pet clothing brand on Etsy and spends half her time in there packaging up parcels. I can't imagine the time/profit ratio is lucrative as she's almost always available to babysit. The twins love her. They're fascinated by her black glossy hair with purple streaks in it, and the way she seamlessly switches into Japanese when she's on the phone. She's gorgeous, like a sexy pop star incongruously found in this Surrey backwater.

I'd prefer to have Marina look after them, but she's in Sardinia and I need more regular help. I'm struggling to keep on top of my posts for Griff – hence why I was over here in the Big House in the first place, looking for a bloody wok. I was midway searching through the cupboards – copper pots and Le Creuset casseroles cast aside – when it dawned on me that it would be much quicker and easier to get the cross-trainer shot done first! Why hadn't I thought of that sooner? I rushed upstairs, borrowed some of Marina's workout wear and sprinted over the lawn to the gym and pool annexe. I must've been twenty minutes, tops. When I came back, Ruby and the twins were in the kitchen, the welly rack dragged in from outside, copper pots turned terracotta as they overflowed with mud.

Who makes a mud kitchen in an actual frigging kitchen?

I could use a nanny agency but it's too fraught with risk, even if they signed a confidentiality agreement. The Mumsnetters would have a field day if they knew I paid for help once in a while. It's not such a risk with Ruby; she's one of those unusual millennials who isn't in to SoMe. I tried to impress her with my media pack stats once when the twins were in bed and I was waiting for Seb to find his Radford tie before the golf club's annual fundraiser (snooze), and she looked totally blank and went back to appliquéing a Sgt Pepper-style jacket for a sausage dog.

I clap my hands on my thighs without thinking. *Shit.* Marina's leggings, now flecked with mud. She won't mind me borrowing them, but she will mind if I stain them. We're close, Marina and I. She's like the mum I never had: considered, calm, curated. And supportive. She would've supported my career choice, like she does now. I often think of Elen's face when I told her my good news, clutching my letter from Horizon, her mouth dropping to the floor like a baggage forklift scurrying over tarmac. 'But how will you ever find a husband with a job like that? It's off-putting. The hours…'

'I don't know,' I'd shrugged. I still remember the tingling on my face, as I realized she wouldn't be proud of me after all. She didn't understand why I wanted it so badly, why I wanted to leave Watford, travel the world, explore new places. 'Who cares? It's my dream.'

'It's your *dream.*' She stretched it, spat it out. 'Of course it is.' She was elated, later, when I couldn't return to Horizon. As if she'd been proved right all along: *I knew she'd only do it until she found a man to take care of her.*

Seb's mother died when he was a toddler, an accident in the lake in the grounds; apparently she'd been free-diving, looking for 'treasure' for Seb. He wasn't there, and didn't know what had happened until he was older, but I often see him staring out at the lake, his expression unreadable. Charles had a string of girlfriends in later years, but none serious until Marina. She was a fashion editor in Italy before she met him, and had never married or had children herself. I owe my whole makeover and look to her. The Missoni cast-offs, the leather cigarette pants – it's all designer vintage, because it's all second-hand. The first hands having been Marina's delicate digits. She created Cassie Holliday really. I guess she felt sorry for me. She called me over one day – 'Bring the twins!' she said. 'Oh, and *fare una doccia*!' 'Sorry?' 'Take a shower!'

I arrived to a crack team of assistants: a hair colourist; hairdresser; masseuse; two nail technicians. I was clipped and cut, buffed and beautified, preened and polished. I emerged like a butterfly from its crinkly old mum joggers chrysalis. It was different to when Elen would put my hair in rollers, or apply clumpy mascara to my virgin lashes, because I didn't look like a princess or a teenage beauty queen. I looked like the me I wanted to be: *cool*, in a way I'd never achieved before. It was a few weeks after that I started posting on SoMe. I could never have done it as the old me. Even in school I was always more of an introvert. Funny really, because you might consider my old job – *my real job* – customer facing, but unless they managed to get a grip on me, passengers would only glimpse me as I flashed by.

I move the welly rack back outside, grimacing at the woodlice scattered beneath it, and reach again for the broom. *Bloody Ruby.* I keep thinking about what Beth said at 2.00 a.m., when she was awake feeding and I was trying to get in with The Pod Bitches, an LA InstaMum collective: 'I don't feel like myself, since having Poppy.'

I've come to look forward to our nightly exchange of messages; there's something intimate about it, like you're the only people in the world. It reminds me of flying. More than once my phone's lit up with a response from Beth and I've had that sense of something magic in the air, a deliciously private moment shared, like seeing the Northern Lights, the bounce of light on the curve of the horizon, while the rest of the plane sleeps. I'm easily lost to memories of my old life, to light illuminating the dark, but something about Beth anchors me in the present.

I know exactly what she means: I remember those early months with the twins, the love I felt competing with the feeling that parts of myself had been ejected at the same time as the babies. I didn't want to change anything, but I needed something for me. Something to feel like I hadn't disappeared completely into a vacuum of misaligned sleepsuit poppers and wandering packs of baby wipes. This has been it; my little corner of Instagram has been the thing that's kept me feeling like me. I see Beth standing on the precipice of it now, the motherhood black hole. I want to stop her falling in, like Marina did for me, but how?

I lean heavily on the broom and sigh. I had a meeting with Griff and Alicia yesterday; we didn't get the traction Griff was hoping for after the Mumspire event. The tension was palpable. They want top-of-her-game Cassie. Not me, crash-landed at sea, hoping someone will push out a dinghy.

'When you were selected, we didn't appreciate how soon the twins would be starting school,' Alicia said quietly as we said goodbye where the exposed brickwork met the shiny lifts. 'What are you going to do once they're in uniform?' She bit on her lip nervously, her eyes casting around the steel-trimmed space for inspiration. 'How about campaigning for gender-neutral school uniforms?' she asked, her eyes luminous, and my stomach flipped at her optimism. 'That's something we could get behind, something… *relevant.*'

I'm still kicking myself about the photo. I usually make sure we stay 'on brand' until we get home, or at least until the train's passed out of London. I thought I was in the safe zone at the train station. The truth is, I rarely get recognized in real life. It's surprisingly easy to go about your daily business, doing boring mum shit, unless you're dressed like a twat. I'd brought a change of clothes for the twins – I knew they wouldn't last in those stupid outfits for long – and of course I'd promised them McDonald's. It's so hard, being a good mum *and* a good influencer.

I look at the post on *Boom!* mag *again.* A series of photos of me and the twins: Scout in a football shirt, Birch in a Batman top, both of them glued to their iPad screens while they dunk their chips in those putrid little pots of sauce in unison; me mid-inhale of a Big Mac, scowling and jabbing at my phone; my face twisted as I berate them, the viewer not knowing it's because we're about to miss the train and Scout's just announced she needs a wee even though I'd asked her five times if she needed one when she was playing on her iPad. Beneath that, quotes from me:

'I call it The Wildflower Approach – children need love and light, to grow, to be nourished, emotionally and spiritually. Can they get that from an iPad? That's all I'm saying.'

'I'm not anti-technology for children – I respect every parent's right to choose what's best for their family – but it's not right for us. I don't want to curb their potential. I want them to be outside, running free, my wildflowers in the wind.'

'We tend to avoid characters and logos etc. We prefer muted shades, natural materials. We want the world to be a blank canvas on which they can paint their futures. Artists of their own destinies.'

The face of free-range, organic parenting Cassie Holliday. Anyone else get the feeling we're all being taken for a ride? #GenderNeutralLittlies #TheUnhappyHollidays

Have I really said all that shit? Christ. I sort of remember it, little snippets here and there, playing up to whatever gig I'd been signed up for, but put together like that I sound like such a tit. And the comments…!

@JembolinaM How do we even know for sure this is Cassie? It looks fake to me

@ChiChi Come on, she's the fake!

@Panini82 Photoshopped for sure!!

@SelBelle Who gives a shit what gender her kids are anyway? She's old news

@FabFrannie She's probably in on it with Boom Mag, sending them the pics. She'll do anything for a bit of exposure

@AartiParty100 What happened to the baby?

@Cassie_No1Fan What's wrong with you people? Of course she wouldn't do that. These pics are FAKE! I LOVE Cassie #peaceandlight #thehappyhollidays

I reason it out: it's most likely an opportunistic snap, taken by someone who saw us in McDonald's and then googled the quotes. But why send them to *Boom!* mag? And what's with the 'unhappy hollidays' thing? A worry needles at me: could someone have followed us from the event, watched us from afar, staying close waiting for an opportune moment? I should never have posted to my Stories in the park.

They're not the *worst* photos. In fact, we look like one of those normal families, where the kids clutch character backpacks and the mum says things like, 'Here you go, sweetheart, have some more ketchup'. That's the problem, though. That's not what my followers come to me for. They don't want to see their own lives reflected: they want me to be *inspirational*, not *aspirational*. And that's what I've built my brand on, that's what my livelihood depends on. Me being a different sort of mum. I bore my fingertips into my temples. *Is* someone following me? I look across the lawn to the lake. I shiver all over.

What the fuck, Cassie? You have two million followers across all channels. Of course someone's following you! That's the whole fucking point!

I flick through Instagram despondently. It's a total shitshow. My own posts are getting hardly any traction while Lucy's *Boom!* mag feed is clocking up more followers and likes by the second. It's like watching my own career combust. At least Griff and Alicia haven't seen it yet.

Meanwhile, the newbies are coming up fast from behind.

Like this Mardy Mum, who suddenly seems *everywhere*. You've got to hand it to her, her persistence is paying off. There's been a flurry of new posts. She's not focusing on the night-time any more, she's posting in the day. There's some baby spam: beautiful fluffy hair fanning out around its head like a lion's mane. I can practically feel my womb pulsing. I want to reach my arms into my phone cartoon-style and draw it into me. I love tiny babies with big hair. That's 50,000 GML right there. Instagram Gold. And I don't use that term lightly. East London-y-looking places. Understated jewellery. No photos of her yet. Working up the confidence. It can take a while. Almost 4,000 followers already and how long has she been going? A few weeks? I get distracted reading a few posts. Damn. She's funny. Self-effacing. Witty. Honest. When you get traction like this it's like magic and stardust and unicorn fucking sprinkles. Briefly you become the sun, pulling opportunities and cash and freebies towards you. She's doing it. In record time.

In a recent post she's bemoaning a lack of cool breastfeeding-friendly clothes. 'Still getting the hang of this social media malarkey' my arse. She's playing the game like a pro. There's heaps of brands asking for her address. She'll have a whole new wardrobe to choose from by next week.

18

#ComeFlyWithMe

Beth

I fold my new breastfeeding tops from my sister – a well-timed work freebie no one else would make use of – and stack them neatly in my drawer. I had two chunks of four hours' sleep last night. I feel like a new person as I potter around the flat listening to my first podcast! An absorbing discussion about anxiety and technology and dopamine hits and how we're all becoming addicted to our phones. Sandy recommended it, she said podcasts 'made boring mum shit better' and I wouldn't put it quite like that but she's right. I've got some craft ones lined up next.

I want to suggest something to enrich Sandy's life in return, but what can I offer in a similar vein? I've told her I don't go on social media and my craft magazines are hardly agenda-setting. Unlike the podcast: I've been so absorbed, I almost forgot it's Friday afternoon. Each day I have to fight the urge to ask Joe to text me as he leaves work, but on Fridays I feel light and free, the promise of the weekend sweeping ahead.

In the living room, I place my forehead on the glass. Increasingly I feel like a country mouse, out of place in my glass box in the city. If only I could customize it, make my mark on the flat in some way. I joked about bringing down my sewing machine so I could run up some curtains and cushions for Poppy's room, but Joe looked alarmed.

'Well, we won't live here forever, will we?' I'd said. 'We'll be able to take Poppy's bits with us, they'll be right at home somewhere more… rural.'

'Babe!' he'd grinned. 'I've been thinking the same, but I didn't think you'd be keen.' He beamed enthusiastically. 'Let's do it! Let's move to the country!'

Happiness surged like electric, light suffusing through my core. I love London but it isn't where I thought I'd be when I had a family.

'Joe!' I threw my arms around him, my face wreathed with smiles. 'What will you do about work? Can you work remotely?' Having him at home more would be, well, it would be fantastic. Especially when we're settling in. Briefly, I wobble – *Could I really go back?* – but the warmth in my core is still there, spreading through my veins, soothing the spikes of anxiety. I realize that with Joe by my side, it's possible. Anything is possible.

'I don't mind a longer journey. We'll get a little place right by the forest. Mum will be made up. She'll find us something.'

'Your mum? She will?' I thought his parents would be the reason he'd be reluctant to go. I pick up another train of thought. 'You can't commute from Yorkshire, Joe.' Sometimes I wonder if he remembers exactly how far away Yorkshire is.

'Yorkshire? I thought we were talking about Epping? Epping Forest?'

The light drains from my body and I feel a strange cocktail of sensations: emptiness, confusion, frustration, relief.

'Joe, Epping Forest is *not* countryside!' Not as I know it.

'Of course it is. It's a big forest with trees and grass and... deer! There's *deer*!'

'*So?*' I'd said, exasperated. Countryside to me is rolling moors, rosehips and red kites. It's God's own country. But I couldn't ignore the relief. I couldn't ignore...

My phone pings in my pocket, bringing me back. A text from Joe:

Drink outside the Palm Tree in 15? J xx

I head straight there and get a spot along the canal path where I know the sunlight will linger the longest. I lay down one of Poppy's giant muslins to sit on and watch the band arrive: a glamorous trio of octogenarians, sharply dressed. When Joe appears, music is emanating from inside the pub and Poppy's awake and propped up on my knees, and for once she isn't crying. I wonder which movie we'll watch tonight: Joe insists on a Friday night romcom with chocolate and wine. A tradition he started with Gloria.

'Babe, I was thinking,' Joe says, as he returns from the bar with drinks. 'That wedding we've got coming up, you should go to the shops tomorrow, get something new. Me and Pops can have some daddy-daughter time.' He grins at her and she stares back sternly.

I feel a buzz of excitement, but it blooms and dies as quickly as snowdrops in February.

'I can't... it will be too depressing.' I picture myself in a brightly lit changing room, the front and back mirrors. 'Nothing will fit.' My self-confidence is a fragile ecosystem, at risk of extinction. I look down at my naked ring finger. Trying on dresses for my ex-boyfriend's wedding to the most popular girl at school is the last thing I want to do. I couldn't feel less enthusiastic about this wedding if I tried. I'd love to not go, but I can't bear to disappoint Dad.

'What?' He draws me into him. 'Elizabeth Jenkins, you'd look beautiful in that dustbin.' He raises an elbow at the squat receptacle overflowing with waste from end-of-summer picnics. 'Take Lucy with you, she'll help.' He pulls a scared face. He's always been a bit afraid of my big sister. I laugh.

She *would* help, I think, but... I puff my cheeks out... I've been off with Lucy since my Amber binge; it's unfair, I know, but I feel she's partly responsible. I hadn't considered looking up Amber until she started blathering on about Instagram. I can tell she knows there's something up. I should explain what happened, but it's easier to ignore it. To pretend that everything's okay. I feel my heart rate flicker, staccato. Besides, I don't enjoy shopping trips with my sister. So many avenues of conversation are blocked with explosives. I need to take someone like Jade with me. Or Sandy. Yes, definitely Sandy. She'd be an excellent shopping partner. Would it be strange to ask her if she's free tomorrow? Guilt vibrates on my tongue. I *should* ask Lucy. I can't avoid her forever.

'I can't anyway. I'll need to feed Poppy.'

'She'll be okay for a few hours between feeds? She's been fine with Lucy.' He sounds put out that I haven't jumped at his offer. 'I could try her with a bottle?'

I feel a niggle of irritation. Ever since she was born, every time she's cried – which is a lot – he's handed her straight over to me, saying 'I think she's hungry', but just as I'm getting the hang of breastfeeding he's suddenly keen to give her a bottle.

'It's one more thing to do, isn't it?' I sigh. 'Buy bottles and a pump, sterilize them, express milk...'

'We could give formula a go?'

'But we said we wouldn't. We said—'

'I know, babe, but it might take the pressure off you a bit? Mum was saying I had formula and look at me, I'm fine.' He pretends to tense his whole body and I smile, biting down rising disquiet: *He thinks I'm not doing a good enough job. And he's talking to Gloria about it.* 'No harm in trying, is there?' he asks.

The opening bars of 'Come Fly With Me' zip out from the pub as I sip the warm lager in my plastic cup.

'Maybe,' I say, squinting as the sun's rays sink into the earth around us, the sky dipping and stretching, the heat of the alcohol suffusing through my veins. I don't want to think about tomorrow. I don't want to think about the wedding. I'm in one of my favourite places with my two favourite people and there's nowhere I would rather be.

I nestle further into the crook of Joe's arm, drinking in the notes of citrus and the sea on his skin, my soul humming as the three of us are bathed in a last bubble of warmth from the sun and the jaunt of the music and we must be doing something right because... I take a sharp intake of breath.

We speak over each other, giddy with beer and sunshine and the simplest but most wondrous of things:

'Babe!'

'Did you see that?'

'She smiled!'

'Joe, her first smile!'

'I need to take a photo for Mum!'

At the mention of Gloria and photographs my stomach clenches, a post-trauma response. Gloria and Ron turned up what seemed like minutes after I'd had Poppy. I learned later that it was actual minutes. They'd been in the waiting room the whole of the previous day, Gloria furiously berating the staff: 'My Jojo has been up now for almost three days! It's not human. You need to end this now!' A midwife told me that bit. 'Your mother-in-law,' she'd whistled sympathetically, her voice with a delicate Caribbean lilt, 'it sounded like she was asking to have you put down.' She chuckled as she took my blood pressure, one hand on my arm, the other checking her upside-down daisy watch.

There was an unending stream of photos as Poppy was passed between Gloria, Ron and Joe, when all I wanted to do was eat toast and stare at Poppy in bewilderment. The absence of Mum had never felt so unbelievable. So catastrophic. It was like someone kicking me in the stomach every few minutes, even though my heart was bursting with love (and actually, physically, much worse had been done to my stomach, my three-day labour eventually ending in an emergency caesarean section). The daisy-watch midwife returned and with a wink mentioned 'colostrum'. That cleared the room. 'Are your family...?' she asked softly, and I bit back tears as I explained that Mum was gone and my sister was in Dubai for work (terrible timing) and Dad was on his way down from Yorkshire. Since then, we've hardly seen Gloria. Not that that matters, as she's always on the family chat group asking for photos of Poppy, so even when you haven't seen or spoken to her directly it feels as though you've been talking to her non-stop. She's sort of omnipresent.

I reach a hand out to stop him. 'Let's just enjoy it. Let's not be those people constantly snapping their kids, missing them grow.'

He looks at me like I've had too much to drink. Draws his eyebrows and lips into a confused, mocking face. I jostle him with my shoulder.

'I'm not saying let's never take photos of her, I'm saying let's enjoy these first smiles, just us. Your mum can see all the later ones.' I look up to the sky, laced with streaks of mango orange and flamingo pink. *I hope you caught it too*, I think.

'True.' He rests his head on mine. 'Besides, I think we'll be seeing a lot more of these.'

He strokes Poppy's cheek and she smiles again. We all do. It's catching. It's beautiful. It's everything I ever wanted.

19

#DiveBomb

Cassie

'You should have taken me shopping with you!' I punch out angrily. 'I'd have told them where to stick their snorkel!' As if Beth – along with all the other first-time mums out there – doesn't have enough to deal with?

Even as I'm typing I know I shouldn't post it: it doesn't fit with my theme – it's too angry and emotive – and I've already posted enough to Stories this morning to satisfy the algorithm (*feed the beast!* as Boardroom Boss Mum reminds us), but I feel *enraged*. That my friend, my new friend, is having to put up with this shit.

I screenshot her original message, scribble over her name to keep it anonymous (Beth won't see it, she doesn't go on SoMe, but still, I can't be too careful these days) and tag @DiveBar. I upload it to Stories, check my make-up and start to record.

'Seriously, Mamas, did you see the text I just got from my friend? You know this isn't my usual vibe but *shame on you,* Dive Bar! For sending a breastfeeding mum *into the toilets* to breastfeed! Would you eat *your* lunch in there?' I shake my head, eyes rolling, picturing heads rolling when Dive Bar HQ sees this. 'You know, Mamas, in this world where we need more love and light, I *despair* at this shaming of a mum who is just trying to do her best. *DIVE BAR, WHAT WERE YOU THINKING?*'

I stop recording and throw my phone down crossly, blood pumping in my veins. I feel protective of Beth. She's the me I want to go back and give a hug to in those startling, early years. She's the countless mothers I've seen walking down the street with shoulders slumped, or staring listlessly into a cup of tea in cafés, that I wish afterwards I'd said 'Hey, are you okay?' to, because if you look, you see these women *a lot*. And that 'Are you okay?' can be the difference between a good day and a bad day. I said it to Beth that day, and my life changed: I remembered how it feels to connect. The truth of it.

I've always thought of myself as someone who supports other women. That's what the Breastfeeding Babe Bombs were about (that and quelling my own anxiety because I only did it for a couple of weeks myself – but I had two babies, I needed four tits). That's what the gender-neutral stuff's about. Equal opportunities for women (and men), from the start. What damage do we inflict with this pinkification of girls from birth? Steering boys away from it? *It's just a colour*. Birch's favourite. It's well intentioned, I want to do my bit, improve the world, but I've been doing all this from my ivory tower. I thought I was super connected, speaking for women, leading the debate, but since I met Beth, I'm starting to wonder if I've allowed the opposite to happen. I've become too worried about what other people think, too wrapped up in my SoMe bubble, too *disconnected* in fact from... well, from life, I guess. I feel pumped up. I feel *good*! I feel...

Oh God, what if it was a terrible idea? What if there's a backlash? I pace the room, phone in hand. What if somehow Beth sees it, or hears about it, and realizes who I am before I've had a chance to figure out how to tell her? I *should* tell her who I am, I know that, but she's cagey about social media, almost offended by it, and when I'm messaging Beth I don't need to be the woman in my Media Pack: Cassie Holliday, Social Media Superstar, Mother to Scout and Birch, Wife to Seb Holliday, Brand Ambassador for the Family Co app... I get to be myself: Sandy, former frequent flyer, increasingly *un*happily married mum of two, trying my best but somehow never quite seeming to get it right... becoming less and less relevant in every aspect of my life.

I can't be both of those women, I tell myself, jabbing sharply across my closed eyelids, stopping my tears before they have a chance to bud. Those two women are not compatible. They are at odds with each other. And I need to keep Sandy, before she gets consumed by Cassie Holliday altogether.

In a short time it's become so valuable, those slivers of reality with Beth intersecting through my carefully curated days: small chinks at night-time, tiny moments where I can be myself without worrying how it looks to other people or if it's on brand. It's like a secret club. And what if, once Beth knows, she doesn't want to be friends with me any more? What if that daily dose of oxygen is taken away? My heart thuds. Why am I risking that? With an emotive post I haven't thought through? *You idiot, Cassie, you idiot.*

I go to delete the footage but can't because the multitude of notifications keep causing the page to reload. I squint, not wanting to look. Thousands and thousands of likes and comments... and all of them... oh God.

20

#Sisters

Beth

'I just don't think this is the best place to come,' I puff, thumbing through the rails of clothes designed for people that look like Lucy rather than me. I pull out a dress printed with hot pink and yellow geometric shapes, spaghetti straps and a low hanging back. Can you imagine the thick band of my nursing bras slicing along the back of this? The outline of my jumbo pants?

She sees the look on my face. Finally she gets it. 'Sorry, Mitts.' She speaks quietly, evoking our childhood nickname for each other, the one I've noticed we use more when we're disagreeing about something or we're trying to say sorry, an instinctive reminder to the other that we love each other, even if we don't always get things right.

Poppy is cosily tucked up in the baby carrier on Lucy's chest, a pudgy hand wrapped around one of her fingers. Lucy insisted Poppy come with us – 'What sort of aunty doesn't take their niece shopping?' she'd asked incredulously – ending my debate with Joe on bottle-feeding. He's probably in the gym now, I think enviously, the fourth time this week as he often goes in his lunch break, when he's not squeezing in a haircut. 'I wasn't thinking. I thought you'd like something fresh and cool and not too...' She hesitates.

'Mumsy?' I finish for her, exasperation peppering my speech.

'I just thought you'd want to wear something *fun*, you know, not "boring mum stuff" like you said?'

A pleated gold skirt that looks like it would stain easily slips through my fingers. I reach for the care label as my thoughts spiral. *What's this trip about? Lucy reminding me that it doesn't matter that she's not a mum, she can still wear clothes like these?*

I check myself. It's not her language, it's mine. *I* was complaining the other day about "boring mum stuff": not just the underwear but the elasticated maternity jeans I'm still wearing to protect my scar, how awkward clothing can be when you're trying to quickly liberate your nipple so you end up wearing the same thing – because it's easy – over and over. I've worn my baggy Oasis T-shirt so much the last few months that Liam's face has faded. I should try my new breastfeeding tops, but I feel awkward. They're not really me.

'You should've seen Common As Mum's Stories the other day! She was at a christening. She'd worn her favourite dress. The Tummy Tucker, she called it.' She snorts. 'But she had to lift the whole thing over her head to feed her baby. She's there, in this stately-looking room, in her undies, feeding the baby and recording it all on Stories – she's amazing – and in walks some old dude! She caught the whole thing!' She laughs, trying to draw me in, but I can't raise a smile, especially not over anything social media related. She thinks it's all so innocent. She doesn't seem to understand the devastation it causes, images of perfection burned deeper into retinas minute by minute, when she of all people should.

My hand begins to shake. I can't stop the feelings bubbling up inside me, the contrast I feel to the women who can wear shiny skirts like this and not have to worry about their scar or whether their first post-labour period's about to arrive (everyone says the first one is *awful*). Suddenly the thought of being at the wedding, back in Yorkshire, trying to pretend that I'm still me, feels overwhelming. It's bad enough in London.

'Loads of boring mum stuff is my life now!' I squeak. Hot tears squeeze out of my eyes.

'Mitts?' She's immediately at my side, both arms wrapped round me as best she can with Poppy between us as I sob into her khaki utility jacket. I feel her arms moving and imagine the looks she's giving to the concerned shop assistant, mouthing over the top of Poppy's fluffy hair, 'She's fine, yep, I'm just going to...' She nods to the door as she ushers me outside and down the road to an artisanal doughnut shop. London is mapped out for Lucy by sweet goods the way Joe navigates it by pubs.

'I didn't know you were feeling like this. I knew you were finding it tough, but you always seem to find the funny side. Why haven't you said anything?'

'It's not all the time,' I say, collecting myself over a banoffee doughnut. 'I just...' I sigh. 'I love being a mum...' I trail off.

'Of course you do. Poppy's *the best*.' She reaches for my

hand, beaming at the mention of her niece, who is on her lap, but I pull it back and cup my brew instead.

'...but it feels overwhelming some days.' I say it slowly, as if I might detonate a grenade. I hate to offload to Lucy. She won't admit it, but it's been hard for her since I moved in with Joe and she had to take a random flat-share. It was always just the two of us, up to then. And on paper, my life is perfect. But then, not everything is written down. 'And there's so much pressure to get it right...'

She takes a sip of her coffee, thoughts flitting behind her eyes as she tries to land on the right thing to say. 'You're exhausted. You'll feel better once Poppy's sleeping and you get into a routine.'

I pick off the small caramel chunks, eating them one by one. 'That's what I keep telling myself. I'm okay if I get some sleep but if I don't, like last night, I'm a mess. I'm too tired to rationalize it. I worry about *everything*... whether she's fed enough, winded enough, napped enough... whether she's *over*fed, *over*stimulated, *over*tired. It's relentless.' I swallow. 'I keep thinking about Mum.' My mouth is empty but my head is full, like a thick rain cloud has gathered in my skull. 'I wish I could ask her about this stuff. Things I didn't realize I needed to ask. Like if I slept in a cot? How things were with Dad... If she ever felt... lost?'

Pop. The questions that can never be answered pierce the rain cloud. Tears start to fall. Not just mine, but Lucy's too. We sit like that a while: a mirror image of tears and loss. Poppy observes us, gripping a paper tube of sugar and banging her fat little fist on the table.

'Oh Poppy, thank goodness we have you,' Lucy says, nuzzling Poppy's cheek. She looks up at me, smiling. She wants us to return to normal but I'm not ready. I still have waves of emotion rocketing through my chest; the tension coursing all the way down to my enormous blooming arse, hot and restless in my plastic seat. Bile spikes up my throat. I thought I'd put it all behind me, but the tiniest threads of my carefully reasoned acceptance have escaped, or maybe they were never properly knotted and tucked away, and now I feel myself unravelling, all the work I've put in with Russell coming undone.

Lucy's eyes are lined with concern. 'I should have been here for you. When you gave birth. I should never have agreed to go to Dubai.'

'You weren't to know she'd come early.'

'Everyone says the first one's late!' she tuts. 'And Mum said *we* were both late. I just thought…' She trails off, frustrated, but I would never have wanted her to pass up the opportunity: she's in the frame for editor when *Boom!* launches there next year and it was basically a week-long interview. I don't want to ask if she's heard anything else about it; I couldn't handle hearing today that she's moving away.

'I still feel it, you know?' I look Lucy in the eye and a strange feeling rushes over me. For a second I think: *I'm going to tell her. Before she moves away. She deserves to know the truth. I always planned to tell her. One day.* 'I feel guilty…' It's a tiny movement, a flick of her eyelashes, but I catch it. I hear her years ago in the quiet aftermath of a thunderous row over something daft, I forget what, speaking softly, and I know that she's thinking the same now: 'It's all about Elizabeth, isn't it?' To be fair, she doesn't know why I really feel guilty; what I did. Is it like this with all sisters? Love. Absolute love. But below it the puzzle of decades-old resentments, like the buried artefacts in the layers of soil and sand beneath us, waiting to be dug up and dusted off, painstakingly pieced back together to tell their own story, their own version of the past? '…that we're here and she's not.' I swallow and quickly change direction. 'I might sign Poppy up to Baby Mandarin… or Mini Mozart? All the hypnobabes are doing classes. And maybe it will help with the crying, if she found her passion?'

Lucy's face explodes, back on safe ground, the resin bangles on her arm jangling as she returns her mug to the table. 'What? She's a few weeks old!' She laughs. 'I don't think you need to worry about that.' She delicately nibbles on her Turkish delight doughnut. She's already got the hang of grasping a baby with one hand and doing everything else with the other. She'd be a great mum, Lucy. Better than me. 'Besides,' she adds, 'Poppy's perfect.'

'Bronagh says—'

'Bronagh has it all figured out, does she?'

'That's what Sandy said.'

'Who's Sandy?'

'My friend from the park. I told you about her.'

Lucy wipes rose dusting from her hands decisively. 'I've had an idea.' She reaches over the table and clutches my forearm with her short black-blue nails. 'Another shop we can try!'

I groan. 'I'm done with shopping for today, Lu. I'm flagging and my boobs are aching. I need to feed Poppy. At home. I can't face a rerun of Dive Bar.'

'At least we got a free lunch.'

Weirdly, after suggesting I feed Poppy in the toilets, the

manager apologized profusely and insisted we didn't pay for our grilled mahi-mahi sub rolls and Ocean Blue martinis (Lucy's idea, the vodka went straight to my head and I regretted it immediately). I feel flat. Is this my life now? Stuck in the loos feeding Poppy, my half-eaten, half-drunk lunch at the table, unable to fit into anything nice, crying over doughnuts, tired, anxious, overwhelmed....

'It won't take long! I saw it on Clean Uddies. It's round the corner.' She's already up, abandoning her half-eaten doughnut (she only ever eats half of anything, but that's still better than half of nothing), the stacks of rings on her fingers catching the light as she expertly rearranges Poppy in the carrier. 'And don't worry if we don't find anything today. There's still time. I'll ask some of the girls at work who've had kids for recommendations.'

'Clean Uddies?' I say faintly.

'Yeah, you know. Uddies. Like Udders. You should follow her on Instagram,' she says pointedly, shrugging as I mock-scowl at her. She flaps a hand at my enormous breasts and sticks up both her index fingers behind her head. 'Moooooooooooooooooooo!' She laughs as I grab her round the neck and pretend to strangle her, to confused looks from Poppy.

21

#TheFarm

Cassie

I love the Farm. We're twenty floors up on the roof of a City building. The place is abuzz with waspy millennials and real bees, hives stacked in the corners of a grassy quadrant. There's an asado grill smoking and a DJ playing music that makes you feel like you're in Ibiza. It's a launch event for the Family Dinners function of the app; Griff's going big with the SoMe chatter for this one. That was always the plan, but I can't help feeling uneasy; they'll be tracking our activity post event and seeing who gets the most likes and views. I *can't* be replaced – I've got to hang on until the end of November to get my fee or I'll have to ask Seb for money again. It didn't bother me that he insisted on keeping our bank accounts separate when I was still working, but now it's a problem. I can't help but feel it's being added on to an invisible tally, along with the costs from my failed enterprise.

Alicia's here, resplendent in an angular, mid-length navy dress in a crisp fabric, square at the top and flaring out at the bottom. It doesn't move as she strides around in her futuristic white ankle boots, stacked golden orbs for heels. She furrows her brow in concentration, fingers whizzing over her tablet, no doubt checking who's here, who needs introductions, whether we've all been sufficiently snapped wafting around looking like besties. She catches my eye and gives me a warm smile despite her weary eyes.

I had to tell her about The Unhappy Hollidays post. She's been so busy on the app launch while still helping me with my SoMe posts so I can keep up with Griff's schedule, but it's had so many likes now, I knew she'd see it eventually and it would look worse if I hadn't told her. She was super nice. Said she'd have a word with their tech guys, see if they could find out who's behind the email account. Agreed we need a plan of action before we take it to Griff. Ever since she's been in overdrive, suggesting post ideas and collaborations. She's on a PR offensive.

Luckily, there's been a wave of goodwill towards me since Dive Bar-Gate. I couldn't believe it when I read through the comments. Thousands and thousands and all of them... good! Applauding me! A journalist from *The Read* (*The Read!* I've been trying to get into *The Read* for years!) had written... '@Cassie_Happy_Hollidays speaking for all women here. This has got to *stop*!' and that in turn accrued thousands of likes in a few minutes. I even gained a few thousand followers on Twitter.

Maybe there is something in this being authentic business? It hasn't escaped me that being my true self, my true cross self in that moment, defending my friend, has made me – I hate this word – *relevant* again, but where do I go with that? Is there a way I could steer my account back to being me, leave this fakery behind? Whichever way I look at it, the answer's no. It's too big a risk if it blows up in my face. Unless I were pregnant. *Then* it would be different. There'd be so much interest in me – and promotional opportunities – I could come clean about everything. I envisage a photo shoot wearing flowing white robes, holding delicate wildflowers over my bump – something contrite, classy, nothing ostentatious – maybe with Buddhist monks either side of me, heads bowed. You can't stay angry at a pregnant person for long, can you? It could be a rebirth. I could turn this whole thing around.

A beard emerges from behind the living wall. Griff. 'Chat and yin in five,' he says.

'Fab!' I didn't think this lot drank before 7 p.m., if at all. I fan out the fabric of my vintage Missoni dress, anticipating a nice craft gin, when Alicia appears and says quietly, 'Don't worry, the yin's optional. Griff finds it more productive to chat and yin.'

'Gin?' I say, hoping the odd pronunciation is something she and Griff picked up in LA.

'Yin. YYYYYin,' she enunciates to me slowly. I must look blank because she adds, 'You do know how to—'

'Of course I know how to chat and yin!' I snap. 'How old do you think I am?' I yank my phone out of my bag, mutter something about checking up on the kids and step behind the living wall, jabbing 'chat and yin' into Google as I do. Nothing. Bugger.

I startle Holistic Flo. Her right arm shoots behind her back. She eyes me suspiciously. 'Are you on Stories?'

'No.' I return my phone to my bag and hold both hands up. She relaxes, moves her right arm back round and draws on her cigarette. 'Just one a week,' she smiles weakly. 'Let's keep it between us, yeah?'

'Sure. No problem. What are friends for?'

She sighs, shaking her head, her braids grazing the bricks.

'What is it, Cassie?' She sounds resigned. She was red-eyed in her Stories last night, saying that Mr Holistic has shacked up with someone new. A faceless person. She doesn't even have an Instagram account. I'm with her on this: how's she meant to know if this *off-grid* woman is suitable to spend time with her kids? Still, I can't let what happened go.

'What was that at the Mumspire event? What the fuck was going on?'

She stubs her cigarette against the wall. 'You tell me. You were the one unprepared. It was a shambles.' She removes a small, clear plastic bag from her pocket, unzips it, slips the fag butt inside and zips it again, squirrelling it into the pocket of her wide-legged trousers. 'We got the email a week before. You had plenty of time to prepare.'

'I didn't get it. But that's not the point. It was obvious you were all ganging up on me.'

'Ganging up on you? How old are you, Cassie? Everyone's busy. Don't you think we've got better things to do?'

Maybe she's right. Maybe they seized an opportunity. Wouldn't I do the same? We work alongside each other but there's an unspoken agreement: work is work. You need sharp elbows in this game sometimes.

'I've other things on my mind, anyways.' She stares at the skyline as her thoughts drift away. 'You're so lucky to have Seb,' she says. We don't spend time with each other's families, but she'll know what everyone else knows: that

I'm happily married to a solicitor in my beautiful home in the country. 'Where did you meet again?'

I fob her off: 'Abroad... travelling.' I'm always vague about my old work; it pains me to think of it, but inevitably my mind reaches for Hong Kong. I'd just flown in. It wasn't the easiest job for relationships, like Elen predicted. (My last one had been with the airline doctor. We met when I had norovirus and I was astounded when he asked if I might consider dinner with him, when I was feeling better. I found love in a hopeless place. But six months on and he wouldn't commit. I later heard from Katya that he had a norovirus victim in every hangar.) As ever, at a slight distance from the rest of the crew, I went for a drink in the hotel bar alone. And there Seb was, also alone. He was a breath of fresh air, not another pilot trying to bang an air hostess.

Those heady first days. Sometimes I think it's the memory of those that keeps us together. Invisible, delicate threads bind the intricate tapestry of the average marriage. We each had the next day free. It seemed so fortuitous, fortune-cookie luck: the universe conspiring to bring us together. We rambled around Kowloon, gawking at the temples and sampling the street food: duck tongue, stinky tofu, chrysanthemum tea. It was only after that Seb confessed he hated Chinese food and an hour later he smiled at me admiringly as we tucked into burgers and milkshakes at the American diner I'd heard the rest of the crew raving about.

'I'm on the 12:20 tomorrow,' he said, mid-gurgle of Oreo milkshake. 'Can I see you when you're back? You mentioned Gatwick? I'm in Surrey, down the road.'

'That's my flight.' I eyed him as I twirled a fry.

'It's fate! I'll see you there.' He flashed a smile. 'Do you turn left or right?'

'Always left.' I smiled back but my eyes couldn't match it. It would change things when he knew, it always did. I was amazed the next day, when I strode up to him in my uniform, that, for the first time, it didn't. It wasn't the scene he was used to (all his school friends had married investment bankers who later became career mummies) but he liked that then. The perks – the discounts and upgrades – meant our first few years of dating flew by in a haze of crisp hotel linen and room service. We were so good together in those days.

Holistic Flo watches me silently. I collect myself, blink hard to clear my eyes. I remember why I sneaked back here.

'Griff wants us to chat and yin in five.' I search her for clues.

She tuts angrily. 'God, I cannot be fucked. Do you know how many times a day I get asked to chat and yin?' I open my mouth to speak but am interrupted as a voice barks behind me.

'Why can't they say "stretch", for fuck's sake?' Boardroom Boss Mum appears, her sleek fitted dress and spiked statement necklace at odds with the boho-Zen scene. How does *she* know what 'chat and yin' means? 'Cassie.' She nods. There's an undertone to her expression that I can't read.

I take a deep breath, my face already tingling with embarrassment.

'I'm glad you're both here…' I force my eyes to meet theirs rather than stare at the floor. 'I don't know if you've seen, but there's someone calling themselves The Unhappy Hollidays…'

They both wince so I know they have, and I wonder briefly if they've liked the post, commented on it even. The thought stops me cold. I'm always so careful to not let these things get to me; to not let bitterness catch me in its web. I'm not the sort of person to trawl through posts checking who's liked what and how many followers they've got. I'm focused on doing *my* best, nothing else. I chide myself: do not become that person, Cassie. Do not become your mother.

'I've not mentioned it to Griff. I want to find out who's behind it first. Could we... keep it on the down-low?'

'No worries.' Holistic Flo's sparky smile makes me strangely nervous.

Boardroom Boss Mum nods, looking bored. 'Come on, let's do this. I've got a call on a major acquisition I'm leading this afternoon and I'm not changing into yoga pants. I've just done Boxfit.'

Once we're all assembled around the Moroccan-themed seating area, Griff thanks us for coming. His left leg is already pressed against his left ear, in an aggressive display of maleness. Alicia, I note, is watching him intently and I feel a small nugget of alarm: young woman starting out in her career, creepy determined boss. I make a mental note to speak to Alicia about navigating these things with grace, not being taken advantage of.

'We're pumped to have you all on board with one of my personal favourite features of the Family Co app: Family Dinners.' The arch of Griff's eyebrows and thick beard conspire to give him an owlish vibe. We sit patiently while he swaps legs. 'We're bringing the soul back to mealtimes.'

Griff's 'vision' is to abandon all technology at the table,

improving communication and time spent together as a family. This utopia is delivered via the Family Co app, which reminds you when it's time for dinner – an alert can be pinged to your teenagers' phones: 'No more hollering up the stairs,' he grunts as he tips forward into Crow – and suggests a new topic of conversation every five minutes while you eat. It sounds like a load of crap to me, but I've got to sell it like it's the secret elixir of life. I just need to get Seb and the kids to cooperate and look engaged and happy at the dinner table for a minute or so. Easy, right?

As we release our legs from Double Pigeon and prepare to go, Griff adds, 'One other thing. You all know Cassie...' Heads swivel in my direction. I flick a peace sign and smile goofishly. Boardroom Boss Mum rolls her eyes and looks at her watch. 'She's doing some great work for the Family Co.'

My smile stretches wider. I love praise.

'But...'

A but! There was a but!

'Her post schedule is intense...'

Um, alarm bells ringing, alarm bells ringing!

'So we're thinking of dividing up...'

Mayday! Mayday!

Holistic Flo jumps in, not giving Griff a chance to finish: 'I'll take the exercise ones. It makes more sense for me to do them anyway.'

'I can do...' They all start speaking at once.

I find some words: 'What are you talking about? I'm on top of my post schedule. I'm bossing it!' I try.

'Alicia?' Griff prompts.

She gives me a sorry-what-can-I-do look. 'We're keeping on top of the Dailies but we're – *you're* – behind on Stories *and* the Monthlies.' She looks down at her iPad and starts reeling off posts I've not done yet. 'No "phone plus Pilates", no "phone plus wok"…' *I never did find a bloody wok.* 'We can cover off "phone plus catching up with friends today" and, Holistic Flo, you're taking all the exercise ones?'

'I've done some of—' I try, but Holistic Flo speaks over me: 'I'm on it!', pulling the splits while doing an 'okay' sign with her fingers. For fuck's sake.

'How did you know there were exercise ones?' I ask, breath short, eyes flashing daggers.

'There's always exercise ones.' Her amber eyes flit away from mine. 'And Alicia flicked me over a copy of your schedule to take a look.'

My head swivels to Alicia, who looks down guiltily. 'Griff told me to,' she says quietly, but she gives a subtle look in Griff's direction, meaning: *Don't push it, Cassie.*

'What can I take?' asks Boardroom Boss Mum.

'I'm happy to help too,' says Common As Mum.

They tussle over 'phone plus hoover' like vultures on roadkill.

'Thanks, guys, this really does feel like a family. Usual flat rate for each post, okay? Bill Alicia once they're done. Cassie, we'll need to talk separately about your fee,' Griff says ominously.

'Hard luck, Cass.' Common As Mum places a cold, spammy hand on my shoulder. 'You've got a lot on your plate, what with this Unhappy Hollidays business. Any idea who's behind it?'

Griff scratches his beard casually, but his eyes are dark and shiny and move between us like restless beetles. 'The Unhappy Hollidays? What's that? New angle, Cassie?'

'I've been meaning to talk to you about that...' starts Alicia nervously, putting down her iPad.

I lie down in Shavasana, dead man's pose, and stare up at the blue sky.

22

#Unarranged

Cassie's Messages

13.10 Keane Bank
A/C****4038 28 SEP
You have reached the maximum amount of times you may enter into an unarranged overdraft in a calendar month. Please visit your nearest branch to speak to one of our advisors as soon as possible.

23

#BirthdayGirl

Sandy 12:01
Happy Birthday! *balloon, cake and champagne emojis*

Have a lovely day whatever you're doing… at the spa, front row seats, cocktails and dancing to the small hours!

Just kidding – hope you get a BIG CHUNK of sleep and a BIG SLICE of cake!

Beth 01:35
Thank you! Just the sleep would be good!

Beth 08:32
My personalized biscuits arrived!

They're so pretty I don't want to eat them! (But I'll get over it, ha!)

I wondered why you wanted my address!

THANK YOU!! XXX

Oh how did that work thing go you were worried about yesterday?

Sandy 09:12
Don't worry about that!

Have a fun day.

Let me know what you end up doing xx

24

#PeriWhat

Beth

The thing about Essex boys is they never move too far from their mums. Pre-Poppy we would regularly find ourselves trekking 'home' for Gossy Gloria's Roast Beef on a Sunday, but we haven't been since Poppy was born, for one reason or another: Gloria's had brunch with her netball team, Ron's at a carpet convention. 'You don't mind, do you, darling?' Gloria will ask in our group chat and I'll reply lightly, 'No, of course not, you two have fun!' while brimming with relief. So it's a bit grating that we're reigniting this tradition on my birthday.

'I didn't think you'd want to cook?' Joe says.

I'm in bed eating a bacon breadcake. The plate rests on my lap while I cup my new 'World's Best Mummy!' mug. Discarded wrapping paper litters the sheets. *And with it my hopes*, I idle to myself before feeling guilty. My gift is perfect: a vintage suitcase with a beautiful floral lining for storing my fabrics and patterns, which are currently spilling out of a box in our wardrobe. I've always wanted one. *I've also always wanted an... Enough. Enough. I'm going to enjoy my birthday.*

'I thought we were going *out* for lunch?' I'm annoyed with myself: I knew I should have planned something. When Joe hadn't mentioned anything, I presumed it was all in hand. I thought I'd dropped enough hints about the new Bolivian tapas restaurant that's opened on Hackney Road.

'Bit awks with Pops, though, isn't it, eating out? I thought this way we could relax? And they want to see you, for your birthday.' He has his towel wrapped round his waist, having just emerged from the shower in a mist of citrus and sea salt. *You mean you could relax*, I think, as he smooths lotion over his broad, muscular chest, since Gloria is appalled if her little Jojo so much as gets his own beer from the fridge once he's crossed the threshold of his family home.

I chide myself. I'm being unfair. It's the lack of sleep. Joe did get up at one point, but it was easier to settle her by feeding her quickly, and him fussing wasn't helping.

'Also...' He sits on the edge of the bed, taking my free hand. 'I have a surprise planned.' I immediately sit up straighter, meerkat-like. He chuckles at my interest and plants a kiss on my head, one hand knotted through the back of my hair. 'Let's get ready.'

It's my birthday, so I dress in one of my new breastfeeding tops from Lucy: it's pale pink with scalloped-edge layers, to make feeding easier, and hand-stitched with delicate sequins. It's not my usual style but it's beautiful. In a double win I'm wearing my pre-pregnancy jeans for the first time since having Poppy! I want to punch the air and shout 'Get in!', the way Joe does when West Ham score.

Poppy's eerily quiet in the car, as if she knows it's my

birthday, and as we hurtle along the A12 towards Essex I allow my mind to wander, *just a little*. Joe's wearing narrow navy chinos with a pale-blue shirt that makes his eyes pop; he knows it's one of my favourites. His hair's looking particularly floppy today, in a good way. I know, I know, I'm a bad feminist, but like I said to Lucy, if I could go to the wedding, to Yorkshire, to Dad, with an engagement ring sparkling on my finger, everything would be so much better. It's not just Sam and Amber's wedding. It's the anxiety. It's the promise I made to Poppy. Mum always said that marrying Dad and having us girls was the best thing she ever did. It would ground me. It would be a counterbalance to the rootlessness I've felt since she died. And Joe and I, we love each other. We're the real thing.

Joe's parents live in 'the nice bit of Essex', as Joe puts it. Where the footballers live. The house is detached, with cream fluted columns out the front. There's a double garage and a line of shrubs fashioned into birds. Inside, there's an abundance of heavy fabrics, thick carpeting (as you'd expect from Ron, Carpet King) and hues of gold and peach.

'HAPPY BIRTHDAY!' Handsy Ron exclaims as he opens the door, using the opportunity to grip me in a bear hug and – I'm sure I don't imagine this bit – graze his hand over my bum. 'Glo's in the kitchen!' he roars as he ushers us in.

'Is, er…' Joe's speech is muffled as they pull in for a hug and clap each other on the back.

'Not yet, son, not yet,' Ron says, arms outstretched. 'Come in, come in!', his arms working like windmills to manoeuvre us inside.

The table's already set, the arrangement as always: peach napkins sit in their pyramid napkin holders, the place mats have a swirly gold arrangement on them. There's a hostess trolley and the vegetables – uniform carrots and parsnips, Jojo's favourites – sit beside a large tray of roast potatoes and Yorkshire puddings (she only started doing those when I started coming on a Sunday, to make me feel at home, she said; I've never told her I can't stand Yorkshire puddings and their horrible, cloggy texture). There's always a big show as she parades the serving tray in with a huge hunk of beef resting on it. 'There she is!' booms Ron, and it's never clear if he's referring to Gloria or the beef.

Gloria hands Ron the fork and carving knife as usual, but then takes me to one side. 'Sorry we've not seen much of you lately, darling. We wanted to give you a bit of space.'

I think of Gloria's daily messages to the family chat group and feel light-headed: how would things be if she wasn't giving us space?

'Can't be easy for you with your mum not around and Lucy not having had kids yet. I relied so much on my mum when I had my little Jojo.'

Her words are kind and well-meaning, but they're still like an ice pick through my chest.

'Anyway, if there's anything you want to talk about, anything at all...' She says, face open and expectant. I feel immediately panicked, like when a teacher calls on you in class and you have no idea what they're talking about.

'We're a very open family, Beth, and you're one of us now, if there's anything you need...'

It's kind. I know it's kind. And I want to be the sort of person who grips Gloria in a hug and asks her questions about stretch marks and constipation, woman to woman,

I do, but it's my birthday and I want *my* mum here. Gloria powers on, all the motherly things she wants to share or thinks I need to hear, and I try not to cry and instead internally curse Joe that we're not eating tapas and drinking pisco sours on Hackney Road.

'And you mustn't worry if things are a bit, er, *slow*, you know, *in the bedroom*, since you've had Poppy...' Gloria gives me a knowing look. I look up to find Joe and give him the evil eye, but through the open double doors all I see is a navy-chinoed leg hooked over the arm rest, football blaring from the large screen.

'I've already said to Jojo, you mustn't rush her. After I had him, me and Ron, I don't think we did it for...'

Why's Gloria asking Joe about our sex life?

'...at least a month or two...'

How can I make this stop? Please make this end.

'Joe!' I call, my voice shrill and rising. 'Is Poppy with you? Is she okay?' I will her to wake.

'...and even then we had to do it...'

Cry, Poppy, cry! Why does she spend all night crying her head off and this one time she won't cooperate?

'Course we made up for it after!' Gloria laughs conspiratorially and nudges my left boob. Pain spikes through my breast; Poppy's frequent feeding has put my boobs into overdrive. 'That's why Matty came along so soon!'

Blooming hell. I close my eyes.

'What's all this about?' says Handsy Ron jovially. 'Stop bending her ear, Glo.' He turns to me. 'Come and get a load of this lovely beef.'

On the table thick slices of beef are fanned out, pink and glistening. I can't stop the recurring image of my placenta, flopped into a clear-glass trifle-shaped bowl, in the operating theatre. My head swims.

We're midway through our meal when the doorbell rings and everyone's heads jerk up. The others glance around at each other. I shift uncomfortably in my chair. Gloria's insisted I eat at least a hundred Yorkshire puddings and I've already had to excuse myself to go to the bathroom and undo my jeans, looping a hairband through the hole and round the button like I used to do when I was pregnant, nervous there's too much pressure on my scar. Defeated by Gossy Gloria's Roast Beef.

'You get it, babe!' Joe says eagerly, his hands holding the edge of the table.

I tug at the scalloped hem of my top, making sure it's covering my makeshift fastening. My legs feel… not wobbly as such, but buzzy, flares of energy zipping up and down them, similar to the icy cold darts that shot up and down my back as my spinal block took effect. Am I about to be serenaded? Has Joe popped out and hidden a ring in a bouquet of flowers? The *Love Actually* doorstep scene flashes in my mind: a boom box, cue cards and Keira Knightley's cheekbones. I find it quite nauseating, but it's one of Joe's favourites.

Four sets of Taylor eyes follow me as I walk. I don't want to look down; I can feel the fabric of my top straining over my breasts and I don't want to have that image forever associated with my special moment. I'm inwardly gabbling. *Stay calm, Beth*, I think. *Be composed. No one likes an hysterical bride-to-be.*

NICOLE KENNEDY

The doorframe seems gilded now. I picture it lined with bulbs, like a movie star's dressing-room mirror. This is why we didn't go for Bolivian tapas! Thank goodness for Joe and Gloria and her blooming Yorkshire puddings! I brace myself for streams of sunlight and sparkling dust fanning into the hallway as I put one hand on the door handle and lower it, relief weeping through my pores, allowing the future – my bright future – in.

A party streamer flaps impotently against my nose.

'HAPPY BIRTHDAY, MITTS!'

There's a sarcastic edge to her tone, as if she knew this wasn't what I was expecting. It takes me a while to recover myself and find some words. Appropriate ones, anyway. It's weird to see Lucy here, in Essex.

'How's it going with Gossy Gloria and Handsy Ron?' she asks leaning in.

She smells fresh. If she were a candle, she would be 'Clean Sheets and Coriander'. She looks great. Her skirt is tight round the waist and blooms out in a bold green and purple print. She's wearing it with a short white top that flashes her midriff and a chunky yellow necklace. Suddenly my own top feels all wrong. Too twee. Too uncool. I wish I was back in a baggy band T-shirt and my maternity jeans. I wish I was in the flat, eating chocolate biscuits and cupping a brew, watching Netflix. That's how I'd really like to spend my birthday. That's where I want to be.

'And what's *that*?' She gestures to a big, pink changing bag decorated with cupcakes and glitter cherries. My gift from Gloria and Ron. 'Tell me you've got the receipt?'

Beneath my disappointment, my brain registers something

else: Lucy's looking thin. My stomach knots, as best it can when it's at capacity. Gloria bustles towards us.

'Lucy! Welcome!' she calls, before rounding on me. 'We're a bit out on timing' – she shoots Lucy a look – 'but I made this especially for you, darling...' She gestures to my place at the table. I'm so uncomfortably full I don't think I can eat anything else, but as the realization that Lucy is my birthday surprise starts to settle, I feel as though, bulging jeans aside, I could do with some cake. I might *need* some cake, in fact. I'll just undo another button.

I can't hide my confusion when I return to my chair and, instead of cake, I see the world's largest Yorkshire pudding. Just the thought of more soggy folds of it in my mouth makes my stomach flip over, but Gloria says, 'Don't worry if you can't put this away, darling, I know you've already eaten quite a few!' She beams over at Joe: 'She can't get enough of my Yorkies!'

Is it a cake in the shape of a Yorkshire pudding? I prod it nervously and look to Lucy for an explanation – realizing as I do that there was a spare space laid at the end of the table – *of course it wasn't for Poppy* – but Lucy's absorbed in her phone. Could she put it down for a second?

'Go on, open it!' Joe looks excited. He doesn't have to eat it.

'Open it?' I repeat dumbly.

'The pud,' he says. I look closer and realize it's like a Yorkshire pudding parcel. There's the World's Largest Yorkshire Pudding and then a smaller one – still pretty sizeable – fitted on top like a lid.

Gingerly I lift the smaller Yorkshire pudding, expecting more blooming beef. Or a swimming pool of gravy. But the contents are... my cheeks flush. Red. Boxed. Square. The contents are a small box with the unmistakable gold lettering of Cartier on them. ONLY BLOOMING CARTIER!!!

My eyes widen and my hands shake as I remove the lid and something big and sparkly blinks at me. A brilliant cut, sparkling diamond band with – unusually, I suppose – a lime-green stone. My face is already splitting into a smile, but my eyes meet with Lucy's. She's ever so slightly shaking her head. Her expression worries me. She looks... wary? Wait a minute – no, she looks... *angry*? I know what she says about getting married but still, this is my moment and if she can't be... No, that's not it. She tilts her head in Joe's direction, widening her eyes. I realize he's speaking to me.

'Don't worry, I know you didn't want me to propose to you just because we had a baby.'

'You independent women.' Ron shakes his head, smiling.

'So think of this as a "Thank You Ring". A thank you for giving me the best gift possible.' He smooths a thumb down the side of Poppy's velvet cheek.

'A Push Present, they say these days!' Gloria chips in.

'Sort of like a commitment ring?' Ron asks. He looks as confused as I feel.

'No, Dad. That's not what she wants.' Joe turns back to me, improvises. 'A "Non-Commitment Ring", if you like. A "Just For Fun Ring"! A "Just Because I Want To Ring"!' He must see my face, crashing to the floor along with all my dreams, because he adds '...not that I'm not committed to you – I am! – that came out wrong! I don't want you to think—'

'Why is it green? Why is it *lime* green?' My mouth twists as though I've bitten into a real lime.

'It's peridot, babe!'

'Peri-what?'

'Peridot! Poppy's birthstone!'

Oh. Okay. That makes this situation marginally better. Marginally.

Lucy puts her phone down and looks at me sympathetically. I feel a tidal wave of pure shame. Weary from the effort of behaving for my birthday, Poppy begins to niggle, chewing on her balled-up fist. My nipples tighten sharply.

'I need to feed Poppy,' I say stiffly, avoiding all eyes as I walk round the table and yank her out of Joe's arms. 'I'll be in the garden.'

I head for the door and the bench under the willow tree, ignoring the clap of thunder from outside. I hope they don't hear the little sob escape as I make it to the French doors and shoulder-barge them to get outside as quickly as possible.

'Took me ages, that Yorkie,' I hear Gloria say wearily as the door swings shut. 'Three attempts!'

25

#HowMayIHelpYou

Cassie

Online Customer Services Query Form #1

Dear Keane Bank,

I would love to know why one of your machines chewed my card up just now?! It's not easy, you know, being freelance! No support, no back-up, no way to get errant companies to pay up without going through the small claims court and do you think I've got time for that shit when I'm working on my industry's biggest campaign to date?!

I'm due a significant sum at the end of November. In the meantime, if you could arrange a new card for me and stop sending me your fucking overdraft text messages I'd be really fucking grateful!

Peace and light.
Cassie Holliday

★ ★ ★

Online Customer Services Query Form #2

Seriously, Keane Bank, if you sort this out for me I'll give you a massive shout-out to my followers! Two million combined across all channels!!

26

Cassie's Twitter Feed

Trends for you

1 #PeriWhat
  85.2K Tweets

2 #MardyMum
  82.1K Tweets

3 #TheUnhappyHollidays
  71K Tweets

4 #TheFamilyCo
  70.8K Tweets

5 #SloshedNewMothersGroup
  51.6K Tweets

OCTOBER

27

Can The Happy Hollidays survive this *unhappy* gossip?

NEWSFLASH! Cassie Holliday is the best mum friend you wished you had… but is that set to change?

Mumspire HQ have just posted their monthly CHIN and Cassie Holliday has slipped from the Top Three and down to number… six. Cassie hasn't been outside the Top Three for the last twelve months. This is BIG. And rumour is things aren't looking too peachy in The Happy Hollidays camp… At last month's Mumspire event Cassie was due to make a special announcement but changed her mind. Things looked pretty awkward on stage. Add to this the photos of Cassie looking distinctly *unhappy* – another Boom! mag exclusive – and we've got to wonder… is there more to it?

If all that wasn't enough, Mardy Mum has exploded onto the SoMe scene, leaping up the CHIN! If you've not seen her fresh take on new motherhood give her a follow now!

Posted by Lucy Jenkins for Boom! mag © 1 October

28

#NumberSix

Cassie

I've never been in a plane crash. Not even close. So why do I keep finding myself in the aftermath of a crash in my dreams? Alone in the fuselage (the only survivor?) as flames lick the carcass of the plane? I know how it sounds but believe me, I'm a rational person. I'm not inclined to explosive melodrama or emotional turbulence. My life is compartmentalized with the efficiency of a food tray in economy. It has to be.

I close my eyes, but the dream returns: me on the plane, an alarm clanging in my popping ears, desperately looking around for the twins, two empty seats beside me, their slack seat belts suspended like spectres in the oxygen-depleted air as the plane plummets. I prise my eyes open, the only way to escape an unimaginable alternative reality.

My hands are still sweaty when the email downloads.

From: Hetty@MumspireHQ.com
To: Cassie@TheHappyHollidays.com
1 October at 05:00
Influencer Update

Howdy, Mamas!

(Urgh. I skip the guff and go straight to the bit about the CHIN.)

Here's your Top Ten CHIN as at 30 September. There's a few movers, a few surprises and – it's not often we get to say this – a new entrant in the Top Ten!

1. Holistic Flo
2. Forest Dad
3. Common As Mum
4. Middle Class Mummy
5. Mummy Likes Clean Plates
6. The Happy Hollidays
7. Boardroom Boss Mum
8. Skinny Bitch Mum
9. Mama Needs A Drink
10. Mardy Mum

Click here for the full list…

What the actual… I click off the email, convinced it must be a formatting error. As I do, my gut knots and twists, like someone wringing out a cloth. I bolt to the loo and sit there in the quiet dark, phone in hand, waiting for the page to reload. It does and I reread it, again and again and again, while my insides register their protest.

Number *six*?

I try to rally. I'm one month down with Griff already; two more and I can collect my fee. I need to keep my head down, work on my profile, so by December I'm in a good position to work with other brands. I have time to turn this around.

It's not until the twins are up, and I'm slathering Scout's toast in a trendy nut-free nut butter I've been sent, that my thoughts turn to the new entrant – *Mardy Mum*. It's unheard of! It's that video she posted. The one that went viral. It had over a million views. I click on to YouTube and type '#periwhat'. It appears before I've finished typing. A woman's shaking hands opening a box, nothing else. The caption is short: 'When you're hoping for an Engagement Ring but instead you get a Non-Commitment Ring!', with a startled face emoji. The only audio is a man saying 'It's peridot, babe!' and a woman's now infamous slicing retort: 'Peri-what?' There's reams of comments and loveheart emojis:

Oh huni! Feel for you

Been there babes

Is that a Cartier box??

What was he thinking?!

What *was* he thinking? What an idiot. Although this clueless man has done this fledgling Influencer the biggest favour of all: he's made her a star (assuming this is organic and not a set-up. It looks authentic, but you can never rule it out). The account's exploded. Over 40,000 followers now. She's become the poster girl for new motherhood and the complicated nuances of modern feminism. She's tapped in to something. She's already written in a previous post how conflicted she feels about getting engaged, questioned whether she's a bad feminist. I don't know why she's so hung up on getting married: husbands are so overrated.

The account's good. I can't deny it. Still anonymous, small fragments of places and snatches of fabric, or random objects – like a nasal aspirator ('however hard I suck, I just can't get it out!') – but starkly photographed to fit with the reportage-style photography of the feed. It looks cool and her flat looks cool: there's glimpses of a London skyline view, details from the nursery, but it's the words that sell it: candid, snappy prose with a friendly, confessional vibe. Like she's speaking to her best friend or sister or something, not the whole wide world. It's very difficult to pull that off without a hint of self-consciousness.

How long until her identity is revealed? She'll be inundated with requests for exclusive interviews, big money offers. Once you've revealed who you are, though, you can never come back, and some of the stuff she's said – it's embarrassing. Not just for her, but for her friends and family too. Her mother-in-law! I can't dwell on this. I need to channel it into motivation: look what can be achieved in a few short weeks with hard work and dedication!

I follow a trail of cornflakes into the sitting room, where the twins are watching CBeebies. I snuggle Birch into me.

'Mummy, can we play' – he breaks free of my embrace and swoops around the room, arms out-stretched – 'albatrosses?'

Birds are the only thing that still him, sitting by the window watching them twitch and flitter, little hops and flutters of their wings. We go together sometimes to the nature reserve on the other side of town. We sit side by side in the hushed darkness of the hides, our eyes and ears searching the spectrum of the lake, breath held in anticipation of something special. Like a kingfisher's flash of blue. You hear the kingfisher before you see it. We wait on tenterhooks, wondering if we'll be lucky. It's one of the few times I don't take out my phone. No point; impossible to catch and you lose the beauty of the thing if you're watching it through a lens.

He prepares to 'take off' from the sofa, back hunched, knees bent, his right leg scraping forwards and backwards. He's in trouble; as he sweeps forward, the hula skirt he's pulled over his jeans gets caught under his foot and he topples down head first. A thick sheepskin rug breaks his fall. A bedraggled Birch looks up, rubbing his head. A baby bird stuck in his nest. 'The Lesser Spotted Hawaiian Albatross,' I say, and he collapses backwards, a big belly laugh. I reach down and ruffle his hair.

He sits up quickly, scratching his head like Seb does, looking downcast. 'What's wrong?' I give him a squeeze. He says nothing. Sullenly pulls the bright strips of his hula skirt through his fingers. 'Why are you sad?'

'Because I can't fly.' He slumps his shoulders.

I hold him to me tightly, breathing him in.

Me too, I think, *me too.*

'You can fly, Birch, I promise. Just in a different way.'

I try to rearrange with Holistic Flo – we'd agreed we'd do some exercise posts for the app together – but she threatens to go ahead without me. 'I'm sorry, Cass,' she says in a voice note, 'but I'm a single parent now, I need the money. I've not finalized sponsorship for the podcast yet. I've had some ideas – how are you with holding a plank?' We agree to meet after her class in Victoria Park.

I dither before messaging Beth: we were meant to be meeting for belated birthday cake today and I want to check in with how she's doing. She's been flat and despondent in her messages since her birthday. Something happened, but I don't know her well enough to press her. Should I cancel? I'm going to be in East London anyway... but I don't know how long it will take with Holistic Flo and I've got so much to catch up on. Time – like my life – seems to be unravelling at the moment, something I can't quite grasp on to. I wish I *could* see Beth today. I might not know *who* I am, but I know who I *want* to be. I want to be the person I am when I'm messaging Beth. I want to be an anonymous, ordinary mum chatting unself-consciously to another anonymous, ordinary mum.

I remind myself to get real: my work, my life, my family, everything's at stake. I have to put all I have into this now. I can't fall any further. I can't risk my fee with the Family Co. This is getting serious.

I stare again at the CHIN, disbelief repeating like the rich Sardinian salami Marina brings back for Seb. A new entrant in the Top Ten and me, Cassie Holliday, at number *six*?

It's the beginning of the end.

29

#ParkLife

Beth

'What are we doing here?' I ask Jade, shaking my head. I look at the toned frame encased in Lycra before me, her pose perfectly mirrored by Priya, who's been at the front of the class for the whole session. You can picture Priya's trajectory at school: Class Rep, Hockey Captain, Head Girl. I reach for my water as our instructor distributes boxing gloves.

I messaged Lucy on my way over to tell her I was coming. She'll be pleased I'm pulling myself together, not wallowing over my birthday and the wedding.

'I wanted to see her up close...' Jade gasps for breath. 'Holistic Flo,' she whispers, gesturing at our instructor, who's shouting: 'Picture those stretch marks, ladies, and go! *Go! Go! Go!*' while she punches the air ferociously. I highly doubt she's in possession of a single stretch mark and I've noticed she only demonstrates the exercises once and then fiddles around with her phone, or equipment, or her shoelace while the rest of us keep going.

That's Holistic Flo? I remember Lucy's profile on her and the accompanying photo: a woman doing the bendy back yoga position with a small child copying her. That Holistic Flo looked glossier, healthier... happier.

Jade drops her arms to her thighs and doubles over. She rolls her head to the side, sweat beading on her forehead: 'I need to soak up some of her holistic vibes. God knows I need them.' She raises herself to standing, hands on hips: 'Can we go to the pub after this?'

Beside us, Bronagh, red-faced and panting, gives a thumbs up.

We start to run again, a herd of hormonal, knackered new mums charging round the park with our buggies, worrying about our leaking uddies and other parts. We stop suddenly and segue into a high-kick sequence and I briefly worry if my uterus might fall right out. I catch Jade and Bronagh's eyes and we share a look followed by nods: let's get out of here.

Jade's quiet after the class and it's not until we're on to our second bottle of rosé that she asks, 'Have you had sex yet?'

'Since Poppy? No.' I screw my nose up. 'I can't even think about it.' When I think of my minnie now, I think of cold steel implements and surgical gowns and highly invasive medical procedures. I still think of my placenta every time I see red meat. I squeeze my legs together reflexively. 'I don't want anything poking around up there for a while.'

'I have,' says Priya, who completed the class and is sipping a coconut water. 'It was' – she tilts her head – 'okay.'

'Why?' I peer at Jade. 'Have you?'

She flushes red, her usual confident demeanour chastened. 'I wouldn't mind… trying it… or doing something,' she says, 'but it's like Liam doesn't look at me that way any more. He just sees these enormous bazookas with a twin hanging off one, and the other kicking around by my feet, and…' She trails off and takes a deep breath.

'It's difficult,' we nod and murmur. I couldn't feel less sexy if I tried.

'The thing is…' She looks around without making eye contact, scratches behind her left ear. 'Liam, he keeps, like, making these little jokes about how I' – she pauses, and in a rush adds – '*shit myself* in labour and it's like, I don't know,' – her voice wobbles – 'like I said, he doesn't see me how he used to…' She rolls her lips inwards, circles her thumbs on her temples, visibly trying not to cry.

We all look at her, not knowing what to say. I never expected Jade to be bothered by anything. She stares into her rosé and I feel a clutch of nausea, suddenly aware of the wine fizzing in my near empty stomach. I want to help but my tongue feels fat and heavy in my mouth.

'If it's any consolation' – *Am I going to say this? To these women I've only known a few months?* – 'I did it too. A poo. In labour.' I feel my forehead wrinkle with discomfort, but Jade looks at me with such relief in her eyes that my whole body exhales and the nausea subsides.

'Really? Because they say everyone does but no one else mentioned it. I thought it was just me.' Her dark eyes are luminescent, round and hopeful.

Bronagh raises her hand. She attempts an English accent: 'Peggy, love, could you just pass the sieve?' She mimes putting on latex gloves, while Priya gives a low, 'Hell, yes'.

Her face and neck flush, but her awkwardness dissolves at the sight of Bronagh's hand, still wiggling into the imaginary gloves, and we all explode into hard, knowing laughter. I feel a buzz of energy, of good vibes circulating between us. It feels intimate, centred, to have a group of women to reach out to like this. My friendship with Sandy has given me confidence: maybe this can be something that happens for me now? But even as I'm thinking it, I don't quite believe it.

My phone pings. Lucy. She's outside the flat. Worry prickles along my hairline. Am I imagining it or is her behaviour becoming more erratic? Whenever I see her now she's glued to her phone, even more than usual, jittery and jumpy when I ask if everything's okay. I hope she remembers that none of it's real. The online world, the photos you see, it's distorted. Fake.

'Sorry, I've got to go. My sister's outside my flat.'

'But you've not finished your drink!'

'You haven't told us about your birthday! Did Joe take you out for lunch?'

I tut when my phone rings but I'm relieved. I've not told anyone about my birthday. I'm too mortified. Thank goodness only my sister was there to bear witness to my humiliation. The ring's at the back of the drawer in my bedside table. The fewer people that know about it the better.

'I'm on my way,' I say, holding the phone to my ear with my shoulder and waving at my friends with one hand while I steer the buggy with the other.

'I have a surprise for you!' She says and don't know why, but something in her voice makes the nausea return.

30

#TakeOff

Cassie

I charge through the gates at Victoria Park, a woman on a mission. In the lift on the way up it occurs to me that I haven't planned what I'm going to say – so much of my life is scripted and rehearsed – but I need to act on my instincts, whatever the consequences. 'I'm sorry about all this,' Holistic Flo had said in the park. 'Alicia sent me over the schedule and a gig's a gig, right?' And the thing that I'd been trying to ignore kept going round and round in my head. Is Alicia up to something? She said Griff told her to send it, but why didn't she give me a heads-up?

'What's going on?' I demand when I reach her.

'Cassie! Hey, what's up?'

Heads pop up around us to see what's going on. Some of my resolve wavers. 'Can we talk?' I ask. 'Alone.'

'Sure.' She leads me to a break-out room, littered with video game consoles and cartons of popcorn. 'Coffee?' she asks, entirely relaxed.

'The Unhappy Hollidays. Do you know anything about it?'

'What?' She looks up in surprise, a perfect eyebrow raised. 'What do you mean?'

'Well, it's pretty convenient, isn't it? Publicity's publicity. The app's climbing the charts.'

'What are you trying to say, Cassie?' She crosses her arms. It's immediately clear I've pissed her off.

'You've been so *nice* about everything and yet...' I begin to feel embarrassed, the evidence I've gathered sounding weak now that we're face to face. 'The email from The Unhappy Hollidays. It was signed off XOXO!'

'Okay...' she says, the way you might try to reason with a belligerent toddler. 'Lots of people do that.'

'And you sent my schedule to Holistic Flo.'

'I had to,' she cuts in. 'Just before I convinced Griff not to reduce your fee.' Her voice is threaded with steel.

'Why didn't you warn me?' I ask, agitated.

'I was going to, after The Farm. I didn't think Griff was going to announce it there like that.'

I feel stupid but there's more to it, I know there is. I'm missing something here. 'Why *aren't* you more bothered about The Unhappy Hollidays?'

Her California tan becomes blushed with pink.

'Well?' I say, leaning on a retro pinball table.

Alicia sinks into a beanbag and gestures for me to do the same, but I stay standing. 'Like you say, the app downloads are doing okay. Not great but okay. And... This is awkward. Griff doesn't know. I played it down to him after Common As Mum...' She rolls her eyes. 'He's not on SoMe, none of the big tech guys are – *go figure* – and it's not in my interests to draw his attention to it.'

'Why not? Isn't that your job?' I join Alicia on a beanbag. It's much harder to keep up the momentum of being cross when you're wedged into one of these, I notice; maybe that's the point.

'My job is to work with you to promote the app and encourage downloads. I have a lot more to gain from you being a success than a failure, believe me.' Alicia sighs, cupping her coffee. 'I was instrumental in you being selected, Cassie. It was me pushing for you. I've always been a big fan of yours and maybe because of that my judgement was clouded when I looked at your stats. Griff had doubts but I talked him round... I put myself on the line. Griff's... tough. And honestly, Cassie? I'm frustrated but I'm trying to be professional. It's hard to feel sorry for you. You don't do yourself any favours. You treat me like an intern for a start.' She frowns. 'I'm new to this – my background's in magazines – but I graduated with Griff.'

'God, that's awful,' I say aloud without thinking, but I don't regret it. Fuck. And I – *proudly* – call myself a feminist? All the times I've felt the sting of society's assumptions because of my own career and I've been doing the same to Alicia. 'Seriously. I'm sorry. I *did* assume...' My voice tails off. I can't say it aloud: *I thought you were his assistant.* 'Jesus. That goes against everything I stand for.'

She looks amazed – and touched – by my honesty, a smile brighter than the Californian sun spreading over her face. 'You're not so bad,' she says, nudging my arm. 'Well, you are...' she grins. 'But there's hope for you.'

I bury my head in my hands. 'I truly am sorry, Alicia. I'm

not on my game at the moment. I've got too much going on, at home, at work. Not that I'm not on top of things. I am. I've got this.' I flick a peace sign and grin and she grins right back.

'I'm glad we had this talk,' she says, and I take the popcorn she proffers.

I feel lighter on the journey home, and my last post is doing well: me holding a plank while Holistic Flo stands on my back pretending to use the Family Co app.

My phone pings with a notification from my fertility tracker app. My period's due any day. I need to speak to Seb. A baby is a fresh start, isn't it? It's early spring, a September stationery haul, salty seaside air. Okay, yes, it's also sleep deprivation, sore boobs and anxiety – *look at poor Beth* – but I've had practice. And – my God, *think of the flat lays*! Instagram wasn't on my radar when the twins were babies. I'm sad about it. Not because of the wasted GMLs (off the chart for twin shots) but for the twins. If only they could look back one day and see their button noses touching, month numbers fashioned from berries and blossom, fig leaves covering their identical little bottoms. You have to wait days sometimes, props in hand, for the right light and two sleeping babies. It's an art form, basically. They would think I spent their early lives floating in a blissed-out bubble, rather than growing increasingly alarmed by Seb's total disinterest in the new little family we created together. This amazing miracle we'd pulled off.

A lump comes to my throat as I realize how much I want another baby. I feel it deep in my womb, a persistent ache I've not been listening to. Being pregnant would fix everything. It would blow this Unhappy Hollidays thing out of the water; the fall in the CHIN would be a dip before I came back on top. I feel sadness dragging me back. The mud shifting on my buried guilt. I need to stay positive. I can do this, can't I? I can find out who's behind The Unhappy Hollidays? I can have a baby; I can save my career *and* bring my family back together?

The enormity of it all feels crushing. Balancing Holistic Flo on my back's a piece of cake compared to all this. She weighs practically nothing.

But I *have* to do it. For all of us.

I have to focus all my energy on lucky baby number three.

31

#SewingAlongNicely

Beth

'Mitts, I need to tell you something.' Lucy puts the pattern for the picnic hamper down and cuts me off. I've been explaining I'm worried I have an under-supply of milk; maybe it's why Poppy's still not sleeping through? Or is it *sleep regression*? Can you regress from something you never really did?

It's been a week since Lucy turned up at the flat with my surprise: my sewing machine. A belated birthday gift. I stood in the hallway, both my hands held in prayer, thumbs tucked under my chin, as I fought back tears, my whole body shaking. Lucy actually looked uncomfortable. She knew I loved my sewing machine, that's why she went all the way up to Dad's to get it, but she didn't know how much. How my memories of sewing are so deeply entwined with my memories of Mum. I found it hard to craft after she died; it was too real, too visceral a connection to her. Unhelpful, since it formed part of my degree. I dropped as many practical modules as I could, swapping them to design-based ones, and when I graduated I tucked my machine away in my wardrobe, closed the doors on that part of my life. But somehow Lucy knew, intuitively, how much I missed it. How much I *needed* it.

I cleared a space in the spare room – more of a store room – and it's become my own little den. I've spent the week walking Poppy round the park, my phone nestled in the folds of the buggy emanating white noise, while I listen out for the parakeets, smiling at their clatter, returning home with her fast asleep and slipping a dandelion thread or a rich jewelled purple on to the spool pin. When I'm absorbed in something like this, time flies. I slip into my own world, just like I used to as a kid: knitting, crocheting, sewing.

Lucy's expression worries me and I suspend my foot over the machine's pedal. I've never been so grateful to have a sister. Navigating life without her around – with her in Dubai – is *unthinkable*. She takes a deep breath, pincering the hairband on her wrist and plucking it away from her skin, like she's drawing a bow and arrow.

'I should have told you sooner. It all happened so quickly…' She pulls the hairband back further, hooking her finger beneath it. 'I wasn't expecting it to and then I panicked.' Beneath the hairband a line of impressed skin circles her wrist, red like a warning sign. 'I had a plan, Mitts. I didn't think it would work out until December and then I could tell you over Christmas when you were in more of a routine with Poppy and you could see…' I'm not looking at Lucy, I'm transfixed by the hairband, still suspended away from her red-lined skin. 'You won't like it, Mitts, but it's an *opportunity*. That's what you have to bear in mind. You *mustn't* go getting all daft about it…'

The hairband pings with a satisfying snap against her skin. Instantly I know this is bad: *I can't hear it.* I can't hear that she's got the promotion and is moving a seven-hour flight away. Not now. Not after my birthday. Life's too raw right now to lose Lucy too.

'Actually, I've got something to tell *you*!' I rush on. 'Sandy thinks I could maybe sell some of my bits online.' I gesture at the cheeseburger and hot dogs I've constructed from scraps of fabric. 'For kids to play with. Her babysitter makes clothes for pets and sells them online. Maybe I will need a social media presence after all!' I add, eager to show Lucy what progress I've made.

Lucy frowns at the change of direction but then latches on it, like she's been saved from something frightening. 'I'm sorry,' – she shakes her head – 'who's Sandy?'

'My friend I met in the park. After I got so upset looking at Amber's "profile".' I can't resist a sneering tone.

'Oh right, yeah, I remember you mentioning her.' She nods, distracted; I can tell she's not listening. She sweeps her fingers around the circumference of her wrist, as if she's just noticed the red line, circling her skin like a tree ring. 'Mitts.' She swallows. 'You need to know…'

It's the way she keeps calling me Mitts. The haunted look in her eyes. Reminiscent of the time she wrote off the car we shared. I cut her off. I can't hear it. I can't hear that she's leaving me.

'Sandy has twins. So cute. Two girls, I think, but I couldn't tell, they were wearing tutus. Poppy's too young for a tutu, isn't she?' I busy myself, fiddling with navy cotton. I don't wait for her to respond. 'And knight tops with graffiti wellies. And alien antennae on their heads.'

I frown, push my foot on the pedal, sewing again, the noise filling the vacuum in the room, pushing out any space that was left for Lucy to say what she wanted to say.

'I guess they *could've* been boys,' I shout over the roar of the machine. 'That's the done thing now, isn't it, all the gender-neutral stuff? In fact, we're in East London, they were almost *definitely* boys. Anyway, we've been messaging *loads*. She works in events. We're going to meet for coffee, talk about my product launch.'

I speak too fast. Not letting her get a word in. *Don't worry about me, even though my heart is breaking. Don't worry.*

Lucy watches me agog, like she doesn't know how to respond. This isn't what she's expecting: she knows I've always struggled making new friends, putting myself out there. I'm pleased I've managed to surprise her, that I'm not as socially inept as she thinks.

'I feel bad for her. She really wants another baby, but she doesn't think her husband will agree. Tricky, isn't it, that sort of thing?'

I barely pause for breath. I want her to know this is the start of a real friendship, how quickly we've exchanged intimacies. Friendships can form like stars and planets, from fast bursts of intensity, like Jade and Bronagh and Sandy. In a few months I'll be part of a solar system – my own Milky Way. I'm going to be *fine* when Lucy goes, just *fine*.

'And risky too, investing in it emotionally and he might say no? I said she should talk to him about it. She sounded surprised – "I hadn't thought of that," she said! Funny how we've all forgotten to talk to each other and yet spend *hours* online deluding ourselves, scrolling through social media looking for the answers on there instead! You know that better than anyone.'

In my eagerness to detract from my terror at Lucy leaving I run off into a tangent, my soapbox spiel about social media and women's magazines. I know I've wandered into unsafe territory. I look at Lucy's face and realize I've stepped on a grenade.

'I didn't mean you're deluded. Or what you do is deluded, or wrong, or anything… I meant you know how much people like reading about that sort of thing. You know, from *Boom!* Sorry, that didn't come out very well.'

I used to love a glossy mag as much as the next person – I still do if I find one at the hairdressers' – but when I hold the shiny pages in my hand, I can't help but see Lucy's skeletal frame bent over, hands gripped as the glamorous creatures stepped out of the magazine and paraded in front of her. Images that replayed in her head and distorted her view of herself and made her feel like she wasn't enough. That's what social media is today. It's millions of people telling you that you're not enough. Well, I am enough. And my sister is enough.

'You think you're so above it all and you can't see what's in front of you.' Lucy's words are sharp, her face twisted. I open my mouth to speak, to explain myself better – it wasn't an attack on her work, or her promotion, or her values – but she beats me to it. 'Why don't you talk to Joe about stuff if it's so easy?'

The fabric in my hand snags. Lucy stares at me fiercely, her eyes filled with challenge. My cheeks burn. 'What do you mean?'

'What could I possibly mean?' Her eyes flick over my

fingers. My eyes sting with humiliation, my nose tingling and itching as I try not to cry. It wasn't a dig at *her*, the mention of social media. It was a dig at the *industry*. But she's poked in a wound that is still too new, too raw, too utterly and hopelessly wrapped up in the fireworks of hormones that rocket through my body.

'Why don't you come back to me when you've actually got a boyfriend? One that lasts past *three* months.'

It's a cheap shot, I know. It's a special gift that sisters have to deliver an insult so cutting, it slices clean to the bone. It's not as simple as I don't want her to go to Dubai. It needles at me. That she feels obliged to look after me. All this little sister stuff. This pretence that she's the strong one. And we both collude in this tired routine, because it's easier to focus on *my* guilt, *my* sadness, more comforting to ignore *her* brittle bones, wondering if *she* might snap at any point.

Who's going to gather up your bones and carry you to the bath when you're in Dubai, Lucy? It was her low point. The moment she needed to finally accept treatment, six months of hospitalization. I'll never forget the feel of her in my arms, her frame loose and disjointed, or the sight of Dad's slack neck as he stared at the floor. I close my eyes as I relive the sight, my anger abating as quickly as it gathered.

'I'm not doing this now,' Lucy mutters, picking up her scarf and slipping her phone into her bag, shaking her head. 'I don't know why I bother.'

As she gets ready to leave, I think back to those days: she *has* to go. She's come so far since. She's still making up for them. And it's a chance for her to make some money, move out of the flat-share, build a foundation for herself, financially and professionally. I've been selfish wanting her to stay here, for me, when I have everything – well, almost everything – I've ever wanted. She'll resent me if she stays. I owe it to her. I sit back from the sewing machine, resigned.

'Didn't you want to tell me something?' I ask. Part remorse, part petulance.

'Don't worry,' she says, smoothing her hair behind her ears and straightening the hem of her silk blouse. She eases into her long camel coat and heads for the door, stepping carefully over some striped fabric I'm using to make miniature deckchair covers. 'It will keep.'

32

#DinnerDate

Cassie

When I tell Seb I've arranged for Ruby to stay later so we can go out, he seems genuinely excited: 'Can we go to the new steak place in town?'

I dither. The thing is, the Flying Gaucho is *all over* SoMe. They keep following and unfollowing me, trying to get my attention. If they see me they'll definitely post it and this is not a time to be pictured with Seb scowling at me over a medium rare rump, especially when I don't know how the baby conversation will pan out.

'I've booked the Otter's Paw.' I hold his gaze.

'Fine.' He rolls his eyes. 'I hope they still do the venison.'

We exit the taxi to a crisp October evening, the sky a vivid coral. I can't help but smile. We had our first date on UK soil here, at a similar time of year. I remember our red wine cheeks, cold hands tentatively reaching out for each other's as they warmed by a real fire. It's the perfect setting for us to reconnect as a couple, to discuss our future. Seb moves ahead to open the door for me and the warm glow in my stomach matches the cosy light spilling through the leaded windows.

'What the…?' Seb stares into the pub, slack-mouthed but tight-eyed.

I remove my beret as I survey the scene. The pub's still large and rangy, but it's divided with various screens depicting fire-breathing dragons – I don't know too much about feng shui, but this strikes me as the very opposite of that. In fact, I can already feel the positive vibes between Seb and me dissipating, shooting out from us like lost sparks and veering headlong into a multitude of potted palm trees. I open a menu: a riot of symbols and even some – *God, no* – photographs of food. The Otter's Paw has become a Chinese buffet.

Seb remains frozen by the door. I link my arm in his and give it a squeeze, drawing him in to the room: 'Well, this is a turn-up!' I chuckle. This is what I've always strived for with Seb, an 'in it together' camaraderie, but as I tilt my head upwards, hoping to meet his smile, he glowers down at me.

'I knew we should have gone to the Flying Gaucho.'

We settle into our chairs and I concede he's right – this is a *terrible* idea. Beside us, a woman is absent-mindedly forking her special fried rice. Her date has his hands under the table and from the tilt of his elbows his hands seem to be working on something frenetically. I see the shiny top of his phone – *thank God* – but my relief is quickly replaced by fear: is he filming me? He doesn't look like your average Happy Hollidays follower, but you never know. I smile furiously just in case and give my hair a flick, laughing at Seb.

He raises an eyebrow: 'All I said was, we don't have to have prawn crackers, do we? It says they're complimentary.'

'Oh, Seb.' I reach over the table to hold his hand but he continues to clasp his menu, looking at me oddly. 'You're such a funny guy.'

I scan the room. We're surrounded by couples not meeting each other's eyes, staring at their phones, berating each other for staring at their phones. Probably all of whom have come here tonight with the same hope as me: to reconnect. Oh shit. This is the restaurant where relationships come to die. I put a hand to my stomach. I can't stop thinking about the baby. I've realized it's not about the money and the opps and the mortification (although it would help with all that, of course), it's about something more. Something more fundamental to me, to my being. We need each other, this baby and me.

'Seb. I've been thinking. With the twins starting school next year and me having so much flexibility with work...' He fiddles with his chopsticks. I take a deep breath. 'Well... we always said, didn't we? We always said we wanted three?'

He furrows his brow, regarding his chopsticks suspiciously.

'Seb?'

'I'm not having pudding,' he says, irritation on his lips.

'What?'

'I hate these blasted things.' He see-saws the chopsticks between his fingers.

'Seb! Are you listening to me?'

'Yes! I'm not having three! It's bad enough having two!'

A waiter sets down a bowl of prawn crackers and Seb smiles and nods at him obsequiously, picking one up and crunching it savagely. 'In for a penny...' he mutters.

I stare at him, my head cocked to the side. 'Not courses, Seb, *children*. We always said we'd have three *children*.' We meet eyes. *Oh. Right. You know what I mean*, I think. There's a long silence as he uses his tongue to scope along his teeth, removing and chewing lost bits of prawn cracker.

I persevere, more to make my point than with any realistic hope of success, my heart already deflating: 'You always said that after being an only child you wanted three...'

The weight of the question drags down his features, like the shutters on a shop front slowly closing. 'I don't remember saying that. Besides, the twins have each other, they adore each other. There's *no way* I want to have more children. I can't believe you do.'

'What do you mean by that? Of course I do.'

'Cassie, I've been there and done that. I'm not doing it again.'

Tears bud in my eyes and I blink quickly to stop them: if there's one thing Seb hates (in among all the other things Seb hates), it's me crying.

After that, our conversation flounders circuitously – me casting the net out, Seb shutting me down as he drains another Tsingtao. I give up and submit to observing my fellow diners. I notice a couple sitting nearby. She has long blonde hair that looks natural. Like, naturally natural. She has that dewy, hot look that Dutch girls have – maybe she is Dutch? – and the kind of body that can wear anything and make it look expensive. In my head I compose her Instagram bio – live simple, live free – and imagine the write-up she would secure in *Vogue*: 'naively dressed Northern European Tilda talks slow living...'.

Her dinner date has rich, hazel skin and short, cropped hair. His plimsol trainers are perfect with his casual blue blazer and white tee, his charcoal-rimmed glasses adding a dash of geek-chic. I conjure an Instagram handle: @ TechyBo. They look young and fresh-faced and – I've not seen this look in a while – in love. It's like a punch to the gut, my envy for them. Were there couples who thought this about Seb and me all those years ago when we met in here? Did detached housewives watch us share our first kiss over the top of their husbands' tipped beer bottles and wistfully try to remember that feeling?

Bo leans in to Tilda, intense but in a good way, earnest but controlled. I picture him last week googling "romantic restaurants in Oatbridge" and the Otter's Paw coming top of the search. The years of positive reviews must still outweigh any recent negative ones. Besides you can buy your way to the top of an internet search quite easily these days. Poor old Techy Bo.

"This is lovely!" I hear Tilda say as she picks up her laminated menu, turning it over in her hands.

'Cassie? Are you listening to me?'

Seb's voice pulls me back. I murmur reassurances, still with one eye on the couple. 'Yes. Marina. The frequent trips to Sardinia. The haircuts...'

'Why can't she get her hair cut here?'

'I don't know, she said she tried once and never again.'

'Who travels abroad once a month to get their hair cut? It's preposterous. How much are the flights costing?'

I couldn't give two shits where Marina gets her hair cut,

and to be fair it looks fabulous. I'd stick with whatever she's doing too if I were her. But I need to get Seb on side so I take a more conciliatory tack: 'I agree with you. There's something going on. But so what? She can stay in the house unless she remarries.'

Placated, he takes another sip from his bottle.

'If we knew she was in a relationship we'd have some hope that she'd be moving on soon! That would be comfort at least. I saw this coming,' he says angrily. 'And now I'm locked out of my father's estate!'

You're not locked out. We could all move in, there's plenty of space. Marina wants us to move in, she'd love to have the kids there in their room, they're the closest thing to family she's got since her husband died, but you're too blinded by pride or whatever it is to do it.

I try to squash down my sadness at how far my reality is from Tilda's. How much wine would it take to drown it completely? *This is old love,* I remind myself. *This is what happens once you've had kids. Don't think you're something special, Cassie.* Elen's favourite refrain. *Don't make the mistake of thinking you deserve more.*

'She'll get bored. We never thought she'd hang around. Maybe it's the twins,' I shrug. Hang on. Tilda and Bo. Something's going on. Bo seems to know the waitress. They're communicating silently.

'They're not even her grandchildren!'

I think of the twins dancing around the kitchen earlier in the Big House to Italian jazz with Marina, tapping their feet and swinging their hips and singing about lemon ice cream (20,403 views at my last check).

'They're very fond of – oh, Seb! Look!' My despondency

melts away. 'It's Tilda and Bo! He's proposing! It's a proposal!'

'Who?' Seb cranes his neck to look at them. 'Do you know those people?'

'No, no, I – that's not their real names, they're probably called Amanda and Steve. I was just imagining—'

A low soulful voice interrupts me. A lullaby for grown-ups, gently drawing all eyes to their table. Techy Bo has his arms outstretched, holding Tilda's hands, emitting the most beautiful sound. On Tilda's plate is a single prawn cracker, a diamond glittering from its curve. A row of waitresses and kitchen staff have formed a line and are gleefully leaning over the table. The woman next to me holds her phone steadily in the direction of the proposal – oh shit! This is perfect for Stories! I get mine out too and in a low voice provide a commentary on the scene: 'So here we are, on a date night in Oatbridge – in *the most* romantic restaurant – and...'

It's impossible to watch a proposal and not feel filled up with love. Unless, that is, you are Seb. He tilts his chair back, waving his empty beer bottle in the direction of the eager line of staff, who are absorbed in the moment. I panorama my phone around the room, taking in the looks of delight from my fellow patrons as Tilda gives a sweet, pink-cheeked 'Yes!' to Bo. I carefully swerve Seb, who is now harrumphing loudly.

Something in the far corner of the restaurant catches my eye. I lower my phone. There's a table obscured by a tropical plant. Its occupants must be the only patrons not watching the proposal unfold. Again I see it: an unmistakable bounce of gel-quiffed hair. Forest Dad! Of course! His Forest

School HQ is out in the sticks somewhere near here. I turn back to Seb but the temptation to see what Forest Dad's up to is immense. What's he doing here? Is he on a date? In the restaurant where relationships come to die? Hang on, what about Tilda and Bo? Their relationship is star-bound. Maybe I've read this all wrong.

When the crowd around Tilda and Bo disperses I tell Seb I need the loo, which is conveniently located just past Forest Dad's table. I stroll over nonchalantly, waiting for him to see me and call me over. I slow as I near his table, giving a quick desperate glance as I go directly past but he's absorbed in whatever his date is saying, and as her words float upwards over the enormous plant, I freeze. I know that voice. Boardroom Boss Mum.

'We need to stick to the plan. So it's taking a little longer than we expected, that's okay.' I have my back to the plant's spine, breath held as I carefully weigh up her words.

'Are you sure?' Forest Dad now. 'It's getting really embarrassing.' I turn slowly, careful not to ruffle any leaves, but the foliage is dense. I still can't see them properly, see *her*.

'It's just business. I knew you wouldn't be cut out for this,' she says softly.

He mumbles a reply I don't catch. I need to see him to lip-read. The wide flat leaves are the sort that squeak with the slightest movement. Through the tiniest gap I can see her. I have a better view of Forest Dad but it's risky now to be this close; his dark eyes are downcast and his hand is palm down on the table.

'I did tell you.' She speaks to him as though reassuring a small child, rather than a sexual conquest. I don't think Mr

Boardroom Boss Mum has anything to worry about. I've never met him, he's always working, another City type. She must have an army of nannies with all those kids. Her voice grows stern. 'Now's not the time to lose your nerve.'

I don't know what to think. They're my friends, aren't they? Surely they're not behind The Unhappy Hollidays? Do I spring out from behind the plant pot and demand to know what's going on? They're hardly going to confess. They stand to leave and I run to the Ladies and hide in a cubicle until I'm sure they've gone. The toilets, I note, remain unchanged. While I'm waiting, I reply to Beth's good luck message: 'Hmm… He wasn't mega keen but I'm sure he'll come round! ☺'

I click on to SoMe. The first thing I see is a post by Mardy Mum – a photo of a stack of Breastfeeding Babe Bombs – who went quiet when that #periwhat thing was trending but is now back and wittering on about breastfeeding and her low supply. *Girls, it's been one of those days. A mardy mum bun kind of day!* God, she's irritating, this 'E'. I'd like to bury her in an avalanche of Breastfeeding Babe Bombs. I can't bring myself to 'connect' with her, like Alicia suggested, but I've followed her back: a small but significant gesture.

I remember Seb back at the table. He hates being left waiting. He'll be furious. I'll never be able to persuade him to have another baby. I remove my knickers. It's cheesy, I know, but… well, he used to love this! I've not done it since we've had kids for various reasons: we never go out and it's not the same to sneak off to the kitchen to take them off; I can't be arsed; and also, leaks. But now I feel some of my old spirit coursing in my veins. The girl who wanted to fly, the girl who fell in love, the girl who took a chance.

You're a woman now, Cassie. You're every woman and you've got this.

I round the corner, my knickers bunched in my hand, ready to slip them into Seb's pocket, but all I see is a plate of cold-looking chicken chow mein at my setting and an empty plate and chair at his. He's gone.

33

#Pumping

Beth

I open the door and Urzula bustles in, a large sports bag slung over her shoulder.

She looks me up and down and says: 'There is a problem with your supply, no?' Instantly I change my opinion on health visitors. She's good.

'I follow you,' she says, as I lead her into the flat. It took me an hour to tidy away my piles of fabric and patterns and works-in-progress. Sandy thinks they could sell. I was worried I'd need an online presence, but she doesn't think I would. In fact, she thinks it would be distracting and a bit pointless. It's refreshing to have a friend who gets it.

While Urzula unpacks her scales, I settle Poppy on her changing mat on the floor and strip her down to her vest, ready to be weighed. I take extra care when extracting her from her clothes, mindful I'm being scrutinized. I silently beg her to behave. Urzula huffily asks me for Poppy's red book. If this was the first time I'd met her I'd worry I'd somehow offended her, but she's been fairly abrasive in all our previous encounters so I think nothing of it and scoot off to get it from Poppy's bedroom.

'You must not leave baby unattended,' she tuts at me when I return. 'What would people think!' she mutters under her breath.

'Okay,' I reply, afraid to add *But you were here*.

'Now. You have breast pump, yes?'

'Yes,' I gulp. Lucy turned up with one yesterday. 'I'm sorry,' she said, as she handed it over, 'about the other day. I was oversensitive...' 'Me too,' I interjected. '...I'm stressed out about work and this promotion and things at the flat are dead awkward...' Her eyes flared as she grimaced. 'Anyway, I was telling Romilly at work you're worried about your milk and she said you could borrow this. Expressing helps encourage more hind milk? It's fattier, so it fills them up more?' She'd waved her arms round vaguely, not meeting my eyes, reminding me of a tourist, asking the way to a bus stop in a language she doesn't understand. Having Poppy has catapulted me into a different world to Lucy's and she's trying hard to navigate it, to immerse herself in its customs and cultures.

'The Super Pump 3000 is the best,' says Urzula.

'That's the one I have!' I'm so eager to please. To pass the test. It makes me hate myself a little bit.

'Yes. Have you tried to use it?'

'Not yet, I—'

'Let me show you.'

Urzula holds what I presume to be the suction end of the breast pump firmly against my nipple. She gestures for me to take over, muttering and shaking her head. Using both her thumbs, she brings the machine to life. The sound is a cross between a mechanical donkey and a ship's foghorn. I sit, breast exposed, ridiculous contraption hooked up, for some minutes. I glance down, expecting a pool of milk. A reservoir of liquid gold. But despite the efforts of the Super Pump 3000, only a small spray of milk is escaping my left breast, nothing from my right. Why can't I get this right either?

'It takes some practice. You do good. Some mums, they get nothing first time. Is best to have baby next to you,' Urzula instructs. She nudges Poppy with her foot. 'Best if she cry.'

After she leaves, I send a photo to Lucy with cow and crying face emojis and write: 'Time for wine!' She video-calls me immediately.

'Not going well with the pump?' she asks sympathetically.

'Apparently this is a good first effort.' I pull a wry face. 'I've got to go, I said I'd meet the hypnobabes. I've not seen them for a few weeks, so I wanted to…'

'Hey, I wanted to ask, how's your friend getting on? The one from the park? Any luck with her hubby and the baby?' Lucy's voice sounds strained. She has a different vernacular when she's working.

'Not great. She took my advice and asked him over dinner, and he left.' I feel bad. I shouldn't have given any advice. I've never even met him.

'Wow,' says Lucy, 'that doesn't sound good.'

'No. She found him at home cosied up with the babysitter.'

Lucy looks scandalized. I don't want to exacerbate her latent commitment issues. 'I'm sure it'll be fine, though. She seems dead nice – a warm, genuine person. I'm sure they'll figure it out.'

Lucy drums her pen on her desk agitatedly.

'Once they see the positives?' she teases gently as she repeats my mantra. Of all the phrases I've picked up from my self-improvement books, it's the one I return to the most: trying to see the positives. I should start listening to my own advice again.

Her eyes shoot upwards and she moves her head, seeing past Poppy and me. When she looks back at the screen, I raise my eyebrows questioningly.

'Alicia,' she says, grimacing. 'She keeps bugging me to go for coffee.'

I pull a face. I've never been keen on Alicia. For a while she and Lucy were always together, in that intense fiery way that women are sometimes: not stars and planets and the freedom of the galaxy – more like a lunar eclipse, their intrinsic pull and alignment blocking each other's light. I was worried Lucy would get sucked in by Alicia's competitive not-eating under the guise of green juices, but it changed after their boss, Griff, sold *Boom!* mag and launched some family tech company, renting office space on the floor above Lucy's, and Alicia moved upstairs with him. Lucy sees Alicia sometimes in the building, but their closeness was never recaptured. For the best, if you ask me.

'Anyway,' Lucy recovers. 'Gotta go! Let me know if you have any updates!'

'I will! I'll get hooked up later!'

'Hooked up?'

'The pump!' What else could I mean? I hold it aloft, its plastic arteries spilling through my fingers.

'Yes! Let me know how you get on, I'll tell Romilly.'

As if Romilly's interested in how I find her breast pump;

she's being nice, helping out another mum. 'I'll send you a photo if you like?' I ask sarcastically.

Her eyes shoot up. 'Could you?' She looks behind me again nervously.

'No!' I shake my head, laughing. She flashes me a grin then quickly hangs up.

'Weirdo,' I say, smiling at Poppy. She blinks.

Things are okay with Lu, aren't they? *Aren't they?*

On the surface we've patched things up, but I feel guilty about our argument: she wanted to share her news with me and I wouldn't let her. Why did I have to jump in like that, banging on about my new venture and friendship?

I rub my hands over my face and into the corners of my eyes. They sting as my moisturizer becomes displaced. This is how it is when I'm tired and anxious: second-guessing myself, questioning my responses. It was nothing, wasn't it? Just standard sibling bickering? I can't help but worry that our spat was the tip of something bigger, something out of our control. We've always been close through the bad times: when I was bullied at school, when Mum died, when Lucy got sick. Haven't we?

For a time at school, Lucy was my saviour. I've never had her confidence, even before what happened with Mum and the panic attacks, so when the cool gang seemed to take exception to me, I didn't have the balls to stand them down as I knew she would have done. As indeed she did, on one occasion, when the outside of my locker was covered in cooking oil. Lucy made it her business to find out who had done it – her future career in journalism obvious – and when she did, tipped a bottle of cooking oil over the perpetrator's – Caitlin Oxenbury's – hair. It went quiet after that. I was spared by virtue of being Lucy's sister. Until that day in sixth form, when Lucy had left, and Caitlin chopped my hair clean off.

My screen is full of notifications: my friends have left the pub. I throw my phone on to the sofa. Only another three hours, thirty-three minutes and forty-two seconds until Joe gets home.

34

#AskFred

Cassie

The dream was different last night. I wasn't *on* the plane this time. I was on the tarmac, ready to check over the aircraft, clipboard in hand, when a crack of thunder split the sky and all gazes – and I realized then that I was surrounded by a thousand faceless people – shifted upwards. Only it wasn't thunder. As I stood immobile, my toes touching a yellow safety line, huge black wheels the size of houses began to fall from the sky. Each one cracking the pavement as it bounced: every particle of air, of dust, of light reverberating with the impact, strong enough to make my body shake. I clutched my stomach with both hands and stared down at my toes as the cracks in the ground snaked towards the yellow line. The noise of it all! I woke with my hands covering my ears, gasping for air. All I could think was: *my baby, my baby*. And then I realized: I'd got my period.

I tell Seb I have a ton of work to catch up on. He begrudgingly agrees to take the twins into town for babyccinos in exchange for nine holes this afternoon. I sit at the kitchen table with my iPad and remind myself to breathe as I look at a new Unhappy Hollidays' post: a horrible series of photos of me taken over the last month and all captured at the right – well, the wrong – angle, with the caption:

> Bump watch! Is Cassie Holliday expecting baby number 3? The snaps certainly look like it, but word is Mr Happy Hollidays isn't too keen – is there trouble in paradise? Is Cassie Holliday's home really a fair-trade, hemp-woven house of cards? And is it about to come crashing down? More soon!

The last photo is of Seb and me scowling at each other, an out-take from our trip to Disneyland, but Joe Public doesn't know it's a year out of date. It's speculation, right? There's no way they could know that Seb doesn't want to have another baby. I've not told any of the other Influencers, or Hetty. I'm careful now to hardly say anything to them. The atmosphere between us is pinched, to say the least. I want to speak to Beth. I want to ask her advice, but the one person I want to be honest with, I can't. Why didn't I tell her about my online persona sooner? I got sucked in by the authenticity of our friendship. I overshared: about Seb, the baby, my dissatisfaction with my life. I don't think Beth would betray me if she found out, but it's a risk. We've not known each other that long; it just feels like longer because we get along so well. It's so easy, so uncomplicated and uncontrived. So normal.

Just as I'm wondering if my life can get any more tragic, I see them: small patches of black mould growing over the damp in the corner. What the…? I google 'black mould' and words like 'toxic', 'infestation' and 'panic' blur in my eyes. I can't keep living like this. Seb went bonkers when I suggested we move into the Big House for the winter. Marina can't understand why he's being so stubborn about it, snapping at me as if it were my fault. Frustration bubbles up. I used to have a proper job. I had means. If Seb insists on us living here, we need to eradicate this mould. If he won't pay for it, I'll ask Marina. I find some local companies and email them, attaching photographs of the walls.

I feel tired and drained as I always do when I have my period, but especially this one. A reminder of what could've been. I stare idly out of the window. How did I get here? In this damp, miserable cottage, my career in free fall, my marriage increasingly fragile, my only true friend not knowing who I really am. And what do I do now?

My eyes flit to the top of the stairs; the loft hatch. I've never given away our baby stuff, it's all up there, carefully stacked in boxes or wrapped in plastic. They say that's the sign. Once you're ready to give away all your baby things, you know you're done. Something buzzes in my jaw and in my stomach: a feeling, of destiny, of truth, of what *ought to be*. Gut instinct, I suppose. We always said… I remember the Family Co app's digital personal assistant function, Fred.

'Fred, when am I most fertile?'

'You are most fertile…' The problem is my periods have always been erratic. That's why I've been tracking them with my app. I click online. Within seconds an ovulation kit is winging its way to me.

'Fred, is it a fucking disastrous idea to have a baby to save my career and my marriage? Actually, Fred, don't answer that.' I close down the Family Co app. It freezes, as I've noticed it is wont to do, 'Fred' repeating:

'It is.'

'It is.'

'It is.'

'Stupid piece of shit.' I click furiously as Fred continues:

'It is.'

'It is.'

Eventually, in frustration, I lift the sash, my lip curling at the tiny black beetles scurrying from their shelter, and hurl my phone out of the window. Even as I'm throwing it, I know I'll go and scamper outside in the muddy grass to retrieve it in a minute, but for a glorious, joy-filled moment it feels good.

35

#RealityCheck

Beth

I lift the receiver and Lucy's face appears on screen. My shoulders slump. I wish she'd stop turning up like this. I can't tell whether she's checking up on me or avoiding going home.

'Joe not in yet?' she asks, stepping inside. She's wearing a nude silk shift dress, bare legs even though it's October, and leopard print ankle boots. Chunky gold bracelets and a statement necklace catch the autumn sunlight as it fans through the window. I look down at my own attire – pale-blue jeans and a baggy grey hoodie – and feel myself shrink inwards.

'No, busy week.' The truth is I've hardly seen him lately. 'Lots on at work,' he muttered on his way out the door this morning, manbag slung over his shoulder. He's even working later on Fridays, which is usually an early finish. I know I need to talk to him about my birthday.

When I found out I was pregnant it was an unexpected

if not entirely unforeseen event since we had, you know, without anything, once or twice. I've worked so hard to convince myself that I'm okay with it happening that way, before we were married, or even engaged. As I said to Lucy over waffles in Bermondsey Market on a gloomy Sunday morning in January, 'It doesn't matter these days if you're not married when you have a baby. I'm a feminist, after all, and I don't want to adhere to some prescribed agenda that society imposes on us.' I was using my best work voice to get my point across.

'Right,' she had said, drawing the word out as she spread syrup over the bumpy surface of her waffle. 'But the thing is, Mitts' – more syrup, more spreading – 'you've *always* wanted to get married, and isn't that what feminism is – doing what *you* want?' She took a small mouthful of waffle. 'Even if it's not very cool.' She met my eyes, smiling with me, but I wouldn't join in. I was looking at how much she had left on her plate while she rested her cutlery. It's always Lucy that suggests these calorie-laden eateries – doughnuts, waffles, macarons – but then only eats the tiniest morsels.

'*This* is what I want!' I'd insisted, poking my fork towards my belly where inside nestled – at that time, according to my pregnancy tracker app – a little poppy seed (we've called her Poppy ever since). 'Why aren't you being supportive?'

'I am! I am! I knew this would somehow end up being my fault.' She sat back, holding her coffee cup with both hands, licking syrup from her lips. 'How many secret boards for wedding stuff do you have on Pinterest?'

I stayed silent.

'There's at least one, you've shown it to me! And that

was before you met Joe. How many now? In total? Look…
I'm not saying it's a problem – you know what I think about
weddings' – she wrinkled her nose – 'but this is about you
– be true to yourself. If you want to get married, speak to
him about it.'

Obviously, I couldn't do that. The only time it did come
up – Handsy Ron inelegantly suggesting it as we shared
our happy news ('I suppose you two will be getting hitched
now!') – I said haughtily, 'I don't want Joe to propose to me
just because I'm pregnant', and after looks were exchanged
his family went back to hugging each other. But now? Now
I am a little bothered. Now I have a baby and the weight
of society's assumptions and the reminder every time I have
to correct a well meaning person who glances at Poppy's
name and then calls me Mrs Taylor: Doctor Shah, Urzula,
the manager at the nursery in the park we're on the waiting
list for. It feels like everyone else out there wants us to be a
family except for Joe, who isn't fussed either way.

Lucy picks up two patchwork bears, shaking them gently.
The bells I've sewn inside them jangle.

'I was chatting to Sandy earlier. She's going to help me do
some product photographs for Etsy.'

'She's coming here? To the flat?' Lucy grasps the bears in
her hands.

'Next week, after the wedding,' I nod. 'I feel bad because
she's dead busy at work, but she insisted. Maybe it's a
distraction from the baby stuff…'

'She's pregnant?' Lucy breathes.

'No, that's the problem, she's obsessed! She's using an
ovulation tracker thing to find out when she's fertile.'

I don't want to, because Sandy's a friend, but I pull a face.

'How will that work...' I asked her earlier, 'if he doesn't want to?' She shrugged. 'He's never asked me if I'm still on the pill, he just assumes I am, pumping my body with hormones every day on the off-chance we might have a shag every once in a while and it *might* happen to fall within my fertile period. *Hell, no.*' It was the first time I'd felt myself judging her.

'Is her husband still not keen?'

I shrug. I don't want to betray Sandy's confidence; she might meet Lucy one day. 'I don't know, she's not mentioned him since.'

Lucy stands very still, as though processing something. I observe her slender frame. I'm worried about her. She's not tried to talk to me about her promotion since our argument. What if the stress of it – her potential move, her snappy sister – gets too much for her? What if she forgets to eat, slowly slipping back into her old habits?

'Lucy, about the thing you wanted to tell me...'

'Oh, don't worry about that.' She looks embarrassed; maybe the promotion isn't in the bag as she hoped? 'I've got something to cheer you up!' Lucy produces something delicate and lacy and not too horrendous in a pale, silvery grey from a tissue paper parcel. 'Isabella at work,' she beams.

'I'm not miserable,' I say, but I take the dress. 'Honestly, I'm happy here in my little bubble, developing my product range, listening to podcasts. I feel like I have a purpose.'

'You'll need these...' She throws a pair of nude Spanx in my direction and leaves the room. I hear her rummaging in my wardrobe. She returns dangling my silver strappy sandals. They look like a relic from another life. Here lived a vibrant young woman, who enjoyed wearing heels in metallic hues... I hold the dress out in front of me. It's beautiful. It has a top layer, which glitters with tiny sequins, overlaying the main dress fabric and a hidden fold, to squeeze my boobs through for feeding.

'It's dead nice.' My voice is small. I hold the fabric between my fingers and try to picture myself wearing it, being back in Yorkshire, with Poppy and Joe and Dad. My heart feels constricted, the knots around it tightening. I can't shut myself off from the world sewing retro ketchup and mustard bottles forever: I've got to go to this wedding and pretend everything's perfect when it's not. But at least, thanks to Isabella, I'll be able to do it in a beautiful dress with no danger of exposing my underwear when I'm feeding.

'I said you were feeling a little... stressed... about what to wear to the wedding so she said you could borrow it.'

I wipe my eyes with the back of my hand. I'm not crying; it's a precautionary measure.

'And it will complement your changing bag,' she smirks. I throw the Spanx at her.

'I'll have to get Isabella something to say thank you.'

'All she wants is a photo. And I can take care of that on the day!' she says brightly.

I hold the dress on my lap, a lump in my throat. 'I don't know where I'd be without you, Lucy,' I say, blinking tears away.

36

#FeelingFestive

Cassie

I shield my eyes from the sun – it's an unseasonably warm day – and scan the sweep of lawn that stretches from the Manor House. Beside me, an harassed-looking man is kicking a machine, which expels the odd bit of white fluff – snow? He has ginger hair and a smattering of freckles, partly obscured by some hastily applied factor 50.

'Have you seen her?' Holistic Flo sways precariously. In her Stories last night she had her crystals laid out by the window. 'I'm charging them in the light of the moon... I like to whisper intentions and manifestations into them, I like to take care of them...' At one point she watered them. 'The super moon is a powerful opportunity to reflect on our desires and plant new seeds for our lives... I'm *so* sensitive to energy and frequency and how we all operate on different ones...' And then she ended the recording with her swearing at the super moon: 'AND FUCK KNOWS WHAT FREQUENCY THAT TOSSER'S ON!', her braids jerking like forked lightning as the crystals cowered behind her. She's slurring now, even though it's only just after lunch. There's no point asking her. There's no way she has it together enough to be behind The Unhappy Hollidays.

'She's everywhere! This Mardy Mum. Rabbiting on about how hard it is with a newborn. I'd *love* a little newborn.' She flicks daggers at me and down at my stomach. I'm wearing a slightly too tight top and I had toast and croissants for breakfast, aggravating my gluten intolerance and supplying the illusion of a mysterious bulge. *I know, I know*, but man, I'm getting *desperate*. This pregnancy gossip is the only positive conversation I'm generating at the moment. Everything's going up in flames. The last Unhappy Hollidays post has thousands of likes already and it's only been up a few days. The story's been picked up by *HuffPost* and *Grazia*. There's a new SoMe account: Cassie Holliday Bump Watch. Ironic really, since I'm sure Seb would rather shag a hole on the golf course than me.

After I finished my chicken chow mein at the Otter's Paw – loudly telling the waiting staff we'd had a babysitter emergency, but my husband was insistent I finish my chow mein as it's my absolute favourite: ('*We met in Hong Kong, you see! Such fond memories!*') – and took a taxi home, I found him on the sofa with Ruby. She was wearing skimpy satin shorts despite the chill, with a matching shirt (pyjamas?), both covered in cats festooned with coned hats and streamers encircled with the words 'Party Cat!'. Her toned legs were elongated by chunky-heeled biker boots. Seb was next to her, another beer in hand, as though he'd been there all evening and our dinner had never happened.

A stream runs along the bottom of the manicured lawn

and – hang on! – there's a man out there, knee-deep in water, a small crowd gathered round as he swings something in the air. His silhouette hints at a not too shabby physique. It's a scene reminiscent of Mr Darcy in *Pride and Prejudice*. The angle of the sun obscures my vision; I can't see who it is striding around, slick with water. I walk towards the lake, curious, and keen to avoid any pregnancy enquiries from Holistic Flo. It's one thing to encourage bloating, it's another to lie to a friend. *That hasn't stopped you with Beth, has it?* I frown. What am I going to do about Beth? I've told her I'll help her with her product launch – she's so motivated by it, her confidence reaching cruising altitude; I can't take that away from her?

I start to pick out voices as I approach the stream.

'We agreed in the contract I would be able to wear my own clothes.'

My heart sinks, the small flutter of interest zipped away.

'Yes, but we assumed you would be wearing *seasonal* attire.' This comes from a dark-haired woman, who has removed her gold round-rimmed glasses and is rubbing her eyes. *What's he doing now?*

'They're waders. You can wear them *any* day of the year.'

'Yes,' – the tone becomes grittier – 'but waders aren't *festive*, are they?'

I reach the bank and let out an audible sigh. He looks up. 'Oh, hi Cass.'

His broad shoulders block the sun and I see the offending items – olive-green wide-legged trousers, presumably waders since he's knee-deep in water, and a fitted black T-shirt in the sort of fabric that looks like you can sweat a lot and it wouldn't leave a mark. Each have an 'FD' logo on them, tilted neon orange lettering. Did I just almost accidentally have a lust-on for Forest Dad? I shudder.

'What are you doing out here? We've got the group shot inside in five.' My tone is brusque, businesslike. After the shoot I'm going to demand he tells me what's going on.

Harassment furls his brow. He's sort of handsome. High-cheekboned, strong-nosed, the sort of face that would always look stubbly no matter how close a shave he had had that morning. Shame he's such a pain in the arse.

Inside, we assemble around a lustrous Christmas tree, thick-branched and adorned with tartan bows and gold baubles. We're being paid top dollar today by a British clothing company aimed at middle-class mummies who shop at Waitrose. We're decked out in what the designers call 'zany' prints (a long-sleeved Breton tee with gold palm trees and teeny red glittered baubles in my case, teamed with faux-leather trousers and gold mid-heel boots) and wide checks, which are doing nothing for Holistic Flo. She's drowning in her dress, wobbling in royal-blue pumps. Forest Dad's still in his wading clothes but with a tweed jacket worn like a cape and a rifle slung over his shoulder, as if he's at a pheasant shoot rather than a photo shoot. A collection of animals – a taxidermist's lifetime's work – are arranged around him.

We're about to begin when an 'Alright mate!' floods the vestibule, reverberating and amplifying around the opulent cornices. Common As Mum. 'Sorry I'm late, traffic was MENTAL' – she drops the 't', of course – 'This is posh!' She sets down a couple of budget supermarket carrier bags by her feet. I eye her coolly. I've seen the home-made oaty snacks poking out of her bag, the 'jam on toast' in her Stories and in the background a Nutribullet, goji berries, rose petals and scattered chia seeds.

It's not that she's common. In fact, I'd like her more if she *were* actually common. I don't come from horsey stock myself. I bet she went to a private girls' school somewhere in the Home Counties. She looks worse now than when she went viral. This is the crux of it. While the rest of us have grafted for years, she rocketed up the ranks after *going viral*: so crass. I watched it, cringing – a cheeky, somewhat *smutty* mash-up of the great works of Beatrix Potter. 'Each squirrel had a little sack and a large oar…' She winked. 'He's a *bad kitten*' was delivered in a Marilyn-addressing-the-President tone. There was *a lot* of innuendo around gooseberry bushes. Her face was far too close to the camera, shiny T-zone gleaming. Okay, it was funny in a someone-give-this-desperate-mum-a-glass-of-Chardonnay kinda way, but it never crossed my mind it might catch on for real. Thirty-seven million views later – *thirty-seven million!!* – and her future was made off the back of a mockery of someone else's material. Ridiculous. Now she presides over a bush-pun-related empire (she gets free haircuts, waxing and gardening year round).

'Hi.' Holistic Flo waves limply, her forearm rising at the elbow, a puppet's hinge, her shoulders slumped forward. She looks dead inside. 'Okay if I lean on the…' 'Tree' becomes 'treeeeeeeeee' as she slumps into its branches, all but disappearing from sight. We all gawk.

'For fuck's sake,' mutters the ginger-haired assistant from outside, 'what's with you people? This is worse than the Kardashians.' He speaks into a microphone on his lapel. 'I need some help in here, guys. One of them – the skinny yoga one – is in the tree. I repeat, she is in the tree.'

The sound of thudding footsteps fills the vestibule. A crack team of assistants arrive carrying mineral water and a fluffy white bath robe. Muffled moans come from the depths of the tree.

'Break!' The assistants scuttle off with Holistic Flo.

Common As Mum pats my shoulder as she shuffles past. 'You alright, Cassie?' She winks as I side-eye her. 'Sorry if I put you in it with Griff. I thought *everyone* knew about The Unhappy Hollidays!'

I hadn't factored her in as a potential suspect – I've never seen her as competition for me at all – but now I mentally bump her to the top of my list while simultaneously smiling and flicking a peace sign.

Finally, Forest Dad and I are alone. Through the ornate windows I see a Boeing 747 fly high overhead, a vapour trail in its wake.

'Everything good with you, Cass?'

I feel my anger rising, like heat on tarmac. I need to ask him. I need to know what he was up to with Boardroom Boss Mum. 'What do you think?'

He steps back, his lips pursed. The fire in my belly ignites, a pure white flame.

'What's going on with you and Boardroom Boss Mum?'

He stands up straighter, as if he's in a police line-up. 'What? Nothing. What?'

'I saw you together...' I keep the pressure on, moving towards him as he backs away. 'Having a business meeting at the Otter's Paw, but that's funny because I searched both your SoMe platforms and couldn't find *anything* to suggest why you'd be out together.' He gasps as I pace towards him, kicking a stuffed badger out of my path. 'You work for different brands and have *no* tie-ins.' There's a clang of metal as he backs up against a knight's armour. He blinks rapidly. His eyes dart left to right, hoping for an escape route. 'So what were you up to at the Otter's Paw?'

I catch his eye. Curious as to whether I will see something there, anything at all, to give some clue as to the inner workings of Forest Dad. We've never spoken about his late wife. In fact, he's never mentioned her, online or in interviews, nothing at all, which affords an awed respect from the masses and especially from his fellow InstaParents, because the opportunities will have been presented to him, for sure. I know of at least two life insurance companies after him for a campaign.

'It's *you*, isn't it? You two are behind The Unhappy Hollidays?'

'She said I couldn't tell anyone...' He strains his head backwards.

'Well, *I'm* telling you, you *can*.' I have a hand cupping his chin now, staring into his eyes. I can feel his breath, warm on my lips, which makes me think of crackling firewood and the reassuring density of thick grass underfoot. His face relaxes on to my hand.

A beat passes. A moment where I'm looking into his eyes and I do see something, and it is not at all what I'm expecting. I take a step back as he leans in. In my haste I stumble backwards, over the badger, falling to the floor. I land heavily on my wrist and yelp as he springs over and gathers me up.

'Are you okay? Do you need to sit down?' he asks quickly,

eyes flashing to my stomach as if remembering something. I suck my stomach in as best I can. Bloody croissants.

'No, I'm *fine*.' The fire reaches my skin, hot and flaming.

He checks my wrist with both hands, then darts around gathering materials: a discarded scarf from the shoot and a vintage-looking wooden angel from the tree. He snaps off its wings, pulling a comical grimace face as he does, and places it along my wrist, carefully wrapping the scarf around it and securing it in a knot around her halo.

'Looks like a sprain. Try to rest it; it should be fine.' He kneels. Our faces are level. My hand still in his.

'It's a business arrangement,' he says. 'I needed some advice on the franchise. The truth is... you'll think less of me for this, Cassie, but... I'm struggling to hold it all together. The business, my family... you know how it is. I would never – could never – hurt you, Cassie.'

He looks into my eyes and I see the look again. A look I'm not used to seeing.

'I can prove it to you.' He proffers his phone, open to his Instagram profile. 'The days those photos of you were taken, I was working...' He looks up at me hopefully. I notice the red dot symbolizing unread messages on his account. I wonder who they're from.

I take my own phone out and open to his feed. He's right: he can't have taken those awful photos of me because the days clash with his various product launches and Forest School sessions. It can't be him. I try to do the same for Boardroom Boss Mum, Holistic Flo and Common As Mum, but the dates don't match up. I can't eliminate them. And besides, they were all at the Park Keeper in September. Any one of them could have followed me after the event and taken those photos. But Forest Dad wasn't there that day.

The ginger assistant hollers for us to reassemble. An hour has passed. We resume our positions, but this time Holistic Flo reclines on a teal chaise longue with a tray of mince pies. My bandaged wrist rests behind her out of shot. She's had a power nap and some food and is looking pretty good, all things considered. You would only notice she's shaking and sweating if you knew.

'Are you okay?' I whisper down. *It wouldn't be her, would it?*

'Sure, doll, I'm good with this, just like Bikram,' she says, her rictus smile never fading. She reaches a thin hand up to my stomach and I instinctively draw back. 'It's you we should be looking after.'

37

#WeddingDay

Beth

'Remind me again why we're surrounded by cow shit in a trailer at your ex-boyfriend's wedding?' Joe asks, smiling cheekily as we bump along in a tractor trailer. A few weeks on from my birthday and we've done what every healthy relationship does after a problem threatens to nuke it: we've buried it under the patio (or in this case, inside my bedside table).

'I told you, only family vehicles are allowed on the farm. The tractors drop everyone off and then come back for us later.'

'So we're stuck here until it ends?'

'It'll be fun!' I release my grip on the buggy momentarily to squeeze his leg. 'How often do we get to spend the day on a celebrity farm?' I cajole, gesturing at the devastating beauty of the North York Moors that surround us, no other buildings in sight. Now *this* is countryside.

Joe rocks a suit well and today is no exception. It's dark blue with a matching navy tie and a shirt in the palest pink. 'To make you wink,' he said to me earlier, kissing me, as he buttoned it up and I kissed him back, enveloped in citrus and the sea. I'm determined for people to see how happy we are together, ring or no ring. I'm determined to convince myself.

The smell of manure isn't something I'd want at my wedding, but the setting is breathtaking. They've remodelled the house since I was here last, extended it with a beautiful pale brick and thick warm wood. Where the house ends a marquee has been erected, one of the posh types, more luxury hotel than tent. The sides are up, showcasing panoramic views over the moors. Inside, it's festooned with the fairy lights and pom-poms in sugar shades that Amber was teasing us with on her Instagram grid.

Simon, Sam's dad, appears at my side as we disembark the tractor trailer. 'Took me all blooming night!' he laughs, enveloping me in a bear hug. His broad Yorkshire brogue is like a soothing balm.

'This is Poppy!' I blink, gesturing to the carrier, my eyes creasing with tears at his warm embrace.

'A beauty of a bairn, just like her mam! And hers before that,' he adds solemnly. Mum and Penny had Sam and me on the same day. They met on the labour ward in adjacent beds. Sam and I grew up together, but it wasn't until after Mum died that I began to see him differently. In some ways it was beautiful: my friend since babyhood, my first kiss, my first time. But in a lot of ways it was sad: overcomplicated when it should have been simple, its edges charred with grief, guilt coursing through the whole thing. I felt too guilty, in the early years of Mum dying, to enjoy anything, when she couldn't. We tried to make it work when I went to uni, but eventually the panic attacks killed it: he didn't understand them and I began to see our relationship in a new light when I had therapy. I needed a fresh start.

I went to school with Amber, but it might as well have been a different school on a different planet, existing in different orbits. She was popular and aloof; she wouldn't have noticed Sam either, at least not until we'd all long left school and Field-To-Plate took off and Simon landed his own TV show and the lucrative opportunities that came with it. Suddenly, the whole family were local celebrities.

Already I feel the need to retreat, my toes beginning the usual low hum, the flutters that signal I'm out of my comfort zone. Luckily, Poppy's awake and cranky, so I ask Simon if I can feed her in the house and leave Joe with Lucy and Dad. Inside has a Scandi-luxe vibe. There's log burners and thick rugs and delicate paintings of vegetables and wild flowers on the walls. I turn left into the snug as instructed by Simon; there's an assortment of squishy-looking chairs upholstered with prints of hares and foxes.

I'm feeding Poppy and yes, sort of idly daydreaming about my own wedding one day, when Poppy lets out a stonking fart. I suspect they can hear it outside over the steel drum band. My hand, hovering on her lower back, vibrates. Two things happen at once: my dress welds itself to my thigh and a stench, rotten and sweet, reaches my nostrils. Blooming hell, *not now*. I'm too scared to look. I gingerly move my hand down. The pads of my fingers meet with thick oozing liquid. *A poo bomb*. Poppy feeds on, oblivious.

I wipe my fingers on my dress and text Joe: 'Come find me. In snug inside house.'

He appears quickly. 'You called? Well, texted?' he

corrects, pulling his most charming smile as he leans on the door frame. 'It's beautiful here, babes. Like something from a film.'

'Look!' I gesture at my dress.

'Wow!' Joe winces, and to his credit his smile drops and he looks genuinely gutted for me. 'That dress must've cost a fortune. Was it new?'

Poppy finishes feeding so I pass her to him and examine the damage. 'One of Lucy's friends lent it to me... She needs winding, hold her upright.'

'Thank God for that.'

'Hardly. If I can't get it clean, I'll have to buy her a new one.' I found it online after Lucy gave it to me. £1,000! I don't tell Joe that.

'Do you have a spare change of clothes?'

'Yes, I'm almost thirty and I carry around a spare set of clothes for myself!'

'Okay, okay,' he mutters, walking to the window holding Poppy with outstretched arms like she's an explosive device, while I use baby wipes to get the excess off my dress.

'You could be changing her,' I snap. Poppy hasn't come out unscathed.

He lays her on the floor, kneels down, and carefully undresses her. Poppy, of course, has two changes of clothes available.

'Babe, can you pass me the wipes?'

'I've used all these. There's a spare pack' – I gesture at the changing bag – 'in the inner pocket...'

Joe sucks in air quickly. 'Oh, babe. I took those out.'

'What?' I say irritably, still trying to soak up the thick, oozing paste with the last of the wipes. '*Why?*'

'You're always saying I don't help get the changing bag ready and it was so full. I didn't think we'd need an extra packet.' He sits back on his feet, hands on hips, a rueful expression on his face. 'I thought I was helping.'

'But this one was half empty! Blooming hell, Joe.'

'Yeah, but we're only here for the day.' He leans forward, softly chuckling as he tickles Poppy's cheeks. 'I didn't realize how much damage you could do, Pops, in a few hours. It's only after lunchtime!'

He beams down at Poppy, but I'm unable to see the funny side. He looks over, a soft look of concern burrowing into the fine lines around his eyes.

'Babe, it's fine, we can sort this out.'

I look away from him, out the window, over the moors, tears prickling in my eyes. I've been on the verge of tears since visiting Mum's grave before the service, but it's this final indignity that threatens to push out all the other feelings I've been bottling up.

'We can sort this out?' My lashes twitch like butterfly wings, keeping the tears at bay, because if I start to unwind now, I don't think I will stop.

'Babe?'

He keeps pressing me and my feelings convert in a fluid stroke from sadness to anger.

'*I. Am. Covered. In. Shit!*' I say, and Joe looks stunned because I rarely swear.

He races over, cups my face with his hands. 'I know it's hard for you being here, babe. I can't imagine it. But I'm here and Lucy's here and your dad's here and Poppy's here, *as we know*!' He gestures down at my dress then back into my eyes, reading me for a softening, a change in mood.

When he sees none, he looks around him. 'I'll sort it, babe, I promise. Wait there a sec.' He dashes from the room.

I stare down at my dress. My breath comes in raggedy gasps. *Why today?* I meet eyes with Poppy and she smiles at me. A big, gummy grin.

'It's okay for you,' I say, running my fingers along my eyelids in an effort to save my mascara.

Poppy's eyelashes flare up and a look of surprise lights her face as she makes a strange gargling sound. I lift her quickly as Joe re-enters the room.

'Joe...' I start, but it's too late: like a scene from *The Exorcist*, she projectile vomits all over my dress, entirely avoiding her own. 'Didn't you wind her?' I cry.

'You said to change her!'

'I assumed she'd already burped! You know what she's like after feeding!' *Although does he, I think, does he have any blooming clue?* There's too much vomit for Joe's tissue offering. I scrunch up some muslins, shaking as I press them against my dress, trying to absorb the liquid, my skin itching as it begins to seep through. It's hopeless.

'Babe, I'm sorry. We'll get a new dress for Lucy's friend. It's just a dress, babe, you still look amazing.'

'It cost a thousand pounds!' I hiss. His eyes bloom open with shock.

He recovers quickly, his brain visibly making the effort to deal with that later. 'Even so, babe, it's pretty funny, isn't it? Typical *us*, here at this wedding on this posh farm and I've ballsed up the wipes and Poppy's messed up your dress?'

I dry the dress off as best I can then check my make-up, reapplying concealer and lipstick, all the while ignoring Joe.

'Your dad and Lucy are here, we can still have fun. Babe?'

I put on the baby carrier, adjusting it to cover as much of the dress as possible. I take Poppy and, without looking at Joe, go to find Dad and Lucy.

The food – as it would be when the father of the groom is a celebrity chef – is exquisite. I spend the meal talking to Dad, surreptitiously watching how much Lucy eats. The speeches are the traditional three plus one by Amber, during which I have to stop myself heckling. It's after these, as we throng around the reception area of the main house waiting for the band to start, that I see Dad looking thoughtfully at a wall of rifles and then back to Joe, now absorbed in conversation with a full-bosomed wedding guest. Her thick dark hair trails down her back in waves as she throws her head back, laughing at something he's said. His dark tie's undone, his sleeves rolled midway up his muscular forearms.

'Y'all right, Dad?' I say. The more drunk I get, the more northern I get. He says nothing, continuing to stare.

'Dad?'

He nods over at Joe. 'Things were different in my day, love. Different altogether.' He shakes his head sadly. 'If your mam…' He stops himself. Sighs. 'No matter, love. I hope you're enjoying the party?'

In that moment, as the band sings out 'I'm Still Standing' and Dad stares sadly into his pint of bitter, I realize that this is unbearable. This situation, which I thought was fine, is anything but. I move to extricate Joe. To get out of here and back home where I can get out of this stupidly expensive poo-and-vomit-stained dress and heels. Everything is hurting.

'Babe!' Joe swings his arm around me as I approach, slightly clipping Poppy's ear. He doesn't notice. 'This is Jazz! We went to school together! She knows Amber from their promo days. Small world, isn't it?'

I survey Jazz. Full lips, thick lashes; please tell me she's wearing a girdle to be pulling off this Jessica Rabbit look. I'm torn between a sidelong dirty look and clinging to her leg until she tells me where it's from.

'Really small,' I nod, eyeing her waist. 'What did you promote?'

Jazz turns to me and flashes a blinding white smile. She's attained the sort of whiteness that would give you a headache if you looked at it for too long. 'Clubs and bars back then,' she says huskily, 'but now I do grids...' She pauses, sniffs the air and looks between me and Joe and then down at my dress. 'Oh. My. Days. I'm sorry to tell you this, hun' – she lowers her voice – 'but I think you've got shit all over your dress.' She looks dumbstruck.

'I know.' She looks more dumbstruck. How could I *know* I've got shit all over my dress and not have changed it? 'We can't leave until the tractors start up again at eleven.'

'Oh, wow, that's really shit!' she cackles.

Lucy strides over purposefully. She's pushing Poppy's buggy, clutching something silky in her hand. She thrusts the buggy at Joe and the silky thing at me. 'Here,' she says to us both, giving Jazz the dirty look I hadn't been able to muster.

'*You're* taking Poppy home,' she barks at Joe. 'You can leave early. I've sorted it with Sam's uncle, he's bringing a Landy round the front. He'll drop you back at Dad's.' She jerks a thumb at me. 'We'll get the minibus back to the village later.'

'But—' says Joe.

Lucy silences him immediately. 'She spent half the morning pumping. You could sell it as gold top. It's all stacked up in the fridge with the date and time on it.' In spite of myself, I smile. Lucy turns back to me. 'You're putting this on and then we're going to have some fun at this party.'

'Lu, that's really sweet and – wow! This is a nice dress, where did you…' I hold it in front of me, a glittering cascade of gold in an Olsen-twin loose fit.

'Beth!' She looks panicked and pushes it back towards me. 'Don't fan it out like that, just slip into the loo and put it on.' She glances over her shoulder to where Amber has two sleepy flower girls holding up a ribbon sash from one of the chairs between them and she's gesturing for them to lower it further while she shimmies underneath it, doing the limbo. Sam is watching his bride from the sidelines, surrounded by a group of lads from school. I catch his eye and he nods, gives me one of his broad smiles that feel like home. And I feel… calm. An uncomplicated calm. I'm happy for him.

'Quickly!' Lucy hisses as I force my gaze away from Sam.

I look apologetically at Joe. 'Do you mind?' I ask redundantly, as he looks very clearly like he *does* mind, extracting his arm from behind Jazz and raking his hand through his hair.

'I have to miss the party?' He looks like he's regretting pushing the bottle-feeding thing now.

I gently kiss Poppy and pass her to Joe, hang the cupcake changing bag over his shoulder. 'Yes, Joe. Like I've been doing for the last few months.' I remember my pregnancy. 'The last *year*!' My eyes are alight, sending out little minimum daggers in his direction. 'And you won't be needing THIS!' I swipe away his champagne glass, knock it back in one and do my best sassy walk to the posh Portaloos. The best cure for anxiety: mum rage.

38

#RememberMe

To: Contact@TheHappyHollidays.com
From: Katya.Peters@horizonair.com
31 October at 15:12
Hello Stranger!!

Cassandra…? Are you there? Is that you? I've been so worried. It's been so long. You never responded to my messages and then your Facebook account disappeared. Your cell rang out. I'd given you up to soft play and jelly sandwiches. And then I joined Instagram and there you were on the grid. I thought, woah, that woman looks like Cassandra, so I clicked on and on and Cass – you have a whole other life! My God, woman, you're like Madonna! The queen of reinvention. You look so different! So polished. It suits you, you look great! I guess you wouldn't want to return to flying now, your life looks so perfect! And hey, looks like you don't need to! The house! You moved in after all? The kids! So cute! I haven't seen them since they were babies. Look… I'm gonna say it because I didn't get a chance to before. I don't know if you left because you were embarrassed or something, but you didn't need to be. No one remembers stuff like that. Three years later and I rarely hear it mentioned.

How many years since we met? There's a few more female pilots now (still not as many as there should be!) and you should see some of them! Look like they belong on a catwalk! That's why I went on to Instagram in the first place. Checking them out. No old gals like us. I can't believe you left me but I don't blame you looking at how well things have worked out. I would dearly love to see you, pal. I'm in and out of Heathrow and Gatwick. Let me know when I can swing by and say hi.

Katya xx

39

#FamilyDinners

Cassie

I push the heels of my hands into my eyes and shake my head as if I can shake away Katya's email. And that wasn't the worst message I've had today: a direct message from Mardy Mum, so excited that she's been asked to be the new Brand Ambassador for the Family Co app! *Does this mean we'll be working together?* she asks. *That would be so cool!* she says. That wanker Griff! Going behind mine and Alicia's backs. Does this mean her job's on the line too? I can hardly ask Mardy Mum what's going on, how humiliating!

Seb drums his fingers on the table. I bore my knuckles into my eye sockets: *Bury it, Cassie. Bury it and figure out a plan later.* I can't put it off any longer. This will be fine, right? We can sit round a table together nicely for dinner as a family. What could go wrong? It's not like I'm about to be replaced on my industry's biggest campaign to date by some no-mark Influencer who got famous by going viral and who may or may not be connected to the unknown entity who has been trying – quite successfully, it turns out

– to derail my career and everything I've worked hard on to support myself and protect my children so I can pay back my miserly husband who hates his life and who may or may not be fucking our fucking babysitter?

'Hey, Scout,' I ask breezily. 'What do you think of the pumpkin soup Mummy's made?' My neck feels sinewy and tense, the map of veins popping around my face.

'Er, guys,' Scout says, in this affected way she's picked up from watching too many YouTube videos, 'it's, like, kinda bisgusting.' She holds her spoon aloft and starts coughing and spluttering into her soup.

'Hey, don't be so rude! Mummy's making a special movie of us and she made us special soup,' Birch protests, pulling at the neck of his Peter Pan tunic.

My darling son. Maybe I can edit out Scout… I spent a torturous few hours with the twins earlier, photographing them in ponchos (the wool from goats up a mountain in Iraq or something, some charity eco-initiative Alicia sorted). I checked wind direction (transferable skill) and set them on course so that, as they ran, the frayed edges of their ponchos were gently picked up by the breeze. My beautiful babies. The poor things were freezing so we had to wrap things up quickly, but I got some footage on Stories of the twins selecting a pumpkin while I talked about all the different pumpkin recipes on the Family Co app. Now I'm tying the whole thing together: top-of-her-game-Cassie style.

'Er, like, guys, the soup packet's on the side! It's from Tesco!' Scout shrieks.

Seb starts guffawing, his paunch wobbling where the tabletop intersects it. I stop recording. Suddenly, fifteen seconds seems like a very long time.

Enter Marina. Dark and voluptuous. Everything looks as though it's been pumped and preened and lifted but I'm fairly sure – and there's been some careful, albeit discreet, inspection on my part – it's mostly natural. Sixty-two and she's still got it.

'Darlings.' She glides, air-kissing me and the twins – three times each, avoiding Seb – before walking to the far side of the kitchen and disappearing from view.

'Tramp,' Seb coughs.

'Right, this won't take long. Please can we do this nicely?'

'Just get on with it,' he says (I've had to promise him he can watch the rugby tomorrow, in the pub, alone, if he participates).

Marina returns from the cellar with a dusty bottle of red. Seb seethes at her, hawk-eyed. She settles herself on a stool at the kitchen island and reads something on her phone, her thumb occasionally flicking while she uses her other hand to drink her wine. I stare longingly at the bottle, remember the pregnancy gossip, and resume recording.

'WHAT SHAPE IS A PINEAPPLE?' intones Griff's voice.

'PINEAPPLES!!' the twins shriek. They've always found pineapples inexplicably hilarious. For fuck's sake. I press stop.

'*Come on,*' I implore. 'No laughing at the man, kids, he's paying the bills.'

'Mummy's legal bills,' says Seb, unable to resist a dig, and I see Marina's head lift in consternation. '*I* pay the bills, actually,' says Seb snippily, addressing the twins, and I roll my eyes because I can't remember the last time Seb paid one without me having to nag him for days.

I notice Marina's eyes narrow at him, the brilliant blue ovals cat-like. 'Actually, darling, that's me,' she purrs.

Even the twins seem to pick up that something's amiss, because they are finally quiet. Seb fizzes with rage, silently turning puce, so I seize my moment.

'DID I PLAY MINDFULLY TODAY?'

The twins remain mute. No wonder. What does that even mean? God, this app is shit. I try again.

'MY FAVOURITE BIRD IS…'

Yes! They can do this one.

'Birds, Birch! Birds!' But I don't need to be so enthusiastic because he's got this, instantly parroting, 'I LOVE TITS! Blue tits, great tits, coal tits, marsh tits – I just *love tits*, Mummy!'

I groan, head in my hands. Can I use this? Sure it's funny, but it's so *Common As Mum*… I try again.

'WHERE DO BOOMERANGS COME FROM?'

'POOMERANGS!!'

'No! Not laughing! *Speaking!* Share what we know about… pineapples… and BOO-merangs.'

'MUMMY SAID POOMERANG!'

Each laugh triggers another episode of Scout coughing, until she's practically retching at the table, the feather from her green felt cap dunking into her soup.

Marina moves over and envelopes her in a hug. '*Povera bambina*! Out in the cold too long.'

It's an Italian thing, she's terrified of the kids being outside. I pretend I haven't heard her and avoid Seb's gaze, expecting it to be reproving, but when I glance up he looks minded to carve up Marina rather than a pumpkin.

'Seb,' I say softly. *Come back to me. Come back.* Not just

now – although that would be useful – but for good. Forget Marina. Forget the inheritance. *Come back*. I lean forward and stop the recording. My face fills the screen, packed with sadness. How did we get here? I feel tears coming and I do not want that to happen. *Pull yourself together. You are Cassie Holliday. You've got this. All the hashtags.*

My phone pings: an alert reminding me I'm about to miss the Chardonnay slot. I need to get this done. I just need a few more seconds of footage. I lean forward, unfreezing my face.

'We...' Griff's voice stutters as the app buffers, trying to catch up. 'We...' I try again. 'We... We...'

'WEE WEE! POO POO!' the twins explode, holding their little jiggling bellies. It should be funny. Really it should. Because it is, right? But it's also Fucking Annoying. It's also...

'FIFTEEN SECONDS! CAN YOU UNGRATEFUL LITTLE KIDS JUST GIVE ME FIFTEEN SECONDS?!'

'CASS!' Seb's voice is sharp. I feel Marina's eyes on me, sense her disapproval at my outburst, but it's too late. I can't stop.

'What? It could have been worse. I could have called them LITTLE SHITS!' I shout it across the table, into their faces, already in motion as I register the shocked look in their eyes, their *fear* of me, at that moment.

I abruptly push my chair back, but I jerk backwards without actually moving, jarring my neck. I extricate myself and bang my bowl on the marble worktop. Orange soup (carrot and coriander, not even pumpkin) sloshes over the sides and in my frustration I pick up the bowl and throw it into the sink, splinters of ceramic smashing against the sides of the deep bowl with a din. The release of tension – the noise – feels briefly, beautifully, sweet.

I'm aware of Marina ushering the twins out of the kitchen, entreating them with tales of bears and wolves up to their bedroom upstairs, as they try to crane their neck to see what's happened; *they want to know if I'm okay*, I realize, my heart breaking into as many pieces as the soup bowl.

I squeeze my eyes shut, as cross with myself now as I am with everyone else, because why is my life like this? How did this happen? My eyes race over the surfaces of the room. The marbled kitchen, the expensive appliances, the things that mean more to Seb than our family does. Sometimes I think this house destroyed us, but Katya's words reel through my mind as if on an autocue. I'm already thinking about that day. My gaze alights on a row of champagne glasses: their tapered stems, their thin hard glass, the shine bouncing off their curved sides: so perfect. Everything here is always so fucking perfect.

I fling open the display cupboard, grasp a glass in my hand.

'Cassie!' I hear Seb's voice as if from far away.

Why can't I get fifteen fucking seconds of footage when I try *so hard*?

So. Hard. All. The. Fucking. Time. With each punctuation I smash another coupe into the sink, another spray of glass delivering a brief respite from the aching and longing that ripples through my body. The rage at my core that's been unsettled, unlocked by Katya's email. Why does everything have to be so fucking difficult?

I shake as the adrenaline leaks out of me and know my

body will soon be wracked with sobs. I know why she sent it today, why she's thinking of me wherever she is, even if she doesn't. I look over at Seb and he's looking down at the table, cowed by my anger: he's remembered what day it is too.

'FIFTEEN *FUCKING* SECONDS,' I say, right into Seb's face as I walk past him. 'You couldn't even give me that.'

40

#SquaresOnAGrid

Beth

'This wasn't how I thought it would be.' I stare woefully into my glass of organic, biodynamic English sparkling wine and I realize that I'm not talking about the wedding, I'm talking about my life. Before me, the valley glitters with lights punctuating the dark. We're sitting up the hill on hay bales outside a little tepee, the remnants of our hog roast breadcakes by our feet – it was a damn good wedding, I'll give her that – with a bottle of bubbles we swiped from the bar. I feel like I'm in a scene from *Wedding Crashers*. 'I want what Mum and Dad had. For Poppy. And for myself. I want a normal family – Joe playing in the garden with Poppy, me washing up, jollily looking out over rolling hills and drystone walls. And I know that's total fantasy because who washes up these days, other than Dad?'

'That's deep, Mitts. Really... deep.' Her head jerks up. She looks at her empty hand, then gropes around the swirly fabric of her skirt before retrieving her phone from the hay bale. She quickly stabs something into it.

'You know your problem... you can't switch off. All day the screen's been lighting up with notifications!' She says nothing. 'And *my* problem? My problem is I fell in love with the wrong man.' This is where Lucy should say, *Don't be silly! Joe's lovely! He loves you!* Instead her profile bobs next to me as she nods solemnly. 'It should've been me today...' I start to cry. *Where is this coming from?* 'It...' – I gasp for air – 'should have been me.'

Lucy lifts her head and looks around as if she's just remembered where she is. She wrinkles her nose in distaste, the way she does at the mention of engagements, weddings and children who aren't Poppy. 'What? Don't be daft. You never wanted to ride that train.'

'What?'

'You know... You can't marry someone you don't fancy.' She's right. I never did. That was part of the problem. 'You've found someone you fancy, who you love, who loves you.' She points out each positive on a new finger, holding three in the air and trying to focus on them. 'He even likes romcoms.' She grimaces. 'And the gym. He's like your soulmate. You've done it. That's it.'

'But what if it's not enough?'

'You're pissed. Stop being melodramatic.' She wraps an arm around me, but I shake it off.

I feel the weight of it all; I'm failing at everything: Lucy, Poppy, Joe. I look in my clutch bag for a tissue – where's that monstrous cupcake changing bag when you need it? Lucy's eyes swim as she stares at her phone.

'*What are you looking at?*' I demand.

'*Nothing.*' She turns her phone over quickly so I can only see the cover – navy, with her initials embossed in rose gold.

'What? What is it?' I forcibly try to take her phone. She moves to clamp her hand on top of it but I'm that bit quicker; it scoots over the hay bale before toppling to the ground. We both grope around in the grass, looking for it. My hands touch a stiletto, something soft and warm that I don't want to think about – we're on a farm, after all – and finally the velvet softness of Lucy's phone case. As I lift it, her initials catch the light. I turn it over quickly and stare at the screen, confused: 'What are you doing with these?'

'Nothing! Just looking.' She looks down, shame cloaking her face like a mask.

'Where are they from?'

She sighs. Releases her hand. It's Amber's Instagram profile: @ThatGirlAmber.

'But how could she…? There's so many…?' Three, six, nine, twelve, fifteen, seventeen… seventeen photos posted today. From the moment she woke up – or slightly after that, unless she goes to bed with a full face of make-up – to half an hour ago, when she posted a photo of her and Sam's first dance, the pair of them silhouetted as he swooped her up high against a backdrop of twinkling lights. All hashtagged #SamberShindig. 'But it's her wedding day. Why would she spend it uploading photos? Why hasn't she been enjoying the day? *I* would have been enjoying the day.' My voice sounds plaintive. Far away. 'What's wrong with everyone?'

'It *is* part of enjoying the day. It's all wrapped up in your memories of it.' She waves her hands for emphasis. They move at separate speeds. 'And Amber's an interior designer. It's good for her business to look cool. That's what effective social media is: it's just business, Mitts. It's squares on a grid. Not something to freak out about. As long as you're in control of the content, what's the big deal?' Lucy doesn't see it as an invasion at all. It's like we grew up in different times. How can she of all people see it as so anodyne? It's a branch of the same industry that contributed to her anorexia.

'What if you're not in control?' I flip back. I know that she understands my meaning, because she closes her eyes and furrows her brow in a way I've not seen since Mum's funeral.

'Beth...' she says, in a drunk, watery voice, but she's drowned out by a growl from the bottom of the field.

'The tractors!' I'm on my feet, yanking her up by the arm.

'But I need to—' She clamps her hand over her mouth as if she might be sick.

'C'mere, let's get you home.' I can't miss the first tractor up to the minibuses because Lucy's leathered. I shove the phone into my clutch bag and link my arm in Lu's to prevent her falling. She grips on to me as if she never wants to let me go. We hobble together down to the field where the tractors are waiting.

An hour later, Lucy tucked up in bed, I notice her phone in my clutch bag nestled against mine and, ridiculous as it sounds, it reminds me of how Lucy and I used to sleep side by side as kids. *Is it ridiculous?* I ponder earnestly, the alcohol still buzzing in my veins. Phones have come to represent so much about their owners: their contents, their covers, their attachment issues. The kettle whistles as butter sinks into my toast – as old a tradition as it gets.

I can't stop thinking about Lucy's phone. *You've had too much to drink*, I admonish myself. *It's a breach of privacy...*

Or is it, I reason, *since I'm only going to look at Amber's profile and that's publicly available?* It's just quicker to view it via Lucy's account than setting one up myself. If I google her, like I did before, I won't be able to gorge on the hashtag: #SamberShindig.

I tap in Lucy's passcode: Mum's birthday. I set myself some boundaries before I dive in, to soothe Russell's voice in my ear asking if this is a good idea: just Amber. And #SamberShindig. I give myself permission to binge: on her photos, her comments, her likes and interactions. Just the time it takes me to eat my toast. And then, I promise myself, I'll move on.

I climb into bed. This is the benefit of a boyfriend who doesn't stir for night-feeds: you can sit in the dark, in the place you feel most safe, your childhood bed, in your childhood home, your favourite floral-printed duvet pulled up over your knees, and you can cup a brew and eat toast while he sleeps soundly beside you and you can *see*. You can finally see what's been going on.

It takes seconds to click on to Instagram and even less time to wish that I never had.

NOVEMBER

41

InstaMum Intrigue!

O. M. G.

Is Cassie Holliday pregnant?
Rumours abound that Cassie Holliday is pregnant. Not only were there pictures in which she seemed to be sporting a bump – another Boom! mag exclusive via The Unhappy Hollidays – but we've heard reports of a bump from a recent shoot. Cassie hasn't confirmed or denied the rumours, adding fuel to an already hot fire. #BirchAndScoutAnd?

Who is Mardy Mum?
She's storming up this month's CHIN and yet we still have no idea who Mardy Mum is, or why she's keeping her identity a secret. Was it a fluke she went viral or is this part of an orchestrated campaign? No one's ever risen up the ranks this quickly. Who is she and what *is* going on?

Where's Holistic Flo?
The rumour mill went into overdrive this week with reports that Holistic Flo has entered rehab for a crystal addiction.

The official word from her camp is she's having some time out following her recent break-up. Wherever she is, we wish her well.

Posted by Romilly Loader-Smyth for Boom! mag © 1 November

42

#BumpOff

Cassie

> From: Hetty@MumspireHQ.com
> To: Cassie@TheHappyHollidays.com
> 1 November at 05:00
> **Influencer Update**
>
> Hello there, other worldlings!

(Oh, piss off.)

> There's been lots of spooky happenings at Mumspire HQ!

(Whatever, whatever, yada, yada. Where's the CHIN? Where's the CHIN? My eyes dart over the text as I scramble to pick out my name.)

> Here's your Top Ten CHIN as at 31 October. There's been a battle at the top and a few bump (offs!) in the night! Mwah haha haha hahahahhhhaaaa!

1. Holistic Flo
2. Common As Mum
3. Forest Dad
4. Mardy Mum
5. Boardroom Boss Mum
6. Mummy Likes Clean Plates
7. Mama Needs A Drink
8. Middle Class Mummy
9. Skinny Bitch Mum
10. Clean Uddies

Click here for the full list…

I AM NOT ON THE CHART. I AM NOT ON THE FUCKING CHART. WHAT THE ACTUAL FUCK? I have to click on the link for the full list – *the shame!* – and even then I'm searching for my name, my eyes blurring.

Where is it? Where is it?

Number 34?!??

My heart plummets as fast as my brand sway.

It's over.

43

#Enough

Beth

Lucy crawls in, on her hands and knees, over the strips of sunlight escaping under the curtains: a slow-moving insect, bug-eyed and angular. She doesn't look up at me, or towards Joe, who's snoring lightly on the other side of the bed, the space between us wider than it's ever been. She stops by my shoes, the stiletto spikes ringed with mud, askew from where I kicked them off last night. She seeks out her phone with the fervour of an addict, silently combing my bag. I feel another clutch of shock when I see it; I wish I'd left it on the hill, surrounded by sheep and fields of heather and the remains of hog roasts; apple sauce and sticky buns.

Lucy sinks back on her calves, cradling her phone in her lap like a baby. She turns her head and our eyes meet. I try to change the arrangement of my face, but too late. She sees it. Besides, I can't change the pool of feeling in my eyes. I can't pluck out my own eyeballs and replace them with ones that weren't glued to Instagram last night as waves of shame and disappointment washed over them, much as

I'd like to. I trawled through the Mardy Mum account, so many posts and words, my brain struggling to keep up, the alcohol meaning I kept rereading and not quite grasping... feeding Poppy while one-handedly scrolling... Crisp accuracy of any of the posts fails me now; it's a mush, a jumble of unpleasantness I will need to pick back over once the shock abates.

She stands quickly and bolts, hand over her mouth. I shove back my duvet and follow her into the bathroom, the white-and-pale-blue tiles unchanged from when Mum decorated it many years ago. More than ever I wish Mum were here. She'd know what to do.

'We need to talk,' I tell Lucy. She's bent over the toilet bowl. She turns her head up to me, her eyes wet and red, her skin pale.

'You've seen it then?' She looks ashen, raking her fingers over her face. 'You need to understand. I thought I was doing the right thing, by not telling you. You were struggling with Poppy...'

She moves quickly, but not quick enough. I pull back her hair, which is falling over the rim of the bowl, hold the soft straw strands in my hands.

'Please don't hate me, Mitts,' she says before retching again.

Each time she vomits I see her ribs beneath her skin in her crop top. I close my eyes. Try to banish the image of Lucy in hospital, each bone stacked on the other so precariously, so little muscle and fat to protect them. I try to stop the images of Mum, still in this house, still alive, still reminding us over and over that we're sisters, that we'll always have each other, that we must take care of each other when she's gone. *My two little mittens.* A childhood joke that stuck. And we were, always either side of her, the string that bound us.

I answer reflexively: 'I don't hate you, Lucy. We're sisters.' But it sounds unconvincing even to me.

I undo my knot of hair and use my hairband to tie hers up. Her forehead rests on her arms, crossed over the rim of the toilet. Her head turns as my feet pad over the circular bath mat, her eyes widening as I reach the door.

'Mitts, please. We need to talk. Before Joe and Poppy wake up. I need to explain...'

I shake my head, my own hangover rattling in my skull. 'I've changed the password. I'm closing it down. Whatever it is, whatever it *means*,' I spit. 'It's over.'

'You can't.' She frowns and winces. 'You... people are relying on you. You have a community! The Sloshed New Mother's Group!'

A vague memory pings. 'You set that up. I don't even get what that is.'

'Using your words!' She speaks quietly, her hands gripping the toilet bowl. 'You've got your own hashtag! Every Friday afternoon mums meet up and join in.'

'What does that mean, "join in"?'

'They have a drink together and take a photo and add it to Instagram with the hashtag.'

I fling my arms out to the side, palms up. 'It doesn't *mean* anything, Lucy.'

'Beth, it means *everything*.' She stops and breathes out shakily, the colour draining from her face.

'Drink some water,' I say. 'Eat something.'

'Please.' She swallows. Her skin grows clammy:

contracting and shrinking before sweat bulges abundantly from her pores. 'Let me explain properly.' The strands of hair I didn't catch stick to the side of her face in wavy lines as she doubles back over the bowl.

'Not now,' I say, my pity for her hardening into something else.

'But…'

I have my hand on the door handle and can hear Dad, filling the kettle in the kitchen, oblivious that his family has once again been transformed. 'There's nothing you can say to make it any better.'

I leave her there, on the floor of our family bathroom, a room in which we've argued over stolen clothes and make-up; where we've sat on the edge of the bath, lamenting boyfriends and bad days at school; where we've fought over her not eating and my not standing up for myself and where we hid, together, after Mum's funeral as well-wishers flooded the house, trying to seek us out. None of those times ever felt as desperate as this. I always knew, then, that whatever was going on we'd get over it. It had never crossed my mind before that we might not see each other again.

44

#FancyDress

Cassie

I've never struggled to sleep before; it's essential as a pilot, being able to shut down and rest at any time. On long-haul flights at Horizon our sleeping compartments were behind the cockpit, above first class, the closest beds to the sky (and proper beds, too). I loved the cosiness of it and would be asleep as soon as my head hit the pillow. I was the same at home, or in hotels, impervious to jet lag. It was a handy skill when the twins were little. I could nap in between feeds, or on the sofa if they dozed off. I can sleep sitting up if necessary. And useful as an Influencer: I can set my alarm to do a post targeting the US market and go straight back to sleep. But for the first time my sleep's disturbed, the lucid dreams recurring. Sometimes I'm on the plane as it plummets to the ground. Other times, like last night, I'm clutching my stomach on the tarmac as debris falls from the sky. I'm always alone.

I check my phone again. Still nothing from Beth. I tried to call her last night; sent a message asking her to call me back, whenever she got it, knowing she'd be up with Poppy in the night. I was so ready to tell her everything, to spill out the whole sorry mess. Just my luck for Poppy to start sleeping through when I cannot.

My eyes feel sore and dry, exhausted from the hours I spent bawling. Not the delicate crying I've been practising in the mirror, which I might post to Stories, but real can't-catch-a-breath sobbing. It was like grief. Overwhelming and suffocating. Did I ever grieve for my career? I should have done. It was there. Buried emotion, expanding and pushing out the light. '*I don't know if you left because you were embarrassed or something.*' That's an understatement. 'Something' was humiliation on another level.

I hear Seb plodding up the stairs. He pauses awkwardly at the door in a grey T-shirt and checked pyjama bottoms.

'I'm sorry about last night,' I say, sitting up in bed in an oversized nightshirt. Now the rage has appeased, I feel exhausted and drained. 'How are the twins?' I need to apologize to them. I'm ashamed at how I spoke to them. Embarrassed for Marina to have witnessed me unravel like that.

'They're fine. They had a sleepover with Marina. I think they loved it, actually,' he concedes. 'Maybe we should let them spend more time over there with her.'

I nod, frowning. I don't have the energy to rake over Seb's change of heart. 'Everything's getting too much for me,' I say quietly, and even though I think I've cried out all my tears, still they begin again.

Seb comes and sits down. 'What's going on, Cass? You don't usually get so upset around…' He tails off, neither of us wanting to discuss that day.

So I tell him about all the other stuff instead. About work, about Mardy Mum, about The Unhappy Hollidays.

He listens. For the first time in years, he listens, and he strokes my hair and he traces his finger over my collarbone and he says: 'I love you, Cassie. You know that, right?' He climbs into bed beside me and draws my head on to his chest and I think of the countless hotel rooms we've woken up in together in happier times.

'Let's do something together today, as a family,' he says. 'We could take some photos for your work. I'll be in some. I'll even smile.' He tickles a finger down my cheek and I feel like I'm being pranked. 'We've got lost somewhere along the way, Cassie,' he says, nostalgia permeating his words.

We're never alone like this any more, I think. *The twins are always here.*

'It's quiet without the twins here,' Seb says, and I have a flashback to when I was convinced we were soulmates because we always seemed to be thinking the same thing.

'Remember Santorini?' I say, because it feels like the last time we were alone. In fact, it probably was. It was just before Charles died. We went away for a week and ate thick Greek yoghurt and figs drizzled with honey for breakfast and watched the sun set and enjoyed some of the filthiest sex – God love pregnancy sex – I've ever had.

Seb lifts my chin and stares down at me in such an intense way that I catch my breath. I know he's thinking about the sex too. I lift his T-shirt over his head, breathing in the familiarity of his scent. It feels like stepping back into another life. I drink him in greedily. He wraps my hair around his hand, gently pulls it back. When he kisses me, my brain says *Yes. Yes, yes, yes.* I shift my body over his. He slowly unbuttons my nightshirt, past my breasts, down to my stomach, every cell in my body tightening as the cool air kisses over my warm skin. He smooths his hand over the curve of my bum until his fingers softly brush against my knickers. I gasp, the sensation acute. We lock eyes again, certain now that we both want the same thing: to erase the past, to glue ourselves back together after the last few years have driven us apart. I want it, I want *him*, so much. I—

The door bursts open.

'Mummy, I need a wee!' shouts Scout, turning to run into the bathroom. It's my job to get the step for her. She stops, open-mouthed. 'Mummy, are you cuddling Daddy?'

Seb and I laugh, falling on to our backs, to suspicious looks from the doorway. 'You're back!' Seb booms. 'I'll go.' He wraps my dressing gown around himself to cover his erection. 'You should…' He smiles suggestively, his eyes still liquid and warm. He closes the door and herds the twins downstairs, asking if they'd like pancakes for breakfast.

I sink my head back into the pillows, pick up where Seb left off, remember the trip to Santorini… Afterwards, I turn on the shower and wee on my ovulation kit while it heats up: habit now more than anything else. A smiley face stares up at me. I was beginning to think I *was* perimenopausal. My feelings ricochet around the room like a squash ball: sadness, hope, grief, love, returning to the same thing: it's a sign, isn't it? I think of the baby in my dreams. The baby I need to protect… *Please let it be a sign!*

My mind whirrs: okay, I won't purposefully try to get knocked up, but if we spend the day together and we pick this back up later, then maybe, just maybe…

★ ★ ★

'There's a charity gala at the golf club tonight...' Seb says casually, only glancing at me once to assess my reaction. I'm scrolling through the photos we've taken in the woods, smiling at Seb and the twins in matching skeleton costumes (it's only taken three years to convince Seb to wear his), highlighting ones to edit. 'It's fancy dress. For Halloween.' I can't remember the last time Seb suggested I come to something at the golf club. 'I'm sure Ruby said she didn't have many plans this weekend...'

I automatically tense at Ruby's name falling so easily from Seb's lips. I open my mouth but quickly clamp it shut: he's trying, isn't he? Maybe a night out and a few drinks is what we need?

'What's the theme?' I ask, mentally rifling through my wardrobe.

Anything goes, Seb said, so I go *all out*: nurse's uniform. I wore this to a fancy-dress party with Katya once. I've never been hit on so much in a four-hour period in my life. I've added a Halloween twist: smoky make-up and a syringe filled with green slime poking out from my pocket. I can tell from the look on Seb's face as he surveys me up and down that I've chosen wisely. He puts his hand on my bare leg in the taxi and a shot of lust ripples up my thigh.

We enter the Churchill Suite at the golf club. Seb spots his friends easily: Hector, always the tallest man in a room, is already here. We make our way through the crowds, sucking in our stomachs and repeating apologies until we reach the others. Predictably, one has come as a zombie Radford rugby player and two, including Hector, have come as zombie James Bonds (black tie, fountain pen, fake blood). They're crowded round Timbo – the joker – laughing and back-slapping, struggling to breathe as they gesture at his costume. I reach the group and peer round Hector's shoulder, only seeing the back of Timbo and his wife, Vanessa (a tall, blonde, thoroughbred type). They're dressed identically, his skirt straining over his hairy thighs, his wig matching her hair. Vanessa is flicking a peace sign.

No one notices me until Seb strides up and claps Hector on the back with a booming 'Hello, chaps!' He puts his arm around me, steering me into the group, and I like to think that for a moment he's proud of his wife who, in her nurse's costume, has still got it going on.

Everyone falls silent. Timbo and Vanessa turn to see why, their shocked faces as much a mirror image as their costumes. 'Seb! Cassie! You said you couldn't make it.'

I take them both in. Their faux-leather mini-skirts, their Holistic Flo cropped T-shirts, Timbo's naval hair like a thousand tiny spiders trying to creep from under the hem. They've constructed oversized mobile phones from boxes wrapped in foil and covered with black card on the front. In white pen, they've written #PeaceAndLight. They're wearing them like necklaces, along with leopard-print caps that say 'YOU'VE GOT THIS' in a block type.

'You've come as...' Seb says, blinking furiously. 'You've come as Cassie?'

'Not Cassie!' Vanessa rushes in. 'We've come as an InstaMum! But not Cassie. Cassie doesn't wear caps. Or crop tops. Or have her phone attached to her all the time.'

All eyes swivel to me, where I'm gripping my phone to my chest like a security blanket. My throat freezes, so dry I can't speak. It's like I'm only inhaling, tiny breaths darting in but no air escaping. I've never been in this position before. I've always been *popular*. I've never felt… 'It's cruel,' I say, when I can find my voice.

'But you never come to these things,' Vanessa says, looking to Timbo for support.

I see the look in Seb's eyes. His pride in me turning to shame. He remains next to me, his arm still around me, but there's no tension in his muscles, no grip that tells me he's got my back. The gesture is as empty and slack as our marriage. I turn quickly, straight into a young waiter with a tray of canapés; I send oat cakes laden with foie gras spiralling into the air.

'I'm so sorry,' I say, grabbing his wrists to steady myself, but too late – I skid on some errant cucumber or oiled rocket garnish and slide effortlessly to the floor and through his legs, landing on my back and looking up at his crotch like a failed *Strictly* contestant. It's only when the waiter tries to help me up that I realize pain is throbbing through my hip and down my side. I don't look back to the group. I can't bear to. The waiter picks up my lost stethoscope and gunky syringe and helps me hobble to the exit, hoping that Seb will follow me.

I glance at my phone while I sit in the foyer wondering what to do. Finally, a message from Beth, stilted, ignoring my plea to call me last night: 'Do you mind if we reschedule the photos? I'm not feeling up to it this week.' It's weird, she's been so focused on her sewing and listing on Etsy, but I don't have time to dwell on it; I've got my own stuff to deal with. Seb appears, white with rage, and heads straight for the exit.

'Seb! Wait!' I call. 'I need some help!'

45

#UnusualActivity

Beth's phone notifications

14 missed calls from Lucy

4 voice messages from Lucy

'Beth… please answer. I need to explain…'

'Please don't tell anyone what I did, it's unethical. I could lose my job… Anyway, you'd be mad to. As it stands Mardy Mum is yours. Brands are banging your door down to work with you. You can do anything you like.'

'Hey I was thinking! Your craft pieces… you could put some on SoMe? You'd sell loads.'

'There's a Mumspire thing in Victoria Park on Friday. I have to go for work. Why don't you come and see what you think?'

* * *

Message from Sandy

'Sure, end of the week? Are you okay? Has something happened?'

SoMe Summary

You have 53,389 new activity items on your account!
Go to Settings to turn on notifications.

46

#YouAndMe

Beth

I click accept on FaceTime. I have no choice: we're mid-messaging so she knows I'm online.

'Hello! That's better! They're driving me round the bend, those messages!' Sandy waves a wine glass in front of the screen theatrically. Her hair is piled high and she's wearing an over-sized sweater from the University of California. She's set slightly back from the screen, her leg propped up on a stool.

'You okay? Where's Joe?' She tries to peer behind me.

'Out. A work thing. And I'd made his favourite dinner.' I raise a plate of cold turkey meatballs to the screen. Guilty Meatballs. Low in fat, high in protein and full of remorse. I haven't told Joe about the account. I know I should, I know he has a right to know, but what's the point? It's an anonymous account. No one knows about it except for me and Lucy. I need to wait until I've processed what's on there and then I'll delete it and Mardy Mum will disappear. No one *ever* needs to know.

'This is where it starts. The first creaking of the gender divide opening… The subtle rub and shift of tectonic plates. You at home with the baby and the meatballs waiting for him to return!'

She's drunk. She reminds me of an overenthusiastic chat show host. She's right, probably, but I can't get mad at Joe. I feel guilty for the things I said to Lucy, which are now publicly available. How would *I* feel if Joe inadvertently told the world how much I'd let him down? My chest tightens thinking of it. I love Joe. What will I do if he finds out? I can't let that happen.

Sandy twists the stem of her glass in her fingers, her red nail varnish chipped and peeling. 'Mine too. Working late. Avoiding me. How's life in babyland?'

'Great?' My voice twists the answer into a question. Should I tell her? Would she understand? 'Great. Everything's…' I picture Mum, her hands on our shoulders: *You'll always have each other.* Pain rips through my chest. 'Honestly? I don't know.' My voice cracks. 'Things are tough at the moment.' *I should tell her. Get some advice on what to do. I can't handle this on my own. It's too big for me.*

Sandy nods earnestly, not understanding it's the plates beneath my feet that are shifting, not the gender divide. 'This is why I like you so much, Beth. You're honest. I'm surrounded by people pretending that everything's perfect all the time. Sometimes I feel like whatever I do, it's not enough.' Her drink sloshes as she sweeps her arm for emphasis. 'Whatever toys the kids get, or places we go, it's never enough. There's always someone doing it – parenthood, motherhood, *life* – better than me.' She gazes off into the distance, then shakes her head, refocuses on the screen.

'I feel like that too,' I say. 'Maybe everyone does.' I twist my hair round my fingers. 'We were at that wedding,' I say, not knowing where I'm going with this or why I'm sharing it with Sandy, '...and he was all over this woman. She looked so hot and *pre*-children. It would never have bothered me before but now, I... I feel jealous.'

'You're having a confidence crisis, Beth. It's normal. You grew a fucking baby and you pushed it out of your vagina. It's going to take some time to get over that. Physically. Hormonally. I'm four years on and I'm not over it yet.' She knocks back her wine, shivers.

'I had a caesarean. She got stuck. But yeah.'

'Same difference,' she snorts.

'He became friends with her on Facebook after the wedding.' I couldn't believe it when I saw it, because Joe never goes on Facebook. He must have logged on just to accept her request. I raise my eyebrows: 'She has an open profile.'

She nods knowingly: 'Slut.'

'They went to school together.' My tone is flat but the unfiltered voice in my head is escalating: *If he finds out about the account, he'll definitely leave me. He'll leave me and he'll crack on with Jazz and while me and Poppy are at home, he'll be off ogling grid girls!*

'Look, he's just trying to pretend he's not got a small baby and a wife and a million respons—'

'Girlfriend,' I cut in. 'Girlfriend.' But I'm distracted: *How could I put this? I just found out my sister set up a secret social media profile for me and she's exploited my trust and all my secrets and hey, you're on there, my new friend Sandy who's trying to trick her husband into getting knocked up. Is that cool with you? No? Oh, well...*

'Right. Husbands aren't all they're cracked up to be, you know...'

Am I destined to be alone? Destined to push everyone away, whether I mean to or not...?

'The thing is...' I repeat, my voice cracking and struggling to emit any discernible sound.

Two whispers in my brain compete:

Come on, Beth. There's no way you can tell her.

She doesn't like social media either, she'll get it. Won't she?

'The thing is...' I say, louder this time but still not loud enough. I swallow, try to soften the sandpaper lining my throat. I try again. 'I...'

She squints at the screen as though there's something wrong with it, because my mouth is open but no sound's coming out.

'Hey, guess what?' she asks, and something about the way she says it makes me feel like this is the point of the call, not rearranging the product photos. 'I had an anniversary yesterday.' She swallows more wine and rubs at her eye, smudging her mascara.

The blood rushes back to my face. I take a deep breath in, shuddering as I exhale. It crosses my mind this relief is what Lucy must've felt when she tried to tell me about the account and I shut her down.

'Did you celebrate?' I ask, buying some time while I collect myself so I can try again. I will not be Lucy. I won't take the easy way out. I'll tell Sandy and I'll ask her what to do. If she still wants to know me.

'Not that sort of anniversary.' She looks down. Covers both eyes with her fingers. When she looks up she looks different, her demeanour sober. 'I lost a baby.' She looks up to the sky. 'I "lost" it. You know, like how you might mislay your purse or your phone. It just fell out.' She reaches for her wine bottle and sloshes more liquid into her glass. All thoughts of social media and Lucy leave my head. This is real life, not virtual life. I feel foolish for being so consumed with something that doesn't even really exist while my friend is grappling with something real.

'I didn't call you. Your message the other night. I didn't realize...' She doesn't say anything, she just stares into the screen, one side of her mouth collapsing into a sad smile. 'I don't know what to say. I'm so sorry.' I wish we were face to face. I wish I could reach into the screen and give her a hug. I feel my usual frustrations with technology: it's not good enough! It's never going to be as good as being in a room with someone.

'There's no words. Heartbreaking, gutting, embarrassing. Nothing cuts it.'

'A miscarriage isn't embarrassing,' I say gently.

'It is when you're working – stuck on a plane with no place to hide!'

I imagine her mid-flight, on her way to an event, a colleague beside her, the shock when she realized what was happening. I wonder what she did? How she coped for the rest of the flight? I would probably lock myself in the loos. Something like that can change a person. *No wonder she's been so caught up in falling pregnant.*

She looks down at her lap. 'It's the guilt.' She pulls the sleeves down on her sweater, hugs her arms in tightly. 'It was my fault... I didn't realize... if I'd have known... I wouldn't have been anywhere near a plane!' She shakes her head angrily, as if shaking away a memory. I feel ashamed. I judged her, for wanting a baby, without knowing the full story. Shouldn't I, more than anyone, know not to do that?

'Where's your husband?' I blurt. 'Why isn't he home?' Why is she always up late, working late, balancing everything with her work and the kids and her husband nowhere to be seen?

'He's working. Or whatever it is he does there. Pretending to work.' Her face falls, sadness dripping from her body, her frame curved inwards.

'Do you think there's... somebody else?'

She laughs, taking me by surprise. 'Who knows? I feel like I don't know anything any more. I had so many ideas about how things would turn out. So many plans... I thought things would be different, you know, from when I was growing up? Don't we all just want to do a different, better job than our own parents?' I realize this is a difference between us; I feel terrible that I'm not doing as well as my parents, Cassie feels bad that she's not doing better than hers. 'My husband hates his life, Beth. That's the truth of it. He hates it. Me, the kids, our home, the lot. I've built this perfect life... and it's a lie. The whole thing is a lie.' Tears cascade down her cheeks, streaking over her skin.

'The kids?' Surely not. I picture Joe scooping Poppy up and blowing raspberries on her belly, so eager to make her smile. I notice the cracks around Sandy's demeanour: her hair greasy, her skin sallower. Whatever's going on is taking its toll.

'He loves the kids, of course, in his own way, but it's like...
like they're my little project. He hates the responsibility of
it. He hates *family life*.'

'Blooming hell. That sounds... weird.'

'It is, isn't it?' Relief passes over her face at my
confirmation. Her eyes look more focused, lucid. '*It is*.
You're the only person I've ever told.'

47

#Gliding

Cassie

I wrap my coat around me tighter as I walk to the train station. I wear it like armour, a magic cloak, as if looking cool can protect me from whatever's going to come. I've been summoned to a Mumspire event today. An opportunity to promote the app since Holistic Flo can't be here, as intended, to promote her podcast. I can't argue with Griff; I'm clinging on to my fee. I didn't deliver on the Family Dinners. The axe could fall at any time. Mardy Mum is clearly lined up to replace me. I've lost my authenticity, I've lost people's trust. Every day brings a new slight: brands I've worked with for years ignoring me, events in my feed that I haven't been invited to. Not a single request to Pimp My Bush.

I'm sure on the silent ride back from the golf club I felt the pulse of an egg jettisoning from my right ovary, hoping – as I did – for one last shot at survival. I imagined it fading away, its edges slowly breaking down, teeny tiny cells eroding and depleting until it was entirely gone, my fleeting fertile window wasted. There is no baby. There will never be another baby. I stared at the peeling ceiling in the night – sleep still eluding me – after talking to Beth, and I knew: it's the right thing. I can never replace the baby I lost, like I can never replace the way Seb and I used to be together. I was a fool to think I could. Beth was right. It *is* weird, being like that. And that's Seb's problem, not mine. I'm sick of papering over the cracks, putting on this charade to convince the world that everything is great when it's not.

The sky darkens the closer we get to London. I rest a foot on my thigh, twist the white laces of my silver shoes in my fingers. I was awake a lot in the night, my hip and leg hurting, listening to Scout cough. She's been coughing all week. I imagine microscopic mould particles aggravating her lungs. The quotes have arrived: the cheapest was £8,000 to strip back the walls, insulate them properly, replaster, repaint. Seb outright refused to pay for it, saying if it was so important to me then I should pay for it, knowing full well that I can't. I'm going to have to ask Marina, further thinning the threads of my marriage. I can't bear as Scout's mother to not be able to fix this.

I couldn't tell Beth the full story, for obvious reasons. Besides, I was feeling too raw, too wrapped up in my memories of that terrible day three years ago. Humiliation compounding my sadness… '*I don't know if you left because you were embarrassed or something…*' I hadn't long been back to work after maternity leave. Just returning to work was an ordeal. I'd been discharged from the simulator and my first long-haul flight was to New York. Everyone expected me to love it. *I* expected I'd love it, but I had to put all my psychological training into practice to get into the car that morning. I felt sick to my stomach, crying the whole way to the airport, dark water-marks pooling on my uniform. I parked and pulled down the mirror. *You can do this, Cassie*, I told my reflection, *this is who you are. You're a pilot. You fly planes. It's your dream. You're a mother and you fly. You can do both. They don't have to be mutually exclusive. Look at all the fucking dads that fly.*

I took a deep breath and I cracked on and I did it. I got through it with multiple texts to our nanny, Becky, when I was on the ground, resigned that she could let them play with Barbies and Action Men and things I didn't approve of at playgroup and there wasn't much I could do about it from thousands of miles away. I did it again and again, for a few weeks. But I didn't enjoy it. I was exhausted, bloated from a return to airline food, and the anxious nausea I'd felt during that first flight hadn't abated – it was getting worse. I was existing, basically, on autopilot (sorry).

The real challenge came the next month: Scout was sick with a fever, all expression gone from her face as she sat curled up on Marina, who had come over to help. I wasn't feeling too great myself, light-headed and sickly, but then I hadn't been for weeks. How much longer could I carry on like this? At the airport, I texted Becky: 'Everything okay?' I gripped my phone, waiting for the dots to appear that indicated she was responding. It was my fingernails that did it. They looked amazing. Like I'd had a French manicure, when I just about had time to brush my hair. My hair... I checked my reflection. My face was drawn and pale but my hair was lustrous: thick and strong. *Fuck.* My stomach lurched and my mouth filled with salty bile, as it had been doing for weeks, but this time I was actually sick.

I had no time. I bought a pregnancy test and got to work. It was later, in a lonely hotel room in Las Vegas, that I took the pregnancy test and felt like I'd hit the jackpot. I had a glorious twenty-four hours, practically gliding over the Strip, avoiding soft-poached eggs and prosciutto at breakfast, my secret tucked up tight in my belly. I would tell Seb in person. Scout was feeling better, but he was disgruntled about being up in the night with her. It wasn't the right time. What would his reaction be? This was most definitely *unplanned*. I'd need to break it to him gently, but once he'd got used to the idea, how could he not be excited? It would be tough, for sure, but we'd get through it. A little gang of us. The Happy Hollidays.

I was packed and ready to go, my car waiting outside, when I felt my stomach start to cramp. I shouldn't be flying, I thought, but I had to get home. Once there, I'd get checked over and signed off work. It would be awkward telling them so soon, but so be it. That's life.

As we taxied to the runway I felt a warm softness, an opening, not too dissimilar to the early stages of labour. The sensation stayed, persistent. As the aircraft climbed to cruising altitude, I felt my uterus contracting and pushing with a pulsating rhythm. It didn't hurt, it felt strange, an unstoppable force. I squashed my legs together and tried to pull myself up and in, as if holding a wee. I needed to get home. I focused on getting the job done.

We finally hit 36,000 feet, which meant I could excuse myself to go to the bathroom. Too late. Blood had flooded my knickers, a dark red stain seeping through my underwear and my uniform to the grey foam seat below. I didn't know what to do. Emotion was rising within me – panic, hysteria, desperation – but something kicked in: survival instinct? My training? *Cassie, you are the captain of this plane. You are flying this plane home.*

I covered my seat with my jacket and grabbed my spare uniform from the wardrobe behind my seat. I tried to clean myself up in the small toilet, fashioning myself a jumbo pad from hand towels. I did this a number of times, ignoring the ripple of confusion along my First Officer's brow (it's not the done thing to take frequent toilet breaks; a nightmare if you have a heavy period, or, you know, are losing a baby). The next time the Cabin Crew Team Leader came to the cockpit I explained to him what had happened in what I hoped were hushed tones but were probably garbled disjointed ramblings, my First Officer's head tilted towards us interestedly. He looked relieved, to be honest. I was having a miscarriage, not a breakdown.

When we'd parked on stand at Heathrow and finished the shutdown checks and technical log, I turned my phone on, quenelles of shame curling from my face. A message from Marina: Scout's temperature had spiked again and she'd gone floppy: totally common and fine, they said in A & E. 'She needed to go to A & E?' I shouted down the phone, as a member of the cleaning team scrubbed my seat beside me. You rarely fly with the same people twice, but as a woman I was conspicuous. The rumours circulated enough for Katya to text me that evening when I was on my way home from hospital, my empty womb confirmed: 'Hey, you're not the pilot that had a miscarriage on a flight today?'

When I checked the dates, it turned out I'd been nine weeks pregnant. I shouldn't have been flying. The chances of it being related were slim, but I knew the risks: the

NICOLE KENNEDY

radiation levels, the nights out of bed. I was so tired, my
caffeine intake was through the roof and it felt like I had
a permanent head cold, so I was knocking back painkillers
and snorting decongestants to get through the long days.
I've always blamed myself. Did I kill my baby?

'Why don't you fly shorter haul?' Seb asked, when I told
him I was resigning.

'You need to be specially trained to fly different types
of aeroplanes,' I snapped. 'It's not like driving a bus.' Who
would look after the twins while I retrained? Not Seb.

Seb did all the right things when I got home. He held me
and made me dinner and brought me tea, but I will never
forget his short, sharp look of revulsion when I said I was
pregnant, or the relief in his eyes seconds later when I told
him it was over. I never let myself think of it. I packaged up
that look on his face and covered it in yellow sticky tape and
sent it someplace else. Because I knew that if I did, I would
wonder if it wasn't just my baby and my career that died
that day on the plane. I would always wonder if that was
when my marriage died too. I feel flooded with emotion;
my body full as though I'm drowning. What was I thinking,
wanting to have another baby with Seb? It's his fault that I
left work, his fault I got trapped in this situation... *his fault,
his fault*... everything is his fault.

I feel like I've betrayed them sometimes. The young
girls like me who dream of flying planes and get told they
can't. Wrong gender. Wrong income bracket. Girls like
Katya would be okay, her family's rich, but girls like me?
No chance. Not any more. You need 100k in The Bank
of Mum and Dad or your own trust fund. Flying is a rich
man's game, like everything else.

I gave it up. Because I had kids and I missed them and my body (and maybe my mind) wasn't up to it at that time. But I didn't just give up on flying, I gave up on something else. I gave up on a little bit of myself. A small but important bit. The bit that thought dreams can come true, if you persevere, work hard enough, trust your instincts. Then I found a little bit of it on Instagram. And for a while, that was enough. Until I met Beth. I started to remember. What it's like to pass through this world with friendship, with connection, with someone on your side. With *love*.

She'll think I've lied. She'll think she doesn't know me. How can I explain that she's the *only* person who knows the real me? I couldn't miss her judgemental tone when I told her about the ovulation test. And I couldn't tell her what happened at the golf club, or on the plane. Our friendship is at an impasse. The roadblock is the lie. If she knew how much depended on it, my alter ego, this other life, she might understand. I need to tell her the truth, about everything. I take a deep breath. I'll tell her today.

48

#DeepBreaths

Beth

I'm trying to concentrate on what the others are saying (Holistic Flo has had an 'epic breakdown', going fully rock star on a photo shoot and demanding a separate dressing room for her crystals) but my mind is elsewhere: on Joe, on Lucy, on Mardy Mum. I thought getting out would be good. I thought it would chase away the anxiety threatening to consume me – *They're just squares on a grid* – but it's having the opposite effect: 'Hey, we should take a selfie, hashtag #SloshedNewMothersGroup!' says Priya. My heart pounds in my chest. Blooming hell.

On the sticky table, littered with cuddly avocados and kale teethers, my phone glows white and vibrates, number withheld: Lucy. She's been calling from work all day, leaving voice messages: she's sorry, she needs to speak to me, she doesn't think I should come to the Mumspire thing today after all as the line-up's changed and not as relevant.

I cancel her call and check my phone: still nothing from

Sandy. I've not heard from her since we clicked off FaceTime last week. I want to ask her advice, but she seemed so sad, so broken. I can't burden her with this too. Then someone mentions 'Mardy Mum'. I tune back in, my skin alive with heat.

'You're right!' Bronagh says, watching a short recording. 'That's our doctors'! She must live locally. I thought it looked like Victoria Park...'

'Maybe I should ask the Hot Doc for some tips #MumLife #HotDoc #BetterThanAskingMyMIL,' Priya read aloud. 'Hey, she's using the nasal aspirator I recommended to you guys!'

On the table my phone lights up again. I turn it face down.

'Is she the one with the poo-ey dress?'

What? A familiar sensation creeps into my fingers and toes. I didn't see a post about my poo-covered dress.

'Yeah. That was on her Stories. You can't see it any more.'

'You can still find it, I googled it to show my sister.'

'What's Stories?' I ask, my voice wavering.

'Mardy Mum, is it?' Jade asks.

Priya turns to me: 'They're little films of footage. They only stay up for twenty-four hours but someone screenshot it and it went viral.'

'Is she the #periwhat one?' asks Jade. 'Did you see "peri-what", Beth?' I shake my head. I can't speak. 'She's had two things go viral in as many months? This is a professional job. That wouldn't happen.'

I place Poppy in her pushchair carefully so I don't drop her and hold on to the edges of the table as the world swims around me.

'Look, the Pavilion! It *is* Victoria Park! I wonder if we've met her! She might go to some of our groups!'

'Have you seen her account, Beth?' asks Priya. 'I think you'd like her, she's very honest, the other day she was saying...' But I don't hear the rest because a buzzing has started in my ears.

Jade locates the account: 'She's funny,' she snorts. 'You know' – she squints at the screen – 'her baby's hair is a bit like Poppy's... I thought she was a one-off.'

'I hadn't noticed that before...' Priya scrutinizes Poppy. You can't see Poppy's face in any of the photos, she's mainly captured from the back, sunlight fanning through her hair, but if you know Poppy, it's unmistakable.

They return to their phones, their gaze shifting, frown lines appearing.

'Isn't that your changing bag?' asks Jade.

I close my eyes. I remember that one. The caption was short and sweet: 'Mother-in-law gift #wheresthereceipt'. Mardy Mum is a more caustic, cutting version of me. Like Lucy.

In my childhood bedroom I'd flicked from post to post, seeing my own words there in black and white:

'It was like giving birth again but with a far less cuddly end product...'

(My first post-birth poo.)

'Pubic hair, don't care!'

(My post-labour waxing regime.)

'The first time she mentioned her little Jojo I didn't know if she was referring to my boyfriend or her vagina.'

(How will I face Gloria and 'Handsy Don' again?)

Things I'd said or written to Lucy. Half the time she didn't even respond, and I thought she was so uninterested, but she was busy transcribing – or copy-and-pasting from our messages – all the personal, private things I had told her.

I could tell them, I think. I could be honest: *I did say those things, but not like that. Not the way Lucy's written them down.* Fear stops me. I can't find the words. Once it's out there, I could never take it back. There must be another way to fix this? I could go home now and delete the account and it will be gone forever. And if I can't do that, if it's too late, then I need to tell Joe first and worry about the hypnobabes later.

I look at Bronagh, nervous to see her reaction – Lucy went to town with some of the Bronagh stuff. Things I'd said because I was wondering whether I should be going the extra mile like Bronagh, because next to Bronagh I feel like an inadequate mum: all whitewashed with sarcasm and ridicule, the context entirely changed – but it's Jade who lays her phone flat on the table and jerks her hand away, as though it's given her an electric shock.

On the screen is an image of a sieve. I'd forgotten. I close my eyes, remembering Lucy's words:

@Mardy_Mum Hands up who shit themselves in labour? *Woman with hands up emoji* my mate Jess did and now her husband won't stop going on about it (or near her). Seriously, dude. Get over it! Anyone else had this? #PassTheSieve #IWishMenWouldHaveBabies #ShowTheMamaSomeLove

All three slowly raise their heads and stare. I have a flashback, edging backwards against my locker, my hair sticky with cooking oil and Caitlin Oxenbury and her cronies staring at me menacingly.

'It's not me!' I say, but my conviction fails me.

'And you've been banging on about how awful the InstaMum scene is? What a hypocrite!' Priya says incredulously. 'You hear about people like this,' she says to the others, 'leading double lives, but I never thought one would be in the hypnobabes!'

They finish their drinks, glancing at each other with big-eyed 'Wow' looks and puffing air out of their cheeks, studiously ignoring me.

'It's not me! There is no double life. I have never – *would never* – make fun of you like that. Why would I? I'm the biggest failure at motherhood of all.' I'm crying, my breath coming out in raggedy clumps, like my hair has started to. The others gather up their things. 'It looks like she's local, perhaps you told her yourself… perhaps you told her about the poo too!' I gabble. I notice the occupants of other tables glance interestedly in our direction, but I persevere: if I can convince them it wasn't me and delete the account, maybe there's still a way out of this.

'*Shut up* about the fucking poo,' Jade snarls.

'What about at Latino Bambino or Baby Swahili Drums?' Jade knocks back the rest of her wine in one, her hand shaking. I reach out for her arm but she pulls away. 'Your twin group! Did you tell someone in your twin group?'

No one speaks as they shove baby paraphernalia under their pushchairs and walk to the door in convoy, Priya with her phone in hand.

'You can't,' Jade says, looking at Priya's phone over her shoulder and back at me.

'Why not? We don't owe her anything.'

'Please don't,' I call out. 'I need to speak to Joe...'

My phone rings again, number withheld, and I snatch it up. *This is all her fault.*

'Lucy, I don't want to speak to you!' I shout.

But it's not Lucy, it's Joe, and he's breathing quickly and he's speaking in a low voice and he's saying, 'Beth, what *the fuck* is going on?'

49

#Commotion

Cassie

When I reach the Park Keeper, there's a commotion going on outside.

'You need to come with me and explain to him,' a woman hisses. She's turned away from me, her long blonde hair pulled into a haphazard bun.

'I'm sorry, *I can't.* I told you. *Please.* It has to stay between us...' She rubs her fingers along her knotted brow line as if to release them. She looks familiar: also blonde, but thinner and slightly taller in leopard print boots. '...I've got to go in, it's starting in a minute.'

She's coming to the event. What's her handle? We make eye contact and she recoils, as if she's afraid of me. That's how bad things have got. I'm grotesque. No longer a spokesperson for other mums, I'm the sort of mum other mums fear being. I put my head down and climb the steps as fast as my injured hip will allow.

'Fine. Go and do your blooming *job.*'

The woman's broad accent catches in my ear. I recognize that voice. *Who...?*

'It's not like that...' The taller woman puts her hands on the other woman's elbows, forcing her to look into her eyes. 'Please.' Her eyes dart nervously in my direction, embarrassed, no doubt, to be having this set-to outside a high-profile event. 'You shouldn't be here.' The wind picks up, billowing her camel coat outwards, whipping her hair across her face.

'The other day you wanted me to come!'

At the top of the steps I side-eye the woman with the messy bun, quickly turning away as my fears are confirmed: *Beth*. I bolt inside. She probably hasn't seen my message yet. I can't tell her *here*, outside the event, with Alicia and Griff around. What's she doing here? And who's that she's talking to?

50

#DoIKnowYou

Beth

I look down at my phone. Something from Sandy and a message from Joe: 'I'm leaving work. Meet me at Mile End station in 20 mins.' No kisses. No nothing.

I turn to leave but Lucy grips my arms. A woman dressed in a ridiculous stringy-looking white coat – she looks like a yeti – with leather pants and silver trainers limps past, entering the Park Keeper. I twist my head and catch a triangle of her face from under her tipped fedora. I stare as she hurries inside. *Was that...?*

'Please don't tell Joe for now. I'll come over later and we can talk about it?' Lucy's tone is desperate.

'It's too late, Lucy!' I shout, my voice climbing. 'He knows. I have to explain!' Little pockets of anger start exploding, like a volcano throwing up rock. 'Why didn't you think of all this?'

'There's something else...' She looks nervously towards the building. I know she has to go.

'Are you joking?'

'It's nothing as bad, just something related, a kind of funny coincidence… I can explain later?'

'No. Don't come over. I need to sort things out with Joe. He and Poppy are my priority now.'

'Mitts,' she says quietly, reeling backwards as though I've hit her.

'I don't think you realize what you've done! It's *not* just squares on a grid. It's my blooming *life*, a life I was piecing back together after Mum…' I tail off. *You'll always have each other. My little mittens. I'm sorry, Mum. I've let you down again. But this time it isn't my fault.* 'I don't want to see you later; I don't want to see you at all! Just *go*.'

I think back to when I first met Sandy in the park, when I asked her to go. The woman in the fedora looked just like her. But it couldn't be. I must need a friend so badly right now my brain's gone into overdrive.

I stop and catch my breath. My heart feels like it's skipping and missing beats, like Joe on his decks in his bedroom at his parents' house. I breathe in and out as slowly as I can. I know that if I keep focused on my breathing eventually this feeling will subside, eventually my heart will beat like my own. *This too shall pass*, I remind myself, hand flat on my stomach. *This too shall pass.*

Lucy climbs the steps of the Park Keeper, her head returning to me uncertainly as I shoot her dirty looks. She disappears under its arches as the sky finally splits with thunder and heavy rain begins to fall, bouncing off the pavement.

I look up at the imposing building. A woman with coral hair and burgundy lips, each set off by her white T-shirt and sequined maxi skirt, rushes inside, a newspaper held over her head.

I secure the rain cover over the buggy and pull my hood up, but something stops me from walking away. Something tugs at my consciousness. Lucy didn't want me to go inside. This is the event she wanted me to come to, isn't it, but then she changed her mind? And she's gone inside rather than staying out here to fight for what's left of our relationship, rather than coming with me to explain to Joe. She's protecting something. More lies, more subterfuge, more whatever this 'funny coincidence' is that she mentioned.

I glance at my watch. Joe will be at the station soon. I need to leave now.

51

#Turbulence

Cassie

Oh God. She followed me. I thought she hadn't seen me. I'm on the stage at the Park Keeper, trapped on my pedestal, looking over the sea of mums, trying to ignore a desperate need to wee. I keep my gaze fixed ahead, not daring to look left to where she's standing in the doorway, mouth gaping open as Hetty introduces me: 'Here she is, chicks, Cassie Holliday! Ready to answer your questions...'

Beth's presence provides a distraction, at least, from the fifty pairs of eyes all trained studiously on my torso, trying to discern whether there's a baby in there. But it's empty. I am empty and lonely, hollowed out by the last few months, maybe the last few years. Thunder cracks outside, loud enough that a few of us look to the windows to check they're secure.

Beth moves into the room, directly into my line of vision, and sits beside Common As Mum. She hates this scene. She told me so herself. So why is she here? I ignore her as she tries to meet my eyes questioningly. There'll be no getting out of telling her today; maybe, somehow, this is a good thing.

Griff's at the back, flanked by Alicia. We're calling this 'An Audience With Cassie Holliday – How To Connect And Grow Your SoMe Following', but really it's another push to get the Family Co app on everyone's radar, driving traffic, encouraging downloads.

I look at Poppy on Beth's lap. Chewing on her fist. When I met Beth in the park, Poppy was wearing that godawful unicorn hat; she's been asleep when we've FaceTimed. Now, without a hat, her hair fans out… like a lion's mane. For the first time, I notice the elbows and nudges tickling the room, the hushed question – 'Is that Mardy Mum? – repeated as the other mums clock Poppy and her distinctive tresses.

I hear Hetty talking about the importance of SoMe to expand your business and all the usual crap, but I stare at the floor. I feel blindsided. Why's Beth here with Mardy Mum's baby? Everything feels upside down and disconnected. My brain feels like an airline destination map, jagged trails looping and criss-crossing, arrows intersecting, nothing making sense. My eyes skitter over the room, searching for answers.

Hetty asks me something. I have no idea what. Instead of responding, I gesture towards Poppy dumbly and in the silence of the room say, 'Poppy's the 50,000 liker?'

The focus of the room shifts from me to Beth. She feels it too, as she seems to shrink inwards. She stares back at me with fire in her eyes.

'What?' She spits. She's furious, crazy with rage. A far cry from the sad figure I met in the park or the person I've become friends with. I didn't think my being involved in

SoMe would be *that* big of a deal. I've not shared anything about her publicly. I should be mad with her. What's the connection to Mardy Mum?

Beside her, Common As Mum watches the action unfold agog; she's had a makeover, her hair a polished coral, wearing the same outfit as in her interview with the *Sunday Read* at the weekend.

I'm E...

Poppy grabs at her sequined skirt with a gloopy fist, but Common As Mum, slack-jawed, doesn't notice.

I love sewing, my sister, and Yorkshire tea...

She can't be E? *The* E? But even as I'm denying it to myself, my brain is processing and reconfiguring facts: Elizabeth... Her full name is Elizabeth. She included it when she sent me her address before her birthday.

'Chicks, is something up? You're kinda killing the vibe here...' says Hetty.

'Don't worry, I'm leaving!' Shouts Beth, clutching Poppy and storming from the room. As she leaves, a woman rises at the back, the same woman she was arguing with outside. Who is that?

Whispers bounce off the stuccoed walls: *That was weird. Was that Mardy Mum? She's not how I was expecting. What's with her and Cassie?* Alicia raises an eyebrow questioningly, darts a glance at Griff, who's watching me. My skin starts to itch. I clench my thighs together as hard as I can: I need to find a bathroom.

'She's... I...'

Beyond the elegant windows, lightning strikes in the sky. The sort so powerful, so fierce, that if you were flying, you would reroute to avoid. What I wouldn't give to reroute now, to change course, divert my life. I can't do this. I can't do this any more. I flee the stage, following Beth. She's in the atrium, clicking Poppy into her pushchair.

'What's going on?' I demand. She ignores me, swallowing repeatedly, using her shoulder to nudge sweat from her face, hair falling from her loose bun. *It's a mardy mum bun kind of day…*

'Why didn't you tell me?' I ask. Rain funnels down outside, clapping the pavement, trapping us in the monochrome tiled entrance.

'Why didn't *you* tell *me*?' she retorts, snapping her head round, standing tall. 'Why is my life *exploding* like this? Who *are* you? *Cassie Holliday? The Happy Hollidays?*'

She rolls her eyes and I stare at the ornately plastered ceiling as if it might cave in. What have I done? Why didn't I see this coming? She knows so much about me. She could say anything, now, here, surrounded by Griff and the other Influencers, and the whole thing will come down, *like a fair-trade, hemp-woven house of cards*. Please don't let her be involved with The Unhappy Hollidays. Please don't let her *be* The Unhappy Hollidays. No. She can't be. My judgement can't be that off. What would be in it for her?

But then why's she here? Why's she befriended me, not told me about her account and who she is? Did she follow me to the park the day we met and then on to the train station? Why is she pretending not to know who I am now? She's been liking and commenting on my photos for months. She messaged me about the Brand Ambassador gig! Of course she knows who I am! This is all totally fucked up. *Why?*

'It was you all along!' I shout. I'm conscious of the atrium filling, smartphones moving around us, people grouping and regrouping like sardines. There's a gap in the rain and we spill out on to the path. 'What's in it for you? Ruining my life?'

I step in front of the buggy, blocking her path, but she doesn't relent. The pavement's slippery; I lose my balance and fall on to Poppy. The crowd gasps. The sound distorts and falls flatly into silence as my perspective narrows to just me and Beth. I right myself, gripping Beth's wrists as she clutches the buggy's handlebars. 'I said, what's in it for you?'

Beth's eyes bulge and flare in fear, the clear tropical sea muddied with tears.

'Let. Me. Go!' A sob escapes between each word, like she doesn't have enough air to breathe. I remember then she suffers from panic attacks. I release my grip just as a flash of glittered cherry and a blinding, shattering pain streaks across the side of my head. I fall to the floor, hard.

Hushed whispers pass through the crowd, a chorus in the round: *The baby, the baby, the baby.*

'Cassie!' Alicia's voice slices through the vacuum, the soft Californian edges gone. 'Are you okay?' She turns and snaps at someone else: 'What are you *doing?*'

I drag myself up on to my feet before anyone can help me. 'There is no baby!' I shout.

'*Leave her alone,*' a woman commands me and I see it's the woman Beth was talking to outside.

Alicia turns to her: '*What's going on?*'

'She's my sister,' she says, and something passes between her and Alicia that I don't yet understand. Beth mentioned a sister. I get closer to remembering where I know her from. A thumbnail that's stepped out of its frame. An avatar come to life. What's her handle? It's there, she's... for fuck's sake, who is she?

'I need to go.' Beth's sister grabs the pushchair and moves to leave. 'Are you coming?' she asks Beth.

Beth stands between us, crying, really crying. All around smartphones are waning, women looking at me with disgust in their eyes. No baby, no sympathy.

'You don't know what she's been doing to me!' I shout. 'She's been pretending to be my friend... feeding information to The Unhappy Hollidays. Maybe she *is* The Unhappy Hollidays...' But even in this state I know they sound like the ramblings of a mad woman; that besides me, and maybe Alicia, no one really cares.

'I don't know what you're talking about,' Beth says, startled. 'Lucy...?'

'I don't know!' the sister shouts. She throws her hands up in the air. 'Are you coming or not?'

Lucy... A face flashes from a bio on the Boom! website. One I look at every now and then when I'm asking myself, *Where is this all coming from? Why's she doing this?*

Lucy Jenkins. *That's* her sister?

Smartphones are still trained on me as I come to a horrible realization: the one thing I thought was real is not.

52

#LetsFlyAway

Beth

'I get that you're cross – I'm cross too – but this isn't my fault.' I remove my hood, shaking the arms of my jacket, dispersing raindrops. The rain has cleared but the sky is grey.

He turns his phone so I can see the screen. On it is a GIF, or meme, whatever they're called, which repeats the image of my hands holding the ring box over the Yorkshire pudding, saying 'Peri—' before it cuts to Homer Simpson saying 'Doh'! It's been retweeted over 436,000 times. 'Mark just sent me this. The whole office thinks it's hilarious. Thank God Jazz warned me so I'd already left the office.'

'Jazz?'

'She recognized your dress from the wedding in the shot that went viral and sent it to me.'

'*Jazz?* How did she have your number?'

He gives me a look that says: Don't go there. 'I hardly think that's the point, do you?'

'Well, you didn't exchange numbers in primary school!'

He ignores me, shaking his head, his eyes flexing with anger. 'So this is all Lucy's doing, is it? It's all made up? You haven't said those things to her? Things that have made me look like a *total dick* to the rest of the world?'

We turn left on to the canal path and pass The Palm Tree. I remember us there, on the star-dotted muslin. How was that only a couple of months ago?

'I did. But not the way she wrote them. It sounds worse, condensed like that.' He shakes his head. 'I'm allowed to speak to my sister if something upsets me. I didn't know she would—'

'What have I done to upset you, Beth? I've done *everything* I could. I supported you from the minute you said you were pregnant. I've made you a part of my family, I've let you take over the spare room with your sewing machine and your mismatched "*vintage*"' – he uses air quotes – 'fabrics to keep you happy. *What more could I have done?*'

I walk beside him in silence, biting my lip.

'You could have proposed.' As soon as the words escape my lips, I feel mortified. Like a layer of my skin has been scraped off and I'm walking along Regent's Canal, grotesquely exposed. It hangs between us, this thing that we've never discussed, like a spider dangling on its silk thread, before suddenly it moves, quicker than you were expecting.

'I thought you didn't want me to propose?'

'I never said—'

'You said: I don't want Joe to propose to me!'

I inhale swiftly and glare at him.

'*JUST BECAUSE I'M PREGNANT.*' I swerve to avoid an abandoned pumpkin that's been smashed by the rain, its rotting innards oozing out of its mouth. 'I said, I didn't want you to propose to me *JUST BECAUSE I'M PREGNANT*.'

An ageing bohemian couple – the woman looks like she's been wrapped up in different carpet samples – pass us and glance at us inquisitively.

I want you to propose to me because you love me.

'I can't win. You're impossible.'

'*What?*' We are doing angry walking-along-whispering-arguing now.

'Ever since we've had Poppy. Or just before. You're up, you're down. You want to move, you don't want to move. You want to get married, you don't want to get married. Now apparently you do! I can't win. The whole world's laughing at me, because of an expensive ring I bought you, and you don't even wear it! I've not seen it since your birthday.'

As we walk along the towpath, attention lifts and sticks to us like prickly burrs. A man with more sideburns than facial skin and an oversized sports cap carefully sidesteps us.

'Because I'm *embarrassed*, Joe!' I poke my finger at him angrily. I don't think I've ever been so angry. Every hormone, every missed minute of sleep, every ache in my body I've worried over, every embarrassing incident I've endured since conceiving Poppy gathers steam and explodes in spitting rage, the volcano that's been threatening since I found out about the account finally erupting.

'I've been too embarrassed to wear it because what am I supposed to tell people? That we just had a baby, but you thought it was a good idea to buy me a *Non-Commitment Ring! A Just For Fun Ring!!!*' My voice doesn't sound like my own. '*Who buys the woman that's just had their baby a Just For Fun Ring?!*' I'm not shouting, I'm screeching.

'You've lost the plot,' he says, and as I stand there, the crowds avoiding us as though we've marked out our own turning circle on the canal path, my heart pumping, my hands shaking, I agree with him. I have lost the plot. I didn't realize it meant so much to me: a stupid piece of metal, a stupid piece of paper. But it does; it matters *to me*.

'I've just had a baby—' I say, my voice low and guttural.

He lets out a noise. An 'aargh' that comes from the back of his throat, aggressively exhaled through his teeth.

'So have I!' he shouts. '*I've* just had a baby too and *I* have to go to work every day and *I* have to come home and not know what sort of mood I'm going to find you in.'

His words fell me. I try so hard to be upbeat when he gets home, to keep a lid on my anxiety, to not expose him to that ugly side of me, but he's seen it and he doesn't like it, just like I worried would happen all along. He really *doesn't* want to marry me. He doesn't even like me.

53

Radford School
Oatbridge Lane, Oatbridge, Surrey

Dear Mrs Holliday,

Many thanks for your letter.

We note that for the purposes of the register your children are to be addressed as Birch and Scout. Your husband did indeed forget to put this on the enrolment form, as you suspected.

Warmest regards,

Mrs Venetia Drake (Head of Admissions)

54

Radford School
Oatbridge Lane, Oatbridge, Surrey

Dear Mrs Holliday,

Many thanks for your letter.

Regretfully, it will not be possible for 'Scout' to wear the same attire as her brother.

It is our dearest wish that this should not 'crush her spirit and stifle her will' but rather shall give her a foundation from which to flourish, uniformly, alongside her peers.

Warmest regards,

Mrs Venetia Drake (Head of Admissions)

55

Radford School
Oatbridge Lane, Oatbridge, Surrey

Dear Mrs Holliday,

Many thanks for your telephone call, it was certainly enlightening.

While we entirely support 'the cause' and are in absolute agreement that equality for women in all respects must be top of the agenda, we have decided to decline the kind offer of your consultancy services with a view to 'updating' the school uniform and our Learning Through Play programme.

On reflection, as the Radford School is a school based on tradition, it may not be in alignment with your values. Perhaps an alternative establishment may suit you and your children better? I have removed them from the roll for September and shall assume they will not be attending unless I hear from you to the contrary.

Warmest regards,

Mrs Venetia Drake (Head of Admissions)

56

#MakingAndMending

Beth

'Beth!' His face fills the screen, his soft Scottish brogue infusing gently through the flat like incense. The lines around his eyes crinkle like silk taffeta. He's always reminded me of a Regency gent, transported into modern times. Today he's sporting a checked blazer, beautifully cut, and a polka-dot cravat. I feel a warmth over my knees, like someone's tucked a blanket around me. 'I'm so glad you booked an appointment. How are things?'

Russell grew up making his own clothes under his mum's careful instruction. He got it immediately. The connection to the fabric, the shared hours learning the craft, how the joy in making extends beyond the finished item: it's pride in each other's work, the perpetuation of technique, remembering the way your mother's fingers pressed down on to the fabric as you make dents in your own.

'Nice jacket,' I say. 'Very dapper! Did you make it?'

'With these very hands.' He raises them to the screen.

Another pause. 'Have you been sewing, Beth?' His eyebrows are high and enquiring.

'It's having Poppy...' I nod and tears bud in my eyes. Russell knows how hard I found crafting after Mum died, so I know what he's asking: Are you still coping with your loss? Still navigating its peaks and troughs? 'I want to teach her stuff, like Mum taught me. I even made some things that I thought I might sell but maybe it's not a good idea...'

'Oh?' The eyebrows rise again.

'Why I booked the appointment...' I swallow. 'Things haven't been going so well lately and... I'm not feeling myself. I'm struggling to stay positive. I'm worried they're coming back. The panic attacks. I had one, in the park a couple of months ago. I've not had one since, but I keep feeling like I'm on the verge of one, the threat's always there, you know? And I know I have to confront them, let the feelings come, but...' I look into the screen. I wish we were face to face. 'I'm worried I won't be able to stop them this time.'

'Anxiety around panic attacks is very common.'

'*I'm anxious about being anxious,*' I sigh. 'The stakes are higher now, I have Poppy. It's not just about me.' He nods, his face open and kind, and I keep talking, surprising myself. 'It feels like... everything's crumbling around me – my relationship with Joe, with Lucy, with Dad, I mean I hardly see him, he hardly sees Poppy...' I think of him rattling around in the house by himself and feel a million jolts of sadness. '...My friendships are a mess... *everything is*, and...' I stare past him, over the screen, to the scrap of blue-white sky. A tear splashes down my cheek, then another and another. He lets me sob, my eyes skywards.

I pull a tissue from my jumper sleeve and blow my nose noisily. 'The thing I'm most afraid of is, I can't picture myself in the aftermath, I can't see myself in the rubble. I just see... nothing. A blank.' He moves to speak. I pre-empt the question: 'Don't worry, I'm not suicidal. It's not like that. I've never wanted to be alive more. To be with Poppy.'

My insides lurch violently and sweat bubbles and slips over my skin, like butter in a pan. I never allow myself to think of it: that one day Poppy will lose her own mum. I pray that I'm old, that she has a family of her own, that it's not too blinding a blow; that I'm not wrenched from her life the way Mum was from mine.

He shakes his head. 'I was going to ask, what's the blank, Beth? What does nothing look like to you?'

I close my eyes, hands under my thighs, the darkness soothing. 'It feels like I'm going to be here forever, stuck in an anxiety limbo, never moving forward... a confused mum, doing my best but never getting it right. Messing things up. And missing things – missing things with Poppy, and with Joe, because I'm inside my head too much. I don't seem to know how to be in the moment any more, to be present.'

'Beth, we know what this is? We've been here before, eh?'

'Catastrophizing. I'm catastrophizing. But Russell, that's because it is catastrophic.' And I tell him what Lucy has done and how I don't know if I can ever forgive her or still have her in my life. I tell him how I lost my mother and now it feels like I've lost my sister too. He doesn't shake his head, or look annoyed, or do any of the things Joe does when I try to talk to him about Lucy, but I note the shift in his features, the sympathy that gathers and passes over his face.

He knows about my guilt, my helpless feelings after Mum died, after what I did. He's the only person who knows what I did, other than Dad.

'You're going to say I need to tell her, aren't you?'

'It might help.'

'What good will it do? Dragging up all that old stuff?'

'It doesn't need dragging up, Beth. It's still there, alive and well.' His tone is robust, jovial almost. 'Lucy's lost your trust and you're trying to figure it out, but this "old stuff", as you put it, is getting muddled up in it. Maybe you *should* take some time apart from Lucy, but I don't think you can make that decision until you've sorted out the "old stuff".'

'It will bring them back, the panic attacks. I can't go through that again.'

'Has Lucy explained her actions?'

'No. I didn't give her the chance. I know what she'd say. She thought it would be good for me. She'd see it as a business opportunity.' I shake my head, rolling my eyes.

We sit in silence a moment, he in his cosy office in Southampton, me in my London penthouse. He puts his notepad down beside him. 'Beth, how many years have you worried now that something bad is about to happen?'

'In capital letters?' I laugh. How many times have I *said* it, to Russell, to Lucy, to Joe, my breath short, my skin hot, my heart hammering in my chest, my thoughts beginning to fracture and split: 'I can't explain it, I just *really feel* like Something Bad Is About To Happen.' 'I don't know,' I say. 'Eight?'

'Eight years.' He rolls his lips inwards, looks me in the eye. 'And in that time, how many bad things *have* happened?'

'Mum died before they started, and it was after Lucy got sick, so...' I think it through. Eight years of panic and... 'None?'

'And Poppy? How's she doing?' I observe her in her bouncer while her mum Skypes her therapist: a modern scene. Her cheeks are pink, her limbs stocky and full, her hands shaking a recycled plastic rattle. She's thriving. When I look up, Russell's smiling. 'We should do some work on navigating change, Beth.'

My heart sinks. 'I feel like I'm back at the beginning, when I thought I'd been "fixed".'

'Change is unsettling, Beth, but change isn't always bad. It won't always result in panic attacks or thinking you're about to faint and fall in front of a bus.' He remembers. I was convinced that was going to happen. I had to stop walking along roads that buses passed through. I feel a stab of sadness for the old me, before I started seeing Russell, lost in the back roads. 'You've got through this once, you can do it again.'

'You're right. I'm not back at the beginning, I'm... *on a journey*?'

'You've lived down south too long.' We both grin.

'Eight years,' I marvel. 'Eight years and nothing bad has happened. Eight years and maybe... Wow, maybe *nothing* has happened? Maybe I've blocked myself off to new experiences, to new opportunities, because I've been afraid?' Suddenly I'm making leaps and connections, rushing ahead, desperate to get started. To be 'fixed' again. Russell raises a hand to slow me down.

'It's something to think about. Don't forget you've met Joe, you've had Poppy.'

'Things aren't so great with Joe.' My voice flattens. We barely speak, passing like ghosts through the flat. Each exchange now awkward and stilted, neither of us keen to acknowledge the growing distance between us.

'He's had a lot of change too, don't forget. Adjusting to parenthood is difficult for everyone. And this account – what happened with the ring – that must have been awful for him?'

'Yeah,' I sigh. 'It was. It still is. He's a meme.' I grimace.

'What are you going to do about the social media account?'

'Nothing,' I say. 'I closed it down – well, disabled it, that's all you can do. You can't see it.'

Russell looks thoughtful, his eyebrows furrowing. 'It does have a currency though, no?'

'If I wanted to *use* it, but I don't. It's Lucy's account, she set it all up.'

'Using things you'd written?' I look up, my expression a question. 'It's a betrayal. No doubt about it. You've a right to be cross with Lucy, but I'm wondering how to best move on, that's all?'

He clasps his hands in his lap; it feels like that's my homework. This is where I'd stand to leave if we were face to face. 'Let's speak again in a few weeks, or sooner if you need. And think about talking to Lucy.'

I nod and I smile and I say that I will, but I know that I won't. I tried once but the words wouldn't conform, refusing to sit side by side in a coherent sentence. It's impossible. I will never find the right words to tell Lucy that Mum didn't kill herself. I did it. It was me.

57

#Stories

Cassie

The timer goes off: ten minutes is up. I delete the video I posted and check my make-up: there but not there. Taking a deep breath, I hit record:

'Okay...' I draw this out while my eyes dart like dragonflies. 'So. The eagle-eyed among you will have noticed that I deleted some of my Stories from earlier. I... went a bit ranty and a bit rambly – kinda like now, I guess, but I just wanted to come back on to say, I'M OKAY.' I stare bug-eyed into the camera. 'Please don't worry. I've had so many messages from you lovely lot. I'm fine, I just' – I smile bravely – 'I just lost it with Birch. WHY DON'T THEY TELL YOU PARENTING IS SO HARD?' I laugh a little manically.

My arms are raised up to ear height with my palms upwards and shrugging. It's a look I got from an emoji. A what-can-you-do? expression, pulling a stressed-out face. I don't need much help to look like I'm losing it – the dark shadows beneath my eyes belong in the outsize baggage area. This is a real departure for me. I like to be cool, calm, curated. I like to be in control. But, like Boardroom Boss Mum says, sometimes you have to try something new. I need to be more relatable, *like Mardy fucking Mum.*

I hear a screech of tyres and rushed footsteps on gravel. Seb enters the room, panting. He looks from me to Birch and back again. Birch is playing happily with his train set. No one wants to hear about that. I stop recording.

'What?' I address Seb, inwardly delighted by his concern. He leans against the counter and wipes the back of his hand across his brow.

'I thought...' He waits for his breath to even out. 'For God's sake, Cassie. This has got to stop. Can't you just be' – he rubs his eyes – 'normal?'

My phone starts pinging:

You've got this.

Oh doll, wish I could give you a hug.

You're a great mum, Cassie!

'I'm serious,' Seb says. 'What kind of mother pretends to lose it with her kids for attention?'

I ignore him, curling my feet up under me, ready to respond. This is key to my new approach: engagement. I've become too stand-offish, too aloof. I see that now.

Seb fishes up a pile of post from the door and sits at the table, exhaling loudly. You wouldn't believe he used to run marathons, would you? I've done him a favour getting his heart rate up.

'Cassie?' The tone of his voice startles me. 'What. The. Blasted. Are. These?' He brandishes some letters. The gold foil of the school crest catches the light. Oh shit.

I stride over and snatch them from him, ostensibly to check their veracity but really to buy myself some time.

'Radford called to confirm whether we still wanted a place for the twins, given our recent correspondence. I didn't know what they were talking about, so I asked them to send me on copies... copies of what I see is an attempt to destroy our good relations at the school! To wreck their education!'

I turn to ask Birch to leave the room and go play upstairs with his sister, but he's already scuttled out. The children are learning to run for cover when Seb and I collide. This is not what I wanted for them.

'I'm sorry, okay? I didn't intend for it to escalate like that, but I can't pretend to not be relieved. I don't want the twins to go to Radford.' I think of what happened at the golf club and am enveloped in shame. 'I don't want the twins turning out like Timbo and Vanessa. I went to state school and I did just fine.'

'Oh? I thought it was a constant battle between being popular and *following your dream*?' He says it in such a withering tone, degrading the intimacies I shared in the early years of our relationship, back when he listened and told me he understood. Was it all an act? 'Get over it, Cassie. This is the real world and in the real world parents want what's best for their kids. Even your mother thought she was doing what was best for you. That's all anyone tries to do. You know what' – he points his finger at me, some wind in his sails now – 'you're an excellent case in point.

If you'd come to Radford, you could have joined the RAF section – one or two other girls did – and you could have got that flying apprenticeship off the back of it without so much hoop-jumping. You'd have achieved all you did at state school, but it would have been easier. That's what a school like Radford gives you: confidence, connections, opportunities.'

He's right. The other female pilots back then were all privately educated. The truth is, being a woman wasn't my biggest hurdle to becoming a pilot: being working class was. The other women had a different air about them. An air like doing this job wasn't a big deal. When to me it was everything.

'I wouldn't have wanted to do it that way. I don't think that's *fair*. We're their parents. Giving them confidence and opportunities, that's on us. We can't farm that out to a school. I want their self-confidence to come from *within*, not from their alumni network!'

Beside me, my phone sounds: Ping! Ping! Ping!

'They're going to Radford,' he says with finality. 'Hopefully it will make them more normal. Why's Charlie always wearing that hula skirt and fairy wings?'

'Because he wants to be a bird,' I seethe. 'He loves birds.'

'We need to start preparing them for real life, Cassie.' He smacks a hand on the table. 'You need to start calling them by their real names. No more of this "tree bark" or "fairy light" or whatever. It's confusing for them.'

I ignore him. We always agreed it was sensible for them to have alternative monikers for my work, so I used the nicknames I've given the twins since birth. They were my preferred names when I was pregnant, but I couldn't get Radford here on board. I can't imagine calling them anything else now.

'And I want you to stop all the social media business. The account, everything. It's becoming extremely *embarrassing*. I was mortified at the golf club.' He's moved to the kitchen and is angrily slicing some of Marina's salami. Never too proud for that.

I follow him, noisily fishing the saucepan out of the cupboard and banging it on the side. '*You* were mortified?'

'Yes. *I* was mortified. Imagine how it will be for them at school, if you keep this up. I've humoured you for long enough.'

Humiliation stings my cheeks. On my phone, notifications are now grouped and stacked into lists. It would be so much easier to dive into that, into the world outside being nice to me, than to stay here in this confrontation with Seb. But I'm realizing I can't exist like that any more.

'This is all about Radford, Seb, and it's academic: we can't afford Radford for two children at the moment. The school money's tied up in the trust.' He looks down at his stack of salami, but for once he doesn't look hungry. He's keeping something from me, wearing that proud lockjaw look he gets when he knows he's in the wrong. 'What?' I ask.

'It's been taken care of. That's all you need to know.' He sits at the table with his salami and a legal magazine. Beside me, the saucepan begins to bubble and overflow.

'What's going on?' I get right in his face. Closer and closer, until we're eyeball to eyeball. He tries to resume faux-reading his magazine, but I meet every jerk of his head.

'Fine, Cassie, fine! I've spoken to Marina. She's signed the relevant forms.'

I don't know whether to be moved or appalled, that his love for his old school has compelled him to suck up his pride and ask a woman he *despises* for money. But I decide quite quickly: 'You can ask Marina for money to send the kids to Radford, but you can't find it within you for us to move into the Big House? Or to get the damp sorted out? You prioritize that school over our daily well-being? Over Scout's *health*?' I think of her coughing all through the night. She's had that cough for weeks now. 'How can I insist on an asthma diagnosis when I know she's living in a damp house infested with black mould?' I drain the pasta, the water fizzing and steaming in the sink, and add pesto.

'I've had enough of this. I'm trying to read.'

'*You've* had enough of this? *You?*'

'You don't *get it*, Cass.'

'No, no I don't. I don't get what the big deal is about a pile of old bricks and stuffy tradition.'

'Almost all the memories I have of my father are tied up in Radford. Not over there.' He gestures his magazine in the direction of the Big House. 'He was always working when I was home, but coming to Radford he loved. The Old Boys' days, the Michaelmas Fayre, Speech Day. He was the first father there, in his school tie, so proud of me. Of *us*, of our family and our tradition and—'

'And that's the kind of dad you want to be? One that turns up for the good bits?' We stare at each other as if seeing one another for the first time. 'Fine. I'm calling Radford. I'll come to an agreement with them. If they have to go, I want them to have the same opportunities. The same sports, the same uniform, the same...'

'You will not! I forbid you! Why are you so intent on sabotaging their education?'

'Sabotage!' I spit. 'It's the school that's sabotaging them! Single-mindedly trying to turn them into creepy little versions of... of' – my eyes alight on his tan deck shoes, jauntily tasselled, despite the weather – 'of people like you!'

'That would be *so bad*, wouldn't it? To be a person like me? You liked me because I was rich and now it's what you hate about me.'

I narrow my eyes. 'I didn't care that you were rich – on paper,' I sneer. 'I had my own money *then*. I had my own life. I sacrificed everything for our family. I gave back my *dreams*, and I was happy to, *grateful* to be here with the twins, but you got to keep yours, Seb! You got to have a family *and* your dream, maintaining your father's legacy, and you're *still* moaning about how awful your life is! Well, I'm sick of it!' He gets up and starts to walk away. I'm not finished. 'You know what, Seb, you're almost right. I don't hate you because you're rich. I hate you for being so fucking blinded by selfishness that you've lost sight of everything that matters. So Marina's living in the house. So what? It's as much hers as it is yours.'

He appraises me coolly, his jaw set, back straight. 'What's going to happen when the kids start falling short of your expectations? Will they be cut loose like me? They don't want to be photographed in lavender fields or sitting in wheelbarrows any more! They're growing up!'

'It's all I've got left,' I growl. 'The only way I can earn my own money.'

'You're a pilot, Cassie!'

'What are you saying? I should go back to flying? It's

too late. My licence has *long* lapsed. I'd have to start at the bottom, find an airline that's hiring, retrain, all on a zero-hours contract. Where would we find the time or the money?'

'I don't know why you gave it up in the first place.'

'Are you fucking joking?' I whisper-shout, banging the twins' bowls down on the table. 'Twins!' I call, my voice shrill.

'And God knows you were better at that than you are at this.'

'What's that supposed to mean?'

'You're not fit to be a mother.'

Scout appears in the doorway but quickly does an about-turn and retreats.

'I'm a good mum!' I feel the growl reverberate. 'I do my best! I turn up every day!' I dig a finger into his chest. 'I *love* them! They'll always know that. How will they remember you?'

He steps back, out of my orbit. 'When did you stop loving *me*, Cassie?'

Something flares in my throat, a lump forming. I want to say the words. I want it to be that easy to get things back to how they were when we did love each other, but they stay lodged inside. I try again. They will not come. I see a box on a beach, yellow tape glinting in the sun, moving further and further away.

'I'm going to call Radford to smooth things over. I'll have to speak to Marina about offering a donation…' He has one foot on the stairs when he turns. 'You didn't seriously want to bring a baby into *this*?'

58

#WhatAHeavyLoad

Beth

The darkness is delicious, intoxicating: it's the first time I've been out in the evening since having Poppy. I sweep my legs, avoiding puddles, tangoing my way from the station until the bookstore looms ahead. Inside, shapes twist and refract in the misted windows. I'm outside and looking in again, but this time there's a difference: I have an invitation. The idea of it, the sense of being included, hums in my chest.

I reactivated the Mardy Mum account – my conversation with Russell replaying in my head – and I slipped into another world. There wasn't just hundreds of thousands of followers and comments and calls for my attention, people asking if I'd like to try their products, join their upcoming event, basically asking me to *be their friend*, there was an invite to *an awards ceremony*: I'm up for a number of *awards*. Yes, it feels a bit strange, but like Lucy said, it's all my copy. They are *my* words. That's got to count for something? It feels like this could be my chance to be popular. To feel part of something. And I need to take it. I need to start grasping life with both hands.

I push my way in. Warm air bathes my face like a hot towel and my clothes grip my skin. Instantly, my heart beats faster. *You can do this. Embrace change. Go with the flow...*

Spiky speech-bubble helium balloons emblazoned with '!@#^!' knock against the ceiling, a sky of neon expletives. Tables are stacked with books titled *What a Heavy Load!* On the covers, a farmer pulls a surprised face as his wife waves a farmyard implement – a hoe? – in the direction of his bottom. I flick through: it seems to be a book of double entendres, loosely grouped around a farm theme.

I recognize the woman from the Park Keeper with long orange hair and dark-rimmed glasses: Hetty? She trails a pink pencil down a list of names. 'Hmm?' she purrs as I approach, smiling.

'Hi.' I stand awkwardly. 'Common As Mum invited me.'

She mistakes me for a friend; gestures behind her without looking up: 'She's over there, signing books.'

I freeze for a moment, the smile dying on my lips – I expected to be recognized after I finally posted a selfie – and my intention wavers.

'Still no Cassie?' a woman with a sharp blonde bob, a tight black dress and vampish red lipstick asks Hetty.

'Nope... not surprising. Honestly, I think it's all over for her. No one wants to touch her...' She shrugs. 'No Holistic Flo, she's still hooked up to her vitamin drip.'

'*Hashtag spon*,' interjects the blonde bob caustically.

My heart sinks. I was hoping Cassie would be here.

'No Mardy Mum... I've got some amazing opps for her,

but she's ignored all my messages.' She draws the tip of the pencil over her brow. 'She's back online, did you see?'

A profanity-laden balloon punches me in the face as someone barges to the table. 'Ooof!' I exclaim into the shiny foil, and a face appears, apologizing profusely – and rather poshly – 'Oh, my goodness, I am *so* sorry! *Oh, it's you! You came!*' Common As Mum. She wraps me up in a hug, all elbows and bosom. I freeze, my hands by my sides.

'They won't like you,' she whispers in my ear.

'Sorry?'

She eyeballs me earnestly. 'The others. They won't like you. They *hate it* when someone goes viral.' She takes two plastic flutes of Prosecco proffered from a passing shop assistant cum waiting staff (who I've noticed warily eyeing the InstaMums) and passes me one. 'Even though there's more than enough work to go round. And Cassie? She's *the worst*. What's going on with you two?' I say nothing, take a large gulp of my drink. 'You must have brands queuing up! I loved "Peri-what?". I retweeted it.' She gives me a pointed look: *You owe me.*

'Doesn't it bother you?' I blurt. 'If they hate you?'

She shrugs. 'You have to play them at their own game,' she winks. 'Are you doing the Beach House?'

'I've been invited,' I say, but it suddenly doesn't sound appealing.

'Mardy Mum!' the icy blonde bob interjects. 'I've been trying to place you.' She elbows Hetty; her poker-straight hair flies up waspishly. '*That's* Mardy Mum.'

Hetty surveys me, perhaps whizzing through her current opportunities. Does she get a cut? Is that how it works? She moves from behind the desk and places a spiky bubble sticker on my top: 'Mardy Mum'. 'Fabulous to meet you, chick! I've got to announce this one' – she puts an arm round Common As Mum – 'but let's speak later. Although, just in case...' Suddenly she is by my side, arm outstretched. 'Smile, darl!' she says, taking a selfie of us, before disappearing into the crowd.

The blonde bob extends her hand: 'Boardroom Boss Mum.' She tilts her head as though weighing me up for a potential acquisition. I swallow.

'You're not how I expected. Less brash.' She sits on the edge of the welcome desk. 'You've created quite an impact. Not good business, though, disappearing like that. Makes brands nervous.'

I raise my flute and realize it's empty. 'Is Forest Dad here?' I say casually, to change the subject. We've been messaging. He's been so thoughtful and helpful that he feels like a friend, even though we've not met yet. He said he'd try to be here tonight, and I admit I got a buzz at the thought. He's the only high-profile man in this circle, and for us to be here together – well, it would feel like I'd arrived.

Her eyes narrow. 'I haven't seen him. Why do you ask?'

Think, Beth. How do these people speak? 'He made a few suggestions to improve my reach,' I improvise. 'I wanted to say thanks.'

'Did he now... well, I can help you with that.' She reaches behind her and produces a bottle, refills my flute. Before we drink, she raises her arm; another selfie, but this time I hold a picture frame with expletive-laden spiky speech bubbles tacked on to the sides. She pokes her head in beside me: 'Say "Green prune"!' she commands as she takes the photo.

I notice other women nudge each other and tip their heads

in our direction. I hear someone say 'That's Mardy Mum', and I realize, in this circle, I'm probably quite mysterious, notorious even. It's an exciting thought. I'm so used to forming the backdrop, rather than being a centrepiece. Soon more women have joined us, larger numbers wanting to be in the shot. I'm flushed with good cheer, by grins and nods, as the group jostles and sways, more and more women trying to fit into the frame, Prosecco leaping from our glasses and splashing on to our shoes. I feel like a coveted prize. A precious jewel. A small voice says: *This is where it starts.*

59

#Critical

Cassie

The tide turns:

> Don't feel sorry for her. Poor kid.

> Parenting's not so hard if you spend less time on social media.

> She should stop exploiting her kids. Maybe they'll behave better.

I bury my face in my hands as the comments stack up. It's not working. My new approach. Nothing is working. The phone rings. Alicia on FaceTime.

'If you're calling to tell me you're cutting me loose, don't bother. I'm out. I can't do this any more.' On the screen I look drained, defeated, my face collapsed.

'What? No way. This is just getting interesting. It was a good idea... you can't predict how people will react.' She sounds so rational, so calm. 'Why resign? You've only got a couple of weeks left.'

'I can't do it any more, Alicia.'

'Look, we can have a pep talk or we can get on SoMe and utilise this. Your accounts are going *nuts*.'

My head is spinning. All I want to do is put on my pyjamas, grab the twins and a duvet and, for the love of God, I feel like watching *Frozen*.

Seb appears behind me, sports bag slung over his shoulder, a suit bag in one hand and his leather briefcase in the other. 'I'm going to stay at the office.'

'You do that.' I stay looking at Alicia rather than at him.

Alicia can't stop a smile after he's left. 'Cassie! This is genius. This will definitely get the public back on side!'

'No, Alicia. It's not… it's not part of the plan.'

'What, this is for real? Woah. I'm sorry. Are you okay?'

'I'm fine,' I say, swallowing the lie, 'but I don't want people to know Seb's gone. Besides, Holistic Flo's been there and done that.'

'She can't have the monopoly on everything: marriage breakdowns, nervous breakdowns. It's selfish. Why's he leaving? Is there someone else?'

'I don't think so.' My mind flashes to Ruby. Her heart-shaped face. Her luminescent eyes. Her perfectly messy hair, secured with *knitting needles*, for fuck's sake. Is it too early for wine?

'The nanny?' She reads my mind, then reconsiders. 'There's heaps of moms doing that, pity.' She drums her index finger against her cheek. 'Hey, he could be one of those guys with a whole other family somewhere!'

'No chance.' That I know. He doesn't like having one family, let alone two.

'He's left you...' she muses, thoughts flying like sparks from a Catherine wheel. 'You don't *think* there's anyone else...'

I know she's well-meaning, but I need to be alone. I need some time to process all this. I hear Seb on a loop: *What kind of mother pretends to lose it with her kids for attention?* It's worse than the voices online saying the same thing, because he knows me. And leaving us! Leaving *me*. He's... My husband's left me.

'Listen, I'm going to arrange an interview with *Boom!* We need some positive coverage for balance. And I'll get you into the Beach House launch.'

'I can't face it, Alicia.'

'Did you see the book launch photos?' she asks, as if I could miss them: hundreds of photos on multiple feeds and in the middle of them all Beth, surrounded by a gang of other InstaMums, all waving glasses of cheap fizz and laughing uproariously. Confronted with her, smiling with all *my* friends, I feel a fresh slug of anger. How can *she* be up for Influencer of the Year and not me? It's a joke. A fucking joke. That woman, whoever she is, is not my friend.

'Maybe next week,' I say. 'For the interview.'

It's tragic, isn't it, my desperation for a friend? How easily I was seduced by the intimacy of a confidante. How desperate I was for Beth to fill the gaps in my life, the gaps where real friends should be. I used to find it easy to fit in, to be the sort of person that my friends, and my mum, wanted me to be. What happened? *You changed, Cassie, because you wanted something different and they didn't get it, and that's not such a bad thing.* I think of Katya's email, still unacknowledged. How can I reply and pretend my life is as great as she thinks it is when it's a disaster?

'Let me see what Lucy says.'

'Not with Lucy. Anyone but her.' Alicia's never asked me about what happened at the Park Keeper, tactfully tiptoeing around it, waiting for me to share. 'Where are we with Pimp My Bush? Who's biting?' I need something to cheer me up before I ring off.

Pimp My Bush is the pinnacle of Common As Mum's topiary-inspired enterprise, whereby companies pitch to her (and now the rest of us) to decorate our Christmas trees. In exchange we promise daily posts and frequent features in our Stories. Brand research has shown it's one of the most lucrative platforms for selling. After a slow start I had a flurry of enquiries from nursery stores and baby product companies.

Alicia whizzes pages across her iPad.

'There must be some interest in my bush?' I titter flatly. The announcements have started trickling through. Forest Dad's with BoBoLa, this achingly cool Scandi brand. Even his announcement was amazing, all the letters hand-crafted from bits of twigs and leaves and strung through the forest. God, to be involved in something like that. I feel a stirring, a yearning I don't want to acknowledge. I think back to the photo shoot when our eyes locked. I've never trusted him, but maybe I've read him wrong all along. God knows it wouldn't be the first time. He's the only Influencer who's checked in with me. Asked if there's anything he can do.

'Sorry, Cassie. After the last event, well, the offers...' She doesn't need to say it. They've gone away. 'There's always the back-up option: we say you don't want to Pimp Your Bush this year, you want to focus on family, decorate your tree together...'

'Will anyone buy it?'

'Hmm, not your fellow Influencers for sure, but the public might.'

60

#SubtleFighting

Beth

'What are you up to today?' asks Joe. He opens the flap of his manbag, peering inside, checking for something, his phone or travel pass or keys.

We're finally getting along better, the icy chill that descended between us warming, and I don't want to lie so I say casually, 'Just heading to this Beach House thing down by Brighton.'

On my lap, my phone buzzes with activity; Common As Mum's added me to a messaging group with some other Influencers. Quite inexplicably they call it a 'pod' and make plans to 'chat and yin'. I've no idea what they're talking about, but it seems uncool not to know so I don't ask.

He frowns. 'You're going to the Beach House? The new place?' He drops the flap and freezes. 'Great,' he says sarcastically.

'What's wrong?'

'Nothing.' He pats his coat pocket. I hear the crush of his keys. 'Who are you going with?' I check my phone: 6.55.

He's already late. 'Babe?' he calls, pulling the front door open.

'Some Instagram people...' I mumble. The door slams. Phew. I rest my head against the headboard.

'I'm not cool with this, Beth.'

Joe towers at the foot of the bed as Poppy stirs: the noise of the door slamming has woken her up. There goes my shower in peace. *Why does he always do that?* I throw the duvet back and spring up, irritated.

'You wouldn't be, would you, Joe? All the better for you if I'm skulking around at home, with your meatballs, waiting for you to return!'

'What are you talking about?'

I yank on my dressing gown, a silky floaty one, not my enormous post-baby fluffy one; I want an air of elegant insouciance as I rail at him for his failings. 'Well, I've got news for you, there's a whole movement going on out there...' I waft past him towards the kitchen and reach for a mug. I need a brew.

'The mama tribe. Yes, I've heard.'

'Don't mock me.'

'I'm not mocking you. I'm just saying. All you seem to do these days is spend your time obsessing over photos of that crazy rich bird. You used to say it was all nonsense and the people were full of shit.'

This is a total exaggeration. It's only been a few days since I messaged Cassie and she hasn't replied, and I might have checked her profile once or twice. It's hard not to after the fall-out from the interview she did with Boom!

'I didn't use that word.'

'Well, I am. The whole thing's bullshit. It's not *real*, Beth. I don't want Poppy involved in it.'

'What do you mean, *involved*?' I fill the kettle, the water thundering in violently.

'I don't want photos of her online.'

'You're being unreasonable.'

'The internet's full of paedos and pervs and I don't want any of them knocking one off at my daughter in the bath.'

The thought makes me want to vomit. 'Why are you being like this? It was a very tasteful photo.'

'Yeah, that's what they look for. Subtle lighting.'

'You don't like me having something for me.'

'Because I don't want Poppy stark naked all over the internet?'

'Clothed, then?'

'What?' Irritation seeps out of him. 'No! Not at all.'

'It was okay when your mum wanted to sign her up for modelling!'

'That was before she was born, and you said no. I didn't think it would be the worst thing, get a bit of money in her account for when she's older, but *you said* it was tacky. Only now it's okay if she's trussed up like a Disney princess, or a hula girl or whatever, as long as you're getting a freebie or, mostly, getting nothing at all except a bit of self-promotion!' He turns to leave. Pauses. 'You know I still arrive to a chorus of "Peri-doh!" every morning at work?' I snigger. I know I shouldn't. 'That reminds me. We need to return the ring.' He goes into the bedroom. I hear him opening and closing a drawer. There's a scuffly sound like mice, a light scratching of paper as he opens the box, checks it's there.

I block his exit: 'You can't take it back! It was a birthday gift.' I reach out my hands for the box but he snatches it away and into his bag.

'It was an *unwanted* gift. You never wear it. Everyone knows you didn't want it. The bloke at Cartier probably knows you didn't want it. It cost a fortune too.'

'Please, Joe. I do want it.' I suddenly feel quite emotional at the thought of not having it. It's part of our history. 'Besides' – a thought occurs to me – 'it might be worth more now, since it's famous!'

'Listen to yourself, Beth,' he says, pushing past me, and then he is gone. What's worse than a Non-Commitment Ring? No ring at all.

61

#LeadingTheDebate

Cassie

The day has been arranged in silver and grey: the sky, the clouds, the road. Everything is on theme, like a well-thought-out mood board. The sun is blinding, low in the sky, as I head towards the coast. I switch on the radio. The warm tones of the lunchtime host emanate into the car. It's some sort of debate on child labour. Sounds depressing. I move to flick stations and hear my own name bounce over the airwaves. They're talking about me.

'Now this is where it gets interesting!' the presenter says, amusement crinkling the edges of his words. I picture parents tutting as they slide sandwich-laden plates over to sticky-fingered kids. It was in the background of Common As Mum's Stories last night as she arranged fish fingers to read '#epicfail'.

'Cassie Holliday is live-streaming an interview with *Boom!* – we all know her blog, The Happy Hollidays, indeed she's a friend of the show – so this is going out across Facebook, Instagram, *Boom!*'s YouTube channel…

reaching goodness knows how many people…'

Two million across all my channels. The figure is a comfort and a wound.

'And initially she has no idea! Little – what's her name? Or his name, we haven't had it confirmed yet, have we? I'm looking at my producer. No. We still don't know what gender the children are.'

My ears pop. Bubbles form and multiply at the base of my throat as I experience the sensation of climbing higher and higher. The last time I felt like this I was trapped in an air pocket.

'So little Scout is there, in the background, shouting – or we *think* he or she is shouting "We want a horse!" Let's have a listen…'

My heart catches at Scout's sweet voice, the steering wheel slipping in my hands. I hear Romilly saying 'What's that, sweetheart?' and me, trying to distract her: 'And you wouldn't believe—', but it's Marina's voice that cuts over all of us, her command of English unusually clear: 'She's saying she wants a divorce.'

The presenter switches gear just as I do, clutch down and into fifth: 'It makes you pause, doesn't it? Hearing those words from a child? But there's more…'

He resumes the recording. My stomach jars. Rises up to my neck. I swallow it back down before it falls out of my mouth.

'Is it true things haven't been going too well with your husband, Cassie?' Romilly's face was open, highlighter-stick bright and engaging. I wanted to claw her to the ground with my bare hands. I still do.

I hear myself gabbling through the airwaves: 'I can assure

you Sebastian and I are—'

'From you.' Marina's voice is steely and calm. 'She wants a divorce from *you*, Cassie.'

'Yes! Yes!' Birch chimes in. 'Daddy says we need be face-painted! We not oddities!' I close my eyes briefly, remember him jumping up and down, repeating this while I signalled to *Boom!*'s cameraman to stop streaming. But Romilly was sensing blood, and before I could stop her she's asking Marina, 'What's that one saying?'

Marina stared at me coolly, as my world caved in. 'She's saying, Daddy says we need to be emancipated. We are not commodities.' The hammer blow. Thanks, Daddy.

Clouds scutter above me, fast-moving and furious, darkening the sky to slate. My eyes start to fill and my tears blur with something scratchy and hard-edged like glitter. I feel the momentum of the car as I slip into sixth. The audio is still playing but it's blurring in my ears. I catch 'sponsorship' and 'exploitation'. The wind abates briefly, crashing silvered leaves to the floor.

'This is, understandably, provoking a very strong reaction. Let's move to a song and pick this up after the break...'

I keep driving, my arms shaking, enveloped in a sense of déjà vu. This is how they were the last time I flew a plane. I'd forgotten. Finally I see the sign for the Beach House. I brake sharply, swing into the car park, dip my head into the hammock of my arms and cry.

62

#TheBeachHouse

Beth

The Beach House is banging. The staff are all in their twenties and look like they've stepped out of an all-American high school. They scream green juices, clean living and bouncy, vertiginous sex. A day here is just what I need, not at home stewing over my row with Joe, worrying about Cassie. Everyone's talking about her. I want to say to the world: that's not the woman I know. That's not my *friend*, because the more time goes on, the more I think that our friendship was real after all. You can't fake that. She wasn't pretending about the miscarriage or wanting another baby or what a miserable arse her husband is.

I'm mid-train of thought when my heart stops. I see her. I see Cassie emerging from the veranda at the back of the hotel with a PR. She's wearing snake-print leggings with an oversized dark roll neck and enormous resin earrings. She looks thin and cold, her usual sparkle dulled. Forest Dad sees her too, a gasp catching in his throat. The fluttering chatter along the daybeds outside the Beach House doesn't stop but its tempo stalls, as voices lower and heads turn discreetly – and not so discreetly – in Cassie's direction, everyone wondering, *Is that really her?*

The PR walks Cassie down to the lounge area and gestures for her to take the daybed next to mine. Forest Dad – who had been sitting on the sand beside me – is now between us. The easy atmosphere shifts, our conversation stopping. I try to make eye contact with him, but he's busy flicking something off his coat.

Cassie brings a frantic energy to the scene, immediately on her phone. I watch her from the corner of my eye, Forest Dad and I silent, as she scrolls and likes, flits to Twitter and occasionally lifts her phone to her cheek and says 'Alicia?' or simply 'Yes?' in a clipped, urgent tone. She's so close I can smell her body odour, sweet and sour like grapefruit, and see her roots and chapped lips. She looks like Sandy but with all the polish worn off. She looks sad, desperately sad and alone. I feel a wave of responsibility as true and unrelenting as the sea. I want her to know it wasn't contrived, that it was nothing to do with me. And I want to ask her why she didn't tell me about her job, about who she really is? But something stops me. *What if I never knew her at all? What if I've got it wrong as I'm so prone to doing?* And what about Lucy? I'm still furious with her, *but* I do believe that in her own misguided way she thought she was doing me a favour. She wouldn't have thought twice about setting up the account in her own name if it were about her. Is it worth her losing the job, and no doubt the promotion, she's worked so hard for?

'Have you posted anything yet?' one of the hotel's PRs asks again and I feel flames of embarrassment: at my general

SoMe ineptitude and because Cassie is witness to it. *She must know that I'm a fraud? She must see that I don't have a blooming clue what I'm doing?*

'Oh! No! Sorry!' The other Influencers make it look so easy, the casual placing of objects on a throw or a rustic table, but you need a degree in this stuff. I found an online tutorial but got lost after a few minutes: texture, squares, direction of travel. I try to capture the flickers from the fire pits dug out along the beach in the ailing November light.

'That won't work in this light.' Her voice startles me: familiar and foreign, honey laced with hostility. She flicks a hairband off her wrist and ties her hair up, pursing her lips as she looks around. 'Try the silhouette of kids playing over there... or if all else fails, order Prosecco and clink some glasses.'

'I'm driving,' I say slowly, my pulse loud in my ears, drowning out the sea. I want to ask if she got my message – details of a therapist local to her that Russell recommended – but not here, with everyone listening.

'We won't *drink* it,' she says as Forest Dad looks at me quizzically. They smile at each other, the small interaction between Cassie and me shifting the dynamic between them, as though they're my parents in the middle of a spat and I've announced I want to be an astronaut.

'If you accepted every glass of cheap fizz offered to you in this game you'd be in trouble,' Forest Dad says, and nods his head towards the shepherd's hut behind us where Holistic Flo's having a spa treatment.

Cassie follows his gaze, a wounded expression crossing her face, as though she didn't expect Holistic Flo to be here.

This is her first public appearance since leaving rehab. She turns her head back and we lock eyes. My stomach jolts. Even without speaking it feels like a tunnel of words – apologies, explanations, acceptances – flurry between us. I didn't conjure our connection; it was real, it's still there.

'How are you, Cassie?' asks Forest Dad gently, a hand on her daybed, and I feel frustrated I didn't ask first.

We continue to look at each other – questions now, each of us trying to figure out the other – before the moment fractures and her attention shifts to him. She can't seem to find the words, emitting a long exhale while she shakes her head. I feel a stab of panic; she's going to cry and then I'll have to reveal everything, right here, on the beach, in front of Forest Dad – *Because any part that Mardy Mum has played in Cassie looking and feeling like this isn't right* – but in the intensity of that look my thoughts have become disordered and I need to pin them down and draw them back into the right order, just like the times I've tried to speak to Lucy about Mum. Why does my brain fragment like this when I need it the most?

'Hiya, guys' says Common As Mum joining us and I look up, frustrated. Middle Class Mummy's a little way along the beach trying to catch Common As Mum's attention, her wave hanging in the air. Cassie's eyes grow stormy, her smile a grimace. She yanks off her boots and socks and strides to the sea.

'Rude,' says Common As Mum and I tut loudly.

'She's clearly upset,' I say, my voice sharp. How can no one see how much pain Cassie's in? It was so clear in the interview, so clear in real life.

'She's always like that. I only wanted a quick word.'

Common As Mum rounds on me from up high. 'I've posted three times and you've not liked any of them.'

'I thought I had? Were two from last night? I liked them this morning,' I say, trying to see past her, wondering if Cassie realizes she left her phone here.

'Then you might as well not like them at all!' She throws her hands up, looking to Forest Dad for confirmation. 'Your response time needs to be under two minutes. That's the point of these pods. Beat the algorithm. I thought you wanted in, but if you're not interested...' She drops her 't's less when she's cross, I notice.

'Heyyyyy!' Forest Dad calls to Middle Class Mummy. His deep voice is like a clap of thunder. Down by the water's edge, Cassie looks up. I try to meet her eyes, to recapture the moment between us, but Middle Class Mummy obscures my view, scuttling over the sand like a crab. 'Nice wrap dress!' he says, as she approaches. 'Lovely print.' She blooms under his gaze and I feel a creeping sensation I'm immediately embarrassed by.

'Thanks! I've not seen you in—'

'I know, I know. Terrible shame. Listen, Common As Mum needs some fresh blood in her pod, me and Beth aren't cutting the mustard...' He steers Middle Class Mummy next to Common As Mum, to furious looks from the latter.

He proffers a hand and pulls me up effortlessly. I avoid Common As Mum's stare. 'Hold this a sec...' He shrugs off his coat, which has a thick borg lining and faux-fur trim; the hood looks like you would need to check for small mammals nesting in it before you put it on. 'It's from the new range,' he says as he catches me appraising it, and I see the little neon orange FD logo circling the cuffs. He picks up a blanket from the daybed and ties it around his waist, crossing over the ends and securing them around his neck. In one smooth gesture Poppy's out of her bouncer and in his makeshift baby carrier.

'You've done this before!' I laugh and he gives me a sorrowful look: 'Too many times,' he replies. He extends his arms and I help him shrug his coat back on.

I turn to the sea and watch Cassie as she digs her toes into the sand and flicks it back up, her hands in her jumper pockets. Occasionally she glances up with a look I can't read; I can't tell if she's looking at us or the hotel behind us.

Forest Dad steers me up the beach, away from Cassie, his hand like a hot water bottle on the small of my back.

'Let's see if we're needed inside,' he says. *Five minutes*, I think, *and I'll find Cassie*.

'Which room are you in?' he asks.

'I'm not staying.' I have to get back to Joe. I realize then how little I want to.

'Didn't fancy bringing the contents of your home for one night?' he laughs. I wonder where his children are. Perhaps with grandparents. '*I* have a room' – he leans in close enough that I can smell his hair, heady as a pine forest – 'if you wanted to put it on Stories? Sounds bonkers, but all the big names are doing it. Boardroom Boss Mum got over 20,000 views yesterday.' 20,000 views! A mind-boggling figure, definitely one for my 'media pack', but I need to speak to Cassie first. I need to explain.

I look back down to the shoreline. I scan the beach, the daybeds, the fire pits. Nothing. 'Can you see Cassie?' I ask.

He shrugs, standing taller as he cranes his neck. 'She was probably in and out, collected her fee and went.'

My heart sinks. If Cassie's gone, perhaps I should too. If I leave now we'll be home for Poppy's witching hour, rather than in the car. Although I could feed her here and hope she sleeps on the journey… Forest Dad looks at me expectantly, an arm extended in the direction of the hotel, Poppy happy in her carrier.

'Just a quick look,' I say. Nothing inappropriate in that, is there?

As we pass the shepherd's hut the door creaks and swings open with a clatter. Holistic Flo emerges in a Hawaiian-print bikini with a long waffle dressing gown slung over her shoulders like a cape. She doesn't seem to feel the cold as a PR appears and starts taking photos of us all chatting. We both tell her how great she looks, really glowing. Do I imagine it, or are we each eager to leave, to be alone together again?

'It's the vit drips!' she purrs. 'Let me give you my code…'

Forest Dad's room is enormous. Sea-facing. The centrepiece is a huge bed styled like a giant piece of driftwood. 'Emperor size…' Forest Dad winks. 'Hand-carved…' he adds proudly, as though he carved it himself. It feels like we've been washed up in our own paradise hideaway. I can't resist sinking on to it, bouncing on its centre. Tiredness clouds my eyes as I flop back, sweeping my hands over acres of brushed cotton.

'It's so… *big*,' I say wondrously. Worried I might nod off, I sit up sharply. Forest Dad's at the foot of the bed, his phone pointed in my direction.

'Here I am with Mardy Mum' – he assumes a low voice – 'checking out the bedrooms at the Beach House.' He walks towards me with the phone still raised. 'And as she says, *it's so big*!' He pans the phone round to where Poppy's suspended from his chest. 'Here's little Pippa – Poppy! Sorry, Poppy!' – he pulls a sort of scrambled-egg face at the camera – 'in a sling I fashioned from a blanket. As we say at FD Forest School, "Craft it real good!"' He croons the last bit, stealing the tune from Salt-N-Pepa. Poppy's arms fly up as he bops around. He keeps filming as he walks to the balcony. 'Now, what do we have over here…?'

I can see that, to Joe, Forest Dad's Stories from the Beach House might look a bit… odd. He puts it less eloquently: 'Why does some knobber have my daughter strapped to his chest while you're checking out the bed in his hotel room?'

'He's not some knobber, he's Forest Dad. My friend.'

'You only met him today… Didn't you?' The vein above his right eye bulges.

'Yes, but we've been in touch. Just via messages!' Joe puts his hands on his hips. 'He's been very sweet, actually, asking if I have any questions, or—'

'You are joking? Sweet? This bloke's a predator. Look at him.' I've never seen him so angry.

'He's a *widower*, Joe. That poor man has experienced more tragedy and heartbreak than you can even *imagine*. You're being the knobber. He's alright.'

'Trading off his dead wife makes him alright?'

'He doesn't trade off her. He never mentions her. Or his kids. Out of respect.'

'He probably doesn't have any kids, Beth. Or a dead wife. This is what I find so frustrating. You don't *know* these people. Just because you've seen them online doesn't mean you can trust what they say.'

'You don't know them either.' I move to him, take his hands in mine. 'It's mad, I know, but I really believe... this social media world... it can be a place for good, in the right hands. And it's given me something I've lost since I had Poppy. Be on my side, please?'

63

#Scoop

Cassie

I park the car round the back of the Big House, in a copse of silver birches. I don't want to go inside and face whatever mess Ruby's made with the twins and, even worse, see their sad little faces when they see Seb isn't with me. They know something's amiss. 'When can we see Daddy?' they ask, over and over.

I don't think I've ever felt as lonely as I did in that moment on the beach, as Beth and Forest Dad walked away together. I needed to move away from Common As Mum, in case I confronted her and embarrassed myself further. I hadn't expected them to leave, the atmosphere between us beginning to thaw and settle. I scrambled up the sand dunes behind a row of beach huts and sat among the long grass, grateful my tears were hidden.

I watch them together on my phone, in his Stories, in his room. Joe must be *very* relaxed. I've never been sure about Forest Dad. So why did I feel like I'd been unzipped and scooped out when they left? Or when Holistic Flo joined Common As Mum and Middle Class Mummy, taking my space on the daybed?

I've not heard from her since she went into rehab. The three of them buzzed around, networking, chatting to PRs, like I used to.

It was so stilted when I returned – Beth and Forest Dad safely inside – to get my bag and phone so I could get out of there. My space is being filled, virtually and physically. The loneliness is acute. What would it take to fix things with Seb? What would I need to do?

I answer FaceTime to Alicia. She groans and emits a 'Fuck, man' by way of hello. It's unusual to hear her swear. She favours an LA patter of big smiles and positivity rather than profanities. 'Have you heard?'

'Heard what?' I say, but it's not really a question because I don't want to know. I used to fly transatlantic every week and I had twin babies, but I never knew it was possible to feel this tired.

'Did you write a new baby media plan?'

I can't answer, my face frozen, my brain working like a juggernaut: *How could anyone know about that? It's not possible. It was only on my phone. I didn't tell anyone...*

'*Boom!* have it,' she continues. 'They're going to post it. So you had a...? You were pregnant?' On the screen her face folds with sympathy, but I don't reply. I'm tapping my fingers over my face, my temples, my cheeks, my brow. *How? How could* Boom! *have this?*

'It was only on my phone,' I say, blood noisy in my ears. 'And I always have it, I've not left it anywhere, I've not...' I tail off, picturing my phone on the daybed at the Beach House, how it had moved to one of the small cubed tables when I returned.

It was one of them. It must be one of them.

64

#ForBetterOrWorse

Cassie

'Cassie!'

Seb's hand flies to his mouth and for a second I think – *she's here* – but his lips curl to a grimace and I take in his stained shirt, the dirty plates and cups littering the room. He's embarrassed. I knew he was sleeping here but it's still sad to see it: the tangle of sheets on the sofa, his shaving brush by the dirty sink.

'What's going on?' I ask, moving quickly, pulling back the fusty, heavy drapes and opening the windows, to stop myself gagging on the stench.

'Nothing. I'm fine!' he snaps, his eyes proud and brutish.

'Why are you living like this?' The beauty of the architecture is in decay; fragments of plaster fleck the sad, moth-eaten carpets. His father's papers and thick-spined legal books are stacked in precarious piles. I lift a dirty cup and a huge spider scuttles from under the saucer. 'Christ, Seb!'

'What choice do I have?'

'It was your decision to go.' I sink on to a Chesterfield sofa, quickly rising as something slides against my bottom. It's a beer bottle, a tied end of salami squashed in its neck. 'I need to tell you something. Someone's got hold of... a media plan... from when I wanted to have a baby...' I drag each word out, mortification coming in waves.

'A *media plan*? For a *new baby*?'

'Yes, Seb, I know.' I put my head in my hands.

'Goodness,' he says, sitting down beside me. 'Are you okay? You look—'

'It was on my phone. I left it, briefly, at an event. One of the others must've got into it somehow. Sent the plan to themselves or took a photo of it or something.'

'Can't you deny it? It could be anybody's!'

'It's quite distinct.' I wince.

'Cassie!' He has fire in his eyes. His eureka moment. 'It's Marina! If you're sure it's from your phone, it must be someone with access to the Shed! You have that thing glued to you most of the time.'

'Yes, but I did leave it—'

He waves me away. 'Ruby? What would be in it for her?' There seems little point asking him if he's been having an affair with Ruby. The idea that she would find him attractive right now seems laughable. 'That American woman you work with?'

I shake my head. 'She's never been over. And she's got too much to lose.'

'It's Marina. It has to be! She wants to drive us apart. She wants you and the kids in the Big House at any cost!' His hair – no longer quaffed to perfection – falls on to his face like an impassioned concert pianist's. 'That interview.

I shouldn't have said those things to the twins, I was cross, it was in the heat of the moment, but saying it like that!' I see some kindness in his eyes. 'She's totally blown it with Radford.' Ah, of course.

I wish now I hadn't told him. Of course it's not Marina. Marina created Cassie Holliday. She's been more like a mother to me than my own mum. She apologized after the interview and I get it. She's upset with me, about how I've been lately, but she didn't understand it was being broadcast *live*, what the implications would be. She wouldn't try to destroy me. What would be in it for her? It's thanks to me she gets to spend so much time with the twins.

Seb begins pacing the room. I can't leave my husband here like this, in this quiet tomb, burying himself alive in the past. This is my children's father. I gather up his crumpled shirts and pants.

'Come home, Seb.'

65

#AperolBitch

Beth

I wearily push open the door to the cocktail bar. Alicia's already inside on a bar stool, bartender hovering like a moth, clearly trying to initiate a conversation, which Alicia's rebutting with her tablet and cocktail.

'Thank you so much for this,' I repeat as she outlines brands she's spoken to, opportunities conjured, events I've accepted and declined: 'Don't bother with that one, no budget, but *do* do this, and say yes to that and *then* they'll offer you...' My head spins as much with the volume of information as with the cocktails. Seeing my near-empty glass, Alicia nods at the attentive bartender, who prepares another round even though Alicia's barely touched hers.

'Honestly, it's nothing. Anything for Lucy's sister.' She smiles but it doesn't reach her eyes.

'What's that look for? You guys are okay, right...? Lucy's okay?' This is the longest we haven't spoken. It feels like my arm's been chopped off. *A gangrenous arm*, whispers the betrayed part of me.

Alicia recovers, beams: 'She's all good. I think. I mean, she looks fine. I've tried to hang out with her heaps of times, but she's not interested.'

Lucy can be weird, I think, feeling bad that I judged Alicia so harshly before. As soon as I reached out to her, she set this up. I've been floundering on social media, I don't know what I'm doing, and I feel a responsibility to make Mardy Mum a positive space: I want it to mean something.

'It's weird, sometimes it feels like we broke up, you know?' She laughs and scoops up her glass, her eyes thoughtful. I know exactly what that feels like. 'So your campaign idea, #BeingABronagh, it's got legs, but you need to pick up your engagement first.' She doesn't need to say it – it's tailed off since I've taken over, the likes and comments and new followers plateauing. 'You need to ramp up the periwhat side of things, your relationship challenges since you've had a baby, that's what's drawn people to your account, that's what your followers want to know more about.'

'I can't do that. Joe would hate it.'

'I see that.' She nods, drumming her fingers. 'The thing is, once you get your stats back up, that's when you can really start to effect change...'

Another two rounds on and despite my best intentions we've inevitably moved on to Cassie. I've been trying to explain our friendship to Alicia.

'So, what was in it for her...' she mumbles to herself, her finger tracing circles on the brushed-steel bar.

'I don't think anything was *in it* for her, we were friends.

Really. Straight up. Just... friendship in it for her.' My iterations fail to shift the dubious look on Alicia's face.

'But then why aren't you friends now...?' She waits for me to fill in the blank. 'She knew, right, that you were Mardy Mum? So what's the problem?' More blanks, more expectation of something juicy, because unless you know that I didn't set up the account, that I was in the dark, that we became friends not because of likes or followers or brand opportunities but because we just clicked, then none of this really makes sense.

'No, she didn't,' I confess. Grateful to share this with someone other than Joe. Someone I can trust to not dig around and make things difficult for Lucy if the truth came out. 'She had no idea. If she did, she would never have told me...' Alicia gasps and leans forward and I stop myself just in time. I can't tell Alicia about Cassie's miscarriage or the reality of her marriage. '...stuff. She would never have told me stuff.'

Alicia sits back, her bar stool wobbling. 'Sorry, Beth, I don't mean to get too personal, I just...' She sighs. Twists the stem of her glass. 'Things are going so badly wrong for Cassie and I want to fix it for her. It's my job, to make her look *better*...' Her face drops and I see the defeat in her eyes. She looks exhausted; so invested, emotionally. 'If there's anything you know that could help, that could make the public see her differently? More sympathetically? I want people to know *the real* Cassie Holliday.'

66

#LightBulbMoment

Cassie

I'm back on the plane, but it's different this time: I'm at the top of the air pocket. Beepers are sounding, the din crashing in my ears, and I know what's going to happen next; I know I will be safe but I also know it will be terrifying and I can't stop it, it is out of my control but something I must move forward with to keep everyone on the plane safe. I glance to my right, to Katya, my co-pilot, but she's gone. Beth's there instead, smiling. I gasp, but before I've had time to process it she morphs, her face twisting and stretching: Marina. Ruby. Holistic Flo. Boardroom Boss Mum. Elen. Twisting and stretching and changing, and while I stare in shock at their morphing faces, all the different versions of my co-pilot do the same thing – they try to grab the controls.

I force my face forward, into the milky sky, my knuckles white as they grip to maintain control of the plane as it climbs higher and higher. I must keep going, knowing that any second now we will hit the top of the pocket; that the only way then is down, down, down and my chest will be battered with the screams of others, but I will know what they do not: this isn't how it ends for me.

Suddenly I'm a passenger again, the twins beside me, an alarm sounding. I know this sequence: the empty seats, the suspended seat belts. I know how this bit ends: me, alone in the wreckage. I force myself awake, dragging myself out of my dream and into that horrible state between sleeping and waking. I clamp my eyes shut until I'm fully awake and the dream has receded and there's no chance I can get caught between those two worlds.

My sheets are drenched through, clinging to me like seaweed. I lie in bed. Finally, here it is, my light-bulb moment. I picture the light-bulb emoji flashing over my bed. I need to save my family. Nothing else matters. I find the details that Beth sent all those weeks ago and bash out an email before I can change my mind.

67

#RainbowsAndMagic

Beth

When I wake, my first thought is: it's light outside. My second: is Poppy okay? And then I realize... *She's slept through*. A weight lifts, floating upwards.

My jubilant feeling lasts all morning. At 10 a.m. I put Poppy down for a nap and am amazed when she simply flops her arms out and closes her eyes. I take a quick photo. I'm sure my followers will be pleased for me: 'I've cracked it!' I write. I punch out a stream of emojis: fist bumps, high fives, smiley faces with sunglasses on, champagne glasses clinking, rainbows and add '#shesleptthrough #alltheemojis #nailingit'.

I make myself a brew, humming along to my favourite indie-rock playlist. Wiggle my head and my hips as I bop around the kitchen. Everything feels different. With sleep I am restored: ready to face the world, to work through things with Joe. Maybe even to talk to Lucy. It's Friday. I wonder if I turned up at the pub what sort of reception I'd get from the hypno-babes? Maybe Bronagh's seen my posts? Heard about the campaign? I know, I'll surprise Joe! I'll take Poppy to his office, we can grab some lunch. He was on at me to do it when he first went back to work.

While Poppy's napping I apply some make-up and run straighteners through my hair so it swings glossily over my shoulders. I try on a dress a company sent me, take a snap and load it to Instagram. Suddenly I worry: what if Joe goes to the gym at lunch? I catch sight of myself in the mirror and smile as the phone rings. For the first time in a long time I feel like *myself*.

'Mark Davies.'

'Hi, Mark. It's Beth, is—'

'Beth!' I picture him leaning back in his chair, legs cocked wide. 'How are you? We're all following you, we love keeping up with your escapades!' In the background hubbub I hear a ripple of 'Peri-what!' I hadn't noticed Joe's work mates following me. 'You've just missed him. He was so anxious about being late that he left early.'

'Sorry?'

'Poppy's appointment. At the hospital. The weekly thing. *You know*… whatchamacallit… the dairy allergy thing?'

I look out through the glass, along the canal, at the throng of life outside while I'm in here, alone. So, so alone. I try to swallow but my throat feels like a balloon's in there, slowly expanding, filling all the space I need to breathe…

'Beth, are you still there?'

'That's great,' I manage, shakily, hanging up. There's a hissing in my ears as all light and excitement slowly escapes until there's nothing left. I zip backwards on to the bed, deflated. There is no appointment. I cut out dairy for a few weeks to see if it helped and it didn't make a blind bit of difference.

Where is he? And why's he lying to work, and to me? I call him but his phone's off. My brain pings: Find My Phone! I charge to the lounge, pounce on Joe's iPad. It's a cliché to say my fingers are trembling and my heart is pumping as I input his passcode, but it's true. Swipe. Swipe. Find My Phone. Blooming hell, technology is wonderful. I hold my hand against my stomach and try to inhale large gulps of air to calm the rising panic. *Where. Is. He?*

I have a sense of being here before, sitting on the edge of the bath staring at a white stick and waiting for a blue line – two blue lines – to appear. It's a magic moment waiting for the results of a pregnancy test, the whole course of your life possibly about to be changed by a second thin blue line. This is the very opposite of magic. This is the death of something, waiting for a flashing dot to reveal the location of your boyfriend when he is, at the very least, somewhere he ought not to be. Like Epping Station. *Epping Station. Why?* My mind flashes: undulating waves of glossy black hair, thick lashes, tanned skin, teeth brighter than the sun. Jazz. It's got to be Jazz. She lives near his parents, doesn't she?

For the first time in her short life I prod Poppy awake, snorting at the irony. Snow begins to fall outside, thick, heavy flakes. Great.

'Wake up, Popsicle. We need to find Daddy!' From the look she gives me, my faux-sunny demeanour isn't fooling anybody. 'Let's see what he's up to, shall we!'

68

#Broken

Cassie

'Sebastian...' Jenna waves her pen in his direction, tracing small circles in the air that reflect her neat chignon. At the top of her pad she's written: *Sebastian and Cassie Holliday – 20 November – 10.00 a.m.* Her script reflects her: elegant, clipped, economic. '...you say things started to change in September?'

Seb shuffled in here with me willingly, agreeing we need to rebuild our marriage, to put our family first, but has so far struggled to answer any of Jenna's questions with any lucidity, *umm*ing and *ahh*ing and sitting instead with the air of a boy sent to the headmaster's office. I'm amazed, not for the first time, how he eloquently led the debating team at university but is unable to articulate a single felt emotion.

'Maybe it was sooner' – his eyes draw in and he rubs the bridge of his nose – 'but September, that's when I started to realize...'

I wait for him to fill the pause, to confess that he doesn't like parenthood and it's impacting our marriage and our family life and he needs to be fixed, so that our broken family can be put back together. He's ashamed – I get it – but we need to discuss it openly so we can move on.

'…that Cassie was…'

I turn the left side of my face to him slowly.

'…struggling…'

My eyes narrow.

'…mentally.'

He exhales loudly, rubs his eyes, cups his hands over his nose, not looking at me.

'That's why I'm here. She needs help and she was adamant I come.'

The benign smile freezes on my face. 'What?' I spit. 'Me? *I* need help?' I turn to Jenna. 'I'm trying to rectify the situation *he's* created.'

'You have no idea what she's like to live with. The constant photos, the pressure to be camera-ready, for everything to be perfect, for me to be a catalogue dad and the kids… She doesn't even call them by their real names, she won't let them wear the things they want to – normal clothes – because they're not "on brand", as she's so fond of saying… She's lost her grip on reality. As soon as one of us steps out of line or doesn't play along, she erupts…'

'Seb' – I am absolutely determined to not lose my cool – 'if I'm "erupting" it's because I'm under intense stress: you, the kids, work. I don't want the twins to feel they have to follow contrived social norms, like I did growing up. Is that *so bad*? And the rest of it, I do that stuff because it's my job now. Since I can't do my old one. My proper one. I'm a pilot,' I tell Jenna. 'I used to fly for Horizon Air, before…'

I want to tell her the truth. I want her to know that I didn't choose all this, that I'm in a desperate situation. But to do so I'll need to say it aloud. The thing I'm most ashamed of. The idea creeps over my skin, predatory and violating. What if she tells someone? What if she breaks her vow of confidentiality? But I'm so tired of pretending. So over being the cheerleader for this family, trying to keep things together and letting myself fall apart in the meantime. And that's how Seb sees this. That it's *my* problem. *I'm mental.* You know what they say: behind every crazy woman is a dickhead man (that's what I should've got printed on those damn T-shirts). I take a deep breath.

'If you want to talk about the start, it was the day I gave birth. He hates having a family. He...' I've promised myself I'll be honest in here. I owe it to my children, I owe it to my marriage, but most of all, I owe it to myself. So I say the words. The words I've only shared once before, with Beth. 'My husband hates his life.' *And it feels like my fault. It feels like I'm not good enough. It feels like Elen was right.*

I expect a shudder of shame to rock my core as it always does when I think of Seb's feelings towards our family, but today, with Jenna here in this airy room, I feel a light buzz at the front of my head. Not the tension sort I'm familiar with – this one feels good, like a release.

'That's ridiculous!' Seb blurts. Now the spotlight's on him, he looks uncomfortable. He interlaces his hands in his lap, the tips red as they press into the backs of his hands.

I know I shouldn't push him, but we only have an hour. 'You don't hate having to make the kids' breakfast, rather than lying in bed? Or helping to tidy up when you get home?'

'Well, yes, I don't love that stuff.' He wrings his hands. 'But who does? The Lego everywhere, felt and pom-poms stuck to my shoes... the *noise*, the fighting over toys...'

'That's family life, Seb! All those little things are the things that make up a family.' – '*Oh come on!*' he interjects, but I persevere – 'You can't hate those things. Those things are *us*.'

'Fine, family life. I hate family life!' His voice comes out in a shout and he throws his hands up in the air. 'I *love* the children' – he stares at Jenna for emphasis – 'but if I'm being honest, and I know that's what this is about...'

'It's a safe space,' Jenna nods encouragingly.

'Right...' he says. I know therapy speak makes him cringe. 'If I'm being honest, I love the children but no, I don't *enjoy* it.' He pauses as if he's only just realized this himself. 'Family life. The restrictions... the compromises... they don't come naturally to me. I don't... I didn't realize what it would be *like*.'

I feel stunned. Almost winded. I knew it was true, I wanted him to admit it, but hearing it ring out in his own voice makes me want to jump on his back and punch and kick him over and over and over.

'I just want my life back,' he finishes, head in his hands.

'Are you joking?' I snap my head to Jenna. 'I've given up a job I love, financial independence and... *bladder control*... and *he* wants *his* life back!'

He reaches for my hands but I pull back and he hangs on to the tips of my fingers as if he's dangling from a skyscraper and only I can save him. 'Do you remember how we were, Cassie? Do you remember when we used to travel and have freedom and sex and fun?'

'Yes! It was when I had a decent job and my own money. That's who you want me to be, isn't it, Carefree Cassie? You want me to be who I used to be, even though you've taken that away from me!' I realize: all our good memories – the moments that make me think this relationship is worth saving – they're all in the past.

'Isn't it better to want you to be *you* rather than someone else? Like you want me to be Forest Dad or Mr Happy Hollidays?'

'Forest Dad?'

'I've seen the pally comments you leave on each other's posts.'

'It's work! I don't want you to be like Forest Dad, believe me,' I say.

He directs his attention to Jenna. 'There you go. They've fallen out or something, some lovers' tiff, she's been skulking around like a lovesick puppy for weeks.'

That he's noticed startles me. 'It's not Forest Dad I've fallen out with, it's a friend. A female friend,' I clarify.

'Those social media women you fraternize with are not your friends, they're your competitors. Look how they all jumped in on your app thing.'

'Not this friend, she wasn't like that. She was different. Or at least I thought she was…' The tears that I can't summon for my marriage come unbidden when I think of Beth. Seb says nothing, brooding silently. I don't want to think about Beth, it still feels too sensitive, a paper cut that won't heal.

This was my idea, but it doesn't make it any less excruciating. I stare at the rug. 'We could still have sex.'

'Ha!' We both redden. Neither of us are the sort to discuss sex with each other, let alone a stranger.

'What? It's not my fault we don't have sex!'

'Do you remember the last time we did?' Seb retorts. I don't. It was a long time ago, I know that much. 'She checked her social media mid-deed.' (*I married a man who refers to sex as 'doing the deed'. For fuck's sake.*) 'She was, you know' – Jenna's face betrays no hint of knowing – 'on all fours...' I'm too embarrassed to check for Jenna's reaction. I look at Seb. Sweat pools at his temples but he's starting to look quite alive at the prospect of sharing this, as if it's something he's been wanting to get off his chest. 'She didn't realize I could see, because I was sort of...'

'Seb!' I bat his hands down. 'She knows what you mean!'

'...but she slipped her phone out from under the pillow and checked her stats!' he booms. '*That's* why we don't do it any more!' He's practically panting.

My face curls up like cling film. He's right. Oh God. I was worried I'd missed the Chardonnay slot. Was that the last time we did it? How could I not remember? Words tumble from my mouth before I have a chance to think...

'What about the way you look at Ruby?' I shoot back. 'All the appreciative little smiles and pats on the shoulder. Why don't we talk about that? Maybe we'd have sex if you weren't drooling over our babysitter!'

'*Ruby?*'

'I'm not stupid, Seb, I've seen the way you look at her!' I'm indignant, the shamed woman resurrected, blazing with vitriol.

'If I'm looking at her appreciatively it's because I'm pleased *someone* is doing something constructive with the twins!'

'Oh right, yeah, it's about the twins, not fantasizing about you two shagging over our kitchen table with her, bloody, knitting needles poking you in the eye!'

He shakes his head, widening his eyes and raising his eyebrows at Jenna as if to say, *Do you see what I mean?* But Jenna is a woman and she will know, as I do, that we women have a sixth sense for these things. If I've picked up on...

'Ruby's gay, Cassie. Her girlfriend's been offered a job in Canada and they're deciding whether to relocate.'

'Gay? Don't be ridiculous!' If either of us were going to notice if someone were gay it would be me, the cool(ish) woke one, not Radford over here.

'She told me.'

'When?'

'When we got back from the Otter's Paw that time, after you disappeared.'

'I told you, I went to the bathroom.'

'For half an hour?'

Jenna's head moves between us like an umpire officiating a tennis match.

'I was annoyed,' Seb continues. 'You'd spent the whole meal on your phone, filming that couple. You say you're going to use the facilities, gone for ages, and then I saw them leaving – Forest Dad and your City chum – and I got it: you're embarrassed by me. How many times have I asked for an introduction to her? I know it's childish, but I left. And when I got back Ruby had just heard the news and we had a good old chat about it.'

'Enjoy yourself, did you?' Not my best comeback, but I'm still reeling a little from the revelation that Ruby's gay. All the time I've wasted worrying about her and Seb.

'Yes, I did. It felt good to give someone counsel for once.

To feel the tiniest bit valued. Your work's a mess and you never ask for my help.'

'I shouldn't need to *ask* for support!'

'You're a fine one to talk about support,' he says and his tone changes and he goes quite sullen, his head drooping. He has an air of defeat about him and I feel sadness, I suppose, that this is where we are after five years of marriage.

'Sebastian?' prompts Jenna, pen poised.

He raises his head. 'You asked when this started? It wasn't September. And it wasn't when the twins were born. It was when my father died. She's never understood – or tried to understand – my grief. It's been an *inconvenience* to her that I've not been on form. That I've not been in the mood for photo shoots or picnics in the woods.'

This is where I should bring up my miscarriage, I suppose. But I can't rip off the parcel tape. I can't unpackage my feelings around the baby I lost and Seb's response and how the look that crossed his face when I told him what had happened damaged our marriage more than any amount of support from me could save it. I opt to leave it where it is: someplace far away.

'Seb, that's unfair! I just don't think that grief should be an excuse for... not doing the washing-up! Or playing with your kids! I think you should focus on the positives...' – *My God, I sound just like Beth* – '...your family, your healthy children – rather than wallowing in self-pity because your dad died...' But my indignation snags on something: didn't I sympathize with Beth that she could feel sad about her mum not being here even though she had a baby, but I can't do that for my husband? That's normal though, right? People are always nicer to their friends than their spouses?

'*I do love the twins*. I feel constantly guilty that I'm not good enough for them. That they deserve better, they deserve someone who it – parenthood – comes more naturally to. Like that blasted Forest Dad, I suppose. Like my own father.'

His voice cracks on 'father' and he hastily reaches into his suit jacket for his handkerchief. His shoulders collapse, like a tent in a storm, as he's engulfed by chest-wracking sobs. I survey the floor, cowed. In all our time together I've never seen Seb cry. Not when Charles died. Not when the twins were hooked up in Special Care. Why have I never thought of that as odd before? Jesus. I didn't bring him here to break him. This isn't what I wanted. I want to scoop him up and put him back together, go back to the Seb he was this morning. I knew where I was with that Seb. I put my hand on his back.

'Seb, the twins adore you. It's... parenthood is *hard*... *marriage* is hard...' I think back to what I said to Beth once. 'But that doesn't mean we should give up trying.'

69

#DontLookNow

Beth

On the Tube I try to collect myself. I need a distraction. Past Woodford I get some patchy signal. I repeatedly drag down my feed to refresh it, breathe a sigh of relief as notifications collate just as we rocket back into a tunnel. There are *loads* of comments: '*Smug bitch*' is the first one I see. '*What a dick*' is the next. '*I used to love this account but lately it's pants.*' '*Don't get me started on the teddy bears' picnic *hotdog emoji**' It goes on and on.

Tears prick my eyes, panic escalating as we shoot into another tunnel. I thought they would be pleased for me. Even as I say it to myself, I realize how wrong I've got it. Like @StressedOutMummy539 says, '*Who cares that she got a free dress? Not what I come here for.*' Alicia was right. They want unfiltered Mardy Mum. They want humiliation and sadness and failing at life. They don't want someone who's nailing it.

While I've been on the Tube, the dot has stopped. At Joe's parents' house. He wouldn't do it there? I feel sick to my stomach as I make the familiar walk from the Tube. It's snowing more heavily here. I skid on some frosty patches as I walk with Poppy, making me more jumpy and alert.

Gossy Gloria thinks leaving a key under the mat is clever subterfuge. Perhaps she's right: what self-respecting intruder would look under the mat these days? I wheel Poppy in over the threshold, gently listing the tip of the buggy and quietly closing the door.

At the living room door I throw my hand to my mouth. The television's paused, a frozen blur of a body on the screen. A trail of Joe's clothes leads to the high back of the sofa. His tie. His shirt. His belt. His trousers are draped over a peach-upholstered pouffe, the hems tickling a row of tassels.

I freeze, my heart thudding in my chest. It feels like a thousand tiny butterflies are jangling in my ribcage. It feels like there's no space for them to go to. What's seen cannot be unseen, isn't that the expression? And I do not want to *see*. Seeing will require action. This is different to squares on a grid. This is real life. The implications feel enormous. This is Poppy's dad. We're bound together forever, whatever his indiscretions, and perhaps... perhaps I've played a part in this? Perhaps this is my fault?

I stumble backwards. I have to go. This is too much. I can't cope with the stress of this; it will trigger my anxiety, there's no way it won't, and what then – how can I be a single mum to Poppy if I go back to a place where I can't walk down main roads?

No, I need to go back to the flat, where I'm oblivious to all this. Joe must never know that I know. I'll have to make my peace with it. I can do that. I can pretend. People can live very fulfilled pretend lives. Just look at Cassie. Okay, maybe Cassie's a bad example.

I reach the door and exit quickly, silently, hand on my stomach and heart in my throat.

70

#Snowflakes

Cassie

The sky's thick, a greyish-white, the snow fall hypnotic. The twins stop mid-run as they fly past the large doors facing on to the garden, performing an about-turn.

'Mummy, is it Christmas today? Is it Christmas?' They pause, eyes wide and hopeful, Scout in an Elsa dress and Birch in racing-driver overalls. What can you do?

'I'm afraid not,' I smile, ruffling their hair. 'It's almost Advent, so not long.'

I make a mental note to dig out the Advent calendar. It's not *just* a calendar, but strings of hand-stitched stockings in thick red and cream felt with gold piping. Little sprigs of holly hang from some, teeny bells from others, which chime and chink as I retrieve them from the loft. Its GML is like 28,000 and it attracts reams of comments tagging in friends and saying 'We should do this' with pointy-up arrows and thumbs-up emojis. Not that they would ever have *any* chance of recreating it since it was a bespoke design and handmade; the craftsmanship couldn't be bettered if it were made by actual elves. I dread to think how much Marina paid for it from an artisan boutique in Finland.

I used to love Christmas, like *truly love it*. I'd start to sniff it in the air in October, jiggle my way excitedly through November, trying not to peak too soon, before gorging on every cheesy bit of festive cheer I could in December.

The thing I used to think about, before all this, was how lovely it would be to have my own little family one day at Christmas: snuggled in pyjamas around the tree, or making mince pies together to leave for Santa. I needed it, to make up for the Christmases spent with Elen; listening to her vitriol towards my absent father increase the more she drank, pretending to be excited about my hairdresser set or new doll rather than the Meccano set I asked Santa for as a child, pretending to ignore the barbed missiles about my career and lack of boyfriends as an adult. And the twins, they look the part. As light bounces off the tree and fans through their hair it's easy to believe they're real angels (and 62,345 likes agreed last year). Each year, Christmas has gotten a little bit harder to navigate, to pretend that everyone is Having The Best Time – and this from me, let's be honest, I've made a career out of keeping up a happy act. But at Christmas it's exhausting.

Through the window I watch the twins, shrieking and laughing, throwing small hard snowballs – snow pebbles really – at a red-nosed Ruby. Thank God she's here today; it looks freezing out there. This will be good practice for her for Canada. The twins are wrapped up in animal snowsuits now: a panda and a bear. God, they look cute. They give me ovary-ache. My poor, shrivelled ovaries. I imagine them deep inside my body, waving two little white flags.

The steam from my matcha tea dissipates in the air. I give Ruby a thumbs up, but she mustn't see as she doesn't return it. The twins are on their backs, making snow angels. I'm so entranced I almost forget to tap on the window and gesture to Ruby to take a photo – 'flat lay' I mouth, then nod; she's got it. That's the thing with these millennials, like Ruby and Alicia, the snowflake generation. They need a lot of direction and hand-holding but with the right steer can be quite useful.

There's only so much a photo of my beautiful snow angels can do and I'm fine with that. I'm so close to the end of my term with Griff. One more week. My fee will tide me over until I figure out what to do next.

The twins bundle back inside. 'Mummy, can we play love-hearts with you later, like we play with Ruby?' asks Birch.

'Yes, love-hearts! Love-hearts!' Scout's breath mists white in the air.

'Soon. Mummy's got to finish something first.' I don't know what playing love-hearts is, they're building a secret world that I'm not part of. But I will do. Our time is coming.

Seb's upstairs. He's still sleeping on the sofa. We're in relationship no-man's land, neither of us wanting to go back to how things have been lately, each of us afraid to take a step further in. If we're serious about mending our relationship, I need a job that doesn't permeate every nuance of our lives. He's right about some things. I've changed, and not in a good way. I only pursued this SoMe thing to spend more time with the children and earn a bit of cash, but it's taken over everything, causing friction in our family. That was never the plan. Would I have kept this gender thing up for so long if it hadn't been lucrative? Hand on heart, I don't know. I need a normal job, a normal career. *Whatever that means...* I think about Beth. Was I too quick to write her off? And is that a thing I do, when things aren't going the way I hoped? Did I do that with Katya? I never did reply to her message.

The thing is, since Beth went public there's been a shift in her feed. The whole tone's changed. It's so nice. A bit twee and misjudged. Like wittering on earlier about Poppy sleeping through. That's not what people go to an account like Mardy Mum for. It's making me wonder... I don't think she could be behind The Unhappy Hollidays. She's not that sort of person. She's... I hate to say it... she's authentic. Like authentically authentic. Not SoMe authentic. I keep remembering the look on her face at the Beach House. It was real, wasn't it? The friendship, the bond between us, was real? Increasingly it feels like she could have been the best friend I'm missing. When did I start to suck at life so much? When I started making shit up for the internet, I guess. I know one thing for sure: whatever happens next, whatever my next move, I want it to be for real.

71

#ForReal

Beth

Outside, the thought of Cassie stops me. She has a fake life and she's dead miserable, isn't she? Maybe that – what Cassie has – is *worse* than anxiety? Is that possible? And is it fair on Poppy, to live like that? Babies are very perceptive, like Bronagh says. What do I do? I can't call Russell; I'd have to schedule an appointment. I can't call Lucy. I do the only thing that makes sense. I call Cassie.

She answers immediately. Her voice tight and hoarse, as if she's been crying: 'Beth?'

It comes out in a rush: 'It was Lucy. She set up the account. I didn't know anything about it. She thought it would help me and… things are complicated. I need your help. Please. I don't know what to do.' I'm speaking very, very fast, as if I'm being fast-forwarded.

'Sure. But-' She pauses. 'Why are you calling *me*?'

'Because you won't judge. Because you'll be honest. He's in there! He's meant to be at work but…' I gulp for breath, like a fish out of the bowl, and that's how I feel: flapping and flailing, my mind turning over, struggling to *exist* beyond the enormous wave of anxiety building.

'Beth, calm down. Breathe. In for one and out for, like, one hundred. You're not making sense. What's happened?'

I breathe in and out as slowly as I can. In for one and out for two. In for one and out for three. Eventually I am out for seven and I visualize a flame, a perfect bulb of orange, flickering and twitching with the force of my exhale. 'It's Joe. I'm outside his house. His parents' house. I called his work and they said he was at his appointment for Poppy's dairy intolerance.' My voice rises and wobbles. '...But she doesn't have a dairy intolerance!' Crashes and rises and wobbles again.

'How do you know he's in there?'

'I went in! His clothes are there! Strewn around! It's Jazz, I know it is.'

'From the wedding? Wow. So what did you say to him?'

'Nothing! I crept out. I hid. It's too much. I can't face this.' At the base of my throat, something flutters: the last desperate twitches of life as I know it. I need to go home. I need to start walking, as fast as I can. I need to...

'Are you fucking kidding me? Get back in there! Find out what's going on.'

'I can't, Cassie, *I can't*. I'm not like you. I can't be on my own with Poppy. It's better if I don't know. Isn't it? Sometimes as an adult you have to get on with things. That's what you do, right? You make the best of an unhappy' – I lurch over the word, physically rising on to my toes and biting down on my thumb knuckle – 'suboptimal situation?'

'Is this about anxiety?'

I stamp my boots, shaking off a thin beard of snow,

realize the energy is so fast, so frenetic, that it's bypassed my feet; it's in my knees, fizzing away in the joints. My legs start to wobble. I spring back up on to my toes, hoping the movement will shift it. I have to go. I start to march away, talking to myself now as much as to Cassie: 'It will come back. If I go in there and I see them and I *know*, I'll have to confront it. I can't be on my own, with a small baby. She's only slept through once!' My teeth start to chatter: it's setting in. It's settling. Soon I'll be buried under, like leaves beneath the snow...

'Maybe it *will* come back – feeling anxious when things aren't going well is *normal* – but so what? If it comes back, you deal with it. Trust me, living a lie, it's not worth it. Nothing's ever worth it.'

Cassie's voice sounds further and further away as snow flurries around me... I need to go home.

'Okay, I don't "get" anxiety, I'm lucky that way, but from what I'm hearing it's still controlling you, Beth. You think your boyfriend's in there with another woman and you're too afraid to go in? It's time to say *no* to that.'

And I wonder: what if I don't make it back? What if it's too late? Should I go back and leave Poppy there? Will she be safer in Joe's amber home, in the comforting spool of his family, rather than with me? I think of Mum. *Maybe...*

'This is *it*. This is your moment. This is when you decide the woman you're going to be. You've been that person broken by anxiety and it doesn't need to define you. You don't need Joe! You've got Poppy, you've got friends...'

Maybe she's better off without me?

'...you've got a budding career going on there on SoMe. Don't let the anxiety win. Face whatever's on that couch.'

Something clicks. I stop dead.

No. No way. Poppy's my daughter. She'll never be better off without me.

I breathe slowly. In and out. My temples fizz. I force myself to be still. To let the waves of emotion wash over me, my skin stinging like I'm being attacked by a cluster of sea urchins, but I force myself to do it, to wait the anxiety out until it slowly drains away, like I learned to do at uni. Like I will learn to do again. *What the fuck was that?* I was spiralling. And over what? Facing the truth?

'*You've got this, Beth.* You march back in there and you tell Joe – and this *Jazz* – you're not putting up with this shit! Do you want me to stay on the phone? I can go with you.'

I look at Poppy's beautiful face, lit by the low winter light and the snow. There's no way I will not be there for her, like Mum was for me. As long as I am living and breathing – and I hold two fingers to my neck and check my pulse to be sure – I'll be there for her. I will beat this thing. Again. But in my own time. In my own way. I don't have to confront Joe to do that. I'll schedule more sessions with Russell. I'll exercise, I'll start off slowly... *I'm as strong as my body, as weak as my thoughts...*

Cassie's voice bursts in over my internal monologue. 'Hey, guess what? I went to therapy! I saw Jenna. Something I never thought I'd do. And I told her... *everything.* How Seb hates his life, how I feel like I'm letting everyone down all the time. How everything's a mess. Because it is. It truly is. But admitting it, confronting it... I can see it for what it is. I'm making positive changes.'

I swallow into the silence. Track back over Cassie's

words, trying to process what's been going on: 'You read my message? You saw Jenna?'

'Look, Beth, I don't want to sound like a dick here, but...' She sighs, a blizzard down the line. 'You've changed my life. Meeting you. It reminded me. Of what it's like to have a mate, you know? Nothing fancy, just someone on your side. The quiet simplicity of it: sharing stuff and sending messages and not having to pretend all the time... I'd got so used to pretending everything was perfect that I don't think I could tell the difference myself any more. Please let *me* help *you*. If Joe is in there with Jazz, you need to know about it. You can *do this*.'

My thoughts swarm. If Cassie can confront her problems like that, surely I can too? I look at the rows of houses. The menagerie of bird-shaped bushes topped with snow. I don't want to always be on the outside looking in. I want to be *in*. In my own life. Whatever that looks like. I need to stop being afraid. Of the truth. Of myself.

The snow stops. Cassie's voice sounds different, amplified, as it bounces over the line: 'Answer me one thing. *One*. What would you tell Poppy to do right now?'

72

#MovingOn

Cassie

I rub my forehead. *Poor Beth*. I had my suspicions about this Joe. I make friendship resolutions: I will have her back. I will be there for her. Maybe she and Poppy could come and stay here for a few days… I glance around the Shed. I've never invited a friend over since Katya, but I can picture Beth here, on the sofa by the fire, or holding a glass of wine in the kitchen. Maybe I could help her out with Mardy Mum?

I watch the twins, waiting patiently while Ruby recreates a crime scene in the kitchen making hot chocolate. My beautiful babies. I can't help thinking there's a poetry to it, my old life interlacing with my new life. It might be a mess but at least it is *my* life, at least I have a life. How tragic for whoever's behind The Unhappy Hollidays that this is how they get their kicks, trying to derail mine? I still have my children, my home, my husband. I'm working on it, anyway. Therapy was the first step. I'll keep at it. I'll work on myself, not just our relationship. I need to speak to Jenna

alone, about my miscarriage, my career, my self-esteem…
my mother. I'll do whatever it takes for the twins to have a
normal life, for us to be a normal family.

I signal to Ruby that I'm heading upstairs. The twins don't
notice as they're absorbed hovering their KidTech cameras
over their hot chocolates and taking photos. Inwardly I die
a little.

I sit in bed, laptop on my knees. If I'm leaving this Insta-
world behind, I'm doing it on my own terms. I don't like
to put the twins centre stage, but what choice do I have?
Alicia's heard a rumour: The Unhappy Hollidays is touting
its own gender reveal. I can't give them the satisfaction of
beating me to it, earning a hefty fee. I've worked for this.
Alicia's right. It has to be now. If the game is up, I'm pulling
the trigger. I'm going out with a bang.

73

#DonnaDay

Beth

She's right. I know she's right. I can't stop to think or I won't do it. I push open the front door with everything I have and walk smack into two raised hands.

'It's not what it looks like.'

Gloria. Gloria's here. Gloria *knows*. What the—

'Mum?' Calls Joe from the living room.

Gloria rushes ahead of me. '*Beth's* here.' She says, her voice pointed and raised.

'Bollo—' He's on his feet, wrapping his West Ham dressing gown around him as I burst into the room.

'Hi, Joe! Hi, Joe and…' I march to the sofa.

'Donna.' He pulls his best sheepish man-boy smile, pointing at a doner kebab, half eaten. Two slices of pitta bread lie open, soggy and forlorn. Nuclear red chilli sauce oozes through the middle, clinging to limp shreds of lettuce and thick slices of grey meat. *Is this some disgusting post-coital ritual?* I shudder.

'Where is she?' I demand.

'Where's who?'

'Do you think I'm daft? Jazz! Where is she?'

'Jazz?' say Joe and Gloria in unison. He laughs. 'Oh, Beth, you've got the wrong end of the stick. You're the only girl for me. You and Donna...' He gestures back to the kebab. Grins. That cute, boyish grin. Why does it have to be like this?

'This is all because I've not been up for it, isn't it?' I crumple on to the pouffe.

'I'll leave you two to...' says Gloria, backing out of the room. 'I'll keep an eye on Poppy.'

'Er, babe.' He gently prises his suit trousers from under me, folding them neatly, and kneels on the floor, looking up at me.

'If I'd been more up for...' I gesture at the kebab.

'What are you talking about?' He brushes my hair to one side, recoiling slightly as his finger meets a trail of snot dangling from my nose.

'I need a tissue,' I gasp between sobs. 'I just... I haven't been *ready*...' Inside my heart hardens, contracts. This isn't fair.

'For what, babe?' He looks confused. 'This isn't about you, it's me...'

'It's not you, it's me! Blooming hell! And that justifies you... where *is* she, anyway?'

'I've told you, babe, there's no one else here. I would never do that to you. I...' He trails off and looks down at the floor. 'I need some time to myself sometimes. To decompress...'

What? I piece it together: 'You take time off work every week for a *hospital* appointment for your *baby daughter* but instead you come *here* to eat kebabs and watch whatever this is' – I wave angrily in the direction of the TV – 'because *you* need *time* to "decompress"?'

He considers this. Frowns. 'I keep an eye on emails. They think I go to the appointment and then work from home…'

'This isn't your home.' I look out over the garden, to the beautiful willow tree where I sobbed on my birthday. I thought him shagging Jazz was bad but *this*, this is a whole other level. This isn't the quick satisfaction of a carnal urge, this is deception of the highest order.

He pulls his dressing gown tighter. 'Is it such a big deal?' he asks quietly.

'Yes, it's a big deal! Don't you think if either of us should be taking some time to themselves, it should be me?'

'I need some headspace, Beth. From all this online stuff, from everything that's been going on.' His mouth pulls into a tight line and I feel my hackles rise.

'It's my fault, is it?'

'I didn't say that. But you're hardly helping matters, are you? Have you done *anything*, a single thing, to make things better for me?' He looks wronged when he should be looking apologetic!

'Like what?' I demand.

'I don't know! A post saying something *nice* about me, rather than implying how much I disappoint you all the time.' His face pinches like it does when he bench-presses eighty kilos. 'You want to make things right with Bronagh, but what about making things right with me?'

I look around, taking in the scene. I don't know what to think. I pick up the remote control and press play, bracing myself for the worst. A young Bette Midler fills the screen.

'Are you watching *Beaches*?' It's Gossy Gloria's favourite

film. '*With your mum?*' My anger escalates. 'And what, sitting here tearing into me about what a rubbish job I'm doing!'

'No. Of course we're not doing that,' he says, but he looks away.

'Pffff,' I manage, anger palpitating in my chest.

'She's trying her best,' he says carefully. 'We all are.' I roll my eyes. 'I know it's unfair your mum's not around, Beth. I get it. But it's also not fair to take it out on my mum. It's obvious you've got a problem with her.'

'I don't!' I say, flustered. I've never thought of it as a problem with Gloria, it's a problem with me. 'How can you say that? We see her all the time! She's... omnipresent!'

'We hardly see her at all. Do you know why we stopped coming over on Sundays? I knew it was hard for you when Poppy was born. After you had that panic attack, I didn't know what to do. I was so worried. But when I suggested you speak to Russell you got all stroppy. So I asked Mum and Dad to give us some space. And then on your birthday...' He swallows and looks away, his face laced with hurt. 'Well, I've not suggested it since.'

'That wasn't about your parents. That was about the ring.'

'The ring! The bloody ring! I wish I'd never bought it.' The anger pumping round my body freezes in my veins when he says that. I close my eyes. 'All I've been trying to do is make you happy. How can you say I haven't? That social media account was the worst thing that ever happened to us. You've changed since you got into all that, Beth.'

'What do you mean?'

'We used to have a laugh together. Now you spend your

whole time glued to your phone, stalking people, staging "flat lays". You don't play with Poppy to make her happy, you play with her to get her to smile for photographs. And I don't like it.' *I was right. I was right all along. He doesn't like me.* 'I miss the old Beth,' he says quietly. 'The one who saw that all that stuff... it doesn't mean anything.'

His words sting, because that Beth was lonely. That Beth felt like a shadow, a ghost in her own life. 'You're here in your dressing gown watching *Beaches* with your mum, Joe! Don't make me out to be the bad guy in all this!' My voice rises a few octaves with the injustice of it. 'You make things *more difficult* for me!' It climbs higher and higher. 'You put pressure on me *all the time*! Like the morning erections.'

His face reddens with mortification. 'I've never tried to—'

'Slamming the door when you come in. Waking Poppy every time you leave.'

'Babe, I don't mean—'

'Mithering on about bottle-feeding when you knew I wanted to breastfeed.'

'To give you a break! And for when we went to—' He stops short.

'When we went where?'

He throws his hands up in a what-does-it-matter-now gesture. 'I booked the Beach House for us, for New Year's. Way before you went. And a spa day for you. I thought if Poppy was taking a bottle by then, you could enjoy yourself and she and I could spend the day together.' I picture them on the beach, Joe giving Poppy a bottle by the fire pits, and my whole body feels cold at the thought that that won't happen now. 'But what's the point? What's the bloody point? You're determined to only see the worst in me, Beth.'

I flinch at the venom in his delivery. 'And I'm not sure how much more I can take.' He begins to cry.

My heart softens but it still seems so *wrong* that he's been doing *this*. 'Joe, you've been coming *here* when you could be at home with me and Poppy!'

'I leave work early so it doesn't impact you! I'm still home at the same time, mostly. I was late *once*,' he sobs. 'I forgot how long *Titanic* is.'

The image is all too real for me: Joe sprawled on the sofa with a kebab while I'm at home trying not to check my phone to see if he's left work yet. It's humiliating.

'Do you know how I found out?' My voice catches as a half-choked sob escapes. 'I was going to surprise you at work, bring Poppy in like you said. Instead, I hear from Mark—'

'You wanted to come to my work?' His head jerks up, aghast, as he wipes away his tears.

'Yes. To show Poppy off. You kept saying—'

'Beth, that was *before*. The whole world knows Poppy now. My mum's friends. My mum's Zumba instructor. The bloke I had driving lessons with when I was *seventeen*. He messaged me on Facebook, a laughing emoji and "PERIWHAAAAAAT?!" You don't need to bring her into the office to *show her off*. You're making quite enough of a show of us all as it is.'

I swing the double doors open and Gossy Gloria almost topples in as I race out. This time, I don't turn back.

DECEMBER

74

Cassie Holliday's New Baby Media Plan

Week 12: Announcement

Me, S & kids – woodland. Clothes: Autumnal palette (matching not-matching obviously).

No hands on bumps (no cheese at all). Light box? Peg board?

Wording: 'Time to jive, four becomes five!' or 'Incoming: #HappyHollidayNumber5'?

Monks?

Week 13: LHOTP

Me, S & kids – all pose side on – Little House On The Prairie theme: broderie anglaise blousons interspersed with pale denim, balloons under S & kids' tops – a little family with bumps! GML: c.28,000? Change outfits each week or keep LHOTP theme? Get spon?

.
.
.

Week 20: GENDER REVEAL?? Would have to be really desperate!!

Comments:

@Lloydella   Can this woman sink any lower?

@TheBillyT   Treating a baby like a product

@CharElle   Social services should be getting involved, this ain't right.

@Cassie_No1Fan   It's fake! Cassie would never write something like this. Would she…? Cassie…?

Posted by Romilly Loader-Smyth for Boom! mag © at 1 December

75

#TopOfTheCHIN

From: Hetty@MumspireHQ.com
To: Elizabeth.Jenkins@email.com
1 December at 05:00
Influencer Update

Festive greetings!

We're just about holding it together over here as excitement reaches fever pitch for the annual Influencer Awards! Hold on to your tinsel! Here's your Top Ten CHIN as at 30 November. Will these be our winners on the night? Follow #TheInfluencerAwards to find out.

1. Mardy Mum
2. Common As Mum
3. Holistic Flo
4. Forest Dad
5. Boardroom Boss Mum
6. Mama Needs A Drink

7. Mummy Likes Clean Plates
8. Clean Uddies
9. Middle Class Mummy
10. Skinny Bitch Mum

Click here for the full list…

76

#DontForgetToFly

Cassie

We're in the forest behind the Big House. It's a beautiful day, the sun filtering in layers through the stripped silvery branches. Scout shivers beside me in her dressing gown.

'Are you still chilly, sweetheart?'

She coughs, nodding. I check her forehead: warm, but it's hard to tell how warm when we're outside. I need a thermometer. 'Do I have time to pop back in?' I ask Oliver, the photographer.

He adjusts his navy beanie, shakes his head. 'Sorry. The light's perfect. We need to do this now.' I look for Marina, who's been buzzing around with flasks of coffee and cantucci, the shoot no doubt reminding her of her old job. She must have retreated back into the Big House.

Lucy checks her watch: 'It's cold. Let's get this moving.'

I bend down to Scout. 'This won't take long and then I'll make hot chocolate, and if you're still feeling poorly we'll call the doctor again, okay?' And I'll insist she takes this cough more seriously, push for an asthma diagnosis, despite Scout's age.

Scout nods, smiling. 'Mummy, shall we do our special dance to warm up?'

I hesitate. The dance is something devised together last week in the kitchen. It's definitely *not* on brand with The Happy Hollidays. And that, I realize, is a perfectly good reason to do it.

'Please, Mummy?' asks Birch, hopping.

I look around. Everyone's busy making last-minute checks of their equipment. Sure, I'm going to look like a dick, but do you know what? I don't care. Fuck 'em. Let them record it if they like. Let them put it online. I won't be on there to see it.

I find the right song on YouTube and press play. 'This?' I tickle Scout's cheek.

'Yes! Yes! Yes!' They laugh and we wave our arms in the air, mimicking a plastic bag, drifting on the wind, as Katy Perry's 'Firework' begins. We dance together, flossing and finger pointing before jumping enthusiastically to the chorus, hands to the sky. Right here, in this clearing, with grins on our faces and music in our hearts, I know it for real: things are going to be okay. I've got my babies and that's all that matters in this world. I take it in turns to pick them up and swing them around, dipping them back, noticing the rosebud pink of their palettes as their wide-open mouths emit the most delicious sound I know to exist: their laughter. Scout starts to cough violently so I lift her back up and hug her into me, still dancing. She nestles her head into my neck and hugs me tightly. I sing softly into her hair... 'Come on, show 'em what you're worth...'

Lucy watches us, meets my eyes, smiles. We've agreed an exclusive on the twins' gender reveal for a significant fee. It's going straight in the twins' bank accounts. I don't ask Lucy about the unspoken connection: Beth. I don't know how things are between them, if Beth's forgiven her for what she did. My friendship with Beth is still fragile. I don't want to risk it. Lucy's manner is clear: business as usual. Neither of us have mentioned the New Baby Media Plan either but I've noticed that the last few *Boom!* posts have been by Romilly rather than Lucy, as if she doesn't want to be involved.

'Are you ready, Scout?' I ask, setting her back down.

'Yes, Mummy!' She punches the air and shrugs off the dressing gown, revealing her superhero costume. It's in muted yellows and greens, a forest palette, a cape streaming behind her. She clambers up the ladder to the tree house. The last of the snow remains stacked on undisturbed branches. Beside the tree, the lake shimmers a pale grey. It's a beautiful scene. I wonder what Seb's mother would have made of this? Made of me? I feel a sliver of sadness she never got to meet them, that my relationship with my own mother is so fragmented, like the thin layer of ice glittering on the lake. I think of my last session with Jenna: *Would you say your mother has narcissistic tendencies?*

'Mummy, can I fly too?' asks Birch. 'You always said I could fly?'

'Of course.' I kiss his hair, inhale his scent. 'But let's see how Scout's feeling after the photos.' He springs up the ladder and settles into his 'nest'. 'What bird are you today, Birch?' I call up. He has the same costume as Scout, but instead of a cape he has wings.

'A blue tit. I love tits!'

Forest Dad claps him on the back. 'Attaboy! Man's man!' he laughs. I roll my eyes. Marina caught my eye earlier, nodded at Forest Dad, winked. The sudden heat on my face failed to convey my true feelings: I don't fancy Forest Dad, I never have. Whatever he gets up to in his own time is his business. He's a colleague, essentially, and I needed his help setting up today.

'Is Scout in position?' Oliver calls to Forest Dad.

'She's all set!' he hollers back. I look to Oliver for the cue. I want to wrap this up. Perhaps I'll head straight to the doctor and call Lucy later to do the interview.

'So a couple just of the kids and then a few with you, Cassie – let's get this right first time, team!' booms Oliver. I adjust my headpiece. I too am dressed like a bird, with long feathers crowning over my head and tail feathers on my back, and I also have a superhero cape – a symbiosis of mother and children. I cock my head to one side, soaking up the beauty of the twins in the forest at this moment. Forest Dad jumps down from the platform and pats my shoulder.

'All clear!' He gives a thumbs up to Oliver.

'Let's do this! Scout, when I get to three, I want you to jump, arms forward like a superhero, okay? One... Two... Three...'

'Don't forget to fly!' I shout, exuberant as Scout bounces on her toes and propels herself forward, arms outstretched just as Oliver instructed. She glides forward, her golden hair fanning back as the wind lifts her cape and it streams behind her. The lake shimmers around us: devastating, beautiful, illuminating Scout's little body. If only she *could* see them... if only she were still here, how different Seb would be, how much happier... but look! They're doing okay, my beautiful babies, here in the present: Seb and I and our mothers and fathers and all those before them, all those tiny complications and idiosyncrasies that make up a person, wrapped up here in these two beautiful souls. The *future*. It feels exhilarating, stretching ahead…

Something in Scout's motion is not quite right. She knows it too. Her eyes widen. She turns her head, trying to find me. Her smile becomes a scream. 'Mummy!!!'

'Scout!' I shout. 'Scout!' I run towards her. 'The harness! The harness has failed!' It's come loose on one side, the rope and pulley rippling in the wind. 'Where's Forest Dad?' Lucy and Oliver don't respond – they just stare, open-mouthed.

For a few seconds she's still, suspended in mid-air, and we collectively sigh with relief. It's premature. There's a clicking sound as the canvas shifts again and begins to unroll like a yoga mat, flipping Scout over and over and tipping her out.

I run as fast as I can, arms reaching, desperate to catch her, to save my baby. As I run, the ropes give up the canvas altogether and hang suspended like spectres in the frozen air. I hear Birch screaming. The pitch of his voice like the screams in my dream. '*My sister! My sister!*'

It's okay, Birch, I say in my head, the words not finding a way to escape. *It's okay, I'm going to get her. Mummy's here, Scout, I'm here.*

But I'm too late.

She is falling,

falling,

falling,

and so am I.

The lake cracks as she hits it, the water enveloping her screams.

77

#SugarRush

Beth

I've hit a wall. Literally and metaphorically. Influencers make it look so easy, but I've been here for hours, against a backdrop of sugar candy, trying to get it right. I saw a picture of Holistic Flo in a Christmas promotion earlier. She was on a chaise longue by a Christmas tree, looking effortlessly glamorous. How does she do it? I look more like a bewildered starfish than a cool mum that other mums might aspire to be. Lucy would know how to do it. How to stand and pose and get the perfect shot. Her pictures looked clearer, fresher, brighter. How? I miss my sister. Like, *really* miss her. And missing her makes me more cross, because she did this. It's her fault.

The first night Joe was gone was strange, even though I often went to bed without him. There was something about knowing he wouldn't be slipping in later on, that I was in it – my bed, parenthood – alone. I called Cassie. 'Call me anytime,' she said. 'I mean it.' And I knew she did, but I also knew this was something I needed to do by myself. My legs shook as the adrenaline built and slowly leaked out of me. I spoke to Russell the next day: 'Remember, Beth, you've done this before, you can do it again.' He was right. The next night my knees didn't knock, and when the thoughts came I sat with them, practising my breathing, and nothing bad happened at all.

A 'NEWSFLASH' appears on my home screen: 'BREAKING: SCOUT HOLLIDAY, DAUGHTER OF INSTAGRAM STAR CASSIE HOLLIDAY, RUSHED TO HOSPITAL AND UNDERSTOOD TO BE IN A CRITICAL CONDITION.'

I unhook the brake on the buggy and run.

78

#DarlingDaddy

Cassie

'How long's she been breathing like this?' asks the paramedic impatiently.

'She sort of always makes that sound... We think she might have asthma, we're keeping an eye on it...' I trail off, realizing how inadequate it sounds. 'We were going to the doctor after this...' The paramedic surveys the scene: our costumes, the tree house, the cameras, the lighting equipment. In the silence, Scout makes a grunting noise, struggling to breathe.

'What's happening?' Seb asks, running over.

'Daddy!' Scout whispers, jerking her head away as the paramedic tries to place an oxygen mask over her face.

'My darling.' His voice breaks as he crouches beside her. He puts a hand on the back of her wet hair and holds both her pale little hands in the other so the paramedic can arrange the mask. Against the warmth of his skin, her hands look blue.

'What on earth happened?' He regards me with such hate he looks like a different person.

'Cold shock, we need to get her to hospital,' the paramedic interjects. 'I'm concerned she may have had an underlying chest infection *before* she fell in the lake.' He shakes his head in disbelief.

'This is all your fault.' Seb scowls as Scout shivers beneath her metallic blanket.

'My fault?' I try. 'I had her out in seconds! If you'd done something about the black mould...'

'This isn't about black mould!' he roars. 'This is about taking a child who was clearly unwell on some ridiculous ill-thought-out expedition to get the right light, or whatever it is. It's not the first time, is it? What about taking her pumpkin-picking half undressed? Why is she dressed like a fairy?' He regards my tail feathers, shakes his head.

'She was in a dressing gown! It was just a few minutes, so we could get a good shot for their gender reveal! It had to be today. I couldn't let The Unhappy Hollidays beat me to it...' I shake with cold, my own hair encrusted with icicles from diving into the lake.

The paramedic looks between us like he doesn't know what to say. 'Let's move.'

We've not even made it to the hospital when my phone pings with a message from Griff:

#CassieHollidayNeglectsHerKidsShocker is trending. Not the sort of brand positioning I was expecting. Afraid I've gotta pull the plug. You're in breach but you'll still get your fee.

Clicks are through the roof.

79

#Scripted

Beth

'Sorry, love, hospital staff only.' A nervous-looking security guard checks passes as they flash by, squinting from camera flashes.

'But I'm a friend...' I try. A reporter clips her leg against Poppy's buggy and I scowl and tut.

'Aren't they all?' The guard says, wearily, turning away and speaking into his walkie-talkie. I try to ease back out of the scrum, but the buggy's wedged in. I have to tug it out like a cork from a bottle, the crowd closing around our vacant spot.

I spy Alicia away from the group, speaking into her phone, pacing the floor, the scene reminiscent of a US government strategist in a Netflix drama. She rolls her eyes at the hospital; she can't get inside either.

'I thought we could keep a lid on it.' She raises her eyebrows and looks away, shaking her head in disbelief. 'I don't know, Griff, *you tell me*! Someone from the shoot?'

A horrible sensation floods my body. I back away. *Lucy.*

It must have been Lucy. Even with what's happened between us – and to Cassie – she couldn't resist. She's been behind this all along.

80

#Crash

Cassie

Maybe, when Scout's better and Seb's calmed down and realized this was a terrible accident and I was trying to do the right thing for all of us, this could still turn out okay?

'I don't understand how this happened!' Seb repeats. His knuckles are white as he grips the rail around Scout's bed. She sleeps soundly between us, tubes snaking over the sheets, rehydrating her, channelling antibiotics, an oxygen mask fixed firmly in place.

'Forest Dad...'

'Does Forest Dad have any actual training?'

'He runs a school!'

'It's negligence, Cassie. Plain and simple! I would never have agreed to this had I been there.'

'You weren't there, were you. You never are, voluntarily.'

'Yes, well, that's going to change. You were right. I need to be more involved. This sort of thing has got to stop.'

'I was stopping! That's the point. It was a final hurrah! I was doing an interview with Lucy to tell her everything.

378

Get it all out in the open. I'm done with all this. I'm sick of pretending. I want us to rebuild our family... don't you?'

He won't meet my eyes. He keeps staring down at Scout, pale and fragile.

'Let's not send the kids to Radford, Seb. Let's do it our own way. Let's move! Start again! We're a *family*, we'll figure it out? You were right. I've not supported you enough since your dad died. We need to get better at supporting each other... but we can do that, can't we?' I plead with him to engage with me, but he remains still and resolute, as though he can't hear me. 'It's not too late... Seb?'

A woman dressed in a dark suit observes us, making notes. I'm painfully aware I'm still in my costume, albeit with the feathers removed and Seb having begrudgingly lent me his suit jacket. 'Mr and Mrs Holliday? Do you have responsibility for these children?'

'Yes. I'm their father.' Seb's large hands rest on Birch's delicate shoulders. This is what I've always wanted: Seb accepting his responsibilities as a father, *wanting* to be there for his children. Only when I pictured it, I was never on the other side of the wall; I wasn't the adversary he was protecting them from.

'Can you explain what happened?'

'Cassie?' Seb glowers.

What can I say? Even to my ears it sounds ridiculous. 'It was... I was doing an interview with *Boom!* magazine... I couldn't get the *Sunday Read*... anyway, we were doing a shoot to accompany the interview... for a gender reveal.' I look at Scout, her body so small in the hospital bed. 'She was dressed as a superhero – that's why she was flying – and my son loves birds, so he was in a bird's nest, pretending to feed his babies... it's still subverting gender expectations, you see, that's what was clever about it...' I close my eyes. It sounds even worse aloud.

'There's nothing clever about this!' snaps Seb.

'I know that! I thought we were in safe hands! It was only meant to take a few minutes, then we were going back inside for the interview. I didn't know the harness hadn't been secured properly...'

'How did that happen, Mrs Holliday? Who prepared the harness?'

'It was my friend, Forest Dad, you might know... no? Okay, well he runs a forest school, he'll have had proper training, you can speak to him. I'm not sure where he is now. He helped set up and then buggered off...'

'Wait until I get my hands on him!' Seb mutters.

'And then what happened?'

'I don't know.' I start to cry pathetically as the image replays in my mind. 'Scout stepped off the ledge to "fly", and she sort of came loose and unravelled...' I still see the blur of Scout's body as she glided forward and then abruptly fell. Hear her scream as she hurtled down.

'And she fell into the lake?'

I nod, tears streaming. I think of the frost still glimmering on the surface; how cold it must have been for her as her head went under. How those tiny shards must have felt in her ears and up her nose when she was already feeling poorly. I'll never forgive myself.

Seb transitions into smoothing-over solicitor mode. I've heard this tone on the phone when he's offering condolences while opening up a new file to execute the deceased's estate. 'I don't know what's gone on here today, I was at work and had no idea about this, but you can rest assured that now I'm abreast of this matter there will be no further business of this sort. I shall see to that. The children will be coming with me.'

'Hang on—' I interrupt.

'I think that's for the best,' the dark suit intervenes, 'at least until we compile our report and discuss further steps.'

'But I'm their mother—'

'We have to act in the best interests of the children. We have a sick child here who has been put in a potentially life-threatening situation. She must be our priority. Mr Holliday, can we have your address, please, where the children will be residing with you?'

'Of course. My family home, Little Oatbridge Manor...' As Seb reels off the Big House address, I think my body starts to go into shock. My heart beats very, very fast. 'Yes, my stepmother, Marina Holliday.' I've never heard him acknowledge Marina as his stepmother before. 'She's aware, yes, I spoke with her on my way here... She certainly is, very happy for us to stay there with her... She's *very* good with them. A natural!'

I think of what Seb said: *She wants you and the kids in the Big House at any cost.* She wouldn't... she couldn't be involved in this?

A security guard approaches and speaks quietly to the navy-suited lady. She nods and turns back to Seb.

'I'm afraid when you're ready to leave you'll need to go through the back entrance. The press are here,' she mouths over Birch's head, pointing at the windows.

I register the shouts and noise and lights – not traffic, then. Lucy must have broken the story before Scout was even safely in the ambulance. I see the look of horror in Seb's eyes and instantly know what he's thinking: Radford.

'Is Mummy coming with us?' Birch asks, his big blue eyes solemn as sweat drips down my face.

The woman places her hand on his shoulder kindly. 'Not today, Charlie. Once the doctor says Amelia's all better, you'll go home with Daddy and your grandma...'

Seb winces at 'your grandma'.

'Who's Charlie?'

She looks at Seb sadly. 'What a shock he's had today, poor little mite. Doesn't know his own name...'

'I do!' he says indignantly. 'It's Birch! My name's Birch.'

Seb speaks into her ear. She shakes her head, makes another note in her pad.

My chest starts to feel funny. Like something is squashing it inwards and I can't get enough air in to breathe. My God! I'm having a heart attack! Jesus Christ, it hurts. I rub at my shoulder hard. Pain shoots up and down my arm. Heart attack or stroke? My mouth isn't working. My lips. My lips are glued together and the glue is slowly seeping down my throat, binding my vocal cords, tightening my tonsils. I can't call for help. I can't do anything. This is a stroke, isn't it? It's a stroke? But then why do I... really... really... really... need... to... breathe...

'Daddy, is Mummy okay?' Birch asks.

The ground shifts, unsteadying my feet. A 'whooshing' sensation whistles through my skull as my head rushes, the heat unbearable. The sky shatters and caves in. I feel a sharp intense pain and the shock of something cold and hard, like metal.

'Daddy?'

It's the last thing I hear.

81

Front page of *The Read*

The social media world is reeling following the admission to hospital of Amelia Holliday, the daughter of Cassie Holliday (known online as 'Scout'). The incident marks the end of an eventful few months for Mrs Holliday. Initially lauded as groundbreaking for her stance on gender neutrality, she recently secured an agreement with the Family Co that made her the highest paid Influencer to date. However, a source at the Family Co reported that her responsibilities had to be shared with other Influencers and she appeared to be struggling with stress in her online posts.

It would appear that Cassie Holliday (née Cassandra Shaw) is a master of illusion. Known at school as Sandy Shaw, she qualified as a pilot with Horizon Air in their inaugural programme to encourage more women to fly. Captain Cassandra Shaw, as she was known professionally, gave up work shortly after having her children. Horizon Air declined to comment but a former colleague, Doctor Marcus Spinks, has described her as being 'very hard work. Impossible to get along with'.

As an Influencer Cassie Holliday was respected by her peers and followers. It appears that in reality her children were neglected, socially isolated and are now reported to be undergoing therapy for gender confusion. It is understood that Mr and Mrs Holliday have separated and the children will remain with their father and grandmother while Social Services investigate the matter further.

The incident has precipitated calls for more stringent regulations to be placed upon social media Influencers and for guidelines to be drawn up regarding children appearing online at an age when they are unable to give consent.

82

#Wreckage

Cassie

The car draws up to the gates and they are already there, swarming the outside perimeter like a SWAT team. If I had pictured this scene, I would have imagined fat, hairy faces pressed against the glass, and there's a few of those, but mainly I'm surrounded by women: sharply dressed, keen-eyed. I shrink back in my seat, use my scarf to obscure my face. It all flashes before me: the ridiculousness of it all.

Their voices penetrate the confines of the car:

'Cassie! Cassie! We want to tell your side of the story!'

'Don't you owe it to your followers?'

I wait for the gates to creak open. Time moves slowly, a filmic glaze snagging the action. Finally, they part and camera lenses crack and squeak across the windshield as we move.

After months of feeling irrelevant, like I no longer mattered, I'm at the top of search lists, the name on everyone's lips... but at what cost? I clench my hands in my lap. My fingers are dry and cracking after yesterday, small red lines of blood loosening at the knuckles. She says nothing, concentrates on edging through the gates without running anyone over. They close behind us and we move on unhindered. I gaze up at the Big House as we pass.

I think back to the forest, before everything went wrong. That's how I want them to remember me: legs bending, hair flying, hips swinging, feeling the joy of the moment. I hope they understand that having them, being with them, is the single best thing in my life. There's a risk that I'll be misunderstood. I *need* them to know. It was all for them in the end, wasn't it?

The car crunches on the gravel, stopping outside the Shed.

'Things will blow over eventually,' she says, cutting the ignition.

'I've lost my children.'

She shifts in her seat. Her hands still on the steering wheel. 'You'll get them back.'

'What if I don't?' I put my head on my knees and wrap my arms around my calves. My body heaves with sobs. I don't want to go inside the Shed without my children.

'Cassie, I need to explain... about The Unhappy Hollidays.'

I turn to face her, the effort exhausting.

'You know what? I really don't care.'

83

#IWantedToTellYou

Beth

I'm in the café in Victoria Park Village that has the excellent French apple tart. My eyes fly to the door every time the bell jingles. She sees me immediately but pretends not to, ordering a slice of apple tart and a coffee. I look down at the table, fuss with Poppy, check my phone – anything to avoid meeting her eyes. For a second my resolve wavers – *am I doing the right thing?* – but Russell's right. I need to tell Lucy what happened.

When she sets down her boxed tart, I finally look up. I realize I'm not crying, my heart is not pounding, bile is not clawing up my throat. Instead, I feel tired. Like someone's let out a plug and all my energy has drained away.

'Thanks for texting,' she says. 'Can I sit down?' I nod, stroking Poppy's hair. It concedes to my touch and springs back up. 'I wanted to tell you. I tried to tell you. In your flat, at the wedding…'

'You didn't try very hard.'

She is ever so slightly shaking, her hands twisting her napkin. 'It was going to be a surprise.'

'Well, you got that bit right!' I raise my eyebrows. 'It was about the promotion, wasn't it? I hope it was worth it.'

'It wasn't like that.' Her voice is small and scratchy, catching on her words.

'You posted a picture of me in that dress? As if I hadn't been humiliated enough?'

She holds her hands to the sides of her face, flaps them lightly against her skin. 'I'm sorry, I'm so sorry. I thought... I thought it would be funny. And I know how that sounds,' she adds quickly, 'but I was drunk. You looked so sad and miserable at the wedding. I wanted to make something good out of something bad. You know, make lemonade. Like Beyoncé. It was before the hay bales, before our chat. And then I tried to delete it – that's why I was so desperate for my phone the next morning – but it was too late.' She winces.

'And my birthday?'

'I was frustrated, Beth. You were off work, you had time on your hands—'

My eyes boggle at her incredulously. 'I had a *baby* on my hands!'

She ignores me. 'I wanted you to have something for you. You know now – the sky's the limit when you do well on these platforms. I thought if I could show you that, it would...' She trails off, air whistling through her pursed lips.

'It would what?'

She pinches her fingers along her nose. 'I thought it would

keep me in your life. I thought it would be a way to keep us *us*.' Tears pool in her eyes.

'What are you talking about?'

She opens the small cardboard box. Plucks a morsel of apple from the tart. 'We were always so close. And then you met Joe and moved out and had Poppy…'

I stare at her in disbelief. *"You were jealous?"*

'No,' she tuts, jabbing her fork into the tart with more force. 'I was happy for you, but your priorities had shifted and I wanted to be a part of it. I love Poppy and being an aunty, but it wasn't enough. I felt on the outside of this beautiful thing.' She waves a shiny piece of apple in Poppy's direction and they beam at each other, happy to be reunited. 'So I created the account. I thought when the time was right I'd present you with this amazing opportunity and we could work on it together. I knew you hated your job.' She digs into the tart, dividing the pastry base, the layers gently falling apart. 'I did some random posts: with Poppy's feet, or nursery close-ups, I was very careful not to use anything identifying…' Which is true. Only Urzula, who had been to the flat and seen Poppy's distinctive princess canopy bed and our hanging rattan egg chair on the terrace (that got a lot of likes), realized it was me. In a post thanking the Super Pump 3000 company, nestled in the comments, @Urzula_the_health_visitor had written 'Excellent! We will try this tomorrow!'

'They did okay,' Lucy continues, 'but it was when I used your copy…'

'They weren't "copy". They were personal messages.'

She pushes on. It feels like she's practised this and she

wants to get everything out: 'The more of your voice I used, the more engagement I got. People loved you! They thought you were so funny, and relatable. Like I do! But then you went viral and everything kicked off dead quick and I didn't know what to do. I wanted to talk to you about it, but you seemed annoyed with me all the time.'

'What do you mean?'

'I don't know… It felt like the more I kept trying to help with Poppy, or when I suggested joining SoMe, the snappier you got and…. it all started to get out of hand.'

'And Cassie?' I ask.

'Yes, when I realized you'd met Cassie there was some self-interest. I needed a scoop and you seemed to be offering it to me gift-wrapped, and you kept digging at me about my job and my love life. Lack of. For a short time, it felt good, in a way…' Lucy starts shovelling in bigger forkfuls of her tart.

'What sort of way?' I snap.

'It felt like something exciting was happening in my life too! You had this big thing going on, this new life, and it felt like my life was becoming smaller by comparison, even though I'm not sure I even want kids. Or if I can have them.' She prods her finger pads with the fork's prongs, leaving tiny white indentations in her skin.

We never talk about it, if Lucy wants children, if that's an option for her after her anorexia. I've always assumed she didn't want to discuss it, but maybe I should have asked.

'It's ridiculous. *Maybe I was jealous!* I don't know. But if I was, it was because I wanted to spend *more* time with you, not less. Not like how it is now.' She spears her fork into the final piece of tart, leaving it upright. That's the most I've seen her eat in one go in years. Silent tears streak down her face as she pushes the box aside. 'I've missed you so much, Mitts. I've been watching you through the squares. In your Stories. I thought... I thought you were happy... I didn't realize Joe was at Gloria and Ron's...'

'How do you... have you spoken to Joe?' From the pushchair, Poppy starts to cry. I reach a hand up and rock her gently.

'No, Cassie told me...'

'You spoke to Cassie?' I've messaged Cassie since the accident – without reply – but I'm so careful not to mention Lucy. I'm not ready to choose between my sister and my friend.

'I went to the hospital. I wanted to help, after... everything. When I got there, she'd had a panic attack.'

I ignore the 'everything'. I don't want to know. I'm beginning to think they're both as bad as each other, in their different ways. 'Cassie?' I interrupt. 'Cassie had a panic attack? *Not* panicking is like her thing.' I can't imagine it.

Lucy nods. 'She had a panic attack and fainted... hit her head on the edge of Scout's bed. They were checking her over when I arrived. No visitors, no one there to hold her hand. Two million followers and all alone. They kept her in to observe her overnight. I stayed with her and drove her home the next day.'

'You stayed at the hospital?' I can't picture Lucy asleep on a chair by Cassie's bed. Poppy's cries grow louder so I stand to leave, Lucy rising with me.

'Someone had to.' She shrugs. 'It reminded me of when you did it for me,' she adds, and I feel a clutch of grief; will that part of my life ever stop hurting? We exit the café and head towards the park.

'How is she now?' It feels weird to be asking Lucy about Cassie.

'Distraught. All she wants is her children back. Seb's saying he'll do whatever it takes to keep custody of them, even though until now he's hardly been interested in them.'

'That's the impression I had too.' I roll my eyes. 'Well, at least she can afford a good lawyer.'

'That's the thing. He can, but I'm not sure she can. He sounds like a dead tight old git.'

We reach the benches on the far side of the park. I lift Poppy out to feed her. The wind bites at my nipple and Poppy latches on. 'Guess who I got a message from...?' I ask, putting off what I have to say. 'Caitlin Oxenbury.'

Lucy raises her eyebrows. 'No! What did she say?'

'Nothing really.' I put on a cheerful voice: 'Hi Beth! Don't know if you remember me, we were at school together! There was an incident in textiles... I liked your hair and yeah. That was it. It wasn't cool. Anyway, I've recently started selling herbal supplements and I wondered if you'd mind doing a post...'

'No way!' Lucy laughs. 'Deleted?'

'Deleted,' I confirm.

'How are things with Joe? Cassie told me about Doner Day.'

I gaze over to the Christmas market stalls. I am back on the bench. Still no ring on my finger but no desire for one either. It doesn't seem important any more. I'm doing okay in the flat by myself, but I miss Joe: his smell, his laugh when he's watching TV, his arms around me in the morning. I thought the flat didn't feel like home because it wasn't in Yorkshire, because it was too full of sharp edges and glass, but it didn't feel like home because I was letting my preoccupation with how things *should* look override how things actually *were*.

'It's a mess. He thinks I'm making him out to be the bad guy, when he needed some time to himself. And because I said I didn't want to get married and then gave him a hard time about it.'

'That's—' Lucy leans forward animatedly, indignant on my behalf.

'I know, I know, but in a way he's right. I did say I didn't want to get married. I'd seen Tiffany rings on Joe's iPad history and I panicked when Ron suggested it. I couldn't imagine doing it without Mum there. I added "just because I'm pregnant" to buy some time, but then it didn't happen... and I grew partly relieved and partly desperate. I spent *hours* on Pinterest; when the proposal came, I wanted everything to be perfect to make up for Mum not being there, even though it never *could* be perfect, because she's gone. I was setting myself up to fail and getting upset when I did.'

'Don't we all?' Lucy sympathizes.

I look at Lucy: 'And it wasn't just me giving him a hard time, it was *everybody*.' I grimace. 'He's still getting ribbed at work.'

'I'm so sorry. I've really messed up.' Lucy presses her fingers over her eyes. And I'm still upset with her, but I also know that she's at a disadvantage: she doesn't know the pain I've caused her.

'Lucy, I need to tell you something.'

She doesn't move but her back straightens a fraction. I force the words out staccato, knowing once they're released in to the world I won't be able to take them back; I'll have to live with their repercussions forever.

'It was my fault. That day. With Mum. I gave her the pills. The nurse didn't leave them there by accident. I took them. I laid them out for her. I followed her instructions. Too weak to say no. Too weak to leave her like that when she was begging me to do it.' Lucy looks at me as if she doesn't know me and my voice thins and breaks as I continue. 'It wasn't the nurse, she wasn't lying, she—'

'I knew it wasn't the nurse, Beth. We all did, didn't we? That's why no one said anything.' Mum was too weak by the end to leave her bed, but she could lift her arms just enough to take the pills, me pressing the beaker of water to her lips each time she asked.

'So who did you...? How...?'

'I thought it was Dad.'

'Dad? He'd never do that.'

'That's what I would have said about you.' Her voice catches and tears slide down her cheeks. She stares at me as if she's reading a map, looking for the sister she's lost. I swallow, a hard lump in my throat, clicking my feeding bra back into place. 'You didn't tell me... because I got sick.' She stares ahead, shock reframing every feature on her face.

'I'm sorry, Lucy, I'm so sorry, I—' Lucy waves me away with her hand. Focuses on Poppy's face as she sleeps. Love blooms and swells inside my chest, almost suffocating. Why couldn't I have it all? Why couldn't I have Mum and Lucy *and* Poppy? The injustice of it still feels overwhelming. That my daughter will never meet Mum. That I'll never see her again... it still seems so ridiculous, so unbelievable, and yet I was there. I did it. I can't lose my sister too. I can't... 'Please, Lucy, I didn't know what to do. She'd asked me so many times by the end. She asked me because I was weak. She knew how pathetic—'

'Beth.' She cuts me off and takes my hands, even though her own are shaking. 'She asked you because you were *strong*.' I see she isn't looking at me with hate – surprise, anguish maybe, but not hate.

'I'll never forgive myself. We could have had another few weeks with her, at least.'

'But like that? Don't you remember the bandages? How her skin had started to peel away when they were changed? Her spirit broken. She didn't want to live like that.' She interlaces her fingers with mine and squeezes our hands into a tight fist. 'That's why you've always felt so bad. I thought it was to do with me... the anorexia... I thought it should be *me* that felt guilty, for putting you and Dad through that, after everything... I thought... I thought you blamed me. For making things worse.'

'You? No! How could I ever blame you? I blamed myself. Do you hate me?' I whisper, terrified of the answer.

Lucy stares ahead at the distance, her head shaking. She dives into my changing bag (a discreet black one I've been #gifted) and before I can ask her what she's doing she retrieves my love-spoon key ring and holds it to her chest. It was Mum's. Mum who picked it up from a shop in Anglesey. Mum who carried it everywhere she went. Mum who gave it to me in her final days, pressing it into my hand: 'It's the little things that matter, love, don't forget.'

'She asked me too,' Lucy says, and I stare at her in shock. 'She asked me too and I couldn't do it. *I* was too weak, Beth, and you, *you* were strong. All these years I've thought that I let her down. Let Dad down because *he* had to do it. But we were only kids... Beth. My God.' And she bundles me into a hug.

84

#IrreconcilableDifferences

Cassie

'What do you think she would say if she were here?' Jenna gestures towards the chair.

'I know what she'd say, because she said it this morning.' I smile, not because I think it's funny, but because the poison in her words hurts less and less. I'm starting to understand that the way things are between me and Elen isn't my fault. 'She'd say how embarrassed she is, how glad she is her new friends – she moves around a lot – don't know I'm her daughter. How much I'm like *him*. Selfish.'

Jenna's face is impassive but kind. A candle flickers on the table between us.

'All I've ever felt like is an excuse. For why her life didn't turn out the way she hoped.' I shrug, my shoulders loosening a fraction. 'I wonder what choices I'd have made if I'd had different parents.' I twist the skin around my ring finger; where my wedding band used to sit. The first thing Seb and I have agreed on in years is that our marriage is over. I picture a box, on a deserted beach, wrapped up tight with yellow parcel tape. Has it been over since that look?

I think of our last exchange:

'Radford have formally withdrawn the offer for the twins! They've seen the coverage!'

'Well, at least that's something positive!'

'I will never understand how you could so willingly sabotage such an opportunity for your children!'

'I'll never understand how you can so willingly be a dick. You see how unfair this is, don't you? That the twins are with you? How ironic the whole thing is!'

My rage was jangling like a lid on a pot of boiling water, but I had to keep it in check. The last thing I need is Seb reporting to Social Services that I lost my temper. So I'm speaking to him – and on occasion to my mother – via the medium of an empty chair in Jenna's office. So far, it's working out quite well.

'How are you feeling about the next few weeks?' Jenna asks.

I think of my phone call with Beth last night, intimacy crackling over the line as we shared everything: our own takes on what had happened, how we felt, what we're going to do next. Most importantly, how to get the children back where they belong: with me. I feel a rush of power, a force so strong it seems to sweep from the outer edges of the room, gathering steam as I take in a deep, deep breath of the delicately scented air.

'You know, I think I'm going to be okay.'

85

#TheInfluencerAwards

Beth

A woman steps on to the stage.

'This is it...' she booms to vibrant applause. '*Ladies...*' – there's whistles, foot-stomping – 'And... *Gentlemen*!' Silence falls as the few brave men attending try heavy-handed claps and non-committal 'Yeahs', while women cast scowls around the room. 'The event of the year... *The Influencer Awards*!' The room regains momentum. A woman calls, 'We love you, Hetty!' 'And' – Hetty grins and points skywards as a neon digital clock illuminates and begins counting down – 'it's almost awards time!'

Fifty-nine minutes to go...

Why am I here? Why am I here? Why am I here? Because Cassie asked me to come, that's why, for moral support, although she's late. 'And if you do win an award, for God's sake, go up there and get it!' she'd implored. I gulp. Lucy said the same, less enthusiastically, given her role in my being nominated. She should be here any minute too. I thought Cassie and Lucy were as bad as each other, but

399

actually they're kind of made for each other – and, well, it seems that through blood and by choice, both destined to be a part of my life. Just not at the same time. At some point, Cassie will have to confront Lucy's role in The Unhappy Hollidays. Whatever that was.

'Boardroom Boss Mum's leading the games tonight, but before I hand you over, a gentle reminder to use #TheInfluencerAwards hashtag when posting.' Hetty claps as Boardroom Boss Mum strides confidently to the stage, all spiked heels and red lips, then leans in and adds in her best low-pitched terms-and-conditions voice, 'Seriously, folks, our sponsors, the Family Co, have asked me to remind you that any deviations from the official hashtag may lead to you being removed from the event and/or your invite being revoked next year.' She steps back again, resumes her usual high-pitched performance mode. 'Happy posting, guys!'

What am I doing here in this old-school swanky hotel in central London when I could be at home with Poppy? Gloria's babysitting. She's been pretty cool about everything with the account, probably because she feels guilty for her part in Doner Day. I get it: Joe's her son and she was doing her best by him. By me even, maybe, letting him have some space. I explained about the things I'd said to Lucy that made their way online; how having Poppy reignited my grief, Gloria's presence making my pain at the absence of Mum more acute. We hugged it out in Gloria's generous bosom. 'Darling,' she whispered, 'if he'd taken me shopping with him, you'd have had the biggest diamond in there.'

I head for the bar but get distracted by a familiar figure leaning against the wall. She's in a silver lamé jumpsuit and cerise pink shoes. She looks so thin. Her arm's outstretched, marked with bruises, trying to take a selfie, but she can't quite get a grip on her phone. It's heartbreaking. I go to help. A technology mercy dash.

Just before I reach her, she slithers down the wall – she's so light it doesn't take long – and sits there, arm taut, phone in hand. Mumbling. Drunk. 'To be honest, guys, I feel like I've given all I can give. I've shown you every part of my home. I've bared *my soul*. Shared *my pain* at my marriage breakdown. I'm thinking, what else is there to give? What more can I do?' Her head slumps downwards and the phone lists in her hand, pointing at her crotch, which, I'm alarmed to see, has a camel-toe situation occurring. 'I've compromised myself. I've lied... I've... done some terrible things.' I turn off her phone and gather her up in my arms, my heart pounding with adrenalin. Now what?

Cassie

I enter the room. Boardroom Boss Mum's on stage leading Bad Birth Bingo, booming bad birth-isms:
  'THIRD DEGREE TEARING!'
  'FORCEPS!'
  'FORTY-PLUS HOURS ACTIVE LABOUR!'
She sees me and stops calling. Heads turn. The room falls still, a gargoyle scene. Most tables have at least one woman standing on them, legs wide, bent over, hinged from their hips with their phones in hand. Below, the tables are littered with expertly placed champagne flutes, invitations and goody-bag paraphernalia, artfully strewn. All to get the perfect event flat lay. I give Boardroom Boss Mum a nod.

'EMERGENCY CAESAREAN SECTION!'
The gargoyles are brought back to life.

Beth

'BINGO!!' someone shouts, and cheers and hurrahs explode as Johnny Cash's 'Ring of Fire' blares from loudspeakers. I can't follow the game. I'm worried Holistic Flo's going to throw up Poppy-style and I can't help but wonder: these terrible things she's done, are they to do with Cassie? Forest Dad had emerged from the disabled toilets as I was half-dragging her, his hair messy and shirt part-unbuttoned. 'I belong in the forest!' he said, eyes lit and wild as he lifted Holistic Flo over his shoulder and staggered to a quiet table at the back of the room.

'I've been watching your Stories,' I say now, my hand on his arm. 'I love what you're doing for Ebola. So worthy!' I practically swoon.

'Not *Ebola. Bo*BoLa.' He scowls and I wince. 'You know? The Scandi brand.' He shakes his head. I realize he's leathered. 'Cassie would know. I tried to bring her in, I thought we could work on it together, but she wasn't interested...'

I move my hand away. 'Cassie?'

He tilts his head to the side and nods, his eyes soft. His usual look, which I had taken for 'charming rogue', but all I see now is 'alarming creep'.

'I've always had a thing for Cassie,' he confesses. 'Always trying to get her attention... As if she'd give me the time of day now...' His face grows desperate. 'I doubt

I'll ever see her again...' he warbles. *You might get lucky*, I think, glancing around. He grips me by my elbows, his breath thick as a pub carpet; sticky with not just today's alcohol but yesterday's too. 'It's not happened to you yet, Belle. You're still glowy and fresh. The years haven't worn you down.'

'It's Beth.' I lean back in my chair to create some distance. I'd given him the benefit of the doubt over the accident. Lucy told me he was there but that's all I know and I feel a buzz of alarm. What lengths has he gone to, to get Cassie's attention? Are they all in on this together? He hangs his head.

'Parenthood changes you. My wife's so far down the rabbit hole she's...'

My ears prick up. *Wife?* 'I thought... everyone thinks...'

'Yeah. I know. My wife's dead. If only.' He raises his glass. 'I tell you what I *would* kill for, some decent beer.' He shakes his head. 'No. She's very much alive. She started the rumour – said it would be good for me, but really she was embarrassed by me and wanted me to know it.'

'But...' I'm speechless. My brain fizzing. I knew, didn't I? I knew this world wasn't real, so why am I surprised?

'You all joke you want a stay-at-home dad, but you know what they say... don't ask, don't get. No, that's not it...' He ruffles his hair. 'You get what you need?' His eyes cross with the effort of concentration. He drains his glass and sloppily tops it up, using the sleeve of his Forest Dad top to wipe up the spills. My gut knots; I've been duped by a man wearing his own brand clothing. 'I was at school one morning with our daughter Araminta, before all the Forest Dad stuff. I was your average stay-at-home-dad. My wife earned more than me, so it made sense. It wasn't just about the money. I was better at that stuff. She didn't enjoy it. I'm a modern man, I can do this, I thought. I hadn't counted on how *lonely* it would be. That's the problem, there *is no* average stay-at-home-dad… no one I could catch up with and moan about the washing pile or this week's craft project. Anyway, Araminta was desperate for us to play bunny rabbits, so we were hopping around the playground, waiting for the bell, when I overheard a mum, in cut-glass English: "He's been on the wacky baccy again." You can't win…' He drifts off, glassy-eyed. 'The mums at school used to look at me with a mix of curiosity and pity. Now – *now* they look at me with *desire*.' His flies are undone and slightly stained. He's a mess.

A shriek interrupts us. '*Help! My hair! I'm stuck!*' A woman standing on a table has her corkscrew waves entangled in a chandelier, like curls of tape pulled from a cassette, furling in the light. There's a burning smell as other women clamber on to the table to extract her. Forest Dad doesn't notice. 'I'd better go, before she comes looking for me.'

'She's here?'

'She's everywhere.' He sidles off.

Beside me, Holistic Flo is still slumped over, head on the tablecloth. 'I knew it,' she mutters.

A squeal emits from a microphone. Hetty spreads her sequinned bat-winged top like a cape: 'Time for the awards, chicks!'

★★★

Cassie

I enter the room behind the stage.

'Cassie!' She says, startled. 'I didn't expect to see you here!'

'No shit!' I lean against the door, my hands clasped behind my back. I thought she'd look different, villainous, but she looks like she always does. 'I don't get it? I don't get what was in it for you? And...' My skin crawls and prickles with humiliation. 'I thought we were friends?'

'Look, Cassie,' she says, businesslike. 'It was nothing personal. People want real life, real problems, not this made-up happy bull. You crash. You rebuild. That's life. It was heading that way anyway, I just speeded things up a bit. And in exchange, it raised all of our profiles.' She shrugs. 'You got something out of it too.'

'What?' I spit. 'I've lost my children, my husband, my career!' Her indifference is mortifying.

'Look at all the coverage you've had the last few months.'

I reel, disgusted. 'For awful, awful things,' I hiss.

Beth

She says my name. My heart is thumping, my head is rattling; not just with the truth about Forest Dad but with everything: because I didn't listen to Joe, because he was right all along, because Hetty has just read out the list of nominees for the Influencer of the Year and she said my name and what if she says it for a second time? What if she repeats my name and it means I've won and I have to approach the stage and stand up there among this sea of vipers?

She says my name. Again. I try to shrink down in my seat; perhaps no one will notice I'm here and I can slip out quietly and find Joe and… All around me heads are angling, necks craning, trying to locate me, and Forest Dad is back at the table, punching the air and enveloping me in a bear hug as he practically drags me to my feet. Even Holistic Flo has summoned the strength to stand and between them they hustle me over to the stage, as flashes of light follow me, and I don't need to worry about whether my legs will give way as I scale the steps because I'm carried up there on surges of claps and good cheer, on hoots and whistles and foot-stomping, and I stand on the stage and my heart is still pounding and my cheeks are flushed and the waves of celebration wash over me, the room a vibrant chorus, and I stand and I clutch my award and I hold the weight of it clasped against my chest and I feel… nothing.

Hetty's using her clicker to change the background screen on the stage to fireworks, indicating to the photographers to capture this moment forever. Or for the ten minutes it's trending. And I can't do it. I can't stand here and accept this award and represent an idea of me that is so far from the truth. I'm not Mardy Mum. She's Lucy's creation. And I don't want to *be* Mardy Mum. I don't want, don't need, *this*. I want to be at home in the flat with Joe and Poppy, drinking a brew and eating chocolate biscuits and watching Netflix. And that's okay.

I turn to Hetty as the wall of applause built for me collapses into silence. 'You know what?' I say. 'Nah. You're alright.' I return the award. As I do, the fireworks stop and

Cassie's face appears on the screen, an enormous floating head. I look over to Hetty, but she looks as confused as me. She looks up at the screen and back down at the clicker and something seems to register.

'Reuben!' she hisses at the hotel's event coordinator, who's been hovering around the stage. 'Where's Alicia?'

Cassie

From behind the stage I hear Hetty announce 'Mardy Mum!' and the rupture of applause, my old life moving further and further away. I grasp the edge of a table to steady myself.

When Lucy told me – that she was suspicious of Alicia at the panel event, that the tone of the Unhappy Holliday emails reminded her of Alicia and, crucially, that she called Alicia to tell her about Scout's accident so it could be kept private, but Alicia broke the story – I was spinning. Free-falling. Now I can see it for what it is. It was her from the beginning. It was always her. She had access to my social media accounts to post for me. She knew my passwords. My whole life is synched to my phone and I frequently granted her access. I gave her the lot. *Why did I not think of that?*

'Yes.' She sounds bored. 'It was me. Mostly, anyway – you were quite the contributor in your own way.' She laughs, her LA tinkle. 'And look, I never wanted you to lose your kids. Those clicks were way beyond my imagining. I wanted you to reveal their gender, get trending again. It was the last bit of interest left in you and the clock was ticking.'

'Did you give the kids the microphone at the Mumspire

event? Did you let them out when I was speaking? Was it all a set-up?'

'Yep.' She flicks her hair. 'I was always one step ahead, Cassie. I moved Hetty's email to your junk folder, suspecting you would never check. Marked it as unread in case you did.'

'What about all the other stuff? Was there ever any interest in my bush?'

'Loads,' she says, her eyes sparking. '*Absolutely loads.*' She flicks her fingers as if batting it away.

I sink on to a chair. This is bigger than I realized. Bigger than Alicia taking some photos from my phone and emailing them to Lucy. This is a carefully orchestrated campaign against me, and I still don't understand why? I begin to sob. She exhales crossly. 'You know people would pay a fortune for the level of coverage you've had the last few months? People *do* pay a fortune. I'm starting out. I've got to build my reputation.'

'How will people even know you're behind it?'

'I'm preparing a case study for my pitch deck… Obviously I'll tone down what I did, brands will assume you were on board, the stats will speak for themselves…'

Griff steps out of the shadows, his phone firmly fixed in our direction.

'Griff? Jeez, you made me jump! I was filling Cassie in on our little project…' she says, but he doesn't respond, he simply presses a finger on his phone screen and slips it into his pocket.

'That was next level,' he murmurs, smiling, sated. 'We're gonna break the internet. Literally, tear the whole fucking thing up!' He drives a balled fist into his other hand.

'What's going on?' I ask, but Alicia, always one step ahead of me, has already bolted out the door in the direction of the stage.

I follow Alicia to the wings and peer out. The room is silent. Hetty's still holding the award and staring up at the screen. I shuffle on to the stage and crane my neck to see what's going on. There's no fireworks there, as in previous years, just my face, frozen, at the end of my confrontation with Alicia. Every other face in the room is staring up to the sky, just like in my dream. But these are not faceless people, these are people I know: people I've worked beside, sat beside, selfied beside for the last few years, and they all have a phone in their hands, filming the spectacle. Filming *me*. I am the spectacle. The heads tilt down and their gaze adjusts and alights on me and I see the thing I hate most of all: pity. Then their gaze shifts to Alicia beside me and I see contempt, because you may think our world is shallow, our lives scripted and curated, our hearts cold, but I know without speaking that we all agree on one thing: she's gone too far.

Alicia stares up at the screen, not yet understanding, although she must feel the glare and heat of eyes upon her. 'What the—?' She starts as Griff appears, clapping.

'Take a bow, people. We're making SoMe history here! The country's 100 most influential parents live-streaming to a combined audience of' – he holds up his iPad – 'twenty-six million users! Brought to you by Griff and the Family Co.' My stomach lurches, my bowels cramping: it was all a big production. I feel like an unwilling participant in a scripted

NICOLE KENNEDY

reality show. These millennials, the snowflake generation: they're ruthless.

'Brought to you by *Alicia* at the Family Co,' Alicia tries, but it's not picked up by the microphone. Griff fixes his gaze on her and shakes his head firmly. Alicia's eyes grow large: she's been played too. I almost feel a tiny sliver of sympathy for her, because it's a tale as old as time: man takes credit for woman's work.

'Griff, mate?' Common As Mum calls, clambering up to the stage. 'No one gives a shit!' As she speaks, I sense a presence around me and realize it's not just Beth and I on the stage; Lucy has appeared, along with Holistic Flo and Boardroom Boss Mum. We stand together and link hands. 'And what's more, none of *us* are going to work for *you* again. So good luck with that app! It was a load of shit anyway. Am I right, ladies?'

The room roars in response. There's a loud thudding sound as phones are dropped on to tables and glasses and bottles are raised; soon the goody-bag paraphernalia is hurtling through the air, missiles of menstruation cups and copies of *What a Heavy Load!* all heading in Griff's direction. He scuttles from the stage like a cockroach, Alicia close behind.

'Fuck the awards!' someone shouts. It might even be Hetty.

'Let's go to the bar!' says another.

The six of us stand on the stage and grin. 'What do we do now?' Beth whispers. 'Are we going to sing "I Am Woman"?'

'God, no,' I shudder. 'We're leaving.'

But, before I go, there's one last thing I need to do.

* * *

We descend the steps together and for a second I have a sense of the familiar: exiting an aircraft flanked by my crew; of being part of a team; of a job well done.

I corner him. Scrawny-necked, with his head slung low. There's a scrap of camouflage fabric snaking through his hair. Is he wearing a Forest Dad bandana?

'Where did you go?' I ask. He tries to move, and I shove him back against the wall. 'When Scout's harness failed, where were you?'

I saw him earlier as I arrived, emerging from the disabled toilets; Middle Class Mummy not far behind, adjusting her pearls and wrap dress. I was right not to trust him. I wonder if there's anyone within a five-mile radius he hasn't tried to shag?

It hits me like turbulence. Disappearing during the shoot. The coy looks. Why didn't I think of it sooner? 'Were you with *Marina*?'

The look on his face says it all. He doesn't get to speak because he's blindsided by a punch from his right. The sort of punch delivered by someone who does Boxfit in their lunch break.

'Not you too?' I say to Boardroom Boss Mum.

Beth leans in: 'I think they're married.'

86

#Unicorns

Cassie

'You're a pilot?' Boardroom Boss Mum repeats, swigging from a bottle of cava, occasionally eyeballing the label and giving it a dirty look. She's lost in thought, her booze-addled brain trying to catch up. 'Why don't you fly now?'

We haven't made it far – we're in the foyer of the hotel, having nicked a crate of booze and snacks from behind the bar. It's on Griff. I'm not staying long; I have an important meeting with Social Services in the morning.

I shrug. 'Didn't work out. Too hard with the kids.'

'Madness,' Boardroom Boss Mum tuts.

'It's okay for you. With your plum part-time role and stay-at-home husband. It's not like that for the rest of us.'

She makes a sound that's a cross between a cackle and a choke. 'I'm a unicorn, Cassie, I don't exist. I'm a figurehead. A symbol. I'm Father Fucking Christmas. I'm there for the kick-off meeting and the closing dinner at the end. I'm the name on the press release. But I'm not allowed to get my hands dirty on the deal. I can't be trusted with that, in case I lose my focus. In case one of my kids gets sick. That falls to the men, or the women who haven't got knocked up yet. And a judgy bunch of bitches they are.' She scowls. 'Lemme tell you how I spent last night. I had Ophelia over my lap, bare arse in the air, cheeks spread, waiting for a fucking threadworm to emerge – they like the light, you see – you've got all this to come when the twins start school.' As she speaks, my own bottom involuntarily twitches. 'I'm armed with a cotton bud, waiting for its wriggly little head to pop out, the whole time conducting a conference call in New York. And I get called a part-timer. Do you know what a dad would get for doing that? A fucking medal. A profile piece in the *FT*, 'How I Make It Work'. What do I get? A paltry bonus, a thirty per cent pay cut and no career progression. The amount of times I've had to mute a conference call while I've puked down the loo with morning sickness for those bastards? By which I mean the company, not my kids; I love *those* little bastards. All for nothing.' She pinches the bridge of her nose, sighs deeply. 'As for my husband, he's a drain. A total drain. I told him he wouldn't be cut out for business.'

I hear her saying it to him. *We need to stick to the plan… I knew you wouldn't be cut out for this…*

'I saw you. At the Otter's Paw. In October.'

She raises an eyebrow. 'Crisis talks. He wasn't shifting anything. I had to bankroll the whole thing. I told him, "When I said create some merchandise, I meant puddle suits for kids! Not Forest Dad branded gilets! No one wants to *be* Forest Dad".' We all nod in agreement, rolling our eyes. 'Do you think real working mums look like this?' Her hand moves from her razor-sharp blonde bob to her pristine navy Chanel suit. 'In the City especially? Do you think they can do Boxfit in their lunch break or squeeze in an hour at the on-site masseuse? You either sell yourself full-scale: eighty-plus-hour weeks, never seeing your kids but having a damn good nanny – and looking like something your kid made for homework – or you're out.' She flicks her red nails. 'It made sense for him to stay at home. When this Forest Dad thing took off, I was pleased. Thought it would boost his confidence. There is no school – the kids in the photos are ours, mucking around in the camp he knocked up. Whenever anyone tries to enrol he says they're full. And all the merch is doing is taking up space at home. Instagram's been the ruin of us. You know our eldest, Cordelia, wants to bring a class action on behalf of the InstaKids? You raise strong women... and they fucking sue you!'

'You think you lot have problems,' mutters Common As Mum, nibbling angrily on an olive. 'At least you have a shot at it. Working-class mums have no choice: they're at home unless their family can help out. Cost of childcare! That's why I like SoMe. It's got its faults but it's a level playing field. Well, as much as anything can be.'

Boardroom Boss Mum turns to me. 'Why didn't you say hello, at the Otter's Paw?'

'It feels weird to say it now, but I thought you two might be behind The Unhappy Hollidays. Plotting against me.'

She frowns, hurt. 'Why would you think that? We're friends... although I did half wonder if it was you. Setting the whole thing up yourself.'

'Why would she do that?' asks Beth, looking genuinely confused.

'It's like Alicia said,' Lucy shrugs. 'Sometimes people go to desperate lengths for exposure.'

I nod in agreement. 'And you didn't try to help. When The Unhappy Hollidays began, you seemed almost gleeful. You both did.' I look at Boardroom Boss Mum and Holistic Flo. We *were* friends. We *are*.

'I was pissed off you weren't there for me over the summer – I only had the kids under my desk because *he'd* sodded off on that Villa promo for Hetty... Or when I went down the CHIN.'

'Neither of you cared when my marriage broke down. Or when I had a breakdown,' adds Holistic Flo dolefully.

'It seemed... convenient. Like I said, I thought you might be behind The Unhappy Hollidays.' We sip our drinks in silence. 'So what's going on with you? Are you alright?' I lift her frail, bruised arm questioningly.

'It's the vit drips,' she says, lowering her arm. 'I think so. I have days where I eat clean and go to the gym and feel good. And I have other days where I want to eat cake and drink wine. But with all this Insta-stuff it feels like I have to keep it a secret, you know?'

'Things can get out of hand,' agrees Boardroom Boss Mum. 'We shouldn't have said Angus was a widower, it just... escalated.'

'How come no one from school has said anything?'

'No one's joined up the dots. I never put the kids in my photos and he only includes them if you can't see their faces,' she shrugs. 'I don't go to school too often – he's always been better at that side of things than me – and when I do I don't look like this –' She gestures at her suit. 'I don't have any friends from school, I've always felt like the other mums judge me for working, so I avoid it. This is the problem with working part-time; you feel like you're failing at work and failing at home. I should put that in my bloody manifesto. *Women: whatever you do, you're fucked!*' She downs her drink.

'What's down your jumpsuit?' Common As Mum asks Holistic Flo suspiciously.

'My tits!' she snaps.

I frown. Common As Mum's right. There's something there. 'Look, we're your mates. If you need some time out, we can help with your account, and the kids... please...'

'For fuck's sake! Fine, fine, here you go...' She rummages around in her bra, producing two clear bags. One with cigarette butts and one with small white rocks. Beth and Lucy gasp. Common As Mum laughs and points to the rocks. 'Whatever these are, you can't smoke 'em!' she cackles.

'They're for positive energy,' pouts Holistic Flo, squirrelling both bags back inside her bra.

'You can like crystals *and* fags, you know?' I say.

'The brands don't like it. You're in or you're out.'

'Fuck the brands! InstaFagMum has a ring to it! Do what you *like*. You're going through a relationship breakdown. How many times have you posted images saying "Do what makes you happy!"? Well, do it!'

'Fine. I will!' She takes the bowl of crisps from Board-room Boss Mum, shovelling a handful into her mouth. We all laugh as Boardroom Boss Mum reaches down for another bottle. Across from me Lucy pulls back and taps Beth's leg, nodding across the hotel's squeaky-floored lobby to the brass revolving door where a man with floppy hair is looking nervously in our direction.

***

Beth

My heart thuds in my chest. Not with anxiety, but with love. It's Joe, with fear in his eyes, looking at the group of women intently pretending they're not watching. He checks his watch as I make my way to him, the lobby silent as snowfall.

'The awards... I thought I was on time? Did they finish early?'

'You came?' My voice croaks. Gloria must have told him where I was.

'I knew it was important to you.' He steps closer. 'I want us to make this work, Beth. I'm sorry about Doner Day. For all the Doner Days. I should have been honest with you about how I was feeling, not going off to Mum and Dad's. Ever since Poppy was born, I've felt this weird pressure.' He presses a thumb over his breastbone. 'I can't explain it.'

'I know that pressure,' I say.

'I thought I had to *be* better, *do* better – because she's, you're both – you're the world to me. And when you started with the online stuff, I thought it was a sign – that I wasn't doing a good enough job. That even though I was trying my best, you needed validation from *strangers*.' He looks down.

'I did. But not because of you, Joe. Because I've never felt like I fitted in. I never felt like I deserved to. And then, for the first time, I did. I got swept up in it.'

'I felt like I was letting you down. I thought if I had some space, some time out, I could be a better boyfriend and dad. And having Poppy – I don't know, it sounds childish, but it made me want to be at my old home, in my parents' house, and' – I see him swallowing down tears – 'I couldn't explain it to you, because I knew you must be feeling the same but worse, because your mum wasn't around...' He trails off and I realize how tired he looks, how his eyes are lined with the absence of sleep. Ironic, really. 'I knew you doubted yourself, but to me you were doing such a great job...' He swallows, pulls down on the cuffs of his jacket. 'It's just... God, it's hard, isn't it, parenthood?'

'Hell, yes!' shouts Holistic Flo, and the other mums whoop and clap. Joe keeps his eyes fixed on me, shuffling his feet, ignoring the mums crunching crisps, agog, and the upright doormen in gold-trimmed suits, their top hats cocked in our direction.

He takes my hands in his and every nerve ending in my body sparks to life, even the ones in my dormant vagina. 'I've missed you, Joe,' I say, and I step closer, inhaling his citrus and seawater musk, needing to feel his lips on mine.

'I was going to propose, Beth. I'd chosen a ring. When you said you didn't want me to, I bought the other one instead. I didn't want to rush you, but I wanted you to know how much you mean to me.' His voice wavers and breaks.

I have the strangest sensation: of my body stretching taller; my organs shifting into the correct spaces; my lungs filling fully with air; my brain fog lifting, my thoughts clear; my heart rate strident and strong, not tightened by fear of the past or the present or the future. I feel like *me*. In a good way.

'But I got it wrong. I'm sorry, Beth. I'm so, so sorry and I'll do whatever it takes to fix this. I miss you,' he says, cupping my face in his hands. 'We belong together.'

I know he's right. In this marble-flanked hotel, in this big, noisy city, surrounded by these women, Joe's arms wrapped tight around me, I am home.

87

Extract from the Social Services Report regarding Amelia and Charlie Holliday

Issues arising:

1. Baby Media Plan
We received a number of concerns raised by members of the public regarding the publication of a 'new baby media plan'. While we note that such a plan is undesirable, given the child to which it was subject did not in fact exist, we will not be pursuing this further.

2. Health and welfare of Amelia Scout Holliday and Charlie Birch Holliday
We note that this is the first incident referred to our services and as such it would be highly unusual to remove a child from a parent unless the incident were of sufficient gravity.

Amelia's health: Following examination by a paediatrician, it has been confirmed that Amelia suffers from asthma. Doctors' records show that Mrs Holliday had taken her daughter to the doctor on a number of occasions, but the doctor was hesitant to diagnose asthma at such a young age. While Mrs Holliday (and indeed Mr Holliday) could have been more insistent here, we do not find her behaviour negligent.

It has been reported that the children were often dressed insufficiently for the weather. Mrs Holliday has explained this was for very short periods – for photographs – but this is not something she will do in future.

We have visited Little Oatbridge Manor and noted that the children are settled there but nonetheless remain distraught at the absence of their mother, their primary caregiver prior to the incident. When questioned as to what they missed, they responded with dancing, watching movies and pretending to be birds. Charlie queried whether their mother had gone because they did not 'get enough love-hearts' (we understand these to be 'likes' on social media posts, which he had seen on his babysitter's phone).

Since the incident the children's mother, Cassandra Holliday, has removed herself from all social media platforms. She was helpful and engaged during our interview and expressed her deep regret at her actions and said more than once that she would do 'whatever it takes' to be reunited with her children.

We understand that there were extenuating circumstances in this case: a work colleague, Alicia Steele, was exerting undue pressure on Mrs Holliday to garner publicity. Furthermore, the harness used on the day of the incident had been secured by an Angus Hunt (known professionally as Forest Dad), a man whom Mrs Holliday believed to have undertaken the relevant qualifications to run his own forest school but who did not hold any such qualifications.

It should be noted that as well as the negative reports to this department regarding Mrs Holliday, we received a number of positive recommendations as to her character, notably from her mother-in-law, Marina Holliday, her nanny, Ruby Suzuki and friends and colleagues: Elizabeth Jenkins (formerly known as Mardy Mum), Melissa Hunt (known as Boardroom Boss Mum), Florence Asante (known as Holistic Flo) and Kirsty Love (known as Common As Mum).

Other issues of concern: we understand Mrs Holliday was paid by *Boom!* magazine on an 'exclusive' basis to reveal the children's gender. This issue is complex; a number of other 'Influencers' have provided 'sponsored content' when revealing their babies' gender – ordinarily done in utero – and this has become accepted practice. We feel this is a matter for the government, rather than this department, to ruminate on and will be referring this issue to the Minister for Children and Families.

We recommend that we leave this report on file and pending no further incidents that Cassandra Holliday share custody with Sebastian Holliday during their separation and subsequent divorce.

CHRISTMAS EVE

88

#Karma

Cassie

'Cassie, please come over to the Big House and help. It's *so hard* doing everything by yourself. There's so much to do!'

'Isn't there just?' I respond, raising my nail file, barely concealing the tremor in my voice.

'Did you see the report? Did you see what they said? They said we could share custody...' He surveys the Shed. The log fire's burning, the room's clear of glitter and face paints, everything decluttered and tidied away. All the twins' gifts are wrapped and ready under my little tree. I've had to fill every second I was apart from them to stop my heart from shattering into a million tiny pieces, and I didn't want Social Services seeing the Shed how it was. I've even got builders lined up to rectify the damp after Christmas; I can afford it with my money from Griff. 'I was thinking, why don't we swap? You could move in with Marina and the twins in the Big House and I could move back in here? We could take it in turns to have the twins at the weekends?'

Amazingly, after all the fuss he caused, Seb wants Marina

to stay in the Big House. She even *wanted* to leave, devastated that Forest Dad was with her when the accident happened, but he insisted she didn't go. I guess when it came down to it, she had his back. That and she's been helping him with the twins. He looks slimmer, his face chiselled. Parenthood's the diet he's been needing.

'Shall we talk about it later?' I've agreed with Seb I'll come over to lay out mince pies and Babycham (the only tradition from my Christmases with Mum I've kept) for Father Christmas with the twins.

'Later...? Oh that. Oh God.' He winces. 'I forgot to get carrots for the reindeer!' He puts his hands over his face and groans.

I put my hand on his arm. 'It's Christmas. The kids love the magic of it, it doesn't need to be perfect.'

He leans heavily against the door frame. 'I've been trying my best, Cass, I have, but the thought of being indoors all day with them, the overexcitement, the hysteria... I'm not sure how I'm going to cope.' I see an idea glimmering. 'We could swap tonight, if you like? You could be there when the twins wake up? And there'll be loads more space for your friends to stay. Marina will love it! She's always saying how much she adores the house being full and the sound of the twins.' He grimaces.

'I'll think about it,' I say, closing the door, but I'm already bounding up the stairs to pack my bags as his feet crunch back over the gravel.

CHRISTMAS DAY

89

#ItsTheMostWonderfulTime

Beth

I sit with Poppy nestled on my lap in her Christmas pudding onesie and survey the room: Ron's regaling Dad with tales of banger racing 'back in the day'; Dad looks happily engaged, as he always does when talking about anything engine-related. Lucy and Joe are laying the table, their jovial chatter not quite as comfortable as before but heading in the right direction.

Outside, the light's already dipping and fading, the sun slowly being squeezed like an orange as it's pushed down by the darkening sky. Inside, the house is warm and cosy, Gloria's multitude of lamps sending out pools of amber light, and filled with almost all of my favourite people. Which reminds me. I check the time and dial. Four faces fill the frame: Cassie, Marina, Melissa and Florence. They're adorned with party hats, strings from party poppers falling over their ears and festive jumpers, cups of mulled wine and flutes of champagne in their hands. Their children – all eleven of them! – are in the background, dancing and playing, one of them skateboarding ('Mind the tree!'), Mariah Carey projected on to the wall, belting out all she wants for Christmas. It's like a fashion shoot gone wrong.

'You look very Instagrammable!' I say, and we collapse into laughter.

'What a spread!' Dad exclaims when we sit down to eat. 'Thank you so much, Gloria and Ron. You've made me and my girls so welcome.' I hear the lump in his throat. I know he feels it and wants to avoid it because he leans over my plate and in a comical tone says: 'Don't mind me, love,' as he spears my Yorkshire pudding. It's our little thing.

A curious silence falls over the table as he holds it aloft. Gloria's eyes narrow and she can't help but look at him indignantly: *Oh right, he's one of those blokes, is he? Controlling!*

Dad senses the frostiness on the fixed, awkward faces. 'Sorry, I don't mean to be rude!' he says shyly. 'I've been having Beth's puds since she was little. She's never liked them. *Can't stand them!*' He smiles. 'I could never understand it myself. And these! These look delicious!' A small bead of gravy slicks down the curved surface of the pudding and splashes on Gloria's deer-grazing-in-the-forest tablecloth. No one speaks.

'I...' I start to say, blushing as red as Gloria's poinsettias, but a strange snorting noise comes from Gloria, breaking me off. We all turn to her but she's silent now, eyes widening and watering, as she tries to swallow her pig-in-a-blanket. *She's choking!* I think, and Lucy must do too because she's on her feet and striding over, but Gloria waves her away, batting her hand furiously and then smacking it in a fist on the table as she tries to get purchase on the pork trimming. Finally, she manages it with a triumphant swallow and takes a small sip of wine to clear her throat.

'Oh my days!' she roars and then begins to shake, literally shake, with laughter. 'Beth! My darling! And you never said!' Tears stream down her face, she can't wipe them away quick enough, and now the rest of us are laughing too, even Poppy, who's looking between us trying to figure out the joke, a mirror image of her grandfather.

'What?' Dad asks. 'What's so funny?'

I gingerly take the fork and ease the pudding on to his plate. 'I'll tell you after dinner.'

'Oh, girls,' he says later, an arm round each of us. 'What a blooming mess. I wish you'd told me sooner. Like your mam always said, *we've got to stick together*.' He places a hand over Lucy's. 'We all make mistakes,' he says softly. 'It's how we fix them that counts. Now, what are you going to do about this promotion?'

'I've decided to turn it down,' she says, and I look to her in surprise.

'But Lu, you've wanted a step up for so long! It's such an amazing opportunity.'

'It doesn't feel right. Moving away, sticking at *Boom!* That place doesn't bring out the best in me...' She trails off. Nibbles on a pecan from one of Gloria's holly-shaped bowls. 'I was thinking, Dad, I might move home for a bit, if you don't mind? Figure out what to do next without the pressure of rent and bills...'

Dad says nothing, looking between us expectantly.

'What?'

'Well, isn't it obvious? Hope I'm not speaking out of turn here, but Beth's got that lovely room in her flat...' I do. I cleared out the spare room, finally emptied all the junk that had been accumulating there, and bought a bed so Dad has a place to stay when he comes down. 'And she needs some help with Poppy...'

My head springs up. He's right. It could be perfect. I'll need to check with Joe, but it wouldn't be forever, just time for Lucy to get back on her feet and for us to adjust to parenthood better. Maybe even have the odd night out together if Lucy didn't mind.

'What do you think?' I ask Lucy, excited now, positivity starting to fold around me like wrapping paper. I picture Lucy and me hanging out together in the flat when Joe's out with work. This could be really, really good. For all of us.

'I think it's great,' she shrugs, 'but what about Joe? What about you? You've loved having a space to yourself to craft again.'

'I'll speak to Joe. And I haven't had a chance to tell you yet, but I've got plans for the sewing machine...' I can't stop the smile that spreads across my face.

'You don't need to speak to me, babe.' Joe ambles over. 'I think it's a great idea!' Lucy looks up in grateful surprise; she wasn't expecting him to agree. 'None of us have been at our best lately.' He reddens. 'But me and Lucy, we're family.'

He squeezes her shoulder and my eyes fill. Since the awards, Joe and I haven't stopped talking, about everything, including what happened with Mum. The unworthiness I've always felt, the buried fear that he might reject me if he knew, was unfounded. It feels as though we love each other more, not less.

Gloria bustles over with slices of Christmas cake and I'm amazed when Lucy takes one.

'What?' she asks.

'And you ate all your Christmas dinner,' I say.

'Are you watching me?' she teases, taking a big bite of the rich cake. 'You don't need to worry about that. I'm good. I know myself. My own warning signs. And when I get stressed... yeah, it's a challenge. But I've found this amazing group online. I can post any time and there's loads of women, and some men, who get it. It's a lifeline, really.' *It's like I thought: social media can be a place for good in the right hands.* 'Mum was always funny about her weight, you know,' she muses, pressing some of the crumbs from her plate on to her index finger. 'I was getting worried about you at one point. You kept saying how fat you were after having Poppy, but you didn't look much different. Apart from the huge boobs.' She grins.

'I felt lost,' I say. 'More Lardy Mum than Mardy Mum.'

'No, you were definitely mardy,' Lucy teases, and I grin.

'But I'm getting there,' I say, stealing some of her marzipan as she tries to move her plate away.

'You can stay here, Stanley, when you come down?' Gloria says, proffering the tray of cake to Dad. 'We have a guest suite.'

'We'd love to have you!' booms Ron, one hand on his hip as he dutifully tops up our glasses. 'I don't know how you can sleep in that flat. I never could.'

Joe rolls his eyes.

'It wasn't the best night's sleep I've had, I'll be honest,' Dad says, with an apologetic look in my direction. 'I do like it here in Essex, reminds me of being up north. Sense of community.'

I know what he means, I think, mentally teeing up a property search app for Poppy's next feed.

'Well, that's it then,' says Ron, as we settle into position for the Queen's Speech. 'This is all working out nicely. Very nicely indeed.'

JANUARY

90

Everything's… 'Normal' (Whatever That Means)

Cassie

'I think there were some product issues. It was a niche offering.'

I laugh, wondering what Beth did with the surplus of hot dogs and miniature deckchairs.

'This is much more me,' she adds.

We're back at the Farm, the floor below the terrace this time as it's cold outside. The room has been set up with sewing machines, knitting needles, wool, fabrics, crochet hooks; you name it, Beth's sourced it.

'Shall I do a SoMe post?' Melissa asks, entering.

Beth nods. 'You do it and I'll repost it.'

'Here for the launch of Grafting and Crafting,' she narrates as she types, 'an initiative led by Elizabeth Jenkins in conjunction with' – she winks – 'Boardroom Boss Mum. They're working together to promote better mental health in the workplace, encouraging workers to spend their lunch break learning a new skill or improving a craft. Come join us!'

An hour later and every work station's full and there's a line snaking out the door. There's the girls from Beth's hypno-birthing group (including a particularly clingy one called Priya who keeps asking me if I need anything) and Joe and Lucy as well as Florence and Kirsty. Everyone, really, except for Hetty and Forest Dad, who have shacked up (it had been going on since the Villa, apparently) and now run a shopping channel together on QVC, and Alicia, who's juggling job offers in Silicon Valley. It turns out she was right: people will pay big money for publicity at any cost and they want to read how to do it too. So it was Alicia who got the book deal, but I got all the people in this room instead. And – finally – a positive piece in *The Read* after the awards, covering the whole sorry saga.

'It's my first step,' Beth says proudly. 'It's a long road, and I'll need to do a course, but I'm going to use the money I make from this to go back to uni – I want to be an art therapist.' She gazes over the rows of crafts, where Lucy is bobbing Poppy on her hip. 'I don't mind it will take a while, I feel good that I'm doing something for me, you know?'

I tap my finger on my phone, still open on my Horizon Air application form. Katya's coming over later to look over it before I hit submit. 'I know exactly what you mean.'

ACKNOWLEDGEMENTS

Thank you for reading this book. It means an enormous amount to me. It would not exist without the support and editorial wisdom of Laura Palmer and Anna Nightingale so huge thanks to them both, along with the rest of the team at Head of Zeus, and to my agent Nelle Andrew who had a vision for this book from the day we met and has provided advice and creative brain-storming ever since.

Thanks to my early readers: my sister Katie Butterworth, my first reader and first friend; Jemma Thomas, who always keeps it real, and who, alongside her husband Super Billy, answered my many questions on social media; Cara Pannell, who read outside her genre (sorry it wasn't a sci-fi zombie bodice-ripper); and the divine Anna Morris who gifted me a joke when she queried whether Gloria's 'little JoJo' was a person or a body part.

Thanks to: Keeley Smith, whose insights into being a pilot were invaluable (any mistakes are my own); Cesca Major for virtual hand-holding throughout; Rebecca, Brendan, Molly, Rosa and Leo Keane who generously let me edit this book in their spare room when my own house was too noisy; my writing buddy Dessa Miller for moral support and coffee breaks; Katie (again) and Lia Harlock, the original mittens, who allowed me to pilfer their nicknames; my Dad, Patsy Conway, for his unwavering enthusiasm in promoting this book across Ireland (we'll make it to The Late Late Show one day); my Grandmother, Ruth Foley, for her warm words and excitement towards this project; and Mrs Bernie Williams, my English teacher at The Sacred Heart of Mary Girls' School in Upminster, Essex, whose persistent urging of me to challenge myself still pushes me to do better.

Thanks to Jodie Williams for looking after my sons with love and care while I was writing and to Delyth and Stuart Kennedy who toured the castles and sea zoos of North Wales when I needed to write during holidays.

I've wanted to write for as long as I can remember but life and love and other stuff got in the way and the dream of holding my own book in my hands became ever more remote. So thank you mostly to my sons (if I hadn't wanted to ~~quit my law job to spend more time with you~~ show you that dreams can come true, I would probably have continued to procrastinate over writing, rather than actually writing, for another twenty years) and to my husband Tom, who makes everything possible. This book is for you. With love, always.

ABOUT THE AUTHOR

NICOLE KENNEDY grew up in Essex and studied Law at Bristol University. She has always loved to write but her efforts were waylaid by work as a corporate lawyer in London, Paris and Dubai. During Nicole's second maternity leave she began writing poems on motherhood and family life, which she posted to her blog 'The Brightness Of These Days'. She completed her first novel during her third maternity leave (by then it was easier than leaving the house). Nicole lives in Kent with her husband and three sons. You can find her on Instagram (@nicole_k_kennedy) and Twitter (@nicolekkennedy).